A PLUME BOOK

RASHI'S DAUGHTERS
BOOK III: RACHEL

MAGGIE ANTON was born Margaret Antonofsky in Los Angeles, California. Raised in a secular, socialist household, she reached adulthood with little knowledge of her Jewish religion. All that changed when Dave Parkhurst entered her life, and they discovered Judaism as adults. That was the start of a lifetime of adult Jewish education, synagogue involvement, and ritual observance. This was in addition to raising their children, Emily and Ari, and working full time as a clinical chemist.

In 1997, as her nest was emptying and her mother was declining with Alzheimer's disease, she became intrigued with the idea that Rashi, one of Judaism's greatest scholars, had no sons, only three daughters. Using techniques developed doing her family's genealogy, she began to research Rashi's family, and the idea of a book about them was born.

Eight years later, the first volume of *Rashi's Daughters* was finally complete, making Maggie Anton a Talmud maven and an authority on medieval French Jewish women. She retired from the lab and spent the next two years researching and writing *Book II: Miriam*, in addition to lecturing at more than one hundred synagogues, JCCs, and Jewish women's organizations.

Maggie lives in Los Angeles, California, with Dave, her husband of thirty-nine years, where she is working on her next historical novel. You can [illegible]t her at her Web site, www.rashisdaughters.com.

Advance Praise for
Rashi's Daughters, Book III: Rachel

"Imaginative and talented novelists have the ability to shed fresh light on corners of history otherwise inaccessible. Maggie Anton's new book, *Rashi's Daughters: Rachel*, takes us once again into the medieval Jewish world of love and learning, and the love of learning. One can only be grateful for such an intriguing and engaging work."

—Dr. Tamara Cohn Eskenazi, Professor of Bible, Hebrew Union College–Jewish Institute of Religion; editor of *The Torah: A Women's Commentary* (2008 National Jewish Book Award)

"*Rashi's Daughters: Rachel* is an enlightened, empowering, and engaging journey of Rashi's youngest daughter, Rachel, who enacts the forbidden during the Middle Ages—studying and teaching Talmud as a female. Thought provoking, research rich, psychologically complex, *Rachel* is a mirror of our own hearts and minds, a tale of pathos that awakens the tenderest of emotions, even if time separates us by nine hundred years."

—Elissa Elliott, author of *Eve*

"This third book of Maggie Anton's brilliantly original trilogy is a page-turning delight. I'm dazzled by the clever ways in which Anton integrates poignant depictions of Rashi's third daughter with obscure yet wonderfully pertinent Talmud texts, fun details about ancient medicines and the complexities of wool weaving, a gripping portrayal of the horrors of the Crusades, and descriptions about the vivid intellectual world of medieval Europe."

—Rabbi Miriyam Glazer, PhD, Professor of Literature, American Jewish University; author of *Psalms of the Jewish Liturgy: A Guide to Their Beauty, Power, and Meaning*

"With only scraps of information about Rashi's daughters, Anton has brought these three women to life. A stunning achievement. You will not be able to put this book down and you may even find yourself rushing off to study Talmud. So curl up in your favorite chair and savor every moment."

—Judith Hauptman, E. Billi Ivry Professor of Talmud and Rabbinic Culture, Jewish Theological Seminary; author of *Rereading the Rabbis, A Woman's Voice*

Praise for the Rashi's Daughters Trilogy

"True to life yet colorful characters and a riveting plot . . . a most informative and enjoyable read. Not to be missed!"

—Eva Etzioni-Halevy, author of *The Garden of Ruth*

"Wonderful . . . a fascinating glimpse into the world of Jewish women long ago."

—Rabbi Elyse Goldstein, author of *ReVisions: Seeing Torah Through a Feminist Lens*

Rashi's Daughters

Book III: Rachel

MAGGIE ANTON

A PLUME BOOK

PLUME
Published by the Penguin Group
Penguin Group (USA) Inc., 375 Hudson Street, New York, New York 10014, U.S.A. • Penguin Group (Canada), 90 Eglinton Avenue East, Suite 700, Toronto, Ontario, Canada M4P 2Y3 (a division of Pearson Penguin Canada Inc.) • Penguin Books Ltd., 80 Strand, London WC2R 0RL, England • Penguin Ireland, 25 St. Stephen's Green, Dublin 2, Ireland (a division of Penguin Books Ltd.) • Penguin Group (Australia), 250 Camberwell Road, Camberwell, Victoria 3124, Australia (a division of Pearson Australia Group Pty. Ltd.) • Penguin Books India Pvt. Ltd., 11 Community Centre, Panchsheel Park, New Delhi – 110 017, India • Penguin Group (NZ), 67 Apollo Drive, Rosedale, North Shore 0632, New Zealand (a division of Pearson New Zealand Ltd.) • Penguin Books (South Africa) (Pty.) Ltd., 24 Sturdee Avenue, Rosebank, Johannesburg 2196, South Africa

Penguin Books Ltd., Registered Offices: 80 Strand, London WC2R 0RL, England

First published by Plume, a member of Penguin Group (USA) Inc.

First Printing, August 2009
10 9 8 7 6 5 4 3 2 1

LIBRARY OF CONGRESS CATALOGING-IN-PUBLICATION DATA

Anton, Maggie.
Rashi's Daughters : Book Three—Rachel / Maggie Anton.
p. cm.
ISBN 978-0-452-29568-1
1. Jewish women—Fiction. 2. Rashi, 1040–1105—Fiction. 3. Troyes (France)—Fiction. 4. Jews—France—Fiction. 5. Jews—France—History—to 1500—Fiction. I. Title.
PS3551.N765 R3 2005
813.54—dc22 2005920049

Printed in the United States of America
Set in Adobe Garamond Pro

PUBLISHER'S NOTE
This is a work of fiction. Names, characters, places, and incidents are either the product of the author's imagination or are used fictitiously, and any resemblance to actual persons, living or dead, business establishments, events, or locales is entirely coincidental.

In memory of my father
NATHAN GEORGE ANTON
Like Rashi,
No sons, only learned daughters

acknowledgments

FIFTEEN YEARS AGO, when I began researching the lives of Rashi's daughters in hopes of discovering if any truth lay behind the legends of their being learned and wearing tefillin, I never imagined that I would end up writing a trilogy of novels about them. I certainly never imagined that *Rashi's Daughters* would be published by a major New York house, that my books would become bestsellers, or that I would be receiving fan mail every day.

There are so many people responsible for this amazing turn of events. I've studied with some of the finest Talmud scholars in America, but I owe a large debt of gratitude to Rabbi Aaron Katz, my study partner and dear friend since 2002. Aaron has taught me so much that there aren't words enough to thank him. My books would not exist without his assistance.

I want to thank my outstanding editor at Plume, Signe Pike, who went over every line of *Rashi's Daughters, Book III: Rachel* and suggested changes that better expressed what I wanted to say. Also much appreciation to my freelance editor, Beth Lieberman, for advice and encouragement that turned this book, and my others, into the ones I wanted them to be, and to Sharon Goldinger, who shepherded this naive author into a successful one. My friend Ray Eelsing and my daughter, Emily, spent many hours critiquing my early drafts. Each brought their own unique talents to the task and their comments were invaluable.

Last, but certainly not least, I offer heartfelt thanks and love to my husband, Dave, who had no idea that his chemist wife with a normal job would morph into an author who wrote late at night and on weekends, who traveled all over the country speaking, and who would get corralled by fans when we went out. Yet his encouragement never wavered. He gave me excellent advice to improve my first drafts, could always think of the right word when I couldn't, and endured countless intrusions of my writing life into our personal lives. Without his support I would have given up long ago.

Now that my trilogy is at long last complete, I must also acknowledge my many fans: you chose *Rashi's Daughters* for your book groups, invited me to speak at your organizations, and validated my belief that women, especially Jewish women, were hungry for books with real, historical heroines. Your e-mails told me how Rashi's daughters touched your lives, taught you so many things you never knew about Jewish women's history, even encouraged you to study Talmud. I tried to answer every one, even the complaints.

And though I have no plans for *Rashi's Granddaughters,* rest assured that I intend to continue writing. I am currently researching a new era and location, with the goal of another historical novel celebrating an unknown Jewish heroine. My readers can look forward to more Love and Talmud, this time in fourth-century Babylonia.

time line

1040/ 4800 Salomon ben Isaac (Rashi) born in Troyes, France, on February 22.

1047 Count Étienne dies; his son Eudes III inherits Champagne.

1050 Invention of horseshoes and padded collars enable horses to plow fields much more efficiently than oxen.

1054 Salomon goes to Mayence to study with his uncle Simon haZaken.

Under Pope Leo IX, split develops between Byzantine (eastern) and Roman (western) Churches.

1057 Salomon marries Rivka, sister of Isaac ben Judah. Leaves Mayence to study at Worms.

1058 Joheved born to Salomon and Rivka in Troyes.

1060 Philip I becomes king of France; Henry IV is emperor of Germany.

Miriam born to Salomon and Rivka.

1062 Count Eudes III found guilty of nobleman's murder; his uncle Thibault takes over Champagne and forces Eudes III to flee to Normandy, where he takes refuge with his cousin, Duke William (the Bastard) of Normandy.

1066 Salomon studies in Mayence with Isaac ben Judah.

Duke William of Normandy becomes king of England (the Conqueror).

1068 Salomon returns to Troyes.

1069 Rachel born to Salomon and Rivka.

Joheved becomes engaged to Meir ben Samuel of Ramerupt.

Isaac (Troyes' *parnas*) becomes winemaking partner with Salomon.

1070/4830 Count Thibault marries his second wife, Adelaide de Bar, a young widow.

Salomon founds yeshiva in Troyes.

1071 King Philip marries Bertha.

Count Thibault and Adelaide's first son, Eudes IV, is born.

1073 Hildebrand, a Cluniac monk, is elected Pope Gregory VII.

1075 Pope Gregory announces excommunication of married priests, suspends German bishops opposed to clerical celibacy, and threatens to excommunicate King Philip.

1076 Thibault and Adelaide's second son, Hugues, is born.

Pope Gregory excommunicates German king Henry and appoints Rudolph as new king.

1077 Isaac ben Meir born in Troyes.

1078 Daughter Constance born to King Philip and Bertha.

1080 Samuel ben Meir (Rashbam) born at Ramerupt.

Archbishop Manasses of Rheims is deposed by Pope Gregory; a blow to King Philip.

King Henry of Germany appoints Clement III antipope.

1081 Prince Louis VI born to King Philip and Bertha.

1083 King Henry attacks Rome, Saracens plunder city, and Pope Gregory flees.

1084 Fire in Mayence attributed to Jews; many move to Speyer.

Count Thibault's oldest son (from his first marriage), Étienne-Henri of Blois, marries Adèle, daughter of William the Conqueror.

1085 Pope Gregory dies in Salerno.

1087 King William of England dies.

1088 Smallpox epidemic begins in winter.

1089 Isaac haParnas and Count Thibault die in epidemic.

	When Count Thibault becomes ill, son Eudes IV takes over as ruler of Champagne.
	Champagne goes to Eudes IV. Blois goes to Étienne-Henry.
1092	Epidemic of infant meningitis in Troyes.
	King Philip repudiates Queen Bertha and marries Bertrade, wife of Count Fulk of Anjou, enraging Pope Urban II.
1093	Eudes IV dies on January 1. Thibault's son Hugues becomes Count of Champagne.
	Count Érard of Brienne starts war with Hugues.
	Solar eclipse in Germany on September 23, followed by famine.
1094	Pope Urban II excommunicates King Philip over Bertrada.
	Terrible drought in summer in Champagne.
1095	Count Hugues marries Constance, daughter of Philip and Bertha.
	Spectacular meteor shower in early April.
1096	Crusades start: four Jewish communities in Rhineland attacked between Passover and Shavuot.
	Lunar eclipse in early August.
1097	Jews converted during crusade permitted to openly return to Judaism.
	A comet is seen for seven nights in early October.
1098	Robert of Molesme founds Cîteaux Abbey and Cistercian Order.
1099	Crusaders take Jerusalem.
1100/4860	Jews return to Mayence.
	Louis VI becomes king-elect of France.
	Paschal II is pope, Theodoric antipope.
	Discovery of alcohol by distillation is made in Salerno medical school.
1104	Assassination attempt made on Count Hugues.
1105	Salomon ben Isaac dies on July 17; Samuel ben Meir heads Troyes yeshiva.

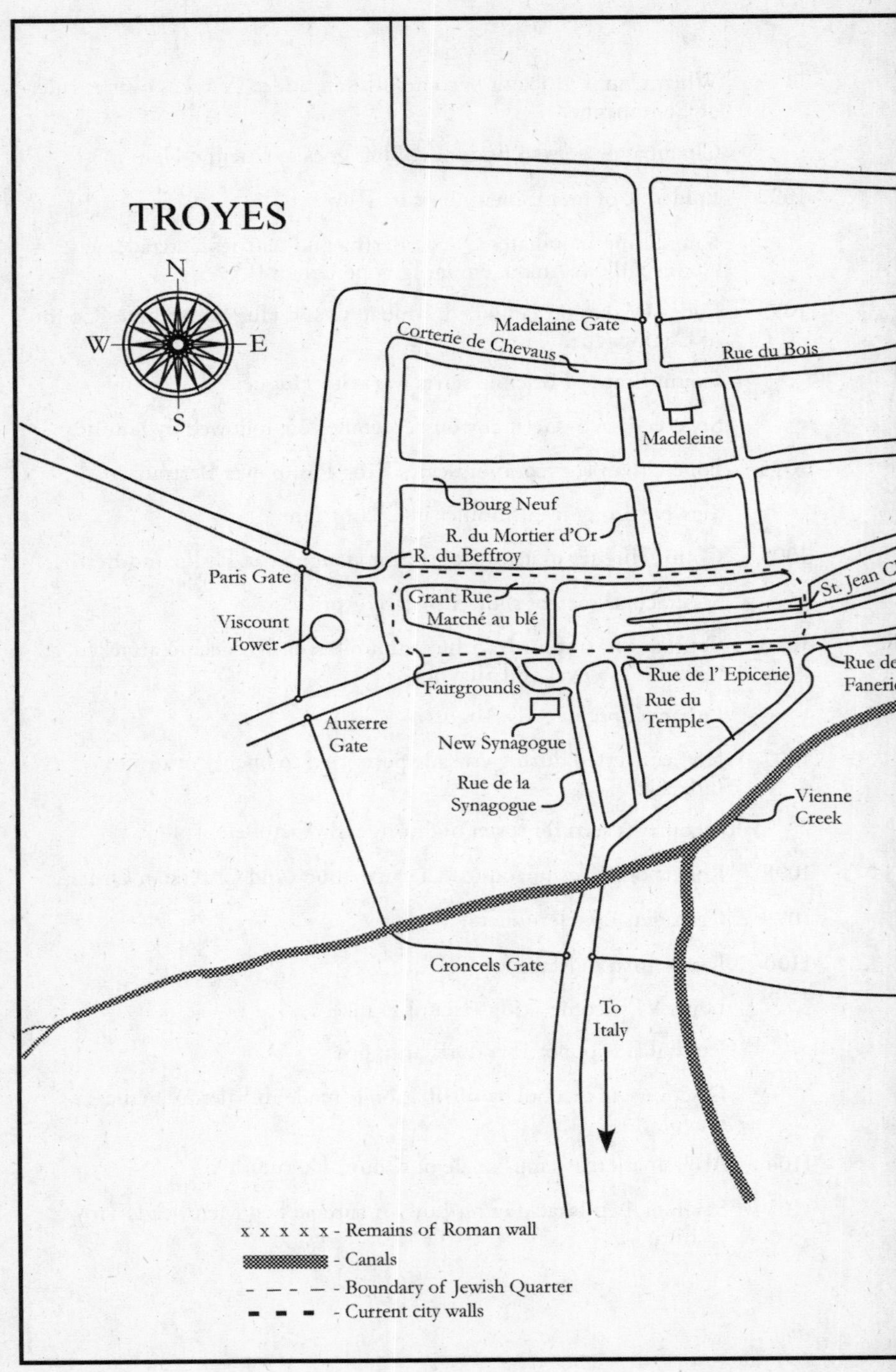
TROYES
N
W
E
S
Madelaine Gate
Corterie de Chevaus
Rue du Bois
Madeleine
Bourg Neuf
R. du Mortier d'Or
R. du Beffroy
Paris Gate
St. Jean
Grant Rue
Marché au blé
Viscount Tower
Rue de l' Epicerie
Rue de
Fairgrounds
Rue du Temple
Auxerre Gate
New Synagogue
Rue de la Synagogue
Vienne Creek
Croncels Gate
To Italy
x x x x x - Remains of Roman wall
- Canals
- Boundary of Jewish Quarter
- Current city walls

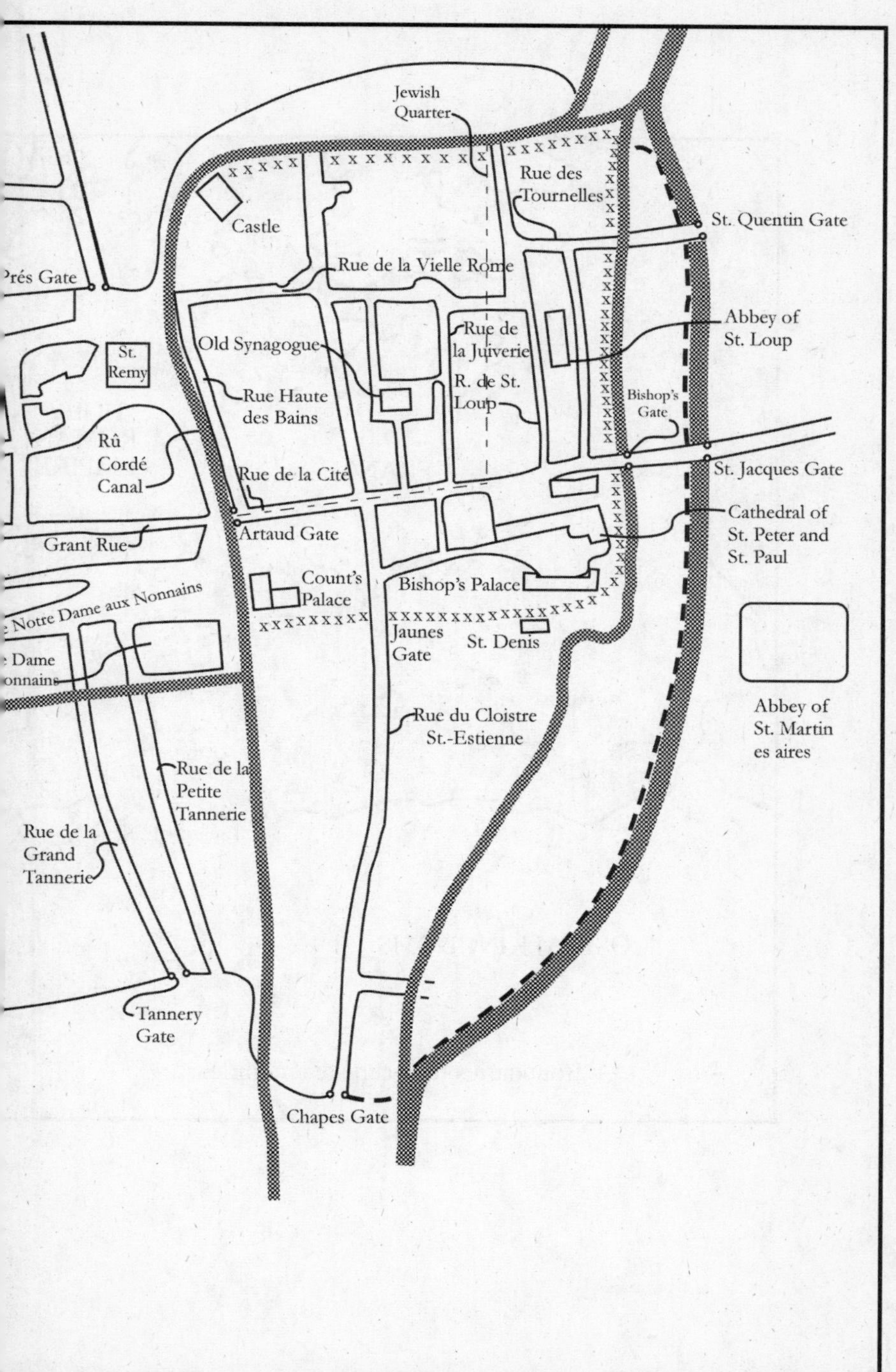
Jewish Quarter
Rue des Tournelles
Castle
St. Quentin Gate
Prés Gate
Rue de la Vielle Rome
Abbey of St. Loup
Old Synagogue
Rue de la Juiverie
St. Remy
R. de St. Loup
Rue Haute des Bains
Bishop's Gate
Rû Cordé Canal
Rue de la Cité
St. Jacques Gate
Artaud Gate
Cathedral of St. Peter and St. Paul
Grant Rue
Count's Palace
Bishop's Palace
Notre Dame aux Nonnains
Jaunes Gate
St. Denis
Dame
onnains
Abbey of St. Martin es aires
Rue du Cloistre St.-Estienne
Rue de la Petite Tannerie
Rue de la Grand Tannerie
Tannery Gate
Chapes Gate

Cologne
Mayence
Worms
Speyer
Paris
Orleans
Troyes
Prague
HOLY ROMAN EMPIRE
FRANCE
Venice
Genoa
Clermont
Arles
SEPHARAD
Toledo
Valencia
Cordoba
Rome
Tunis
MOSLEM KINGDOMS
Boundaries between sovereignties

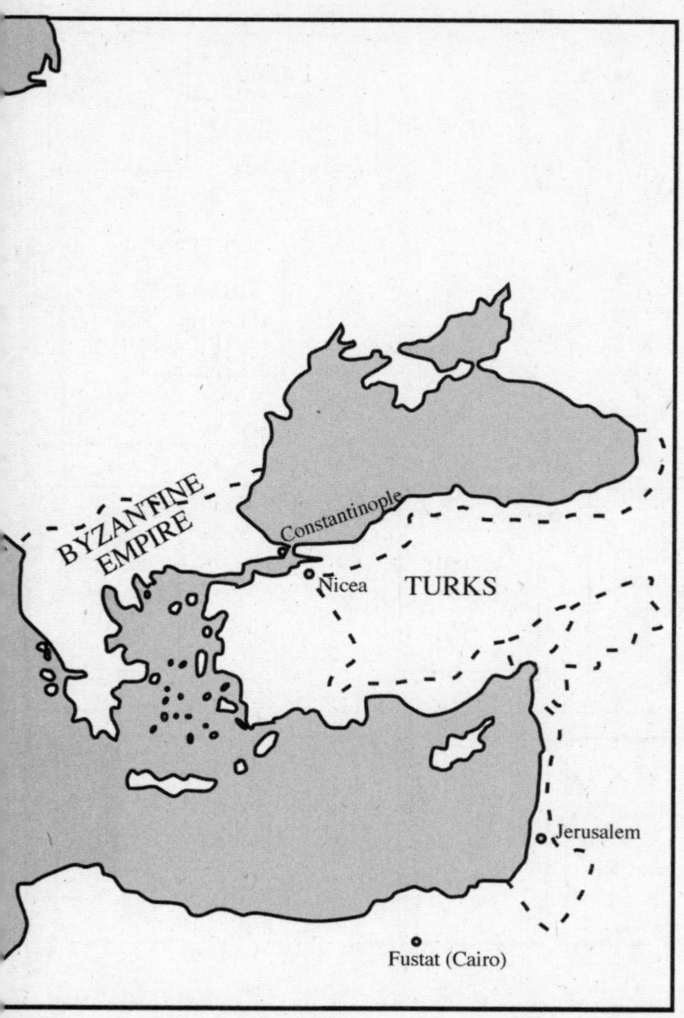
BYZANTINE
EMPIRE
Constantinople
Nicea
TURKS
Jerusalem
Fustat (Cairo)

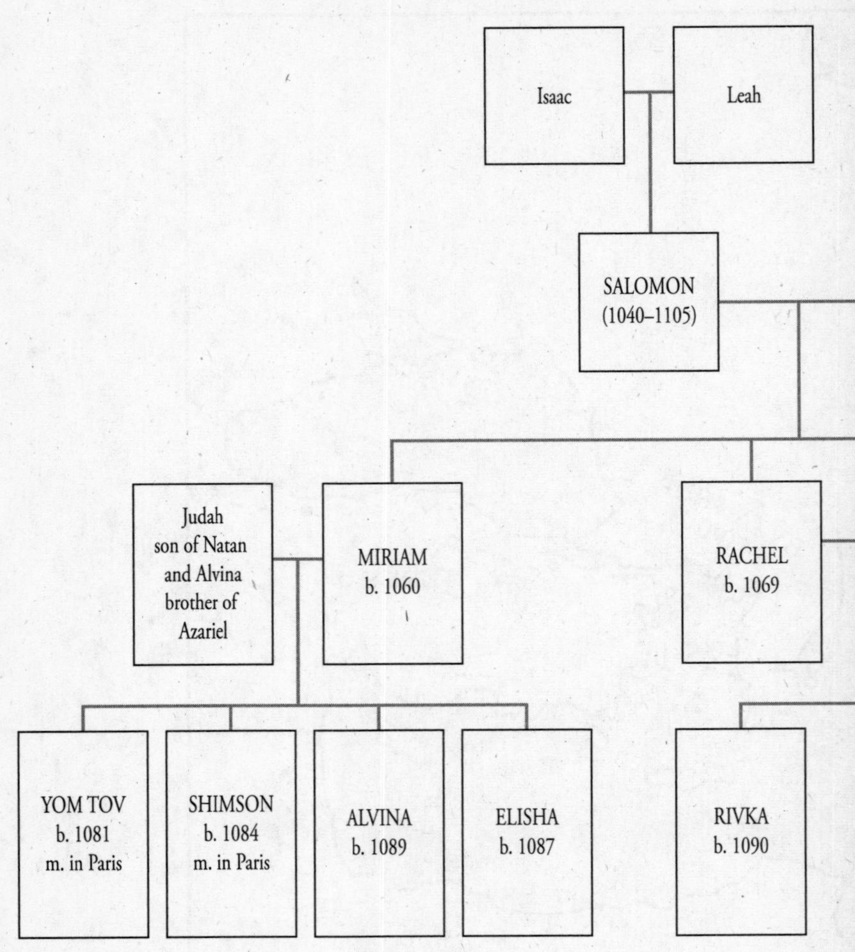

Isaac
Leah
SALOMON
(1040–1105)
Judah
son of Natan
and Alvina
brother of
Azariel
MIRIAM
b. 1060
RACHEL
b. 1069
YOM TOV
b. 1081
m. in Paris
SHIMSON
b. 1084
m. in Paris
ALVINA
b. 1089
ELISHA
b. 1087
RIVKA
b. 1090

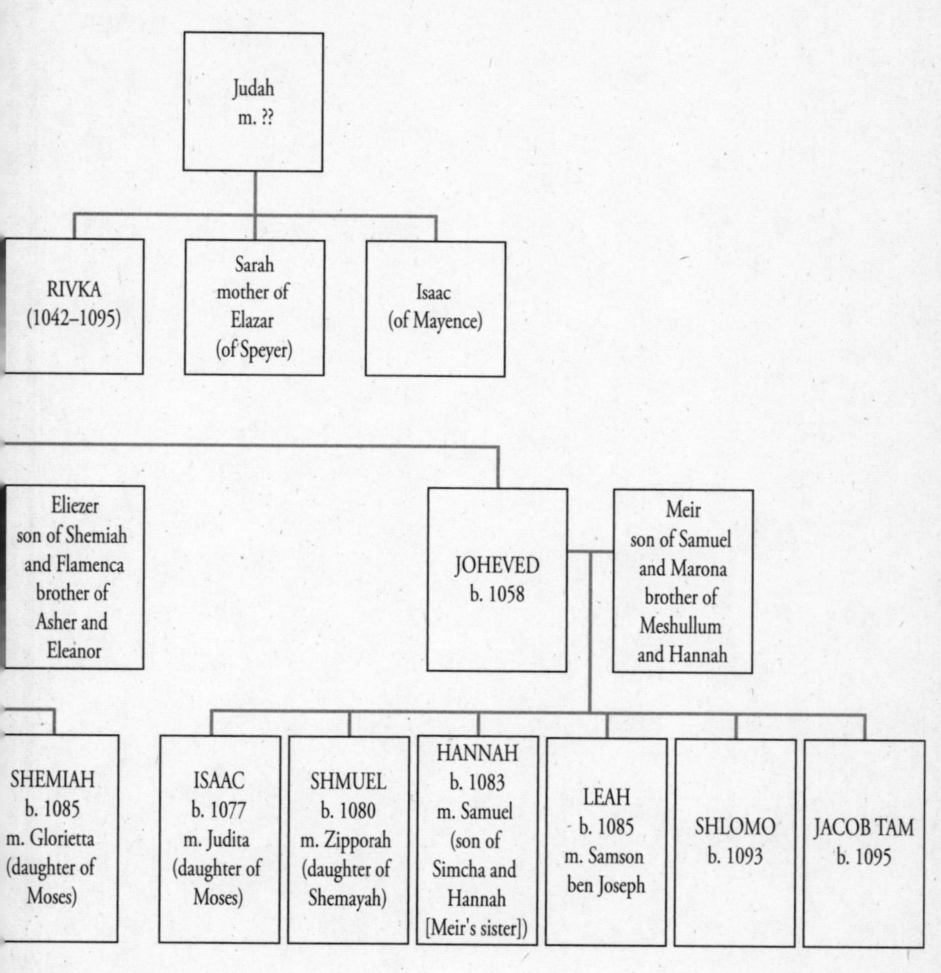

Judah
m. ??
RIVKA
(1042–1095)
Sarah
mother of
Elazar
(of Speyer)
Isaac
(of Mayence)
Eliezer
son of Shemiah
and Flamenca
brother of
Asher and
Eleanor
JOHEVED
b. 1058
Meir
son of Samuel
and Marona
brother of
Meshullum
and Hannah
SHEMIAH
b. 1085
m. Glorietta
(daughter of
Moses)
ISAAC
b. 1077
m. Judita
(daughter of
Moses)
SHMUEL
b. 1080
m. Zipporah
(daughter of
Shemayah)
HANNAH
b. 1083
m. Samuel
(son of
Simcha and
Hannah
[Meir's sister])
LEAH
b. 1085
m. Samson
ben Joseph
SHLOMO
b. 1093
JACOB TAM
b. 1095

When love is strong, we can lie together on the edge of a sword. When it grows weak, a bed sixty cubits wide is not big enough for us.

—Sefer Haggadah (The Book of Legends)

prologue

The final decades of the eleventh century saw the Jews of Troyes, France, entering a time of unparalleled financial prosperity, political security, and intellectual achievement. No armies had invaded the region for generations, and the last multiyear famine was already more than fifty years in the past. Under the enlightened sovereignty of Count Thibault and Countess Adelaide, the great fairs of Champagne attracted merchants from throughout the known world, fueling a local economic boom that would continue for almost two hundred years.

Elsewhere in Europe, discovery and innovation was likewise on the rise. European scholars had discovered the lost Greek philosophy and science that had been translated into Arabic and improved upon by their Muslim counterparts, setting the stage for what is now called the Twelfth-Century Renaissance.

Jews living in Muslim lands eagerly immersed themselves in this new knowledge, producing great poets, philosophers, astronomers, and mathematicians. Their compatriots in Ashkenaz (France and Germany) eschewed secular subjects and devoted themselves to Torah study. In particular, they established great yeshivot, advanced academies for learning and discussing Talmud, the Jewish Oral Law.

One of these yeshivot, albeit a small one in Troyes when our tale begins, was founded by Rabbi Salomon ben Isaac, who would be known and revered centuries later as Rashi, one of Judaism's greatest scholars, author of commentaries on both the Bible and the Talmud. Having no sons, Salomon broke with tradition and taught Torah to his daughters, Joheved, Miriam, and Rachel. While his wife, Rivka, worried that no man would marry such learned women, Salomon had no difficulty finding husbands for them among his finest students.

His two older daughters entered into arranged marriages. Joheved was betrothed to Meir ben Samuel, a lord's son from nearby Ramerupt, while Miriam agreed to a match with Judah ben Natan, a Parisian orphan whose mother had supported herself and her son by pawning jewelry and lending money to women. Rachel, Salomon's youngest, insisted that nothing but a love match would satisfy her and married Eliezer ben Shemiah, the son of a wealthy merchant from Provence.

With the eleventh century drawing to a close, Salomon's yeshiva thrived as more and more foreign merchants studied with him while attending the two seasonal fairs held every year in Troyes. And they sent their sons to him for the rest of the year, so these young men could one day learn sufficient Talmud to allow them to enter the upper echelon of Jewish society. Salomon's sons-in-law helped with the burgeoning population of students, which gave Salomon time to write and edit his now authoritative commentaries. In addition he and his relatives worked in the family vineyard—tending the grapevines, producing wine from its fruit, and selling the vintage from his cellar.

Like her older sisters, Rachel continued to study Talmud with her father, though there was no longer need for secrecy. She bore Eliezer a son and a daughter, and partnered with Miriam to establish a jewelry and money-lending business in Troyes similar to the one Miriam's mother-in-law still ran in Paris. Rachel's future seemed nothing if not rosy and assured—after all, she was her father's favorite, adored by her husband, and the eventual matriarch of a large family of scholars.

Regretfully for Rachel, however, fate seemed to have conspired against her.

Part One

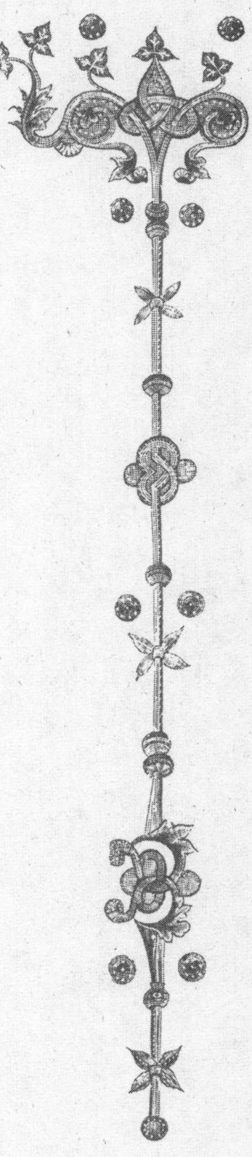

one

Troyes, France
Summer 4851 (1091 C.E.)

Rachel's fingers rifled through the chest that held her most valuable belongings, searching once more for the parchment she had dug out no less than ten times that week. Taking a deep breath, she forced her shaking hands to steady themselves so she could read from the conditional divorce's text.

> In case I do not return after an absence of six months: . . . I, Eliezer ben Shemiah of the town of Arles . . . , being of sound mind and under no constraint; I do release and send away and put aside you, Rachel bat Salomon, who have been my wife from time past to the present . . . that you may have permission and control over yourself to go to be married to any man whom you desire. . . . This shall be from me to you a bill of dismissal, a document of release, and a letter of freedom, according to the Law of Moses and Israel.
>
> Shemayah ben Jacob, a witness
>
> Moses haCohen, a witness

After a night of fervent lovemaking, she and Eliezer had kissed good-bye on the last Sunday in December, following the close of the winter Cold Fair, which meant that the six months would be over next week. Already merchants were arriving for summer's Hot Fair, but none of them carried a letter for her. Clearly her thoughtless husband could not be bothered to write that he would be delayed. Had he never considered how much she would worry?

Rachel started to clench her fists but caught herself before crumpling the precious document, her conditional *get.*

A pox on Eliezer! He had no idea what it was like for her, all those anxious days and long lonely nights, wondering what could have detained him.

It would serve her husband right if she went to the *beit din* on Thursday, six months and a day since he'd left, presented his conditional *get,* and became divorced. Of course she'd have to wait another three months before remarrying, by which time he'd surely have arrived home. Then Eliezer would be the one to wait and suffer while she took her time deciding whether to reconcile, or not. The thought was a delicious one, but would she dare go through with it?

She took another deep breath. He was probably waiting for a ship to arrive with his merchandise, or he was negotiating a contract with someone who might well take advantage of his need to hurry. Rachel could think of a dozen legitimate reasons why Eliezer had not yet arrived.

She scowled down at the paper in her hand. When a decent husband, a loving husband, knows he'll be late, he makes an effort to inform his wife. Her anger flared once more as she imagined Eliezer going about his business in Maghreb, perhaps enjoying a tryst with a local serving wench, with nary a thought of his faithful wife fretting at home.

But there might be another reason for the delay, and it was one she shuddered to merely consider. What if something awful had delayed him, something that rendered him incapable of writing her? Rachel suddenly envisioned Shemiah and Asher, Eliezer's father and brother, swept away in a rain-swollen river six years ago after their ferry capsized during a routine trading mission to Prague.

Please, mon Dieu, protect my husband and bring him safely back to me.

Perhaps sensing her disquiet, little Rivka began to stir in her cradle. Rachel hurriedly locked the paper away and gathered her one-year-old daughter to her chest. The baby pawed at her chemise to find her breast as Rachel lay back in bed to nurse. Stroking the small head of dark curly hair, she told herself to be patient. Eliezer had never missed the opening day of the Hot Fair. Surely he'd return before the week was over. And when he did finally show up, she'd make sure that he'd never be late again without informing her.

She let out a soft sigh. Stop agonizing over Eliezer, she told herself sternly. Think about how your daughter's smiles make you melt inside, of how proud you are that five-year-old Shemiah is learning to read Torah so quickly. Imagine the prices you'll get for the jewelry you've taken in pawn.

But none of these lovely thoughts could keep her mind from churning; whatever had happened to her husband?

Eliezer woke to the sound of birds twittering above and thanked Heaven he was still alive. He could smell something cooking and his empty stomach clenched in pain. There was a cramp in his right leg, but when he tried to stretch, he couldn't move. They had tied him even tighter than usual last night.

How many days had he been a prisoner here, tied to a tree somewhere in the Forest of Burgundy? One week at least. How long before some merchants rode through here, Jews who would ransom him?

Eliezer heard the crunching of leaves and cracked open an eye to see who was coming. He had learned to feign sleep whenever his captors approached, as two of them were crueler than the others. Fortunately, these worn boots belonged to one of the youngest members of the gang, a youth barely into his teens who brought water several times a day.

"Jehan," Eliezer whispered, and the youth squatted down next to him. "Can you loosen the knot on my right leg?" When Jehan did nothing, Eliezer added, "Just a little so I can get rid of this cramp."

Jehan helped him sit up and drink from the battered tin cup. "I can't right now. They might see."

"Can you at least help me up so I can piss properly?"

As Jehan pulled him to his feet and lifted his chemise, a man called out, "Hey, what are you doing with the prisoner?"

"Can't you see?" he yelled back. Then he whispered to Eliezer, "I told you they were watching."

Eliezer was so weak he could barely stand, but at least he didn't have to relieve himself on the dirt where he lay. Most of the men found it amusing when he messed himself. "Tell me, how did you come to live among these thieves?"

Jehan bowed his head to whisper. "Besides me, there were five brothers and sisters, too many for our father's small plot to support. When our mother died, my brother decided to make his escape and I came along."

He winced at the memory. "The gang discovered us in the forest, lost and starving, and we've been here ever since."

Eliezer nodded. Jehan's story was similar to that of many runaway villeins. He sank back down and waited. *The first thing I'll do when I'm ransomed is have a bath. If I'm ever ransomed.*

Fear began to gnaw at him once again.

Soon the daily ritual would begin. Someone would come and offer him a handful of bacon. The first day, Eliezer politely reminded them that Jews don't eat pork and asked would they please bring him something else to eat. The pork was removed, but nothing replaced it. The same thing happened the second day, and the third. Why were they torturing him like this? Even out here in the forest the men must have other foodstuffs.

By the fourth day, Eliezer was so hungry that he began to consider eating the bacon. The mitzvot were to live by, not die by, and if he didn't eat something soon, he would starve. He knew very well that some Jews did eat pork, especially if they were in a tavern far from home. He'd been tempted to try it himself when the other fare smelled rotten.

But he wasn't just any Jew. He was a Talmud scholar. And not just any scholar, but the son-in-law of Salomon ben Isaac, the rosh yeshiva of Troyes. It would need to be a matter of life or death before he sinned so publicly. *And if I don't have something to eat soon, it will be.*

He barely had the strength to roll over to face the main camp, but he wanted to see who would be offering him breakfast today. *Merde.* It was Richard, one of the cruel ones, whose grating voice made Eliezer's skin crawl.

"Here, Jew." Richard grabbed Eliezer's head by the hair and waved the bacon under Eliezer's nose. "You must be hungry by now. Have some nice hot bacon. We cooked it just for you."

Eliezer might have been tempted if Jehan had offered him the food, but he wasn't going to give his tormentor such satisfaction. Usually he turned his head away, but this time he spat on the bacon. He managed to spit on Richard's hand as well.

"Damn you." Richard slammed Eliezer's head to the ground, and Eliezer saw stars. He curled himself into a ball as blows continued to rain upon him.

Suddenly an authoritative voice bellowed, "Leave him alone. I told you to offer him the bacon and report his response back to me."

"He didn't eat it, Master Geoffrey."

"I can see that, you idiot."

From his position on the ground, Eliezer couldn't see who his protector was. His head spun. Why were his captors starving him? It didn't make sense. If they'd wanted to kill him, they could have done it days ago.

Trying to ignore the pain, Eliezer considered his situation. This disaster was his own damn fault. Just before he'd planned to leave Fustat, he'd learned of an alum trader due to arrive from Damascus any day. With alum always in short supply, the profit at the Hot Fair would be worth the wait. When the trader with the alum arrived the following week, Eliezer was sure he could get home to Rachel in time. But the ship carrying him and his stock across the Great Sea was harried by storms, and reports of pirates kept her close to the coast. By the time he reached his mother's house in Arles, all the merchants had already left for Troyes. His only chance to get there before the fair opened was to ride out alone, leaving his goods to follow.

His mother warned him not to ride through Burgundy, that the woods were infested with rogues and bandits. So many merchants had been waylaid that now only the largest, most well-guarded caravans would attempt it. But he was in too much a hurry to travel by the safer, slower river route. Rachel had been furious the last time he'd been late, accusing him of thoughtlessness and worse. If he missed his six-month deadline, she might be angry enough to divorce him, just to make him woo her again.

So he hired the fastest horse in Arles and for the first few days savored his good luck. That's when the highwaymen surrounded him. He fought the best he could, but they threw a net over him and dragged him off his horse. Immediately he was disarmed, blindfolded, and carried off to their camp—where they offered him nothing to eat but bacon.

Eliezer groaned and tears welled in his eyes. He'd only gotten into this fiasco because he was so worried about being delayed. Now he'd never get back to Rachel in time. He'd starve to death in the God-forsaken forest, and his family would be left with no answers. They would have no idea what had befallen him.

Jehan appeared above him. "Master Geoffrey wants to see you. Can you walk?"

"I won't know until you untie me."

Even with Jehan's support, Eliezer could only take a few steps before he grew faint. The youth ran off toward the main camp, telling him to wait. As if he had any other option, Eliezer thought bitterly.

It wasn't long before he heard several men making their way through the brush. Jehan reached him first, helping him sit up against a tree. Three other men squatted down next to him, including Richard and another fellow that Eliezer recognized as Jehan's older brother. Eliezer had never seen the third man before, but the way the others were looking at him, waiting for him to speak, he was clearly their superior.

"Shall I feed him, Geoffrey?" Jehan's brother asked. "Or do you want to question him first?"

Geoffrey nodded at Jehan and his brother. "Feed him."

Jehan untied Eliezer's arms and his brother held out a cup, followed by a plate. The cup contained ale, not water, but Eliezer gulped it down without a thought of its quality. The stuff on the plate looked like fish, but he sniffed it to be sure. There were also some mashed roots, probably turnips. Eliezer didn't care what they were. He forced himself to eat slowly; who knew when he'd eat again, and Heaven forbid he should vomit up this meal.

He had many questions, but instead he forced a smile and said, "I don't suppose you have any bread."

Geoffrey chuckled. "*Pardonnez-moi*, but we have no bakeries in our forest."

Those few words were enough for Eliezer to identify Geoffrey's accent as belonging to a member of the nobility. "I'm Eliezer ben Shemiah of Troyes." He bowed slightly. "I'm sure you'll understand if I don't say what a pleasure it is to meet you."

"My name is Geoffrey . . ." He hesitated.

"Geoffrey de . . . ?" Eliezer revealed that he recognized the man's noble status.

"I was raised in Saulieu, but I'm Geoffrey de Bois now." He motioned for Jehan to pour Eliezer more ale.

"So Geoffrey de Bois, what are you planning to do with me?"

"That's what you're going to help me decide," Geoffrey murmured. "My original intent was to ransom you, but there have been so few other merchants that I've despaired of finding one to send for the payment."

"Of course there are no others coming by. Between Duke Odo's henchmen and yours, these woods are so dangerous people will go days out of their way to avoid them."

"I realize that now, which is why I had to test you."

Eliezer swallowed hard. "Test me?"

"I assumed that you were a Jew, and I knew I was right when you refused the bacon. But I needed to know how pious you were, whether I could trust your word if you took an oath."

"What sort of oath do you intend me to take?"

Geoffrey locked eyes with him. "I want you to swear that if I let you go, you will return with the ransom we agree upon, not in coins, but in food and supplies for my men."

Richard jumped up, his face burning with anger. "Have you lost your mind, trusting a Jew like that? You let him go and we'll never see him again."

"And what do you suggest we do with him?" Geoffrey's voice was icy.

"Kill him. Sell those jewels he was carrying."

Eliezer paled and fought back his panic.

"You idiot," Geoffrey said. "The reason the Duke of Burgundy tolerates us in his forest is because we haven't killed anyone, and it's far too much trouble for his sergeants to track us down when we're just trifling with merchants. But if we try to sell such obviously stolen property as jewels—first, no Jew will buy them because he knows they belong to another Jew. Second, we have no idea how to find somebody else to buy them, someone who won't cry out 'thief' and collect a reward from the Jews for his effort."

The recipient of this lecture remained silent, sulking at his rebuke. Jehan's brother rubbed salt in Richard's wound by pointing out that none of them had any idea what Eliezer's jewels were worth, so that even in the unlikely event of finding a fence to buy them, they'd never get as good a price as his ransom anyway.

"If we don't kill him, if we just let him go," the gravelly voice snarled. "How do we know he'll come back with the ransom?"

"You have my jewels," Eliezer spoke up. "Keep them as security against my return. You may not be able to sell them, but if you have them, I can't sell them either."

As the three men considered this, Eliezer turned to Geoffrey. "You'll have my oath. I will return."

"Bah!" Richard spat. "You can't trust the word of a Jew."

Eliezer's mind was working furiously. "Wait, I have another idea."

"Go on," Geoffrey said.

"What if, instead of attacking Jewish merchants and holding them for ransom, you charge them a toll for safe passage through the forest?" Eliezer took a breath before continuing, knowing full well that his life depended on his ability to persuade them. "You have plenty of men. If there are enough to escort a caravan and protect it from Odo's henchmen, most merchants will gladly pay for the service."

"They might," Jehan's brother said. "Since it's the shortest route from Marseille to Troyes."

"Duke Odo won't like it if we stand between his men and travelers in his forest." The brute's raspy voice rose into a whine.

"On the other hand, Odo's men have stooped to assaulting pilgrims, and I wouldn't mind putting an end to that," Geoffrey replied. "Especially if it meant more income for us."

"If you offer to share some of your fees with Odo, I bet the duke will take his cut and not bother you," Eliezer said. "And that's where I can be of use. Members of Odo's court always attend Troyes' fair, and I can negotiate with them for you."

"Don't believe him." The cruel one's eyes narrowed with suspicion. "The Jew will lie through his teeth to escape, and then he'll lead Odo right to us."

"Let me give it some thought." Geoffrey began to walk away, then halted and leaned in to Jehan. "You can feed the prisoner whatever the others are eating, but no more bacon."

Salomon ben Isaac was pacing.

"Shall I go and get them?" Meir, Salomon's son-in-law, asked. "We don't want the visiting scholars to wait too long for today's Talmud session."

The tension was palpable, and each small noise caused Meir's eyes to jump nervously up the steep staircase that led to the women's gallery. Standing next to Meir in the synagoue entryway, a merchant shifted and removed his cloak.

Judah, Salomon's second son-in-law, shook his head. "Meir, today's lesson will be delayed in any case once Rachel hears the news."

Salomon, feeling older than his fifty-one years, looked up and sighed. "There's my wife coming now."

Rivka, her plump face unlined despite the grey curl that escaped her veil, stood at the top of the stairs, her two oldest granddaughters supporting her on either side. A moment later, Salomon's three daughters followed.

Joheved, the eldest, leaned heavily on the banister as she turned the corner, and Salomon smiled at the telltale bulge at her midsection. So she was finally pregnant again. The loss of her baby boy, Salomon's namesake, to smallpox two years ago had been devastating for her and Meir, and Salomon prayed regularly for another son to replace him. But Joheved had barely survived the child's breech birth, and with two sons and two daughters, he had begun to suspect that she was drinking a sterility potion.

At least we have some good news to balance the bad, he thought, as he watched Rachel and Miriam walk down. Each carried a little girl in her arms whose straight or curly locks matched her mother's. How had he managed to father two such dissimilar sisters? Miriam was slim, almost skinny considering that she was the mother of four, with long reddish brown hair and hazel eyes. She and Joheved were not unattractive, but neither of them could compare with their younger sister's beauty.

Rachel's perfect oval face, framed by bouncy black curls, was lovely enough, but it was impossible not to be captured by her striking emerald green eyes, a feature she emphasized by wearing that color regularly. As for her figure, she was plump where a woman ought to be plump.

Now that he thought about it, each of his daughters was unique. His eldest, Lady Joheved of Ramerupt-sur-Aube, ran Meir's small feudal estate as if she were born into nobility instead of the family of a poor vintner. Calm and competent, nothing seemed to rattle her.

Miriam was the compassionate one, the curious one—good traits for a midwife who was always looking for new herbs and treatments for her patients. Rachel had barely known Salomon's mother, Leah, but she was the one who followed in her grandmama's entrepreneurial footsteps.

Clever and resolute, Rachel not only helped to manage the family's wine-making enterprise, but she also ran a business that lent money to women.

To be honest, she had been his favorite daughter since she was little, and he had long since given up trying to hide his preference.

Three daughters and no sons; yet Salomon couldn't imagine trading any of them for a boy. One quality they shared equally, the one that most filled him with pride, was their devotion to Talmud study. Scholars themselves, each girl had married a man even more learned than herself, and between them he now had six grandsons.

His reverie was cut short as Rachel reached the bottom of the stairs. Dark circles beneath those green eyes marred her beauty, and her usually smiling face was drawn. He knew what was worrying her, and it still pained him to see the physical proof of her anxiety.

"Rachel." He cleared his throat. "There is someone here to speak with you."

The merchant wasted no time on pleasantries. "I have some disturbing news for you, Mistress Rachel." He paused as she instinctively reached to clutch Salomon's arm for support. "I accompanied your husband from Fustat to Marseilles. He asked me to bring his merchandise to Troyes along with my own." The merchant swallowed hard and continued, "He said he was in a hurry, that he would ride on ahead."

Rivka grabbed the baby as Rachel grew pale and her legs nearly gave beneath her. Blinking back tears, she whispered what all of them were wondering. "If Eliezer left first on horseback, while you traveled with the loaded carts, please tell me why he isn't home yet."

two

iriam picked up her midwife's basket. "Be sure to let me know if your wife feels feverish or if she starts bleeding heavily."

"Are you sure you won't spend the night?" Simon the Dyer asked. "I heard Matins chime a while ago, and it is Wednesday."

"*Merci*, but *non*." She smiled at the new father. "I expect there are still people about, even at this late hour. And I expect that my husband is among them."

Miriam remembered the warning against demons from Tractate Pesachim:

> One should not go out alone at night on Wednesday and the Sabbath because the demon Agrat bat Machlat goes abroad with eighteen myriads of destroying angels.

But the text continued with how the sage Abaye later encountered Agrat and, because of his Torah learning, was powerful enough to forbid the demon from passing through populated areas. Troyes, one of the biggest cities in France, should be safe.

If it had been winter, or the weather bad, she might have accepted Simon's offer, since the dyer lived at the far western side of Troyes, near the Vienne Creek. But during the Hot Fair, Count Thibault made sure the city streets, especially those between the fairgrounds and the Jewish Quarter, were well lit and patrolled by his men. Merchants thus felt safe to conduct business late into the night, with the Jewish ones staying up to study as well.

"I'll ask Cresslin to walk you home." Simon gestured to one of the men praying with him for a safe delivery. "He lives the closest to the Old Synagogue."

"*Merci,*" she said. "I'll be back tomorrow afternoon."

Once the courtyard gate closed behind them, Cresslin turned to Miriam. "So Simon finally has a son. Did he say anything about you performing the circumcision, or do you think he'll want Avram to do it?"

Miriam sighed. She'd been a *mohelet* for almost four years, but Judah had been right when he said that she could wait twenty years and perform a thousand circumcisions, yet some men would still complain that brit milah was a man's mitzvah. "Dyers like Simon must have good relations with all cloth merchants, especially foreign ones who are less accepting of me."

"I suppose your doing a brit at the New Synagogue during fair season would upset the foreigners," he said. "But they will have to accept a woman eventually; Avram won't live forever."

Before Miriam could reply, she was distracted by a disturbance ahead of them. "What's that yelling?"

"Wait here. I'll see what the trouble is."

Cresslin bolted down the street while Miriam slowly followed. He had only been out of sight for a few moments when she saw him running back. Except that when he grew closer, she could see that it wasn't Cresslin at all, but her husband, Judah.

He grabbed her hand. "We've got to get Eliezer home right away. I've already sent for the doctor."

"Eliezer?" Miriam gasped. "Where is he? What happened?"

"They've probably gotten him to the fairgrounds by now. He arrived a little while ago, at the Croncels Gate, so ill that he could scarcely stay on his horse. When the guards realized who he was, they sent to the New Synagogue for help. I happened to be there, thank Heaven."

Miriam had to run to keep up with Judah, but she wished they could have gone faster. "What's wrong with him? Is he sick or is he injured?"

"I didn't see any injuries, but that doesn't mean he has none." He pointed up the road. "There he is now."

Miriam saw two men supporting another between them, slowly walking up rue de la Fanerie toward the old city. A fourth man carried a large saddlebag.

"The four of you can carry him," Miriam shouted, tying up her skirt and grasping her basket tightly. "I'll get Rachel."

She ran past the convent of Notre Dame, crossed the bridge, and soon reached her family's courtyard. Her heart beating wildly, she banged on her younger sister's front door.

Where are the servants? Are they deaf?

By the time Rachel's elderly maidservant called out, "Who's there," Salomon had rushed to the door to meet Miriam, plying her with questions. But Miriam raced desperately up the stairs, only to nearly crash into Rachel on the landing outside her bedroom.

Before Miriam could catch her breath, Rachel cried out, "Can't anyone get some sleep around here? Why are you running around in the middle of the night on Wednesday? Have you been attacked by demons?"

"Quickly now, put on your cloak." Miriam hurried into her sister's room and retrieved the garment. "Eliezer is in Troyes, and he's ill."

Rachel stared at her for a moment, bleary-eyed. Then she grabbed her cloak in one hand and Miriam's arm in the other. "Take me to him. Immediately."

The maidservant was still standing at the gate, waving the shoes Rachel had forgotten, as Troyes' doctor, Moses haCohen, caught up with the two sisters and their father at the end of the street. A moment later, turning the corner, Rachel could make out the shadowy figures approaching in the distance and, ignoring whatever she might step in, bolted toward the man she loved.

The next afternoon, Rachel's voice rose in dismay as she refilled her husband's wine cup. "You're actually planning to pay the ransom?" It was all she could do to keep from screaming. He'd barely made it home alive, and now he wanted to put himself in danger again?

Eliezer helped himself to another slice of lamb. "I vowed an oath that I would return with food and supplies worth twenty-five dinars."

"Twenty-five dinars? I thought the standard ransom around the Great Sea was thirty."

He squeezed her hand under the table. "Luckily Geoffrey doesn't appear to know that."

Rachel had waited impatiently while her husband slept through breakfast and morning services, and now their entire family crowded around the table to hear what had happened. Shemiah's eyes opened wide at his father's adventure with bandits in the Forest of Burgundy, but Rachel only felt grateful beyond measure that he'd managed to escape and come home to her.

"Surely an oath given under such duress can be annulled by the *beit din*." She appealed to her father. "He would have been killed otherwise."

"The only reason bandits and pirates don't kill Jews as they do their other prisoners is because we pay ransom." Eliezer took her hand. "We must pay it, Rachel. Otherwise we'll be setting a terrible precedent. Besides, Geoffrey kept at least twenty-five dinars worth of jewels."

"I don't care about the money. You were captured in Burgundy, so Duke Odo must indemnify our losses." She looked up at Eliezer, her eyes pleading. "Please don't go back there."

Salomon turned away from his daughter's display of concern for her husband. One of the reasons the Troyes fairs were so popular, and thus so successful, was that if any merchants were attacked in another province on the way Count Thibault would prohibit anyone from there to trade at the fairs unless the sovereign made restitution.

"Eliezer isn't expected to return until the end of the Hot Fair," Salomon said. "Maybe Geoffrey's gang has harassed enough merchants that by then Duke Odo will have sent some knights to drive them from his land."

Eliezer shook his head. "Geoffrey has plenty of his own men, and if Odo were going to arrest them, he would have done so by now. Geoffrey isn't a bad sort, actually, although I wouldn't mind seeing some of his men swinging from the gallows."

Salomon stroked his beard in thought. "Let me remind you of the discussion between Rabbi Meir and his learned wife Beruria in the first chapter of Tractate Berachot."

Eliezer immediately began quoting it.

> "Certain brigands in Rabbi Meir's neighborhood used to trouble him so greatly that he prayed for them to die. Beruria, his wife, said to him: What is the reason for your prayer? He replied: Because it is written (in Psalms), 'Let sinners cease (from the earth).'"

Rachel knew the text as well and chose this point to interrupt him. "Then Beruria said:

> Is 'sinners' written? Rather 'sins' is written. And further, look at the end of the verse, 'And they are wicked no more.' Once their sins cease, they will no longer be wicked. So pray instead that they repent and be wicked no more. He prayed for them, and they repented."

Eliezer frowned at his father-in-law. "You can't mean that I should just pray for Geoffrey and his men to repent?"

"But it was your idea that the highwaymen should charge merchants for safe passage through the forest," Judah said.

Miriam leaned forward eagerly. "Now you must find out how large a bribe Odo will need to leave Geoffrey's men alone. Once you arrange it, they can become toll takers instead of bandits."

"And you will have done a great service for all the merchants traveling to Troyes from the south," Salomon said.

Eliezer paused. He'd been desperate when he made that suggestion. Now that he was home, did he really want the bandits rewarded instead of punished? But Beruria was right, and he sighed in resignation. "I expect Geoffrey can earn more money this way than as a thief."

Rachel scowled. "What's the difference? Most toll takers are no better than thieves anyway."

"Now that we've agreed." Eliezer locked eyes with Rachel. "You see why I must keep my oath."

Her gazed shifted between Shemiah and baby Rivka, whose lives would be jeopardized if he broke his oath. She nodded slowly. "This must all be in place before the Hot Fair closes. The sooner we get your jewels back, the sooner I can sell them." She continued planning, speaking to no one in particular. "We'll sell the alum and arrange for the ransom with some men-at-arms to guard it. Then we'll take it to Geoffrey."

"Not you," Eliezer said. "It's too dangerous for a woman."

Rachel smiled sweetly, but there was steel in her eyes. "I'm not letting you out of my sight, not after all the nights I spent worrying about you instead of sleeping."

Salomon stood up and put a hand on each of their shoulders. "Hire some extra men, and Rachel can go with you as far as that inn at the forest's edge. You shouldn't need more than a day to pay your ransom and explain the duke's terms to Geoffrey."

"And if you haven't returned to the inn by *souper.*" Rachel shook her knife at him, her eyes smoldering. "I'll hire an army to bring you back."

Eliezer nodded and returned her passionate gaze. Through all his travels he missed Rachel and their marriage bed almost painfully, and he knew she'd be sharing it far more willingly if they were in agreement.

Besides, the thought of going back into that forest alone terrified him.

Eliezer sold his alum quickly and had less trouble than he'd anticipated making a deal with Duke Odo's chamberlain. Meanwhile Rachel arranged sufficient credit to pay for twenty-five dinars worth of provisions and men to accompany them. Eliezer protested again when he saw her packing swaddling for little Rivka, but Rachel insisted the baby was coming—their daughter wasn't weaned yet.

Under other circumstances, their short trip to the travelers' inn would have been a pleasant diversion. But it seemed that far too soon the moment Rachel had been dreading arrived. While the cocks were still crowing, she watched helplessly from the gate as Eliezer, his guards, and their carts disappeared into the dangerous dark forest. Long afterward, she stood there, staring at the empty road in the growing light.

"Mistress, please . . . you must come inside. Breakfast is almost over," the serving maid announced, jostling Rachel from her vigil.

"Of course. *Merci,*" she murmured, reluctantly following the girl inside.

With little Rivka sleeping peacefully through her morning nap, Rachel brought out her father's Talmud commentary to study while she waited. But try as she might, her mind wouldn't focus on the text. *What is Eliezer doing? Has he met Geoffrey yet? How soon will he be back?* She tried to feel confident that Geoffrey would be grateful for their help, tried to ignore the terrible fear that once he had his supplies, he'd kill Eliezer without a second thought.

She paced the inn's main room, taking in the well-worn tables and benches, the long counter littered with pitchers and mugs, the twin cabinets filled with more cracked and chipped dishes than whole ones, and the large stone hearth that was mostly coals on this warm summer morning.

Everything looked exactly the same as the last time she'd been here two years ago. And exactly the same as the first time she'd stayed here, four years before that.

She sighed. It was now six years since Eliezer's father and brother died outside Prague, six years since she and Eliezer brought the two men's effects back to Arles. Until then she'd never realized there was such a large world outside Troyes. Of course she knew that merchants came to the fairs from many faraway places, and she, like other Jews, prayed daily for the rebuilding of Jerusalem. But to travel so far herself—who would have imagined such a thing?

To distract herself from Eliezer's fate, Rachel let her thoughts roam back to those innocent days during their second year of marriage. The inn's salon was warm and, half-dozing, Rachel settled into her memories. Back then she'd been more excited than nervous when they'd left at the Hot Fair's close, baby Shemiah on her hip, one cart loaded with woolen cloth and the other with casks of Papa's wine.

It had been difficult saying adieu to Papa; his eyes looked so sad and his face was creased with worry. But she'd fought back tears and hugged him tight. Eliezer was her husband; to be separated from him for months would have been agony.

Riding through the forest on her hired palfrey had been pleasant, and the gentle movement kept little Shemiah content in her lap. Sleeping in the forest was both exciting and scary, and when they reached the Saône River, where their things were loaded onto barges, the water appeared too gentle to be dangerous. Still, she gave a prayer of thanks that Joheved had taught her how to swim.

Her anxiety began when they arrived in Lyon, where the mighty Rhône River joined the Saône. Here the current was much swifter, faster than a man could run. But Eliezer assured her that the river was only treacherous in the spring. She squeezed his hand and kept her fears to herself; after his father's drowning, Eliezer might be more frightened than she was.

Indeed, after only a few days on the Rhône, the river's constant pull was rather soothing. The ever-changing scenery fascinated her—vast forests interrupted by vineyards, fields of grain, fruiting orchards, and small villages. Eliezer preferred to study Talmud, and their son's lengthy naps provided plenty of time for her to join him. Rachel was almost disappointed when, two weeks later, they disembarked in her husband's hometown.

If Eliezer was shocked at his mother's appearance, he said nothing to Rachel. Of course Flamenca was in mourning, having lost both a son and husband, but Rachel scarcely recognized the plump and rosy-cheeked matron who'd attended their wedding the previous year. Flamenca was a shattered old woman: her hair grey, her face wrinkled, her thin hands lined with veins. The woman who had danced so joyously now walked haltingly.

As soon as Eliezer's mother saw him, she burst into tears, and he began to cry as well when they embraced. Little Shemiah elicited more weeping, and Rachel gulped in alarm as she considered that Eliezer might now be the head of his family, responsible for supporting all of them. But her anxiety eased when Eliezer's sisters arrived. Eleanor, the eldest, was obviously the one in charge.

"We have ten days until Rosh Hashanah," Eleanor declared. "That gives us time to decide what merchandise my husband will take to Sepharad and what you will take to Maghreb."

Eliezer gasped. "I'm going to Maghreb?"

Her husband Netanel nodded. "And if the proper ships land in Arles this week, we should be prepared to leave as soon as a good wind permits." He turned to Eliezer and explained, "No ships sail in the winter; it's too stormy and the sailors can't see enough stars through the clouds to navigate."

Standing next to her husband, Rachel tried to stifle her surprise. Not only would they be spending Yom Kippur at sea, but a journey to Maghreb and back would prevent them from returning to Troyes for the Cold Fair. She felt her excitement and anticipation growing. Ships didn't sail all winter, so they wouldn't be home until after Passover.

Eleanor eyed her brother sternly. "Netanel has spent several years establishing his business contacts in Sepharad. Papa's associates were in Tunis, and he had just started to turn that territory over to Asher when . . ." Her chin began to quiver and she could no longer speak.

"I understand." Rachel stood up tall. "Our family mustn't lose such valuable connections. Eliezer and I will travel to Tunis and assure your father's clients that nothing has changed."

"You're taking the baby?" Flamenca asked. "But I was expecting you to stay with us."

"Wherever I need to travel, Rachel and Shemiah come with me," Eliezer replied. Now his voice was firm.

Rachel sighed with relief. It wasn't just a matter of preventing their separation. Eliezer had almost no commercial experience, while she had been partners with Miriam's mother-in-law in a jewelry business for years. Without Rachel's expertise, Eliezer would be at the mercy of the sophisticated Maghreb merchants.

She and Eliezer continued to present a united front to his family until Shabbat. They were sitting at Flamenca's dining table, where Rachel was enjoying the food, so different from the fare she knew. The olive trees that flourished in the Provence countryside yielded massive quantities of olive oil, and the fried fish included ocean varieties she had never sampled before. Citrus trees also thrived there, and several dishes were infused with the sweet pulp of oranges or the tart bite of lemons. There were delicious vegetable sauces, rich with olive oil and eggplant. And some wonderful desserts. Rachel couldn't help but wish Papa were there: he loved sweets almost as much as she did.

She was wavering between another piece of lemon cake and an almond pastry when Eleanor announced to Netanel, "Rachel taught us the most beautiful blessing for lighting the Sabbath lamp. It's just like the one for Hanukkah, except you say '*ner shel* Shabbat' instead of '*ner shel* Hanukkah.' "

Before Netanel could respond, Eliezer burst out, "What are you talking about? There's no special ritual in the Talmud for lighting the Shabbat lamp, and it's against Jewish Law to make up new blessings."

Rachel could feel her face burning as everyone at the table stared at her. "This isn't a new blessing," she countered. "My mother and my grandmother both said it." How dare Eliezer berate her in public? As if he were the only one who studied Torah. "And how do you know it isn't in the Talmud?" she shot back. "You haven't studied every tractate."

Eliezer's eyes glittered with anticipation. The gauntlet had been thrown. "I've studied enough to know that I've never seen it." He sounded very sure of himself. "Considering the lengthy debates the Sages have about the Havdalah blessings said on Saturday night, I can't believe they would ignore one for the Shabbat lamp when they discuss the blessings said on Friday night."

Rachel had been arguing Talmud with Eliezer since he first came to Troyes, and she wasn't going to back down because they were away from home, where people thought women shouldn't study the Oral Law. Especially not when he acted so patronizing. She tried to think of what Papa would have said.

"Maybe the blessing was so well known that the Sages didn't need to mention it. After all, when they talk about women dying in childbirth for neglecting the women's mitzvot, they include the Shabbat lamp along with *mikvah* and challah, both of which do have blessings."

Eliezer smiled broadly and rubbed his hands together, his objection ready. "The Sages also list lighting the lamp along with setting *eruv* boundaries and tithing Sabbath food, neither of which require a blessing." He proceeded to quote the relevant passage from Tractate Shabbat.

> "A man says three things in his house before dark on Shabbat eve. Have you tithed? Have you established the *eruv*? Light the Shabbat lamp."

Ha. Women can also quote Talmud. Ignoring her in-laws' looks of astonishment, Rachel leaned across the table and said:

> "Rav Huna says: One who regularly lights the lamp will have scholarly sons, one who is conscientious about mezuzah will merit a beautiful home, one who is conscientious about tzitzit will merit beautiful clothes, and one who is conscientious about kiddush will merit casks of wine."

Sure she had bested Eliezer, she grinned. "Mezuzah, tzitzit, and kiddush are all mitzvot that require blessings."

But her husband would not admit defeat so easily. "Rav Huna is talking about a normal house lamp. If a family keeps it burning, their sons will be able to study Torah late into the night. Besides, nobody in the Talmud calls lighting the Shabbat lamp a mitzvah. Certainly the Holy One never commands us to do such a thing." He crossed his arms over his chest triumphantly. "Lighting the lamp on Friday night is no different from lighting it on Wednesday or Thursday, except that on Friday it must be done before sunset."

Now Rachel had him. She didn't care that his family was staring at her with frank disapproval; she wasn't ashamed of her scholarship. "But Papa says that it *is* a mitzvah. In his commentary on that passage, he writes:

> As it is written [in Proverbs], 'For the mitzvah is a lamp and the Torah a light.' Through the mitzvot of lighting Shabbat and Hanukkah lamps, the light of Torah comes to us.

So of course it requires a blessing."

Eliezer couldn't contradict Salomon, his teacher, and he bowed graciously in her direction. "And what does Rabbenu Salomon say about this blessing of yours?"

"Papa told us that he saw it in the prayer book of Amram Gaon from Bavel and that Amram calls it a *minhag*, a 'nice custom.' So Papa didn't stop the women from saying it."

She gave her husband a seductive smile. Under the influence of the planet Venus, Friday night was considered particularly auspicious for marital relations. Sparring over Talmud first would make using the bed even more exciting.

Eliezer had returned her inviting gaze and chuckled: "As if any man in Troyes could stop the women there from doing what they want." He turned and addressed his bewildered family, "Including, of course, studying Talmud."

three

achel sighed as she recalled those heady days in Arles. Netanel knew which ships had the best reputations, and when one of the most seaworthy docked on the Sunday after Selichot, bound for Tunis, he arranged for their passage. If the wind held, they would board Tuesday evening and leave at dawn.

"You must be careful to step onto the ship with your right foot, never the left," he warned them. "Don't cut your hair or nails at sea either, and that includes trimming your beard."

"Anything else?" Eliezer said.

"Don't whistle: it brings on a storm. And don't expect a ship to leave port on a Friday: it's bad luck."

Rachel twisted her sleeves with anxiety. "How long do you think the journey will take?"

"If you have a steady wind, perhaps a month. That reminds me . . ." Netanel paused and handed Eliezer a thick book. "Here's an Arabic translation of the Bible, written in Hebrew letters. When you reach Tunis, you may be able to understand their language."

"*Merci.*" Eliezer nodded at Rachel. They both knew the holy text by heart, so using it to learn Arabic shouldn't be difficult.

"Speaking of the Bible, there are several verses from Moses's Song at the Sea that you should remember." Netanel leaned toward them and lowered his voice. "To calm a storm, recite:

> At a blast of Your nostrils, the waters pile up.
> The floods stood straight like a wall.

And if, Heaven forbid, you're attacked by pirates, pray:

> Pharaoh's chariots and his army He cast into the sea.
> You made Your wind blow, the sea covered them;
> They sank like lead in the glorious waters."

Unlike some other biblical incantations she'd learned, Rachel thought these from Exodus actually made sense. Still her stomach had knotted with fear at the mention of storms and pirates. But their first ocean journey was like nothing she could have imagined. It was wonderful, with magnificent sunrises and sunsets, and enormous flocks of seabirds wheeling over the water in the wind. True, the ferocious east wind sometimes blew them off course, but the delay was slight and six weeks after putting out to sea they docked safely in Tunis.

Suddenly a commotion outside the inn interrupted her pleasant recollection. She jumped up and raced to the window. *Please, mon Dieu, let it be Eliezer.*

But it was only a motley group of travelers dismounting in the courtyard. Including some wealthy ones, Rachel decided, as she noted the copious baggage and retinue of servants and men-at-arms. Just in time for *disner* too, if the smells emanating from the kitchen were any indication.

She took little Rivka upstairs to change her swaddling, and on the way down she could hear the innkeeper and his wife exchanging whispers in the hall.

"I don't care if they are pilgrims," the wife hissed. "Why should they eat for free? We're not a hospice."

"Because we're good Christians," her husband said. "It's our duty to support them on their perilous journey while we stay safely at home."

"But there are too many of them. We can't give away all that food, not with business so poor this summer."

"I know we don't get so many merchants as we used to—curse those bandits in the forest—but it's not right to charge pilgrims for their food." The innkeeper's voice was firm.

When Rachel entered the main room, the other diners were already seated, including several with crosses conspicuously sewed on their *bliauts*.

A pair of well-dressed women, the likely owners of the luggage outside, sat at a table with a third woman in nun's habit. They waved her over to join them.

"*Bonjour*, I'm Belle Assez of Troyes." Rachel saw no need to advertise her Jewish identity and used the pet name Eliezer called her.

"*Bonjour*, I'm Lady Margaret of Norwood, and this is my daughter-in-law, Jane." The elderly woman had an English accent. "This is my cousin, Prioress Ursula." She indicated the nun.

Rachel nodded and sat down.

"We just came from the Bethany abbey in Vézelay," Margaret continued proudly. "We viewed the relics of Mary Magdalene."

Rachel was sure she'd heard wrong. "Excuse me, but didn't Mary Magdalene die in the Holy Land?" She carefully used the Edomite name for Eretz Israel.

Margaret sat up straight, as if imparting something of great import. "Not at all. During the persecutions that followed the death of Jesus, the Magdalene came to Provence with her sister Martha. Eventually she died and was buried there, but a monk rescued her relics when the area was devastated by Saracens and brought them to Vézelay."

"It's not so strange a story," Ursula said. "After all, the body of St. James the Apostle was brought to Compostela from the Holy Land by his disciples."

Rachel turned her attention to feeding herself and Rivka. What bizarre stories these gullible pilgrims believed. She tried to hide her boredom as Margaret expounded the family's sad history and how she was on pilgrimage to atone for their sins.

It was much harder to hide her mirth when the garrulous old lady said, "And before Vézelay, we went to Coulombs for Jane to smell the holy prepuce."

"The what?" Rachel nearly choked with suppressed laughter.

"The foreskin of Jesus," she answered. "Its sweet scent enhances fertility and eases childbirth."

The subject was preposterous, yet so intriguing that Rachel couldn't resist asking how such a relic had come to Coulombs.

"Charlemagne received it as a wedding present from Empress Irene of

Byzantium, and he in turn gave it to the Coulombs Abbey," Ursula explained, while Rachel fought her urge to giggle.

Lady Margaret expressed concerned at how their party had grown as they traveled. "While there is security in numbers and most of these people seem pious enough, one can't always tell about these things," she said. "I expect most are merely going to Rome. They don't look like they can afford the voyage to Jerusalem."

Rachel looked at the dowager with respect. The majority of pilgrims visited local shrines, while those undertaking a long pilgrimage usually went to Compostela or Rome, and the roads leading to them were populated with monasteries and hostels devoted to succoring pilgrims.

Margaret must have interpreted Rachel's expression as one of interest, because she began to explain how she'd decided on Jerusalem. Avoiding the riffraff who frequented the roads to Compostela and Rome was one of her motives, but she was also compelled by the greater spiritual reward she would receive for the more dangerous trip, plus the status she would attain on returning from the Holy Land, a place few pilgrims visited.

Rachel grew so irritated by the woman's monologue that she couldn't resist saying, "I traveled to Jerusalem three years ago. It is indeed a long and difficult journey."

Immediately she regretted it. She was now the center of attention. Rachel couldn't bring herself to disappoint her audience by reporting the Holy City's squalid appearance—an earthquake fifty years earlier had left much of the city in ruins. In addition Turks had ousted the Fatimid rulers only fifteen years ago, destroying even more of the city, and *that* was followed by years of pestilence and famine.

Even worse, decades of infighting between the rabbinic communities of Jerusalem and Ramleh had undermined their financial support to the point where neither yeshiva functioned. She and Eliezer were horrified to see that a small study hall in Tyre was all that remained of the once great Palestinian Talmud academies.

Rachel put away thoughts of Jerusalem in ruins. "I won't say anything about Jerusalem itself," she began. "To fully appreciate the experience you must have no expectations." She paused, grateful for not having to lie to these hopeful fools.

"But I can tell you about the journey, about what you can expect and how to best prepare yourself," she offered as all faces turned to her expectantly. "You might think that no one would be so sinful as to try to injure a pilgrim, but there are evil innkeepers who will rob you in your sleep, while others are in league with thieves who will attack you once you leave. And not all who wear a pilgrim's garb are what they seem."

"But what can we do?" Margaret's chaplain cried out. "We're sheep among wolves."

"Send a servant ahead to determine which places have a good reputation. And be very careful who you trust on the road." Rachel shivered. Eliezer, after all, had been captured by Geoffrey and might, at this very moment, be in grave danger from the bandits. Her listeners' faces darkened at her display of fear, so she composed herself and added, "With any luck you will reach your port safely. Where are you leaving from?"

"Genoa."

Rachel nodded. Venice and Genoa were common pilgrim ports. The ships headed south along the Italian coast, picking up fresh water and provisions as necessary, and leaving behind the corpses of anyone who died. Captains tried to avoid taking on sick people, who believed that dying on pilgrimage was a guarantee of salvation; yet there were always a few on board in their final days. It was one of many reasons Rachel and Eliezer tried to avoid ships carrying pilgrims.

She said nothing about death; the group looked frightened enough. "You will need to sell your horses before you arrive in port."

One of the men-at-arms started to protest, but Rachel cut him off. "No captain will allow the beasts on his ship, and you will receive a better price if you don't sell at the last moment. You should buy a mattress before you board; otherwise you'll be sleeping on the bare wood."

"What's it like, inside the ship?" Margaret's maidservant asked. "Do we all sleep together?"

"Passengers sleep below deck, in berths just wide and long enough to lie down in. Try to find a place on the upper decks; they don't stink so much."

Ursula was clearly a practical woman, because she asked, "What do we use for privies on board?"

"You bring your own pot, which you use for seasickness as well," Rachel said.

One of the two white-robed canons nudged his companion. "After enough passengers spill the contents of their pots in the dark below, the stench must be horrific. I can well imagine why you recommend the upper decks."

"You don't have to go below. The sailors also rig up a basket overhanging the sea, which you sit in to relieve yourself." She shuddered at the memory. "It's terrible to use during a storm."

"Are storms at sea very common?" Margaret's chaplain asked, his brow creased with worry.

"No more common than they are on land," Rachel said. In truth the most likely time for a ship to flounder was while negotiating the waves and rocks near port. "But if you do run into a storm, praying the Twenty-fourth Psalm can save you."

Her audience looked at her expectantly and Rachel immediately regretted mentioning the powerful words of scripture. None of these people would understand the Hebrew, and of course the procedure wouldn't work unless the psalm was chanted in the holy tongue. Before Rachel could decide what to do, the prioress rescued her by reciting in Latin:

> "The earth is the Lord's, and the fullness thereof;
> the world, and they that dwell therein.
> For He hath founded it upon the seas,
> and established it upon the waters.
> Who shall ascend into the hill of the Lord?
> Or who shall stand in His holy place?
> He who hath clean hands, and a pure heart . . ."

The group nodded at each other in agreement, apparently understanding the Latin and approving of how the words both mentioned the sea and alluded to pilgrims. Rachel tried to hide her annoyance. How dare these heretics who worshipped the Hanged One consider Jerusalem their holy city and assume their sins would be forgiven by traveling there? And now she had given them encouragement by telling them about Psalm 24.

Rachel recalled Papa's commentary on the psalm and was reassured that the Holy One would not listen to His psalms recited in a strange language by heretics. Papa pointed out that in the first verse, *ha-aretz*, "the earth," refers to the Eretz Israel, which belongs to the Jews, while "the world" means the other lands and their peoples. As to "who shall ascend" and "stand in His holy place," Papa said that while all people of the world are His, not everyone deserves to come near to Him.

Thank Heaven she'd mentioned that psalm only, not any of the many others said for protection on a journey. Each of the 150 psalms has a specific protective effect. And Rachel had learned all of them. Reciting Psalm 20 to a woman laboring in childbirth helped ease her pain, and birth amulets were inscribed with Psalm 126. With any luck she would never need Psalm 39, to thwart an evil design on the part of the king, or Psalm 73, against forced baptism. But the Eighth Psalm, to calm crying children, was useful, along with the Third, for healing a headache. There were many psalms for protection against the Evil Eye, as well as several to awaken love.

She grimaced as she recalled all the men who'd been attracted to her against her will—sailors who pawed her below deck, merchants who insisted on showing her special merchandise in private, strangers with a message that they needed to tell her in secret—every kind of excuse a man could invent to be alone with a woman. Why wasn't there a psalm to stifle love? The closest thing was Psalm 11, against evil men.

Rachel pulled her attention back to her tablemates when she heard herself being addressed by Ursula. "Belle Assez, you warned us about many possible dangers. Are there any agreeable events we can look forward to?"

Rachel answered in an instant: "On a cloudless night at sea, with a myriad of stars in every direction, it is impossible not to stand in awe of creation." She sighed at how overwhelmed she'd felt on her first sea journey. "But then you've seen these things; you came from Angleterre."

"During our brief trip across the channel, it was so cloudy that we rarely saw the sun or the moon." Lady Margaret stood up and shook the crumbs from her clothes, staring sternly at the other pilgrims. "We are going to the Holy Land to receive indulgence for our sins, not to enjoy the sights."

The rest of her party rose with her, and soon the only guests left at the inn were Rachel, baby Rivka, and their guards. A horse whinnied outside, and Rachel rushed toward the door. *Eliezer is here—mon Dieu, let this be him.*

* * *

But the front door opened to admit Miriam.

"I was checking on a baby nearby that Avram circumcised a few days ago, and I though I'd see if you were still here." Miriam gave her sister a reassuring hug. "When I saw your horse, I thought you might appreciate some company."

"You have no idea how glad I am to see you." Rachel signaled to the serving girl for more food.

"That's not necessary. I've already eaten."

"Then come upstairs with me while the baby naps."

They settled themselves on the bed, little Rivka between them. Miriam searched her mind for a topic that would distract her sister from Eliezer's activities in the forest.

"You've traveled so far, Rachel. But this inn is the farthest I've ever been from Troyes," Miriam said. "I admire you, taking Shemiah with you when he was just a baby."

"A babe in arm travels easily, and I never considered leaving him with a wet nurse. To tell the truth, there were times when I would have gone crazy from boredom in Tunis if not for his company."

"But surely living in such a strange country was exciting," Miriam said in surprise.

Rachel shook her head at the memory. It was true she was thrilled when they arrived at the mysterious foreign city, never suspecting that her excitement would fade into tedium and finally evaporate as she felt increasingly trapped. "Arriving in port was fascinating, with all the different boats loading and unloading, but I was worried about how we'd get in touch with the men who worked with Eliezer's father."

"What did you do?"

"We were blessed in that Safik, his most trusted business associate, met us and escorted us to the apartment where Eliezer's father had lived. You can imagine my surprise when I learned that both he and the Nubian housekeeper, Dhabi, were slaves who now belonged to Eliezer. And then I realized that Dhabi was actually my father-in-law's concubine."

"Eliezer's father had a second wife in Tunis?" Miriam's voice rose in dismay.

Little Rivka whimpered at the noise, and Rachel patted her gently.

Then she whispered to Miriam, "It still infuriates me to think of the argument Eliezer and I had over how Flamenca could bear her husband taking a concubine and whether she even knew that he'd betrayed her."

"What did Eliezer say?"

"He told me his father's slaves weren't my concern, and what his mother didn't know wouldn't hurt her."

The last thing Miriam wanted was Rachel thinking about Eliezer. "So besides owning slaves, what else was different between Tunis and Troyes? How did you spend your days?"

"Visiting other women." Rachel sighed. A major disparity, one that irritated her more the longer they stayed, was that Tunisian women seldom left their homes except to visit other women. They rarely saw men outside their families.

"Did you meet any learned women?"

"None," Rachel replied with disgust. "Even worse, women there only attend synagogue on Shabbat. If it weren't for Eliezer's need to ingratiate himself with those people, I would have gone on weekdays and ignored the consequences." Instead she'd seethed in frustration inside the beautiful prisons the Tunisian Jews made for their wives and daughters.

Miriam tried again to find a subject that wouldn't irritate her sister. "So you visited lots of women. What were their homes like? How did they live?"

"It's funny, but at first I thought that the Jews possessed great wealth," Rachel said. "Their houses were many-storied buildings of brick and clay, decorated with the most luxurious silk curtains and cushions. They had copper and brass dishes, and their floors were covered with elaborately woven mats."

She turned on her side and whispered, "Despite all my experience in the jewelry business, I was amazed at the amount of gold and number of gemstones and pearls those women possessed. And nobody in Troyes, not even the count and countess, owns such magnificent clothes."

Miriam exhaled in awe. "And I thought Jews in Troyes were prosperous."

"We are. Eventually I discovered that silk and gemstones are far more common there than in France and thus less precious than I thought," Rachel said. "Would you believe that wood is a great luxury there? That a simple birch bowl is more valuable than one made of silver?"

"Really?"

"There aren't any forests in Maghreb: lumber has to be imported from great distances."

Miriam nodded. "No wonder people there sit on silk cushions. Wooden benches and tables would cost a fortune."

"Here's another strange thing about having so little wood," Rachel said. "Women do almost no cooking for their families. Men shop for food, bringing home hot dishes from vendors selling prepared items in the marketplace. The master of the house carries several empty pots, arranged in layers, which he fills with whatever he wants for that day's meal."

"I bet women serve the food and clean up afterward," Miriam said.

"True. And when I explained how women do the shopping in Troyes, my hostesses were appalled that proper women wandered about freely in the marketplace. In Tunis only slaves and harlots behave so brazenly."

Miriam stared in astonishment as Rachel continued, "Only poor women work for a living there, at occupations they can do from their homes, like dyeing and weaving, or for other women in *their* homes, making dresses or helping to prepare a bride for her wedding. I couldn't believe how many women support their families that way, spending hours applying a bride's makeup and dressing her hair." Rachel gazed over at her sister, so thankful that Miriam had come to wait with her, for their mundane conversation that was helping the time to pass.

"What was the strangest thing you saw there?"

"Hmm . . . Actually, one custom shocked me so much I never would have believed it if I hadn't witnessed it myself."

"What was it?" Miriam asked eagerly.

"Jewish women there, and apparently in Cairo as well, don't visit the *mikvah*."

"Impossible. You must be mistaken."

"Here's what they do instead." Rachel's voice carried her disapproval. "Seven days after a woman starts her flowers, not seven days after she's finished them, she goes to the bathhouse at sunset with another woman, one who's not *niddah*. She bathes and has the clean one sprinkle her with warm water. Then she goes home to her husband."

"Women sprinkle themselves with water? After only seven days?" Miriam sputtered.

"I was still nursing Shemiah, so I was never *niddah* while I was in Tunis. And several women asked me to sprinkle them."

"Maybe the others immerse in the river or the sea if they don't use the *mikvah*?"

"*Non*, they don't immerse at all." Rachel doubted that any of these women knew how to swim. "None of their synagogues have a *mikvah*."

Miriam's jaw dropped. "And the men permit this?"

"Clearly they do; otherwise they wouldn't build a synagogue without a *mikvah*," Rachel said with contempt. She and Miriam both knew that some women in Troyes didn't use the *mikvah* either, especially in winter. When they finished bleeding, they considered it sufficient to bathe at the stewes. But their husbands probably didn't know about it.

The sisters' loud voices were disturbing the baby again. Rachel, who'd gotten little sleep the night before, yawned widely, causing Miriam to suggest that she would wait for Eliezer downstairs while her sister and niece napped together.

Rachel cuddled her daughter and closed her eyes. After that winter in Tunisia, she couldn't stand it anymore. One night in bed with Eliezer, the only time they got to spend together, she'd told him, "I don't want to come back here next year. Do we have to?"

"Maybe not." He'd stroked her hair. "I've been impressed with Safik's performance. Do you think he is competent to manage our affairs here by himself?"

"Safik's more competent than we are," she replied. "I hear it's common for slaves to be freed at their master's death. Perhaps you should make him your partner."

"My clever wife! I'll ask him tomorrow."

She chuckled. "Lucky for you that most men's wives don't study Talmud."

"Luck has nothing to do with it. I deliberately sought the most intelligent woman I could find." When Rachel looked at him skeptically he added, "And the most beautiful."

"We can sweeten the deal for him," she said, blushing at Eliezer's compliments. "Free Dhabi as well and give her to Safik for his wife."

That solved two problems. The Nubian girl was greatly anxious about her future since Eliezer wouldn't need a concubine if he traveled with his wife. Not that Rachel had any intention of letting such an attractive young woman remain in Eliezer's possession—not the way he kept eyeing her when he thought Rachel wasn't looking.

In Ashkenaz, a man could only have one wife at a time; Rav Gershom had made that decree years ago. But in Maghreb, men had both wives and concubines. Just the thought of Eliezer taking a concubine in some faraway place made Rachel's stomach churn, and she was glad she'd gotten Dhabi settled safely out of his reach. She would never share her husband with another woman, never.

These unpleasant thoughts were cut short by the door slowly creaking open. Heart pounding, she sat up and reached for the knife at her belt. Who dared enter her room at the inn without knocking?

"Who is it?" she called out, her body tensing as she tightened her grip on the blade.

four

liezer stopped short when he saw the knife in his wife's hand. "Rachel, *mon amour*. It's me. I'm so sorry I startled you. Miriam told me you two were sleeping."

Overjoyed, Rachel sprang from bed into his arms. "Don't worry, I wasn't asleep."

They clung to each other, savoring their familiar scents as the forest nightmare slowly drained away. She sighed into the cloth of his chemise. "Your trip was successful?"

"Completely." He stroked her disheveled curls. "Geoffrey is eager to begin collecting tolls and was impressed at how cheaply Duke Odo could be bought off."

"That's a relief." She hugged him again. "I was afraid something terrible had happened to you."

"I would have been here sooner if Geoffrey hadn't been out hunting. It took us hours to locate him."

"What's the matter?" she asked as his smile was replaced with a flicker of pain.

"I had two well-armed guards with me; yet those hours waiting in the forest today were almost as terrifying as the week I spent there before." He shuddered. "Even after this road is safe, my memories will make it difficult to travel."

Rachel caressed his shoulder. "So don't go that way. We did very well last year when you went east to find furs to sell at the Cold Fair and then bought swords and armor to sell in Sepharad." Her pulsed quickened. If only she could convince him to take a route that would allow him to spend more time at home.

"So we did. And Sepharad is still an excellent market."

Sadly, continual warfare in Sepharad produced a continual demand for weapons. Ever since the Castilian king, Alfonso, took Toledo from the Moors seven years ago, neither side had been able to vanquish the other.

"You could send a message to Safik to meet you there with his dyestuffs." Rachel thought she would overflow with happiness at the mere thought of it. Her husband was safe in her arms, and last year he'd finished his business in Sepharad so quickly that he was home for Passover.

"Good idea." He patted her reassuringly. "He can come with one of the winter caravans." Eliezer stood back to gaze at her. "It seems once again my wife has proven that she is as clever as she is beautiful."

Eliezer was so eager to see Rachel again, and to keep her from worrying, that he completed his fur buying that fall in time to arrive home at the end of October, a full week before the Cold Fair opened. Rachel was elated to see him, but the rest of Salomon's family was focused on two new yeshiva students.

Most new pupils elicited little excitement, but these two, Simcha de Vitry and his son Samuel, were not only father and son, but also Salomon's close relations.

"What is their story, Rachel?" Eliezer was sure he'd never met these men before, although they were kin to his wife.

"It's a sad one," Rachel replied. "Simcha's first wife, Hannah, was Meir's sister, and she died when Samuel was born. I haven't seen either of them since her funeral, and I was only seven then."

Eliezer's face clouded. "Poor Simcha."

"Miriam must know more about it. She's a midwife," Rachel said. "I'll ask her at breakfast."

Judah was as ignorant of the men's identities as Eliezer, so Miriam explained Simcha's unhappy history over the meal. "Hannah was only a couple of years older than Meir, like the age difference between Joheved and me."

"Then Meir must have felt close to her," Judah said.

Miriam gave Eliezer a sympathetic smile. He too had lost a sibling. "*Oui*. Simcha and Hannah were newlyweds when Joheved and Meir got betrothed. I met them at the feast and saw them regularly at Rosh Hashanah and Yom Kippur, since they lived at Ramerupt with Hannah and Meir's parents."

"She died in childbirth." Eliezer's words were more statement than question.

Miriam nodded. "Hannah went into labor in the middle of the night, and Meir rode to Ramerupt at dawn."

Miriam's audience was staring at her, their eyes wide. She took a deep breath. "Hannah's womb was blocked by her baby's placenta, and once labor started, nothing could prevent her from bleeding to death. Aunt Sarah had to deliver Samuel by cutting through Hannah's belly."

Rachel gasped and clutched her abdomen. She was sure she was pregnant.

Eliezer took her hand and squeezed it. "What happened to Simcha after that?"

"A widower with three small children needs a new wife, so he returned to Vitry and remarried."

"Did they ever come back to visit?" Judah asked.

"They came to console Meir's mother after his father died."

"If Simcha was at all attached to Hannah, Ramerupt would hold terrible memories for him," Judah said sadly.

Rachel rolled her eyes in annoyance. "But Hannah died fifteen years ago. Simcha and Meir must have stopped grieving, and Samuel never knew his mother. I don't see why we all have to tiptoe around them now."

Miriam and Judah stared at her in dismay, but it was Eliezer who spoke. "It's been six years since my father and brother died, but I doubt I will ever stop grieving."

"I intend to treat Simcha with the same welcoming demeanor I would display to any other relative arriving in Troyes," Rachel declared. "If his past is too painful to discuss, I won't bring up the subject."

"I'd like to know how a man his age decides to start studying Talmud," Eliezer said.

"I wonder what Papa is going to do with him." Judah scratched his head. "I can't imagine Simcha studying together with the thirteen-year-olds."

* * *

Despite his son-in-law's misgivings, Salomon placed Simcha and Samuel in the beginners' class. When the Cold Fair ended with no sign of the pair returning to Vitry, Meir's younger son, Shmuel, began to tutor his uncle and cousin in the vineyard while they pruned the vines together. Simcha and Samuel might have much to learn about Talmud, but they were experts when it came to viticulture.

The final day of the Cold Fair, Rachel stood shivering in the street, watching forlornly as Eliezer's silhouette disappeared into the falling snow. Next month he would be in sunny Sepharad. Her advanced pregnancy would leave her housebound soon enough, so she tried to accompany Papa to the vineyard every day. This was the rare opportunity she had to talk with her father in relative privacy.

"Papa, I hate it when Eliezer is gone," she said. "I want him back for Passover, or at least for the baby's birth, but he has to go all the way to Córdoba to meet his agent."

"*Ma fille*, I know it's difficult for you, especially when your sisters' husbands remain at home."

"How do I get used to it?" She paused to study the vine in front of her, and then cut off several errant shoots. "You were away from Mama for all those years when you studied in the Rhineland, and the two of you were recently married then. Didn't you miss her? I know Eliezer would rather stay with me than travel."

Salomon sighed. "My situation was different. I loved my studies at the yeshiva, and when I came home for the festivals, I usually couldn't wait to return to them."

"You loved Talmud more than your family," she accused him.

"I love Talmud *and* my family." He gave her a quick hug. "But I knew I would only have a few years at the yeshiva, while I expected to spend the rest of my life with my family."

"But Eliezer will always have to travel."

"Will he?" Salomon turned to apply his full strength to cut through a thick branch. Only new wood was fruitful, so all the previous year's growth had to be pruned away. "Your husband is the youngest child in his family; doesn't he have some nephews who can take over for him eventually?"

"I suppose so, but that will be years from now." Rachel's frustration showed as she slashed at the vine in front of her.

"Be careful. Remember how my father died."

"*Oui*, Papa." She blushed with shame. When she was little, Papa had often reminded her that his father had died of blood poisoning after he cut himself in the vineyard.

She decided to change the subject. "I'm glad that Joheved had a healthy baby boy, but I would have liked to name a son Salomon after you."

He smiled at her. "There's nothing to prevent you, *ma fille*. Meir's father has two grandsons named after him."

"*Oui*, and now that they're both studying here it's confusing to have two Samuels, even if one does prefer to be called Shmuel."

His expression clouded and his voice dropped. "Joheved's baby seems well enough—may the Holy One protect him. But pairs are unlucky, and naming this boy Salomon after the previous one died of smallpox . . ." He stopped, reluctant to say anything to provoke the Evil Eye.

"I thought Miriam did the circumcision beautifully." Rachel quickly found another topic to discuss.

Salomon shook his head. "She is adept at the procedure, but honestly I wish there were a qualified man in Troyes to be our junior mohel."

Here was a topic they could debate all day. "But you have us sit in the sukkah and say the Shema; you bought us our own tefillin—you taught us Talmud. The Mishnah says that women are exempt from all these."

He chuckled at her vehemence. "The Mishnah doesn't say anything about women studying Talmud. But Tractate Kiddushin says:

> A father is obligated to teach his son Torah . . . how do we know that a mother is not? Because it is written [in Deuteronomy]: *v'limad'tem* [you teach], which can also be read as *ul'mad'tem* [you study]. Thus a man, who is commanded to study Torah, is commanded to teach his son. And a woman, who is not commanded to study Torah, is not commanded to teach.

Because Hebrew is written without vowels, different words can be spelled identically—in this case 'teach' and 'study.' The Sages of the Talmud regularly used comparisons of this kind for exegesis."

"But this assumes that women are not commanded to study Torah," Rachel objected.

Salomon smiled and raised one finger in the air as he made his point, quoting more of the Gemara.

> "How do we know that she is not obligated to study and teach herself? Because it is written: *v'limad'tem*, which can also be read as *ul'mad'tem*. Thus a son, whom a father is commanded to teach Torah, is also commanded to study, and a daughter, not commanded to be taught Torah, is not commanded to study."

"That argument is circular and you know it." Rachel's voice began to rise.

"True. This contention hinges on the premise that a father is not commanded to teach his daughter Torah." He looked Rachel in the eye. "You know the next line as well as I do," and they quoted the text together:

> "How do we know that others are not commanded to teach her? Because it is written [in Deuteronomy]: 'You shall teach them to your sons [*benaichem*].' And thus not to your daughters."

Rachel looked at him, an earnest expression on her face. "Papa, why did you teach us?"

"Some interpret *benaichem* to mean children, and thus fathers without sons can perform the mitzvah of *v'limad'tem* by teaching a daughter Torah."

"Maybe they teach only one daughter? You taught all three of us."

"You and your sisters are all competent to study Talmud. You're not light-headed like most women."

"Most men are no better."

"Which is why their fathers are obligated to teach them Torah," he said. "If not for Torah, a man would be unable to control his *yetzer hara*. Look how violent the Edomite lords are, always attacking each other."

She smiled and shook her finger at him. "You've managed to avoid answering my question about women doing mitzvot they're exempt from."

"If women want to fulfill the men's mitzvot, if it gives them *nachat ruach*, 'spiritual satisfaction,' then they are of course permitted." He playfully shook his finger back at her. "Not that we could prevent them."

"But in Maghreb they do prevent them." Rachel's voice was suddenly serious. "You should have seen the way the women looked at me when I put on tefillin—like I was some kind of demon."

"Every community has its own customs, which eventually take on the force of halachah."

Their conversation ceased as they saw Simcha approaching. "Excuse me, Rabbenu. I have a question about this morning's lesson."

Rachel discreetly backed away, but not out of hearing distance. Papa treated every student's questions with respect, which is why the older man often came to him. She hadn't heard Simcha ask a silly question yet, and sometimes they were quite interesting.

This time Simcha's question was easily answered by encouraging him to be patient; the Gemara would address his issue a few pages later. And when several young pupils quickly followed with questions of their own, Rachel realized that they had been reluctant to interrupt the conversation she'd been having with her father.

It seemed that Papa's answer to Simcha was her answer too. Somehow she must wait and keep herself from becoming bitter like Mama, who, despite Papa's words to the contrary, never resigned herself to her daughters performing the men's mitzvot, a situation she hated but couldn't change.

The days went by and Passover concluded with no sign of Eliezer, but Rachel refused to give up hope that he might return before their child was born. And when she gave birth to a boy on May Day, she still harbored hopes that he would arrive in time for the brit.

But that was not to be. It was Papa who held the baby while she climbed up to the *bima* and took her seat on one of the two elaborately carved chairs. The other was reserved for Elijah the Prophet; the only people who used it were bridegrooms. The bride sat in its mate, everyone hoping that she would soon occupy it again with a son to be circumcised.

While Papa recited the father's traditional introduction, "Behold, I am prepared to fulfill the mitzvah of circumcising my son, as the Creator, blessed be He, commanded us," Rachel sighed. She regarded the empty chair and recalled how Eliezer had filled it on their wedding day. But then she brightened; less than ten months later, she was sitting on the bride's chair again with newborn Shemiah on her lap. And now there was another son for them.

She gently settled the baby on her lap and spread his legs. Papa might prefer that a man perform the brit, but Rachel was glad that it was a woman leaning in so close to her thighs. When she felt comfortable, she nodded at Miriam, who made the mohel's blessing and picked up the *azmil*, the two-sided circumciser's knife.

Rachel was determined to keep her eyes open; yet when the moment came, instinct made them close. Only the sound of her son's cry made her realize that she had missed his brit milah as well as Shemiah's. She looked down in time to see Miriam take a swig of wine and then bend over the howling infant. This was *motzitzin*, drawing the blood, and according to the Talmud, any mohel who did not cleanse the baby's wound with his mouth is a danger and must be dismissed.

Now Miriam was smearing the cut with a salve of olive oil and cumin, the same as she applied after cutting his cord. Since no father was present to whisper the chosen name to Papa before he made the final blessing, Rachel had told him earlier that the boy would be called Asher. When the ceremony was complete, tears of disappointment wet her eyelashes. The cumin Eliezer had imported was here, but he was not.

Seven days had passed since the birth of her son, and though she was still bleeding, she was no longer considered *niddah*. According to Torah, her blood was *dam tahor*, "the blood of purity," and she was permitted to her husband. Talmudic Sages wondered why a woman giving birth to a boy was impure for seven days, while a girl made the mother impure for fourteen days, and give the answer in Tractate Niddah:

> Why does the Torah say that milah is done on the eighth day? So that it does not happen that everyone else is joyful while the father and mother are sad.

Papa explained that if the circumcision were done earlier, while the mother was impure, the guests could enjoy themselves at the feast afterward while the parents were forbidden even to touch each other.

So instead of snuggling close to Eliezer, Rachel sat between Papa and Mama at the banquet, baby Asher asleep in her arms, as all her guests ate and drank and danced and laughed and enjoyed themselves—and as she tried to hide the tears welling up in her eyes. She was rescued by Miriam, who had seen quite a few new mothers grow inexplicably melancholy.

Miriam announced, "It's been three hours since Asher's brit. I'd like to check if he has wet his swaddling."

"I'll come too." Joheved followed her sisters, her six-month-old son on her hip.

Mama had just joined them at Rachel's door when they heard a loud masculine voice drunkenly call out, "You are to be congratulated, Rabbenu Salomon. For a man who started out with no sons at all, you now have acquired a minyan between your grandsons and sons-in-law."

All four women, as well as many in the crowd, gasped in horror. How could anyone, even inebriated, be so reckless as to praise a man's quantity of male descendants? Such a declaration would surely provoke the Evil Eye to lessen the number.

"Who the devil was that?" Mama's eyes were blazing.

They strained to see the man, but none of them recognized him.

Rachel could hear voices in the courtyard, hushing the stranger. But he would not be silenced.

"I am certainly correct," he shouted. "The eldest has three, as does the middle daughter. The youngest now has two, plus their three husbands. That's ten males—a minyan."

Mama blanched and Rachel had to bite her tongue to keep from blurting out that he was not correct, that his count totaled eleven. She saw Meir, flushed with fury, forcing his way through the celebrants, and then Miriam took her by the arm and led her sisters inside.

By the time Miriam had checked Asher's swaddling, which thankfully was wet with urine, and after both Rachel and Joheved had nursed their babies, calm had returned to the feast.

Meir was pacing the floor when they came downstairs. "Nobody knows that boor's name." He swore under his breath. "It seems that he heard about the brit milah while attending the May Fair in Provins."

"What does it matter who he is?" Miriam asked.

"It matters to me."

Joheved took hold of his hand, hovering close to the knife at his belt.

"You're not going to challenge him. The less attention we pay to him the better."

"I expect you're right, but, even so, I asked Shemayah to inquire at the New Synagogue."

Rachel agreed with Meir. "Once your study partner discovers who this fellow is, we can ensure that his business in Troyes is both brief and unsuccessful." The drunkard had so much as cursed her new baby, and he would pay for it.

Mama fingered the amulet she wore around her neck and said, "Amen to that."

At *disner* the next day, Shemayah reported grimly that the fellow was known as Adam, a merchant from Roanne. "According to those who lodge with him, Adam drank so much wine at our banquet that he has no recollection of anything said there."

Salomon sat quietly at the table while his family awaited his decision. If told to ignore the incident, they would do so.

Suddenly Judah scowled. "Wait a moment. Adam of Roanne—that name sounds familiar."

Salomon half closed his eyes and stroked his beard. "*Oui*, I have heard it too . . . One of my responsa, I think."

"I'm sure that I have never heard of him," Meir said.

"Then the query must have come while you were at Ramerupt, not during the fair seasons." Judah's face froze with concentration. "I have it. Last year, after Passover, you received a letter complaining about a merchant named Adam, asking for your legal opinion."

Salomon shook his head. "That Adam lived in Vénissieux."

"But the people of Vénissieux said that he had moved to Roanne." Judah walked to the cupboard and brought out a small chest. "These are the responsa from last year. I should have the one we want in a moment."

The room was silent as he rummaged through the chest. "Here. I believe this is the letter in question."

He handed a sheaf of parchment to Salomon, who read it aloud. "The Jews of Vénissieux complain about a merchant named Adam. He travels behind various rapacious barons and their knights when they loot their rivals' villages. Adam buys the spoils cheaply and resells them at much higher prices, often to the very people they were stolen from."

Rachel scowled. "Such an unscrupulous man menaces every Jewish merchant. With so few Jews in the countryside, Edomites who encounter this fellow will believe we're all that greedy."

"Exactly." Salomon continued reading, his voice rising in anger. "Adam's activities have aroused the hatred of the plundered villagers, and of their lords, who say: 'This Jew, because he is always ready to buy looted goods, entices our enemies to attack us. He is the real cause of our troubles; yet he walks in safety.' "

"But what was the responsa about, Papa? What did the Jews of Vénissieux want from you?" Miriam asked.

"The Jews there were outraged at being associated with Adam, particularly since several of them were taken captive and held for ransom on his account. They placed him in *herem* and banished him, but he merely moved to Roanne and continued his evil ways." Salomon held out his hands helplessly. "They turned to me for support, but there was nothing I or they could do. Each Jewish community is independent, and if Roanne chooses to tolerate Adam's behavior, despite the danger, it is its prerogative."

Joheved didn't need to hear any more. "The Jews of Vénissieux have put Adam under *herem*, and for good reason. What if he starts buying stolen property in Champagne? Next the petty nobles will be pillaging each other's villages to sell to him, and we will have no peace in Ramerupt."

"Don't worry." Meir patted Joheved's hand. "We will denounce him at services so everyone will know his history."

"Adam is an uncommon name," Miriam pointed out. "But we can't accuse him without proof that he's the same man."

Salomon turned to Shemayah. "Go back to the New Synagogue and find out whether Adam of Roanne once lived in Vénissieux, and if so, did that community excommunicate him?"

"He *must* be the same man," Rachel said. "There couldn't be two men so wicked with that same name, and the sooner he leaves Troyes the better."

Mama whispered what they all were thinking. "I pray that it's not too late."

A stab of fear pierced Rachel's heart, and she hugged her new son close.

Surely Papa's piety would protect his family from the Evil Eye. Yet demons hated Torah scholars above all and seized any opportunity to harass them. When Joheved gave birth to a boy less than a month after Miriam had her youngest son, the bad luck of pairs brought on Lillit's attack. Joheved nearly succumbed to childbed fever, and her first baby named Salomon died a year later. All of Papa's Torah study wasn't powerful enough to save his namesake then; would it be powerful enough now, with eight grandsons in jeopardy?

Walking home from Shavuot services, Rachel pulled Joheved aside and whispered, "Now that Adam has left Troyes, do you think we still have to worry about our babies—may the Holy One protect them?"

Little Salomon squirmed in Joheved's arms, and she shifted him to her other hip. Her son could walk while holding on, but she wasn't about to put him down in the muddy road, filthy with every kind of garbage a person could throw in it.

"I don't know. My worries over him never cease." A smile lit her face as she watched Meir take hold of their daughters' hands and cautiously cross the street. "I worry about all my children."

Adam from Roanne had proved to be the very man that the Jews of Vénissieux had put in *herem*, and it took less than a week before Troyes affirmed the ban. Once everyone in the community refused to speak to him and made sure they stood at least four cubits away, it became clear that he would do no business in the city.

Rachel checked that the red threads around Asher's wrists weren't too tight; he was growing so fast. Though Adam had only given the Evil Eye to Salomon's male family members, Mama saw to it that all her grandchildren wore red threads these days.

Mama also insisted that Papa inspect every mezuzah within their courtyard; never mind that they were written less than three years ago. And each night, after Rachel nursed Asher and tucked her older children in their beds, Papa blessed them with verses from Numbers that were especially effective in protecting children from the Evil Eye.

> May Adonai bless you and protect you. May Adonai make His face shine upon you and be gracious to you. May Adonai lift up His favor upon you and give you peace.

In the morning, before they headed for synagogue, Papa followed the advice that the Sages gave in the ninth chapter of Tractate Berachot.

> He who fears the Evil Eye—let him put his right thumb in his left hand, and his left thumb in his right hand. And he says, "I, A son of B, am of Joseph's seed, and the Evil Eye has no power over me. As it is written: May they be teeming like fish." Just as the waters cover fish and thus the Evil Eye has no power over them, so too the Evil Eye has no power over Joseph's descendents.

When Rachel asked how he knew they were descended from Joseph, rather than another of Jacob's sons, he explained that all Jewish people were Joseph's progeny and that the Evil Eye is easily fooled. Thus the incantation works whether a man is of Joseph's seed or not.

Rachel wished she shared Papa's confidence a few days later when Shemiah came to her complaining, "Mama, I don't feel good."

five

Rachel's chest tightened. "What's the matter?"

"I feel hot and my throat hurts." Shemiah sneezed and blew his nose onto the ground. "And my nose is dripping all the time."

She reached out and felt his forehead for fever. It was warm but not burning. "Go on up to bed. I'll have Cook prepare some chicken broth for you."

Just to be sure, Rachel checked her daughter's forehead too, but little Rivka seemed fine. So she headed for Miriam's, to obtain whatever herbal infusion her sister would recommend for a mild fever with an overabundance of phlegm in the nostrils.

"Broth boiled with parsley for a light fever, and sage to reduce the phlegm," Miriam replied. "If there's a cough as well, I recommend adding some water mint. As a matter of fact, I have a pot on the hearth right now for Elisha."

Rachel gulped. "Elisha's sick too?"

"He's just a little warm, with some excess phlegm." Miriam took in Rachel's fearful expression and tried to sound calm. "With a diet of foods that are mildly warm and dry, to balance the cold and moist phlegm, I would expect our children, may the Holy One protect them, to be better in a week."

"Do you have enough broth for Shemiah too?"

"Of course."

But things were not to be so easily mended. By the end of the week, all Miriam's children were sneezing, coughing, and complaining how bad they felt. Meir sent word that his too were suffering the same malady, and that he was needed in Ramerupt to help Joheved care for them. Papa reported that few women were in synagogue these days; they were all home caring for sick children.

At Rachel's house, Shemiah was neither better nor worse, and his sister was ill as well. Little Rivka burned with fever and was so fussy that Rachel, who was nursing Asher every three hours, needed Mama to look after her.

It was Mama who had the first inkling of what troubled the children of Troyes; that it was not merely a common case of excess phlegm. She was sitting at Miriam's dining table after *souper*, trying to rock her cranky granddaughter to sleep while Miriam hovered over a pot of some new medicine. That's when they heard the coughing sounds coming from upstairs.

"Miriam, who's making that noise?"

"I'm not sure, Mama." She cocked her head to listen. "It could be Elisha or Shimson."

A short while later, the coughing began again, although this time it seemed to be a different child. Mama left little Rivka in her cradle and rushed upstairs, Miriam and Rachel at her heels. They arrived in the boys' room in time to see that it was Elisha whose body was doubled over in a coughing fit. He couldn't seem to stop, and each spasm was followed by a strange hooting noise as he struggled to breathe in enough air.

Miriam took her son in her arms and tried to soothe him, but his coughing continued until, with another desperate gulp of air, Elisha began to vomit. Rachel was terrified that he would choke to death in front of her, but his coughing spell eventually subsided. She began to relax until she saw the horror on Mama's face.

"Heaven help us." Mama was clutching the amulet at her neck. "Shibeta has returned."

Once the three women were downstairs, Rachel turned to her mother, her eyes wide with fright. "You're certain?"

Mama's chin began to quiver. "I'll remember that sound if I live to be 120: the awful cough that goes on forever while she's choking them, and then that dreadful yelp they make when she lets go for a moment and they try to catch their breath."

Miriam put her arms around their weeping mother, who continued,

"You and Joheved were strong enough to fight her, to survive her nightly attacks, but not my little boy. For three months I thought I'd finally given your father a son, but Shibeta was determined to take him."

Rachel felt a wave of dizziness wash over her. Shibeta! The only demon that new parents dreaded more was Lillit. Shibeta, who strangled infants and young children in the night. Shibeta was here in Troyes, in their own courtyard. "How can we fight her?" Rachel could not bring herself to name the demon. As she feared, Papa's pious efforts had not prevented the Evil Eye from summoning her.

Miriam stared at Rachel sternly, defying her to give up hope. "Like the Evil Eye, Shibeta is dry and cold. Keep a pot of simmering water on your hearth, and as soon as she attacks, bring a bowl of it to your child's face so he can breathe in the steam."

"You can also use a steaming wet towel," Mama added.

"We must be diligent in our prayers," Miriam said. "And give our children as much broth as possible so Shibeta doesn't desiccate them."

"How long until she leaves?" Rachel felt sick with dread.

"Maybe only a week, but it might be as long as a month or six weeks," Mama replied.

Rachel stared down at the now sleeping baby in her arms. How was she going to protect Asher from the demon? Already his stuffy nose made it difficult for him to nurse, and his fretful crying was a clear sign that he wasn't getting enough to eat.

When Papa came that night to bless her children, she begged him to stay, not to leave her to face the demon alone.

"It would be better if the four of you stayed with us, *ma fille*," he replied. "Then your mother can help."

"*Merci*, Papa. With all the holy books you have, we should be safer there."

So the battle raged. During the day, but mostly during the night—sometimes as often as three or four times an hour—the demon tried to strangle Rachel's children. And each morning, more exhausted than the day before, Rachel gave thanks that all three, as well as Miriam's four, were still alive to greet the dawn.

Yet Asher continued to have trouble nursing and grew increasingly lethargic. One night, just after the bells chimed Lauds, he woke up crying with hunger. Before Rachel could get him to suck, his cries were cut short by a fit of coughing that didn't stop, the spasms coming so close together that he couldn't catch his breath. Rachel lit the lamp and raced down to the kitchen for a steaming towel. She held it over his face, but his coughing continued, interrupted only when he gagged on the thick mucus dribbling from his lips. She froze with horror as her baby's lips and nails turned blue, and then his face started turning blue as well. She began to scream.

Papa and Mama found her moments later, her son's limp and lifeless body still clutched to her breast.

As Córdoba loomed in the distance, Eliezer eagerly anticipated meeting wealthy buyers for his furs and woolens. Among them he would find a suitable host, with whom he'd stay while he waited for Safik to arrive with a supply of dyestuffs. On his previous trips to Tunisia, Eliezer's formidable Talmud knowledge had opened many doors for him, and he expected similar doors to open in Córdoba. He'd heard enough about the city to know that behind its doors were lavishly furnished salons inhabited by men who drank fine wines and dressed their wives in expensive silks, men who wielded power in their communities.

Before a week was out, Eliezer met a man like that named Hasdai.

Hasdai had studied Talmud in Kairouan during its yeshiva's zenith, and to him Eliezer's words were sweet as those of a long-lost lover. When he discovered that Eliezer knew much of the Talmud by heart, the two of them quickly reached an agreement: Hasdai would provide Eliezer room and board in exchange for teaching his two grandsons Tractate Berachot. When they finished Berachot, they would continue with Tractate Shabbat.

"But Shabbat is too difficult for beginning students," Eliezer protested. "I would suggest studying Rosh Hashanah instead."

Hasdai shook his head. "This is how we learn Talmud in Sepharad—first Berachot, and then, in order, the tractates about festivals that follow."

"Then what tractates do they study?"

"At this point, rather than becoming overwhelmed with discussions whose conclusions are not always plainly stated, we prefer our students to learn from responsa of the Babylonian Geonim," Hasdai replied.

Eliezer barely contained his shock. "But how will they learn to make legal decisions if they haven't studied the tractates concerning women or damages?"

"If they base their verdicts on the writings of Rabbi Hai Gaon or Rabbi Hananel, who rendered judgments in clear language, they will not err," Hasdai said.

Eliezer allowed his host to take his silence for agreement. But as far as he was concerned, Talmud was properly studied in Ashkenaz, where yeshiva students and scholars argued until the law was clear to all.

At first Eliezer gave no thought to what Hasdai's grandsons studied when they weren't learning Talmud, but after less than a month in Cordova, it became evident that the men in Hasdai's circle had intellectual interests besides Talmud. Several nights a week, Hasdai either invited other men to his home or he and Eliezer went out. Women never attended these soirees, whose main entertainment was conversation, and for the first time since childhood, Eliezer found himself unable to hold his own among Jewish men.

Of course he added nothing to the gossip, which seemed to concern whether one of the local cantors had been frequenting brothels even though he lived with his wife (if true, the fellow should be dismissed, or at least cautioned to be more discreet), and if a certain man had taken one of his wife's maidservants as a concubine (not very considerate behavior, but understandable since the wife had stopped bearing).

But he also had no reply to their other questions, ones he had never even contemplated.

Why is seawater salty while rivers are not? From where do the winds arise? Why do all men die? How is the earth held up in the middle of the air? How are voices carried through the air and heard by us? Why must all animals sleep?

Hasdai's friends debated questions like these with great enthusiasm. None of them knew the answers, but they all knew scholars who studied such things. There were also questions that did appear to have answers, although the men disagreed on which answer was correct.

Is the universe eternal? Was the world truly created from nothing? How do the celestial bodies act on the world? Does nature obey certain laws? If so, how can man have free will?

Various authorities were cited reverently—names that Eliezer had never heard before: Philo, Aristotle, Plato, Ptolemy, al-Zarqālī, al-Khwarīzmī, al-Jayyani, al-Haytham. These scholars' works must be what Hasdai's grandsons were studying, and Eliezer left these gatherings with a burning desire to know what the boys knew, what Hasdai's friends knew, and more.

Later, when Eliezer was alone with his host, he struggled to ask about these things without exposing his terrible ignorance. "Do boys here study Aristotle at a special school?"

"No," Hasdai replied, apparently finding nothing unusual in the question. "We have many tutors of Greek philosophy in Córdoba."

"What about al-Khwarīzmī?" Eliezer chose an Arabic name.

"They study mathematics with a different tutor."

Eliezer was sure this subject was far more complicated than learning to keep accounts or use an abacus. Suddenly he had an idea. "What texts do they use?"

This was definitely the right question to ask because Hasdai grinned proudly. "Come, I'll show you."

Eliezer followed him out of the salon and into an adjoining storeroom that held the extra cushions and small tables used at large gatherings. Hasdai rearranged the cushions and pushed against the now bare wall, which slowly began to move. Moments later they stepped into a long, narrow room lit by a skylight.

Eliezer gasped in astonishment. Each wall was covered with shelves of books.

"Córdoba's caliphs spent years stocking their royal library." Hasdai sighed. "Some say it contained over five hundred thousand manuscripts written in Greek, Arabic, and even Hebrew—translations of the great works of antiquity and original treatises."

"You said 'contained.' What happened to it?"

"When the Berbers—illiterate scum filled with contempt for the Moors—threatened the city, the library's contents were dispersed and hidden. As I'm sure you know, the Moors prefer poetry and philosophy to warfare. We Jews saved many of the Hebrew volumes."

"Incredible. And you obtained these." Eliezer stared at the walls of manuscripts in awe. Salomon's library in Troyes was a fraction of this size.

"As well as some Arabic texts, including several copies of al-Khwarīzmī,

Philo, and Aristotle. I hope my grandsons and great-grandsons will eventually want their own copies," Hasdai said. "Some of my friends have similar collections, but who knows where the rest of the caliphs' library resides?"

Eliezer didn't care. There were more than enough books here to keep him occupied until Passover, when he would need to leave if he hoped to be home for his third child's birth. The problem was where to begin. He didn't dare lower Hasdai's opinion by asking for recommendations, but—he grinned at his own cleverness—the man's grandsons were another matter.

"Tell me about your other studies," he asked them nonchalantly, after services. "Which subjects do you like best?"

"Mathematics," the younger one replied immediately. "Philosophy is boring."

"That's because you're too little to understand it," his brother retorted.

"I'm tired of Aristotle. I want to study somebody else for a change."

"But you have to understand Aristotle before you can study Abraham ibn Daud, Philo, or Solomon ibn Gabirol." The older one sounded like he was quoting a teacher.

Eliezer now knew where he should begin, at least for philosophy. But before he could ask about poetry and the sciences, he found out that there was more he needed to know about Aristotle.

"I've already studied his *Metaphysics*, *Politics*, *Ethics*, and *On the Soul*," the younger one complained.

"You're almost done," his brother said. "You only have his writings on logic left to go."

Eliezer made a point of remembering the titles he'd just heard. "So you like mathematics," he said to his younger student. "Which text are you studying?"

"I finally understand al-Khwarīzmī." The boy's eyes were shining. "He's amazing. Now I can go on to Ptolemy and al-Haytham."

"Who are your favorite poets?" Eliezer asked. The Jews of Sepharad were fanatics about poetry; every man considered himself a poet.

"Grandpapa says we can't study poetry until we're older." The brothers exchanged looks of frustration. "They're all about wine, women, and death."

Eliezer chuckled. But the mention of women brought Rachel to Eliezer's mind, which led to vivid memories of their last night together. Once the boys had left for their secular studies, he walked briskly to the Street of Harlots.

Eliezer couldn't wait to begin his new studies. He selected Aristotle and al-Khwarīzmī to start, and as he expected, Hasdai's library contained these elementary texts. But it was soon apparent that he would need a tutor for mathematics. The gift that allowed him to memorize pages of Talmud was appropriate for Aristotle, but solving quadratic equations was not something he could learn to do by reading about them. Reminding himself that few men discussed algebra at parties, he put mathematics aside and concentrated on philosophy.

As his Arabic vocabulary grew, Eliezer realized that Aristotle, who took pains to explain his ideas clearly, was far easier than Talmud, where the text was deliberately obscure, with many words missing and no punctuation. He spent his spare time in Hasdai's library and came to recognize Aristotle's ideas when he heard them. He also came to disagree with many of them.

He conducted his business leisurely, banishing any remorse for not coming home for Passover or the birth of his child. He convinced himself that he needed to remain in Córdoba to make more contacts with the local merchants, many of whom would only be arriving after the Great Sea opened to shipping in the spring. But eventually his guilt mounted to the point where he announced that he was leaving the following Sunday.

"But you can't go yet." Hasdai appeared stricken. "Not all the merchants have returned, and I've promised to prepare a great wine party in your honor once everyone has arrived."

"In my honor?" Eliezer couldn't insult his host by leaving before the event. Not if he hoped to do more business in Córdoba. Rachel would understand the delay—he hoped.

"Of course. You're famous; everyone wants to meet you."

Eliezer sighed and gave in. "Tell me, my friend. How is a wine party different from a regular party?" Every gathering Eliezer attended served wine.

"Ah." Hasdai smiled. "A wine party is actually a poetry party. On a warm spring evening, at some outdoor venue, we celebrate the beauty of nature."

"I hope you don't expect me to compose any poetry." Eliezer laughed.

"Don't worry. I know you've lived among the Jews of Ashkenaz, who have no appreciation for man's intellect. Their minds are so permeated with vinegar and garlic that it leaves little room for fixed ideas—except regarding sexual relations and eating, which they seek to restrict."

Eliezer, who still considered himself a Provençal, thought of the German Jews he knew and nodded. "Perhaps you can suggest some books of poetry for me to read in advance."

"Of course." He beckoned Eliezer to the library.

"I think I will hire a boat," Hasdai mused as he removed books from the shelves, only to reject them and put them back. "A cruise on the Guadalquivir will be very scenic."

"How can we appreciate nature at night?"

"We will contemplate the heavens in all their glory, and sunrise over the newly green hills is truly an inspiration." Hasdai took down some volumes and handed them to Eliezer. "Here we are."

"I thought Samuel haNagid was the vizier of Granada." Eliezer glanced at the books' authors. "And that Solomon ibn Gabirol was a philosopher."

"That is true. But they are also excellent poets."

The week before the wine party, Eliezer alternated poetry with Aristotle, memorizing poems about wine and springtime in case he was expected to speak. The day of the event, Hasdai took him, not to the bathhouse they usually patronized, but to a larger establishment outside the Jewish Quarter.

Compared to Edomites, most of whom never immersed in water again after their baptism, the Jews of Troyes were clean people. They washed their hands after using the privy, and many bathed monthly. But the Jews and Moors of Córdoba, who bathed several times each week, would have considered French Jews filthy.

Eliezer followed Hasdai into the bathhouse's long, narrow entry, called the cold room since it remained unheated. They undressed and an attendant handed them each a robe, towel, and pair of wooden sandals. Eliezer had frequented many bathhouses, but the grandeur of the warm room stopped him in his tracks.

The vaulted ceiling was at least twelve cubits high, with arched balconies below and clerestory windows providing diffuse light. The floor was paved with multicolored marble tiles, each area displaying a unique pattern, and in the center stood a tall fountain that spilled into a shallow pool. Eliezer could have spent hours right there, listening to the fountain and admiring each section of floor, but Hasdai hurried him on.

They proceeded down another hall, lined with cubicles where men lounged about chatting with one another, before arriving at a closed wooden door. As soon as Hasdai opened it, a cloud of steam engulfed them, and once inside the hot room, they were surrounded by sweating naked men. The heat blasted up from steam pipes in the floor, making Eliezer glad for his wooden sandals.

Soon he too was covered in sweat, which was the signal for a heavyset man to begin his massage. Eliezer groaned with pleasure as the masseur expertly kneaded muscles he didn't even realize were sore. Eventually the massage ceased and soapy water splashed over him, sending Eliezer reluctantly to one of the many bathtubs. There another attendant shampooed his hair and trimmed his beard.

When Eliezer returned to the warm room Hasdai was already there, deep in conversation with friends who were also preparing for the wine party. Not everyone was talking; several of the men were sleeping on their benches, and Eliezer lay down nearby.

"I have excellent news for you," Hasdai announced. "One of the finest poets in the land will be entertaining us tonight, all the way from Granada."

"You found Moses ibn Ezra?" The speaker sounded elated.

"Indeed."

Eliezer had never heard of Moses ibn Ezra. Relaxing against the warm wood of the bench, he dropped into a dreamy doze as the men raved about the fellow's poetry.

Eliezer could hear the music in the distance as they approached the riverbank, and his pulse quickened with anticipation. Finally, in the last glimmer of twilight, he saw the boat at the dock, the orchestra playing as the men boarded. The deck was covered with woven mats and plush silk cushions, with small tables scattered throughout. A handsome youth helped Eliezer find a place to sit, and almost immediately a wine pourer, even more attractive than the first servant, offered him a drink from a large cup.

The wine pourer flirtatiously pressed Eliezer's hand as he drank, and then suggestively offered the cup to the next guest, who praised the youth's beauty with a poem before drinking. With everyone's applause the evening began. Poems exalting wine and love, some addressed to the young servants, flowed from the men's lips. They challenged each other to compose verses on various aspects of wine—color, fragrance, taste, and the feelings, usually melancholy, drinking arouses. After each round, the orchestra played while fruits and cheeses were served.

Eliezer gazed up in appreciation as the sky gradually darkened and stars blinked into view. How different life was here in Córdoba, how urbane.

Before the guests grew too tired, Hasdai introduced his star, the poet Moses ibn Ezra, who was immediately provided with a cup by the most beautiful wine pourer. Moses, who had an air of sadness about him, took the youth's hand and, gazing into his eyes, began to speak.

These rivers reveal for the world to see
The secret love concealed in me
Passion has disheartened me; cruel of him to part from me
A fawn is he with slender thighs
The sun goes dark when it sees him rise

The young man blushed and preened in front of him as Moses continued his poem, which grew progressively darker with the fawn deceiving the poet and eventually leaving him for another. As if to bring the poem to life, the wine pourer turned to Eliezer and gazed at him with adoration. Luckily Eliezer was sober enough to remember an appropriate poem by Samuel haNagid and drunk enough to not care if the others disapproved.

"How exquisite the fawn who woke at night
To the sound of viol's thrum and tabor's clink
Who saw the goblet in my hand and said,
'The grape's blood flows for you between my lips;
Come drink.'
Behind him stood the moon, slim and curved,
Inscribed on the morning's veil in gold ink."

But there were no frowns at Eliezer's lack of originality, only applause. Thus the revelers passed the night, as they cultivated a state between sleep and waking, their poems flitting from the joys of wine to the grandeur of the night's sky to the sadness at time's passing. Gazing in awe at the vast darkness above him, Eliezer wondered if the stars were truly animate, the same species as angels.

Dawn was breaking when Moses composed a final poem, which brought tears to Eliezer's eyes.

Beware of Time—the gifts that he bestows
  are venom mixed with honey to taste sweet
Beguile yourself at morning with his joys
  but know that they will vanish with the sun
So drink by day till sunset
  washes the silver with golden light
And drink in the night until dawn
  puts all its dark troops to flight

Along with the other intoxicated guests, Eliezer and Hasdai staggered home to their beds. Sadness born of too much wine overwhelmed Eliezer, and as he sank beneath the covers, he was haunted by another of ibn Ezra's poems—about a woman.

She stole my sleep away from me, altogether wasted me
Never will I forget the night we lay together in delight
Upon my bed till morning light
Passion has disheartened me, cruel of her to part from me

He imagined Rachel, just rising from bed, dawn illuminating the dark curls that fell over her naked body. Was she as lonely as he was? Was she thinking of him? Thank Heaven he would soon be going home. He had been gone far too long. Next year he wouldn't stay so long in Sepharad.

But despite his excellent intentions, the week before he left Eliezer realized his stay next spring in Córdoba would be an extended one. For there in Hasdai's library were the collected works of Philo of Alexandria, a Jew.

SIX

thin stream of smoke rose in the distance, and with a sigh of relief, Eliezer urged his horse onward. He'd been fairly confident he could reach the *fondaco*, an inn and warehouse that catered to traveling merchants, before the Sabbath. The smoke ahead made it a certainty.

As he reached the stables, he was pleased to find them jostling with carts and pack animals, undoubtedly the property of other merchants headed for the Hot Fair. There were probably enough men here to make a minyan for Shabbat services, all waiting out the holy day when travel is forbidden. It would also be a time to exchange news.

But instead of a hubbub of gossiping merchants, Eliezer was alarmed to find the atmosphere inside the inn somber and tense. Men with serious expressions gathered at tables near the hearth, listening intently as a tall man addressed them.

Eliezer settled at a table and signaled for ale. "Why the grim faces?" he asked the serving wench.

"That big fellow talking just arrived from Troyes. There's some kind of pestilence in the city."

A pestilence in Troyes? Eliezer's heart leapt into his throat as he moved within earshot of the speaker.

"Normally I wouldn't dream of leaving a wedding before all seven days of celebration, but I couldn't bear another two days in that city." The speaker grimaced. "Everywhere I went I passed a funeral procession, every coffin so small that it could only hold a child's body."

"The pox?"

"*Non.*" The tall man shook his head. "They say that one of Lillit's minions is abroad in the town."

"Oy," another man muttered. "Business at the Hot Fair will be terrible this year."

The other merchants began discussing strategies for making a profit despite the plague, allowing Eliezer to question the wedding guest privately.

"Quickly." Eliezer took him by the arm. "Tell me everything you know about this baby-killing demon."

The man looked down in alarm, and Eliezer quickly added, "Please, my family lives in Troyes and I've been away since the Cold Fair."

The tall man's expression changed to one of pity. "From what I heard—and believe me, guests at a wedding are not eager to discuss such an evil subject—the pestilence has been in the city for over a month."

"What kind of pestilence?"

The man shrugged. "All I know is that the demon does her worst during the night. Adults aren't affected, and while many children have been attacked, only the youngest have succumbed."

"I have two young children, and my wife was pregnant when I left." Eliezer's voice was shaking.

The man leaned down and dropped his already low voice to a whisper. "Are you thinking of violating the Sabbath? I won't tell anyone if you leave."

"What good would it do me to ride for Troyes now? Whatever happened to my family has already happened." Eliezer held his head in his hands. "And should my child's life hang in the balance, committing such an *averah* might condemn him."

"Come you two, the sun is setting," a voice with a Provençal accent called out. "Enough of death and evil spirits. On the Sabbath we should speak of pleasant subjects."

Eliezer joined the men in prayers that welcomed the day of rest, but although he drank more wine than usual at *souper*, it was not enough to let him sleep peacefully. After morning services, his mind was so unsettled that, instead of leading a Talmud discussion, he sat back and listened to the men's idle gossip. Two textile dealers from Tours were eagerly sharing the latest news about King Philip and Bertrade de Montford, for whom Count Fulk of Anjou had divorced the mother of his heir. Eliezer only half listened as the men chortled over how, while visiting the Count of Anjou, King Philip had suffered a lecherous attraction to the beautiful new countess.

"Within four days, the king abducted Bertrade, divorced the queen, arranged for Fulk's divorce from Bertrade, and then married her."

Eliezer felt utterly helpless. Leaving could mean a death sentence for one of his children—that, he could not risk. But he could think of nothing but Shemiah, Rivka, and the baby he'd never even seen, suffering in Troyes. His colleagues continued to debate how even a king could arrange two divorces so quickly without the Church objecting.

Eliezer was so sick with worry and frustration that he barely noticed when a man from Provence asked, "Have you seen this Bertrade? Is she truly as beautiful as all that?"

"*Oui*, she is indeed lovely . . . although I've only viewed her from a distance," one of the Tours merchants replied.

"Bertrade has something else about her," his companion said. "Nobody can see her without wanting to tear her clothes off."

"There's a woman in Troyes like that, a Jewess." A raspy voice grew low and confidential. "The rosh yeshiva's daughter."

Eliezer's jaw dropped as the merchants began to discuss his wife. He was seething with fury and curiosity; yet he forced his expression into a mask of indifference.

"Where is the best place to see her?" someone asked.

"Her family attends the Old Synagogue, so you might catch a glimpse of her there. But it's better to go to their house, where they sell wine. In the summer, when women don't always wear veils at home, you may closely observe her fairness."

"What does she look like?"

"She has black curly hair, skin like cream, and eyes like emeralds." He sighed. "Of course she's married, with a few children as well, but her husband often travels on business."

Eliezer's blood was boiling, and he clenched his seat with both hands to keep from jumping up and assaulting the speaker. *How dare he speak of Rachel as though she were a harlot?*

"I've purchased wine from the rosh yeshiva several times," one of the Tours merchants said. "The women I saw there were quite ordinary."

"Perhaps her hair was covered." Eliezer tried to lean in, desperate to hear more about Rachel's conduct. Did she encourage strange men while he was away? Had she been unfaithful?

"None of them had green eyes. I'm sure of it."

"I'm not surprised you haven't seen her." The raspy voiced man chuckled. "This beauty of Troyes is careful not to be alone with a man . . . unless he's a Ganymede."

"How did you manage it?"

"I never said I was alone with her. I was buying wine with my aunt."

"I must admit that I too had heard of this woman's beauty," the man from Chartres said. "So I attempted to procure some wine before I left Troyes. But the family was gone; the servants said they were sitting shiva somewhere in the country."

Eliezer gasped. Joheved and Meir must have lost a child. *And what of my children?* Surely Rachel wouldn't have gone to Ramerupt if they were ill? But perhaps Rachel and Miriam had taken the children away to avoid the pestilence in town. After all, Miriam sent her boys to Paris when the pox struck Troyes.

Mon Dieu—what if it's not Joheved and Meir's child the family is mourning?

The walls of Troyes loomed in the distance, but instead of the happy eagerness that viewing them usually brought, Eliezer was filled with dread. His trepidation only increased when he passed a funeral just outside the city, the tiny coffin confirming what he'd heard at the *fondaco.*

The streets of the Broce aux Juifs, the Jewish Quarter, were eerily quiet. The few peddlers on the road offered their goods without shouting, and no merchants called out for customers from those shops with open shutters. Nearly choking with fear, Eliezer reached his courtyard gate and braced himself for what he would find within.

A cat stretched out on a bench and a few chickens lazily pecking at the ground were the only inhabitants. He was washing his hands at the well when Salomon's kitchen door opened and Anna, the maidservant, poked her head out. She and her husband, Baruch, had come to Salomon from

Romania as slaves years ago, payment for Eliezer and his brother Asher's yeshiva educations. Salomon freed the couple soon after, before the birth of their son, Pesach, and the family had worked for him ever since.

Anna took one look at Eliezer and burst into tears. "Thank Heaven. You're finally home." She blew her nose and wiped her hands on her apron.

"Where is everyone?" he asked.

"They've gone to Ramerupt." She broke into fresh sobs. "Shiva for Joheved's baby boy."

Anna was crying too hard to answer, but he had to ask. "My wife and children?"

She looked at him with such pain that he knew the demon had not spared his family. "Please, you must tell me."

She was still weeping when the gate opened to admit Baruch and Pesach, returning from the vineyard. Baruch took in the scene and hurried to embrace Eliezer. "May you be comforted among the mourners of Jerusalem."

Eliezer could feel the tears welling in his eyes. "Who died? Please. Your wife can't stop crying long enough to tell me."

Baruch took a deep breath. "Your infant son died a few weeks ago. Shemiah and little Rivka, may the Holy One protect them, still live."

"Rachel named him Asher," Pesach added.

"And the others?" Eliezer was afraid of the answer.

"Shibeta only claimed the two babies, Meir's and yours. Rabbenu Salomon's other grandchildren were spared." Baruch no sooner finished speaking than his expression abruptly hardened with anger.

"What's wrong, Papa?" Pesach asked.

Baruch motioned for Anna to come closer. "Remember that drunk merchant—Adam I think his name was—who got into such a row at Asher's brit milah?"

"*Oui*. He had the audacity to joke about Rabbenu Salomon having his own minyan of grandsons and sons-in-law," Anna practically spat the words out.

"He doesn't now," Pesach whispered.

"Shh," Anna hissed. No stranger to sorrow, her two daughters died of the pox during the last epidemic.

"Tomorrow is the seventh day of mourning, so everyone should be coming home soon," Baruch said. "But I expect you'll want to ride to Ramerupt while it's still light."

Eliezer, too overwhelmed to speak, could only nod.

Baruch headed toward the gate. "Anna, can get you something to eat while I fetch a fresh horse."

Pondering his feelings, Eliezer followed Anna into the kitchen. A stab of remorse assailed him. His new baby was gone, a son he never met. But Rachel would have become attached to the babe: cuddling him, nursing him, and doing all that mothers do for a newborn. She had never experienced a close family death before. She would be heartbroken. And he hadn't been there to console her. Eliezer took a deep breath and tried to appreciate that his two older children were spared.

By the time he had wolfed down his food and used the privy, Baruch was back with the horse. "I'm glad you returned to us safely," the manservant said as he helped Eliezer into the stirrups. "Adam brought down the Evil Eye on you as well, but you didn't know to take the precautions Meir and Judah did."

Several times on the way to Ramerupt, Eliezer stopped his horse, put his right thumb in his left hand and his left thumb in his right hand, and recited, "I, Eliezer son of Shemiah, I am of the seed of Joseph, and the Evil Eye has no power over me."

The death of Salomon's grandsons may have dropped the number of male descendants to nine, but if the Evil Eye counted the patriarch himself, there would still be a minyan's worth in the family.

As Eliezer approached Meir's manor a new worry added to his troubles. Rachel was already unhappy over all the time he spent away from Troyes. His missing their son's birth, circumcision, and funeral would have dealt her further blows.

He was met at the gate by a handsome, slender youth, tall enough to show that he was past puberty, yet lacking the beard to prove that he had reached manhood. Despite the fellow's dexterity at helping him dismount, Eliezer sensed that he was no servant.

"Welcome to Ramerupt-sur-Aube, sire . . ." The youth paused.

Eliezer approved of the youth's discretion, not calling him *lord*, but still suggesting that he was some sort of noble. Eliezer realized that his dark complexion—darker now that he'd been riding outdoors—revealed his foreign, southern origin. Often people weren't sure what to make of him.

"I'm afraid you've arrived at a bad time," the youth said somberly. "The lord and lady are in mourning,"

"I'm their brother-in-law, Eliezer ben Shemiah, just returned from Córdoba. And you are?"

"Excuse me for not recognizing you, Master Eliezer. I'm Milo de Plancy. Come with me." Milo made a small gesture and a groom hurried to take custody of Eliezer's horse.

"No offense, Milo. I didn't recognize you either. It's been over two years and you're at least a head taller."

"But I should have recognized you." Milo looked like he was about to cry. "I should know all my lady's relations."

Eliezer followed Milo to the house. Joheved and Meir must be quite upset to make their squire so unhappy. "Is Étienne a good teacher? Joheved says he's an excellent steward."

"Étienne died of dropsy just before Candlemas," Milo whispered. "Enter quietly. The family is saying their prayers."

Eliezer waited at the doorway behind Milo. Salomon's salon would have been crowded with all the students here, but Meir's great hall could easily hold twice as many. Eliezer searched the room for Rachel but he couldn't find her; she must be sitting against the wall near Salomon. Eliezer couldn't see his father-in-law either, but he could hear him.

Salomon was teaching a Midrash on Proverbs 31, one particularly appropriate for a family mourning the death of two boys.

> "A good wife, who can find?" Rabbi Meir was sitting in the house of study on Sabbath afternoon, when his two sons died. What did their mother, Beruria, do? She laid them on the bed and spread a sheet over them.
>
> When the Sabbath ended, Rabbi Meir came home and said to her, "Where are my sons?" She answered, "They went to the house of study." He said, "I did not see them."
>
> Beruria gave him a wine cup for Havdalah, and he recited the prayer. He again asked, "Where are my sons?" and she replied,

"They went somewhere and will soon return." She put food before him, and he ate and said grace. Then she said, "Master, I have a question for you."

He said, "Ask your question," and she said to him, "Master, some time ago a man gave me something to keep for him. Now he comes back and seeks to take it. Shall we return it to him or not?" Meir told her, "Whoever has an object in trust must return it to its owner." She said, "Without your consent, I would not have given it to him."

What did Beruria do? She took him by the hand and led him upstairs. She brought him to the bed and removed the sheet. When Meir saw the two of them lying dead, he began to cry and wail, "My sons, my sons . . ."

So she said to Rabbi Meir, "Master, did you not tell me that I must return the item to its owner?" He said, "Adonai gave and Adonai has taken away; blessed be the name of Adonai." [Job 1:21]

Rav Hanina taught, "In this way she comforted him, and his mind was set at ease. Regarding such a woman, it is written, 'A good wife, who can find?' "

Joheved's sobs echoed through the room, and Meir's arms tightened around her. The couple stood flanked by their sons Isaac and Shmuel, along with daughters Hannah and Leah. But where was Rachel? Eliezer stepped into the salon, his anxious gaze sweeping the room.

He stopped short when Rachel came into view, and his heart broke. She had lost weight and her beautiful green eyes were rimmed with red. Silent tears streamed down her face as she leaned heavily against Salomon, his hand gently patting her shoulder. Eliezer's throat tightened with grief and guilt. He'd delayed his return to enjoy life in Córdoba, and now his new son was struck down before he'd even held him.

He focused on Rachel until she lifted her head and their eyes met. He'd hoped that she would exhibit some pleasure, or at least relief, when she saw him. But Rachel stared at him with such a baleful expression that Eliezer knew it could be a long time before she was able to forgive him for returning so late.

After greeting her with an affectionate hug, which she returned with a distinct lack of enthusiasm, he thanked Heaven that at least she was not *niddah.* Eliezer expected to be baited by Rachel's scowls and curt remarks that evening, even anticipated how he would reply, but she maintained her stony silence.

At *souper* Eliezer was as solicitous to her as possible, keeping her wine cup filled and serving her those dishes he knew she enjoyed. Filled with gratitude that their older children had survived, he showered them with affection, telling Shemiah all sorts of fanciful tales about Sepharad and bouncing little Rivka on his lap. Yet Rachel's melancholy did not abate.

After the meal he played with little Rivka and helped Shemiah review his studies, and then offered to put their son to bed so Rachel could attend to their daughter. Apparently she'd begun nursing the girl again after the baby died.

When he finally entered their bedroom, he was not surprised to see that Rachel had put out the lamp. It didn't matter; he was perfectly capable of doing what he intended in pitch dark. He took his time undressing and hanging his clothes on the pegs on the wall—let his wife wonder why he wasn't more eager to join her in bed after their six-month separation.

Indeed her petulant voice called out from the darkness, "What's taking you so long? Are you coming to bed or no?"

"Shush." He climbed in and let the bed curtains fall behind him. "You'll wake little Rivka."

He didn't expect her to reach for him, and she didn't. He leaned on his side and caressed the curve of her bosom, gently pinching her nipple as his fingers passed over it.

Rachel had promised herself that she wasn't going to let him seduce her so easily, but the resulting sensation between her legs caused her to gasp, and she couldn't bring herself to stop him when he continued to toy with her hardening nipples. *It's been such a long time.*

Curse Eve, the first woman, who had eaten the forbidden fruit and doomed all of womankind so that:

> Your desire shall be for your husband and he shall rule over you.

Eliezer's tongue was probing her mouth, and, despite the anger Rachel felt at her weakness, the fire below was growing stronger. She clung to her husband's neck as her passion mounted, and though she willed them to be still, her hips pressed and ground against his. His lips began to move, first to her neck and then slowly down her body. When he reached her breast, his tongue teased her nipple so exquisitely that she couldn't bear it if something didn't address the need that assailed her in that hidden place below. Yet at the same time her mind screamed at her for not fighting her desire.

As if reading her thoughts, his hand began making its way down her belly. She tried to resist him and keep her legs closed, but her body betrayed her and spread them wide as his fingers approached. Her breath was coming fast now, and she moaned as he stroked the sensitive skin of her inner thighs, moving closer and closer to her *ervah*, yet never touching her there. *He wants me to beg him, damn him.*

"Please," she whispered, at the same time furious that she wanted him so badly.

Immediately he sucked hard on her breast, and his hand reached up to probe her secret opening. But his meticulous exploration only increased her torment, and she whimpered as his delicate caresses fueled her passion.

"Please," she begged him again.

Eliezer withdrew his fingers, but instead of positioning his body above hers, he slid off the bed and pulled her legs toward him. Then, her thighs gaping open before him, he knelt on the floor in front on her.

"Eliezer." She tried to sit up, but he pushed her back down on the bed.

"I want you to emit your seed first." His voice was husky with desire. "So we will have another son."

The next thing she knew, he was kissing her breasts again. Then his hands replaced his mouth and his lips began moving relentlessly down her belly. *Mon Dieu, he is going to kiss me there!*

Suddenly his lips reached a spot that sent her mind reeling, and her entire being was instantly focused on the ecstasy his mouth was generating. She moaned and cried, and grasped the linens convulsively, but couldn't pull her hips away. His fingers kept playing with her nipples and his tongue was a flame licking at her, turning her *ervah* into a furnace stoked ever higher.

She was transported to a world where the only thing that existed was the inferno between her legs, which continued to rage hotter and hotter until, suddenly, her *ervah* began to swell and pulse with paroxysms of such intense pleasure that she thought she would explode inside. When she couldn't take any more, she pulled away and lay gasping on the bed, her loins and nipples throbbing as the spasms slowly dissipated.

Eliezer sat back for a few moments, and then gently stroked her inner thighs to rekindle her desire. He knew he should wait a little longer, but pleasuring Rachel this way was too stimulating. He had been keenly aware of her increasing excitement, and when he'd felt her climax, it had nearly sent him over the edge himself. Her breathing began to quicken again and he couldn't wait. He flipped her legs back onto the bed and climbed on top of her, somehow compelling himself to enter gradually.

Her damp warmth gripped him, caressed him. Rachel groaned deeply and wrapped her legs around him, so he drew back and then penetrated fully. She moaned again and began to breathe faster as his movements became more vigorous.

Soon she was panting beneath him, her cries of delight growing louder with her increasing urgency. Eliezer had hoped to restrain his ardor and make her climax first this way too, before finally bringing them both to the zenith together. But then he felt her sheath begin to spasm around him, and he gave himself over to the passion that forced him to sink his entire length into her as rapidly and as forcefully as he could.

Rachel's ecstasy erupted in waves, each more powerful than before, a crescendo that would surely shatter her body into pieces if it continued. Then she heard him moan as he slammed into her one last, overwhelming time before he collapsed on top of her.

seven

or a long moment they lay together, unable to move or make a sound. Rachel reveled in the crush of his body against hers, the soft prickling of his beard on her shoulder, the smell of his hair—and she began to weep.

"I hate you," she whispered between sobs. "Why can't you be here when I need you?"

Eliezer kissed her cheek and gently stroked her hair. "I hate being away from you, I hate that I never got to see our new son before he was buried, and I hate that there's nothing I can do about it until my sister's sons are able to take my place." *And I hate the number of men who know I have a beautiful wife at home alone while I travel.*

"There must be some occupation that you can do in Troyes."

He sighed. "None I can think of that will provide for our family so well."

Rachel sniffed back her tears. Her husband was right. Papa's wine production was sufficient to support him and Mama, and in a good year there was profit for her and Miriam. The sisters also divided the revenue from the money-lending business that Judah's mother, Alvina, had set up. But Alvina was old, and instead of contributing to their income she now needed their support.

"I'm not going to give up. I'll find something," she said. "And if it's not quite as lucrative as what you do now, I'll just have to cut back on expenses."

Eliezer chuckled. "Belle, we both know that you do not share your father's and sisters' simple tastes. I can't imagine you wearing badly dyed *bliauts* to save money. And I certainly can't imagine you giving up your jewels, nice clothes, or fine foods." He wouldn't want to give them up either.

"I suppose so." Her tone was grudging.

"Even if you did spend less, we still couldn't live on the same income as Miriam and Judah. They have only one daughter to dower, and who knows how many more girls you will bear?"

"Judah will also inherit all Alvina's wealth, while your father's went to pay your brother's widow and your mother their *ketubah*." The *ketubah*, a woman's marriage contract, stipulated how much she would receive if her husband died or divorced her. The amount was often so large that there was little left over for the man's children.

"You're still angry," he said sadly.

"I'm not so angry at you anymore." She sighed and paused a moment. "I just wish things were different."

He leaned over and kissed her neck. "Remember what it says in the tenth chapter of Tractate Eruvin."

She pretended to misunderstand him. "You mean where Rami bar Chama said:

> A man is forbidden to force his wife in the holy deed, as it is written [Proverbs 19], 'He who blunders with his feet is a sinner.' "

Eliezer was sure his wife knew exactly what he meant, but in between kisses he quoted it anyway. "*Non*, the Baraita just following that.

> 'He who blunders with his feet is a sinner' refers to one who performs the holy act and repeats it. But can this be? Rava said: He who wishes to have only sons should perform the holy act twice."

Rachel allowed him to pull her close. If she had to share Eve's curse, she might as well enjoy it. Before she kissed him back, she whispered,

> "There is no contradiction. With Rava, the woman consents, but in the Baraita, she does not consent."

She too wanted another son.

* * *

Eliezer's sleep was disturbed several times by coughing children, but Rachel assured him that this was nothing compared to before. Shibeta was weakening, and they could leave for Troyes in a day or two. Eliezer devoted most of this spare time, when he wasn't playing with the children, to reviewing Salomon's latest Talmud lessons. For when the Hot Fair opened, the section Salomon was teaching would require more effort than simply memorizing the text.

Salomon had chosen Tractate Shabbat, starting with the seventh chapter, which describes the various kinds of labor forbidden on the Sabbath. He began with the Mishnah:

> The main types of work are forty save one: sowing, plowing, reaping, gathering sheaves, threshing, winnowing, cleansing crops, grinding, sifting, kneading, and baking; shearing wool, whitening it, combing it, dyeing it, spinning, stretching, making two loops, weaving two threads, separating two threads, tying a knot, loosening a knot, sewing two stitches, and tearing in order to sew; hunting a gazelle, slaughtering it, skinning it, salting it, tanning its skin, scraping it and cutting it up, writing two letters, and erasing in order to write; building, pulling down, putting out a fire, lighting a fire, hammering, and carrying from one domain to another.

"These are the labors the Israelites performed in the desert to construct the Tabernacle," he explained over *souper*. "All work prohibited on the Sabbath is derived from them."

"Excuse me, Rabbenu." Simcha blushed with embarrassment. "I know the first group of eleven have to do with preparing bread for the altar, and the second group of thirteen with making the Tabernacle's curtains, but I'm not sure what each word means."

"You're not the only one," Rachel said. "I don't know the difference between threshing and winnowing."

"Of course you do." Eliezer gave her a suggestive smile. "Your father teaches that in order to avoid impregnating Tamar, Onan threshed on the inside and winnowed on the outside."

Joheved and Meir exchanged glances, then he waved for her to speak.

"Threshing is beating the husks to separate out the grain, and winnowing is tossing the grain in the air so the chaff blows away and the heavier wheat remains."

Meir's estate produced wheat, along with sheep and wine, so he easily explained the first twelve terms. "Whitening the wool is the Mishnah's name for washing it, which we do in the river."

Joheved held up her distaff, identical to her sisters'. As children, she and Miriam had lessened their mother's complaints about girls studying Talmud by spinning thread during their father's lessons. "Before placing the wool on the distaff, we comb it into parallel fibers."

"That makes it easier to draw a good length onto the spindle." Miriam demonstrated the action, pulling a tuft of wool from the distaff and twisting it around her spindle. Then she let the spindle fall, where it stretched and tightened the thread as it rotated. Finally she wound the thread onto the spindle and began the process again.

"Why does dyeing come before spinning?" Judah asked. "I thought cloth was dyed after weaving."

Eliezer, expert in dyestuffs, provided the answer. "These days we dye the whole cloth, but in the past it was common to dye the wool."

Next came "stretching" and "making two loops," but nobody volunteered an explanation.

"They clearly come before weaving." Miriam turned to her father. "Does the Gemara explain it later?"

"I'm afraid the Gemara is not helpful." Judah proceeded to quote it.

> "What are loops? Abaye said: two times for the heddle loops and once around the heddle."

"The heddle?" Rachel scowled. "Now I'm more confused than before." She looked at her father questioningly.

Salomon stroked his beard. "I need to see some weavers at work. Once I understand what they do, I can explain it properly in my *kuntres*."

"Our clients include weavers," Rachel said. "They borrow money during the year to buy flax and wool but don't get paid until the cloth is sold. When they come to repay their loans, I'll ask some if you might watch."

* * *

As foreign merchants arrived in Troyes and began struggling with Tractate Shabbat, Eliezer felt a secret pride at knowing both Torah and Greek philosophy. He thought of Hasdai's grandsons and wondered what it was like to study Aristotle and Plato while simultaneously learning Talmud? What questions would such a student ask?

The morning session was almost over when Salomon tapped his shoulder and pointed to Rachel waving frantically from the door.

It had to be important for her to interrupt their studies.

"Your sister Eleanor is here," she exclaimed.

"She couldn't wait until I came home?"

Rachel's irritation matched his own. "That's what I asked her, but she insisted on my getting you immediately."

"My sister still tells me what to do and expects me to do it," he muttered before lapsing into a fuming silence.

They hurried through the crowded streets, waving off the many peddlers who accosted them on the way. They rushed through the front door to find Eleanor sitting in their dining room, drumming her fingers on the table.

"So you've finally decided to visit Champagne's biggest fair," Eliezer said, giving her a perfunctory kiss.

"That's not why I'm here." She fingered the neckline of her *bliaut*, drawing his attention to the torn edges. "Our mother is in Gan Eden with our father and brother now."

Eliezer sagged as if she'd punched him. But instead of embracing his sister to share their mutual sorrow, he leaned on Rachel for support. "When did she die? And how?"

Eleanor showed no sadness. "Last winter, of a fever."

"Our mother died six months ago and you're just informing me?" Now it was too late for Eliezer to observe shiva or *sheloshim*; Jewish Law allowed merely one day of full mourning when learning of a death after thirty days.

"I sent a letter to Tunis."

He fought back tears of anger. "I was in Córdoba. I wrote Mama about it." She had probably died without ever reading his letter.

Eleanor stared knives back at him. "You were supposed to be in Maghreb. Sepharad is Netanel's territory."

"I'll conduct my business how and where I like."

Rachel didn't dare speak. Her husband and sister-in-law looked like they were going to tear one another limb from limb, not like siblings mourning their mother. Why was Eleanor so angry? Surely Sepharad held more than enough commercial opportunities for the two men. And why didn't Eliezer try to placate her by explaining his perfectly good reasons for preferring Córdoba to Tunis?

"So why are you here?" Eliezer asked. "You obviously didn't come to pay a condolence call."

Eleanor thrust a piece of parchment at him. "Here's your inheritance, payable as a credit at the Troyes fairs."

Eliezer scanned the document and his expression clouded. "Mama saved all the money I sent her."

"While spending the money we gave her," Eleanor retorted. "But I shouldn't be surprised. You always were her favorite."

"So you've always insisted. But I don't have to listen to your accusations in my own home." He headed to the door. "If you can't offer me any sympathy, I've missed enough Talmud already."

The next moment, Eliezer was gone, the slamming front door echoing behind him. Before Rachel could offer Eleanor something to eat or ask if she needed a place to stay, Eleanor stood up and stalked out, leaving Rachel sitting alone.

So Flamenca loved Eliezer more than her daughters, left him more in her will; that's what lay behind the siblings' antagonism. How sad that they couldn't even mourn their mother's death together. She must be careful not to favor Shemiah over little Rivka and to prevent Eliezer from doing so as well.

Then an alarming thought assailed Rachel—could Joheved and Miriam harbor similar grudges toward her for being Papa's favorite? Or did they pity her for all the years she suffered Mama's resentment?

Eleanor must have left Troyes immediately, because Rachel did not encounter her in town again. Rachel wanted to ask Eliezer about their estrangement, but he refused to even mention his sister's name, only reiterating his intention of returning to Córdoba in January.

When he left after Sukkot on his now annual autumn trip east for furs, Rachel suspected she was pregnant. After baby Asher died, her breasts were so swollen that she began nursing little Rivka again for relief. The girl thrived on mother's milk, and if Miriam could continue to nurse Alvina, six months Rivka's senior, then Rachel would nurse her daughter too. Thus she avoided being *niddah* for the entire summer that Eliezer was home, but that also meant she couldn't use a missed menses to confirm her condition.

But she'd know for sure by the time Eliezer came home for the Cold Fair. It ought to cheer him after his mother's death, just as the thought of another baby in her womb lifted some of her grief over losing little Asher.

She was also pleased with a plan she'd devised that might make it possible for Eliezer to live in Troyes most of the year and still make as much money as before. The idea came to her while talking to Sybille, a lanky middle-aged widow who borrowed money from Rachel and Miriam to finance her weaving business.

As usual when the Hot Fair closed, Sybille came to repay the money she'd borrowed in the spring to buy flax. "Here's what I owe, plus interest." She counted out the coins.

"Did you have a good season?" Rachel asked as she wrote the amount in her account book.

"Better than most," Sybille admitted, "but not as good as some. Flax is getting more expensive, but there is always demand for well-woven linen."

"Have you thought about weaving woolens? They bring more money than linen."

"I'd have to buy a different loom, and I don't want to get further into debt than I already am. Besides, it's mostly men who weave wool."

"Really?"

Sybille nodded. "Weaving is divided by gender, with women making linen and men making woolens."

"So is the rest of the cloth business," Rachel said. "At my sister's estate, men shear the sheep while women wash and comb the wool, which male dealers buy."

"Spinsters are always women, no matter which kind of thread they spin," Sybille added.

"While the dyers and clothiers are men." Rachel noted that men performed the most profitable tasks. "Sybille, who controls the cloth-making process?"

The weaver paused to think. "Nobody does. The craftsmen perform their parts independently, buying their own supplies and then selling the product to the next one in the chain."

Rachel smiled and nodded. "Oh. I nearly forgot. I have a favor to ask. My father would like to see the weaving process in person."

"You and your father are welcome in my shop anytime."

Sybille gave directions on how to find it, which Rachel automatically wrote down. Rachel's thoughts were focused on a daring idea—what if one person provided all the various craftsmen's supplies and paid them individually for their labor. Then all the profits could go to her.

Another woman arrived so soon on Sybille's heels that Rachel knew the newcomer must have been waiting for privacy. A lady, actually, because her rich clothes and fine pointed shoes proclaimed her noble station. She was heavily veiled, and Rachel noted that her veil was merely loosened, not removed, once the door closed. This one would surely have expensive jewels to pawn if she needed to hide her identity.

"How can I be of service to you, Lady . . ." Rachel waited to write down the name of her new client.

There was hesitation before she whispered, "Marie."

"Ah, another Lady Marie." Rachel made it clear that she recognized a pseudonym. "Won't you sit down?"

As Marie awkwardly seated herself on the bench, Rachel observed that the woman was heavily pregnant.

"I've come to you because I need money." Lady Marie pulled a purse from her sleeve and deposited the contents on the table.

Rachel had learned to never show emotion at a client's jewelry, neither admiration nor disappointment, but inside she was exultant at the magnificent matched set of diamond earrings, brooch, and necklace. *Who is this woman?*

"Do you need a loan with these items as collateral or are they for sale?" When Marie didn't reply, Rachel added, "I can give you more for a sale than a loan."

"A sale then." There was no regret in Marie's voice. "But I must insist that they not be resold in Troyes. My lord mustn't see anyone else wearing them."

"My husband will take them to Córdoba." Rachel made an offer, lower than what she would ultimately be willing to pay if Marie were a shrewd negotiator. It would be more difficult to bargain with her opponent's face hidden.

But Marie didn't balk or make a counteroffer. She filled her empty purse with Rachel's coins (clearly Marie wouldn't want a credit at the Cold Fair), pulled her veil and cloak tightly around her, and let herself out.

Rachel sighed. Lady Marie either didn't know the value of her diamonds or didn't care. Was she a nobleman's wife or mistress? Probably the latter since most wives, even noble ones, didn't refer to their husbands as "my lord." Probably she had gambling debts; that was why most of Rachel's wealthy clients pawned their jewels. If Marie had needed to pay someone to end her pregnancy, she would have come earlier.

Papa found the weaving process fascinating, and when Rachel told him there were two types of looms, one operated by women and the other by men, he insisted on observing both. When Alette, a client whose brother wove the wool she spun, came to repay her loan, Rachel arranged for them to examine his as well.

Sybille's two looms were located in her courtyard. They hung next to each other, suspended from tall tree branches, their bases almost touching the ground. Each was slightly less than two cubits wide and worked by a woman who sat on a stool in front of it. One loom contained mostly woven cloth, while on the other a great many threads hung parallel to its length, each pulled taut by a weight at the bottom. There were two rods suspended in the middle of each loom, perpendicular to the threads, forming openings for the threads to run through.

Sybille urged them to come closer, where they could see that the women were weaving linen. She introduced them to her daughter, seated at the second loom, and encouraged Salomon and Rachel to run their hands over the threads. "These make up the warp. They support the cloth, so their yarn is heavier than the weft."

"The weft?" Salomon asked.

Sybille held up a bobbin with thread wound around it. "This is the shuttle, and by sending it under and over the warp, the weft is woven into it." She pointed to her daughter, who was deftly passing the shuttle from one side of the loom to the other.

"What are these rods and ropes for?" Rachel asked.

"These are the heddles," Sybille said. "Their loops keep the warp in place so the weft can easily move between the threads."

She pulled one of the heddle rods toward her, taking every other warp thread with it. She sent the shuttle across the warp, released the rod, and pulled its mate, carrying the other half of the warp, toward her. Immediately she passed the shuttle back to the other side, and pushed the weft down tight toward the ground.

Rachel and Salomon watched as Sybille slowly repeated the motion several times. At the second loom, where Sybille's daughter did the same thing but much faster, the cloth grew before their eyes.

"So that's what heddles are." Rachel pointed to the rod. "And the rope must form the heddle loops."

"*Oui*, these heddle loops keep alternate warp threads separated, so the weft moves between them perfectly." Salomon nodded. "This is far more efficient than passing the weft between each individual warp thread by hand."

Rachel examined the nearly finished cloth on the second loom. "What happens when it's finished?"

"We either sell it to the dyer, who colors it and sells it to a cloth dealer, or if the linen is to remain in its natural color, to the dealer directly."

"Now we know what the heddle and its loops are," Rachel said as she and Salomon walked onto the street. "But I still don't know what stretching is."

"I expect that refers to how the warp is fastened to the loom. That step comes before the loops, and I could see the warp threads stretching from the weights attached to them."

"But we don't know that stretching comes before the loops today. The Mishnah places dyeing before spinning; yet dyeing now comes much later."

Salomon sighed. "Maybe we'll learn what stretching is when we see Alette's loom." He looked at Rachel with disappointment as she turned left at the corner. "Aren't you coming to the vineyard with me?"

"Not today, Papa. Miriam has to check on a brit milah, so I'm staying home to sell our wine."

Usually by October, while the new vintage lay fermenting in the family's cellars, little remained of the last year's. Rachel and Miriam would calculate the amount needed to sustain the Jewish community until Hanukkah, at which time the new vintage was opened. Any extra wine, and some years there was none, they sold at a high price.

"*Ma fille*, I'll see you at afternoon services then."

Rachel barely had time to use the privy (thank Heaven Anna knew a secret place near the river where moss grew even at the end of summer), wash her hands (Heaven forbid she forget and the demon Shayd shel Bet-Kisay enter her body by way of her dirty hands), and assure herself that the cellar windows needed neither opening nor closing to maintain the proper temperature, when she heard her mother calling for her.

"Rachel, are you still in the cellar? Anna says that the count's new cellarer is coming down the street."

Rachel groaned and patted her hair into place. "*Oui*, Mama. I'm here."

Raoul had been young Count Eudes' cellarer for three years, since Count Thibault's death, but Mama still called Raoul the new cellarer. Despite Rachel's efforts to avoid being alone with men, and certainly not with her hair uncovered, this was not the path to take with such an important official.

The first two times Raoul bought wine for the count's table, both she and Miriam had served him, as befitted his high position. His third visit came sooner than they expected, while Miriam was out, and he not only stayed longer than necessary to complete the sale, he paid a higher price than usual. On his fourth call, he requested Rachel directly, and when she arrived with her braids covered, asked if she truly needed a veil indoors.

Raoul continued to visit Salomon's cellar far more often than Thibault's cellarer used to, always asking for Rachel. He only tithed the wine in Salomon's cellar, although he must have suspected that the family stored more wine elsewhere. In gratitude she made sure to greet him with exposed tresses and a big smile.

There were hurried steps on the cellar stairs, and Rachel looked up to see her mother anxiously scanning the darkened room for her. Rivka's face was a mask of fear, one that Rachel hadn't seen since Shibeta began her attack.

"*Mon Dieu*, Mama. What's the matter?"

"Raoul isn't alone," Rivka hissed urgently. "The count himself is with him."

eight

achel swallowed the lump in her throat. *Whatever is Eudes doing here?* She barely had time to smooth out her *bliaut* when she heard the men's voices upstairs, declining Mama's offer of refreshments. Then there were two sets of well-polished boots on the stairs, followed by two pairs of men's legs encased in fine silk hose topped with knee-length *cotes*, one blue and the other scarlet. Of course it was Eudes who wore the scarlet, the most costly dye in Troyes. Only Tyrian purple, extracted from shells of a rare murex snail that lived on the shores of the Great Sea, was more expensive than scarlet, but that dye was rarely available outside the Levant.

Rachel wasn't sure how to address a count, so she gave him a small curtsy and waited. The young count had light brown hair, which he wore fashionably short, and a full, but neatly trimmed, beard. Despite his twenty-two years, he still had the look of an adolescent about him. She would have considered him handsome enough, except that when he turned to smile at her his teeth reminded her of a farmer's fence: a jagged row of not quite matching stones.

For the first time in Rachel's life, a man's smile frightened her. Eudes was looking at her with the satisfied confidence a wolf must feel when he comes across a fat ewe unguarded in her pen. He might not be hungry at the moment, but he knows where his next meal is coming from.

Raoul, on the other hand, had never appeared so nervous. His eyes darted back and forth between Eudes, Rachel and the wine casks as he twittered around the cellar. He finally realized that they were both waiting for him to introduce them.

"Your Grace, this is Mistress Rachel, Salomon the Vintner's daughter." His voice sounded more high-pitched than usual.

Rachel curtsied again, more deeply. "It is an honor to have you in my family's wine cellar, Your Grace."

Eudes strolled around the cellar, as if tallying its contents. "Raoul tells me that you have no free-run wine left."

Rachel tried to treat the count no differently from any other customer. "True. It is our most popular wine, despite being the most expensive."

"Don't you find it odd that the free-run wine, which pours out of the vat by itself and requires less labor than the wine extracted by the winepress, should cost more?" he asked.

Raoul stood there speechless, but Rachel rose to his challenge. "Most of the vintner's labor occurs in the months before the grapes reach the vats, so producing free-run wine is only minimally less work than pressed wine." To make sure he wasn't offended by her bold answer, she smiled and added, "But truly, the buyer only cares how the wine tastes, not the amount of effort involved."

Eudes ran his fingers through his hair. "A quick wit. I like that in a woman."

Rachel quashed the temptation to grin and give a flirtatious reply. This man was sovereign of Champagne; all its inhabitants belonged to him—men and women. She would have to control her behavior carefully.

She kept her tone professional. "Would Your Grace like to sample the pressed wine? We have some from grapes of our own vineyard and some from the abbey at Montier-la-Celle."

"The abbey's produce does not interest me. I am only tempted by your own vineyard's." Eudes' smirk made it clear he was not discussing wine.

"But our best produce is taken," she replied in kind. "Surely anything less would not be appropriate for Your Grace's refined palate."

"I would like to taste whatever your vineyard has available. Tomorrow you will ride with me and bring a flask of your father's wine." Eudes was stating a fact, not offering an invitation.

Raoul's gasp was audible, but Rachel remained silent, her mind working furiously. "I'm dreadfully sorry, Your Grace, but I cannot ride with you." Before he could voice his displeasure, she smiled and said, "I am enceinte and have no horse gentle enough to ride in my condition." Aunt Sarah's fine mare had died years earlier, leaving Miriam to hire a series of less-than-satisfactory replacements.

"I will have my stable master find the gentlest palfrey in Troyes." He nodded curtly and began climbing the stairs. "I will bring your mount when the bells chime Tierce, the day after tomorrow."

Rachel walked the men through the courtyard. "Surely Your Grace will allow me to say my morning prayers first," she said sweetly.

Eudes scowled. "How long will that take?"

She knew better than to lie—the count could easily find out when services ended. "Perhaps until an hour after Tierce."

"Very well," he said, slamming the gate behind him.

Her heart pounding, Rachel exhaled the breath she hadn't realized she had been holding and collapsed against the wall. Eudes intended to have his way with her, perhaps even in the field while they were riding. Yet what could she do to stop him?

Desperate for advice, that night Rachel turned to the one person she could always count on.

"Help me, Papa," she pleaded after he'd blessed her children. "How can I keep from sinning with the count—other than by killing him or myself?"

"I'm not sure how you can escape our sovereign's attention, but our Law says you need not kill anyone to avoid sinning." Salomon drew on every measure of self-control to hide his deep dismay from his daughter. As abhorrent as he found the possibility of her lying with Eudes, dying to thwart him was infinitely worse. He was determined to be a pillar of strength for her, and that meant utilizing Torah, the ultimate source of strength.

"But a Baraita in the second chapter of Tractate Pesachim teaches exactly that," she said.

> "Just as a betrothed maiden must be saved from rape by taking her assailant's life, so too should a murder victim be saved by killing the would-be murderer. And just as someone told to commit murder must die rather than sin, so too must a betrothed maiden die and not sin."

Salomon patted her shoulder in reassurance. "That text has been emended. Just as a man told to kill another must die rather than comply, a man told to lie with a married woman must die rather than do so. However, she is not considered an active participant and is therefore not obligated to sacrifice her life." Salomon sighed. "It's a small comfort, but if Eudes forces you to submit, you've committed no sin."

"If I don't fight him, if I just submit and lie with him, I'll become forbidden to my husband," Rachel wailed. "Papa, you know as well as I that a woman who lies with another man during her husband's lifetime is prohibited from resuming relations with him. No matter if she's an adulteress or a divorcée, she may not return to him. There is only one exception, as it says in Mishnah Ketubot concerning a husband's obligations to his wife:

> If you are taken captive I will ransom you and take you back again as my wife.

Though the wife is assumed to have been raped by her captors, she remains permitted to her husband, who must take her back."

"I'm sure there's something about this problem in the Gemara in the fourth chapter of Tractate Ketubot." Salomon stroked his beard for a moment. "I don't think you've studied it.

> Rava said: If in the beginning she was coerced, but in the end she consented . . . she is permitted to her husband.

"But if I submit to Eudes, won't I be consenting in the beginning?"

"*Non*, it's different with bandits or a king. Here's what our Gemara says later:

> Rav Yehuda said: Women captured by bandits are permitted to their husbands. The Rabbis objected: But they bring their captors bread and hand them arrows. Rav Yehuda answered that they serve out of fear. Only if the bandits free the women, yet they return to the bandits, are they forbidden to their husbands. So it is for captives of the king; they are permitted to their husbands."

Salomon took his daughter's hand and squeezed it gently. She must perceive only compassion from him, not the dread for her that gripped him. "A woman taken by a king to be his concubine is also assumed to serve him out of fear." He added softly, "So if you submit, you'll still be permitted to Eliezer when Eudes tires of you—which I pray will be very soon."

"But the Notzrim follow the same Ten Commandments that we do. Eudes would be sinning gravely by committing adultery." Rachel brightened a moment. Perhaps she could appeal to whatever piety the man possessed.

Salomon shook his head. "You must never mention adultery to the count. He might decide to save himself from sin by making you a widow."

So far Rachel had managed to control her tears, but now she began to cry. "Then I have no choice. I'll leave for Mayence tomorrow and wait for Eliezer there."

For years Salomon had feared that his daughter's beauty would put her in danger, but he never imagined that it could jeopardize them all. For whether she refused Eudes or merely angered him with delays, he could—Salomon shuddered, not daring to consider all the terrible punishments Champagne's sovereign could inflict on his Jewish subjects.

"*Ma fille*," he said softly. "You and your children would certainly have to quit Troyes forever, and our whole family might have to flee as well."

"Leaving Joheved behind in Ramerupt to reap what I'd sown." Rachel wiped away her tears. "At least I can try to thwart Eudes' efforts as long as possible."

"When you can no longer thwart him . . ." Salomon paused to control his emotions. "You should consult with Miriam so you won't bear any of his bastards."

Now Rachel squeezed her father's hand. "That's one worry we won't have. Eliezer has already filled my womb."

Rachel used her remaining day of freedom to visit Moses haCohen, court physician in both Troyes and Ramerupt, and his wife Francesca. Surely they would know all the gossip concerning Eudes and his reputation with women; perhaps they could advise her. And doctors could be relied upon to keep confidences.

"Eudes already has a mistress; her father is one of his vassals." Moses poured Rachel a cup of wine. "However, the young lady is very pregnant at the moment, which explains Eudes' sudden interest in other women."

Rachel's eyes opened wide. The mysterious Lady Marie was probably the count's mistress. No wonder she had such opulent jewels.

"Bah." Francesca flicked her hand as if shooing away a fly. "The count has never limited himself to one woman."

"True." Moses turned to Rachel and shook his head. "You cannot refuse him, but I have an idea of how to delay him."

"Tell me."

"At court the Countess Adelaide has some troubadours from Provence who are singing about something new in the affairs of men and women: 'courtly love.' "

"Courtly love?" Rachel rolled her eyes. "I've never heard of it, and I've been to Provence."

"I have no idea if courtly love is popular in Provence, or if it even exists there, but it's the latest fashion in Troyes. The countess and her ladies insist that knights participate."

"So how does the countess's new diversion help Rachel?" Francesca's tiny scowl brought her husband back to the point.

"Courtly love has many elaborate regulations, but the gist is that a knight devotes himself to a married noblewoman who feigns indifference to preserve her reputation," Moses replied. "The code requires that, should the lady accept him as her lover, he must remain discreet and faithful despite all obstacles."

"This is nothing more than a set of rules for committing adultery," Francesca retorted.

"Eudes will have more difficulty remaining faithful than I will in feigning indifference," Rachel said.

"Exactly." The doctor took a leisurely drink of wine. "Once he realizes that you are familiar with courtly love and expect him to obey its rules, he will be honor bound to do so."

"And if he fails, you will have an excuse to reject him." Francesca held up her wine cup in triumph.

"But I'm not a noblewoman." Rachel's growing relief waned. "Eudes won't be obligated to follow the codes of courtly love."

"He is a nobleman; that's what matters. And Frankish Jews have the status of knights." Moses paused and added, "Besides, your sister is a noble lady and that puts you in her class."

"I hope the rules aren't too complicated to learn by tomorrow morning."

"Believe me, it's not as complicated as Talmud," he said. "First comes the knight's secret attraction to the lady, but his passionate declaration of devotion only provokes the lady's virtuous rejection. Next comes renewed wooing with oaths of fidelity and complaints of lovesickness, until finally he performs a series of gallant deeds that win the lady's heart. All this must be done with utmost discretion; no one but the lady must know of his love."

"And then?" Although Rachel knew very well what the ultimate result was expected to be.

"Lastly, the couple consummates their secret passion, which is followed by endless subterfuges to avoid detection."

"How does courtly love end?"

"The same as any infatuation." Moses set down his empty cup. "A new love puts the old one to flight."

Moses and Francesca spent an hour playacting various courtly love scenarios with Rachel, until a servant announced the doctor's next patient.

"*Merci* for your wine and your advice," Rachel said as she bid her hosts adieu. "Both were excellent."

"I hope you can put my advice to good use." Moses's expression became somber. "Never forget that Count Eudes has ultimate power over our community. He can confiscate property, order vineyards burned, establish new taxes, take away our profitable fair positions, and even banish us if he wishes."

Rachel needed to think, and preferably in a place where she wouldn't be disturbed. Instead of returning home, she walked to the vineyard, where there were rows and rows of vine props to be pulled out and stacked as she considered various strategies and rehearsed those she thought Eudes would find most compelling.

She would lead him on a merry chase of courtly love, first rebuffing him with protests of virtue and then assigning him task after task, each more arduous than the last, until he was finally distracted by a new, more biddable love. With any luck, his old mistress would give him a son and he would joyfully return to her.

There was no sign of Eudes when Rachel returned from synagogue the next morning, and she was about to return the flask of wine when a stranger rode into the courtyard.

"Mistress Rachel?" he inquired.

When she answered, "*Oui*," he dismounted and handed her the horse's reins.

"His Grace hopes you find this mare sufficiently gentle. He awaits you at the St.-Jacques Gate."

Rachel considered rejecting the animal out of hand, but then decided that it would be best to ride a short distance first. So she allowed the groom to help her into the saddle and rode around the courtyard a few times to test her seat. The palfrey seemed tractable enough, so she swallowed her trepidation and rode into the street. Thank Heaven Eudes was following the primary rule of courtly love—discretion.

He was waiting just outside the city walls, accompanied by several squires and servants. He gestured to the flask tied to her saddle. "I see you haven't forgotten the wine."

She waited while he took a long drink and burped with satisfaction. "This is indeed excellent wine," he said. "I would never guess it came from the winepress."

"*Merci*. My family works hard to make it so."

Eudes kicked his horse's side and the party set off toward the forest, his retainers following at a distance. "Perhaps you can explain to me why it is that wine is so expensive compared to ale. Are they not both fermented from fruits of the field?"

"I am no expert on making ale, but according to my sister Lady Joheved of Ramerupt the process is quite simple," Rachel replied, glad of an excuse to remind him of her noble relatives. "The alewife merely adds barley grist to water, heats it briefly as the mixture mashes, and then allows the brew to ferment for a week or two. Almost any barley will produce a decent ale, but a wine's quality depends on the excellence of its grapes, cultivated for that specific purpose."

"So it is the grape grower who is responsible for a good wine, not the vintner?"

"Both of them are," she said. "No vintner, no matter how skilled, can make good wine out of bad grapes, while a poor vintner can ruin the finest grapes."

Rachel took a moment to glance back over her shoulder. To her dismay, the city walls were now far behind them. Only Eudes' servants would hear if she screamed. Was the count truly interested in winemaking, or was he trying to lull her into conversation in hopes she would lower her guard? But as they rode farther into the forest, its foliage a riot of rich fall colors, Eudes continued to question her about viticulture. And he appeared to listen with interest as she described how they pruned the vines in the winter, trained the new shoots and trimmed the excess leaves that shaded them in the spring, attached the limbs to trellises in the summer, and harvested the grapes in the autumn.

She was about to explain how they trod the grapes in the vats, when Eudes pulled his horse to a stop. "Mistress Rachel, for many weeks I have looked forward to this day, determined to tell you how great are my continual thoughts of you." He turned and looked at her directly. "Your love alone can crown me with the diadem of a king."

Rachel had been hoping for such a fancy speech, but still it was a surprise to hear from the count's lips. She drew herself up tall. "But what a strange falcon we would consider him, who ignores partridges and pheasants to seek his quarry among the sparrows," she began.

Her heart was pounding; yet she kept her voice calm as she continued with more of the courtly love ritual's strange formality. "I am honored that a count finds a humble woman such as myself worthy of his love, but I am afraid to accept a man of such a grand and lofty family."

Eudes' eyebrows rose in surprise, then his expression slowly changed to one of grudging respect. "Every man ought to ask for love where its persuasion impels him. Surely a falcon flies better when it takes a resourceful lark than when taking a fat quail that runs in a straight line."

"But it is not natural for a man of such high rank to faithfully love a woman of a lower one, and if he does, he will soon come to loathe her." She turned her palfrey around and began riding back to town.

Eudes quickly caught up with her. "Love that arises solely from delight in a woman's beauty is excellent in any class and not sought from the privilege of rank alone."

Was the count threatening her by mentioning the privileges of rank? Rachel fought her fear to answer him properly. "Your great haste seems to violate the custom of courtly love, for the wise lover, when conversing for the first time with a lady whom he has not previously known, should not ask specifically for gifts of love but should show himself pleasant and courteous."

Eudes seemed taken aback by her words, and they rode in silence while he fashioned his response. "I now see that all I've heard about you is true, for it is clear from your answer that you are as wise as you are fine in character."

"Yet I believe you have spoken thus because you think I will be only too willing to grant what you ask. Therefore there is good cause to be suspicious of your love." Rachel smiled inwardly. *Does he really think his kind words will win me so easily?*

Eudes was not so quickly dismissed. "If my feelings are too strong to resist, I plead necessity as a defense against your charge of unworthiness. If I have any lack of judgment in love, I must seek the love of a woman with great wisdom and worth to remedy this."

They were fast approaching the city walls, and Rachel had no intention of riding past them in the count's company. He seemed willing, perhaps even amused, to participate in this courtly love pastime, so she dare not repudiate him outright.

"Though you might, by your arguments, compel me to love you," she said. "There is another reason that keeps me from doing so. Suppose you did win my love? If it came to the ears of the people, they would ruin my good name. It is better, then, to refrain from entering into such an affair than to suffer so much that we must end it after it has begun."

"I ask only for you to consider my suit and not reject the love of a count, for only a man of such high rank is worthy of a love such as yours."

Rachel remembered how she'd planned to delay him. "A woman whose love is sought should either promise it to her suitor or deny it outright. But if she is in doubt as to the character of the man she may say to him: do good deeds before you seek the reward for good deeds."

Church bells ringing at midday prevented Eudes from replying. Intending to walk the rest of the way home, Rachel started to dismount.

"Wait," Eudes called out. "Keep the horse so we may ride and discuss this matter again tomorrow."

"Tomorrow is our Sabbath." Now would come the first test. Would Eudes easily accept the limitations of her religion?

"Then we'll ride again on Monday morning." He paused, apparently realizing that he had been too forceful for a courtly lover. "If this palfrey pleases you, I ask you to keep her as a small token of my affection." He smiled at her expression of astonishment. "I hope that by Monday I will have more good deeds to my credit."

Rachel nodded and waved Eudes adieu. Lost in thought, she almost rode past her destination, the stables where Aunt Sarah's horse used to board. She had been so worried about possible punishments for rejecting the count that she had not considered the rewards she might receive for accepting him. Look at those diamonds he'd given Marie.

Would it be so terrible to become the count's mistress?

Papa himself had told her that it wouldn't be a sin, and that Eliezer would have to take her back afterward. But what would happen when Eliezer returned at the end of the month? She shivered in disgust—how could she possibly shuttle back and forth between Eudes' bed and her husband's?

nine

or three weeks Count Eudes wooed Rachel with increasing fervor. He sent more gifts—perfume, silk hose, a pearl necklace and earrings. She rode with him several times a week, he making new protestations of love and she finding new ways to discourage him without entirely rejecting him. But with the Cold Fair only days away, Eudes growing impatient, and Eliezer due to arrive anytime, Rachel knew the moment had come to take the action she so dreaded.

When they arrived at the St.-Jacques Gate at the end of their afternoon ride, she gazed up at the count in what she hoped was an expression of adoration. "Your persistence and devotion have indeed moved my heart, Your Grace, and I am inclined to accept your proposal of love."

"I have devoted myself to your service." His eyes glinted with lust. "Nothing could give me greater happiness than knowing that my deeds may obtain from you the reward I desire."

Rachel took a deep breath. "I ask of you merely one more deed, one that requires great nobility of spirit."

Eudes looked at her with distrust, so she reached out and took his hand, something she had never done before. "My husband will return to Troyes any day. If you can restrain your passion until the Cold Fair ends, if you can hide your love so well that all believe it has died, then when the year begins and my husband is gone, I will be yours."

"Today I am the most joyful of men." He didn't try to hide his triumph. "Rest assured that your love will be safe with me." He bent over to kiss her hand, and it was clear that he intended to kiss her lips next.

Rachel pulled just far enough away. "I am pleased that my answer has given you happiness, but to keep anybody from having reason to suspect evil of us, it is proper that our discussion should end here."

He took a swig from the wineskin hanging from his saddle, and then saluted her with it. "To the New Year, my beautiful Mistress Rachel. I eagerly await celebrating it with you."

With a great sigh of relief, Rachel rode toward home. She would leave her mare at the stables, where everyone assumed the animal belonged to Miriam. At afternoon services, she thanked the Merciful One for sparing her so far, and she prayed fervently that Eudes should forget about her and that word of their liaison never come to Eliezer's ears. When Eliezer arrived in Troyes that evening, she greeted him with greater enthusiasm than when he'd escaped from the bandits in Burgundy.

With her husband's return, Rachel was even more determined to learn about becoming a cloth merchant. It wasn't just that she missed Eliezer while he was gone: their children suffered from his absence as well. Little Rivka barely remembered who he was, while Shemiah should be learning Torah from his father. If Eliezer continued spending so much time away from home, their children would see Salomon and Judah as father figures. But what frightened her most was the fact that each journey Eliezer took entailed a risk that he might not return at all.

So Rachel suggested to Salomon that they visit the widow Alette and see her loom.

"If we earn enough in Sepharad, Eliezer can use our profit to buy kermes and indigo from Maghreb." Rachel's eyes shone with excitement. "Luxury woolens bring the most money, but they require the finest dyes."

Despite his anxiety over her deception with Eudes, Salomon couldn't help but smile. "If we get a good price for this year's vintage, perhaps I can also invest in your venture."

"Oh, Papa." She threw her arms around him. "That would be wonderful. And if the vintage is very good, we might be able to buy some Tyrian purple."

When they reached Alette's home, they saw that her brother Albert did the weaving while she, her daughters, and her neighbors spun the wool.

"It takes eight of us to spin enough yarn for one loom," Alette told Salomon.

Their workroom was located in the front room of the house, with the loom taking up most of the space. Unlike Sybille's vertical loom, this one was set up like a long table. The many warp threads were pulled taut parallel to the length of it, toward the end where Albert sat. In the center, two square frames were suspended perpendicular to the threads. From these hung many small rings with one warp thread running through each. Albert held up a shuttle similar to the one Sybille used to weave linen.

"What are these frames for?" Rachel asked, and then added to Salomon, "The Talmud didn't describe anything like this."

"These are the heddles," Alette said. "Their rings keep the warp threads in place so the weft can easily move between them."

She gestured to her brother, who pressed a foot pedal underneath the loom. Abruptly a pulley hoisted one of the heddle frames, its rings lifting half the warp threads up with it. Albert sent the shuttle between the raised warp threads and the remaining half below. Then he worked another pedal, which caused the first heddle to lower and its mate to rise.

Immediately he sent the shuttle across to the other side, and pulled the weft tightly toward him. As with Sybille's linen, they watched with appreciation as Alette's wool turned into fabric. Eventually Albert paused and rolled the woven cloth onto the rod in front of him while Alette unrolled more warp threads from the rod at the far end of the loom.

Salomon smiled in approval. "I thought Sybille's loom was efficient, but this is clearly an improvement."

Albert nodded. "We can weave twice as fast as on my sister's old hanging loom. But it needs a man to work it. First to pull the warp threads tight and tie them on the end rods—"

"Which means the warp threads must be both strong enough to support the weft and elastic enough to stretch onto the frame," Alette interrupted. "That's why we prefer to spin our own thread, so we can control the quality."

"Attaching the warp threads must be what the Mishnah means by 'stretching,'" Rachel whispered to Salomon.

"My brother is also useful to lift the heavy finished cloth off the loom at the end. But mostly we need his long arms so we can weave a wider cloth." Albert held out his arms and indeed, he just touched both sides of the loom.

"May I try it?" Salomon asked.

Albert offered the older man his bench. Salomon tapped the foot pedals a few times, watching intently as one heddle rose and then the other, each taking half the warp threads with it. He lowered the appropriate frame, took up the shuttle and carefully pushed it halfway across the warp before reaching around with his other hand to pull it through the rest of the way.

Salomon nodded slowly. "Now I see what you mean."

Albert resumed his position at the loom. Rachel felt hypnotized as she stared at his feet pumping the pedals, the heddles bobbing up and down, and the shuttle flying across the warp.

"How long is a finished bolt of broadcloth?" she asked.

"About forty to fifty cubits," he replied, his pace not slowing in the slightest.

"And how long does it take to weave?"

"About two weeks," Alette said. "Our family can produce twenty such pieces a year; twenty-five if we're lucky."

"I have a proposal for you." Rachel addressed both siblings. "Would you be willing to weave for me if I supplied the combed wool?"

Alette and Albert exchanged puzzled looks. "You'd buy all the fabric we weave?" he asked.

Rachel grinned. "And you'd have no expenses at all."

"Where's your profit?" Alette asked.

"We'll pay everyone by the piece and take our profit on the finished dyed cloth."

The proud look on Papa's face as they walked home made it clear that he understood her idea. "Joheved's manor can provide the wool, our family and Alette's spin it, Albert weave it, and Eliezer can import the dyes. Then we'll pay the dyer by the piece and sell the finished product at the Cloth Fair."

Rachel took his arm and her voice rose with excitement. "Then we'll hire more spinsters and more weavers and more dyers until we're earning so much money that Eliezer never has to travel again."

Eudes was true to his word and left Rachel alone for the month of November while Eliezer was home. She was grateful for being able to push her troubles with the count out of her mind, but it wasn't long before she had other concerns to occupy her. Mama was ill with ague, leaving Rachel to host the many guests who dined with Salomon during the fair. She and Miriam also had to supervise the servants as they scrubbed clean the wine-press, utensils, vats, and casks. Heaven forbid that off-odors should result from their negligence.

In addition every pruning knife had to be cleaned and sharpened, and all the straws prepared that they would need for tying up the vines in the spring. But these tasks required little intellectual skill, leaving Rachel vulnerable to increasing anxiety over Eudes' future designs. In desperation she asked Miriam to discuss Talmud with her while they worked.

Her sister agreed readily. "Let's review the section about Hanukkah."

"I thought you already studied that with Joheved."

Miriam's cheeks flushed pink. "When Joheved and I were learning it, I wanted to stop because it was too hard. Now that I'm more experienced, I'd like to see how difficult it really is."

"I'd love to," Rachel replied, glad that Miriam had chosen a demanding *sugia*. "I only got to read Papa's *kuntres* to myself."

So they turned to the second chapter of Tractate Shabbat, where they soon came to a discussion over what action constitutes the mitzvah of Hanukkah. Was it, as Rava argued, placing the lamp where it can be seen to publicize the miracle? Or was it kindling the flame?

> Rabbi Yehoshua ben Levi said: A lamp lit for Shabbat that burned the entire day, when Shabbat ends he should extinguish the flame and rekindle it for Hanukkah. This is fine if you say that kindling constitutes the mitzvah, but if placement is the mitzvah, he should have added, "lift it and put it down" before rekindling.

"I disagree with Rava," Rachel said. "If placement were the important thing, then there would be no need to relight the Shabbat lamp for Hanukkah. You would just leave it burning and move it to where it will be seen."

"The Gemara agrees." Miriam pointed to the text that ended the debate.

> Furthermore, since we bless before lighting, saying "*Baruch ata Adonai* . . . Who commands us to kindle the Hanukkah light [*ner shel Hanukkah*]," we derive from this that kindling fulfills the mitzvah.

Rachel nodded. "So if putting the lamp by the door was really the mitzvah, we would make a blessing over that."

"Which we don't," Miriam said.

Suddenly Rachel's eyes opened wide. "Miriam, this is where the Shabbat lamp blessing comes from. The words are exactly the same—except on Shabbat we say '*ner shel Shabbat*' instead of '*ner shel Hanukkah*.'"

"What are you talking about?"

"Eliezer and I got into a big argument over this, at his mother's house of all places." Rachel's voice rose with excitement. "He said women shouldn't bless the Shabbat lamp because there's no such blessing in the Talmud."

Miriam grinned. "And you made the blessing anyway."

"Of course I did, just like Grandmama taught us. I meant to ask Papa about it when we got back." Rachel shrugged. "But now it doesn't matter. We've found the blessing in the Talmud."

"But it's not the same blessing."

"It's almost the same. Only one word is different. Look further down the page. There's the blessing again, only this time the Gemara has all the words, not just the final ones." Rachel pointed to the passage.

> Rav Chiya bar Ashi said in the name of Rav: One who kindles a Hanukkah light must make a blessing.

Then she continued reading:

> "What blessing does he say? He blesses: *Baruch ata Adonai* . . . Who sanctifies us with His commandments and commands us to kindle the Hanukkah light. But where did He so command us?"

"The Sages question how we can have a commandment to kindle the menorah, since Hanukkah is never mentioned in the Torah," Miriam said.

"I remember this." Rachel nodded. "Now they give us two different

Torah verses to justify it, both of which teach us that rabbinic mitzvot are as important as biblical mitzvot."

"And that we have to say blessings over their mitzvot too, just like for Torah commandments," Miriam added.

"Wait, we skipped the part about women." Rachel began reading again.

> "A woman may certainly kindle the Hanukkah light. Rabbi Yehoshua ben Levi said: Women are obligated in the mitzvah of Hanukkah for they were involved in that miracle."

"Papa told us about a Jewish woman who served as an instrument of the deliverance," Miriam said. "In those days, virgin brides had to submit to the local Greek commander first. So when the high priest's daughter was betrothed, the general demanded that she lie with him. She went to his tent, gave him so much wine that he passed out drunk, and cut his head off. When his army saw that their general was dead, they fled."

Rachel said nothing. The story of the high priest's daughter came too close for comfort. *Does Miriam know?*

But Miriam continued innocently, "I still remember how Joheved and I stayed up talking. It was just after she and Meir were betrothed, and I asked her what she would do if Count Thibault insisted on lying with her."

"What did she say?" Rachel tried not to sound too interested.

"Joheved thought the idea was ridiculous, especially since Thibault was as old as Grandmamma Leah. So I asked her what she'd do if we had a young count, if she'd get him drunk and then cut off his head."

"And?" Rachel asked. She was so close to confiding in Miriam. *After all, she turned to me when Judah wanted a divorce.* But it was easier somehow to confide in strangers like the doctor than in family, and if she told Miriam then she'd have to tell their judgmental older sister.

"Joheved said that if a lord instituted such a policy, we'd have to move away."

"That's easy to say when you're a child, when you don't understand what's involved in packing up everything and moving." Rachel spoke with such vehemence that Miriam looked at her with concern.

"I didn't mean to upset you. I thought you might want to talk about it."

Rachel looked into her sister's compassionate eyes and sighed. "How did you find out?"

"Didn't you think I'd be curious about that lovely new horse that the stable hands said belonged to me?" Miriam asked in return. "When they told me that you rode her several times a week, I decided to follow you."

Rachel covered her face with her hands. "*Mon Dieu*."

"Rachel, I'm only sorry you couldn't unburden your heart to me."

"I haven't done anything sinful."

"Of course not," Miriam said. "According to Tractate Ketubot, a woman captured by the king to lie with him isn't sinning."

Rachel's green eyes flashed. "But I haven't lain with the count . . . yet. I've managed to put him off until after the Cold Fair." She explained how she'd used the subtleties of courtly love to thwart Eudes so far.

Miriam frowned, but then her brow relaxed as she turned to her sister. "Do you think you'll enjoy it with him? After all, one of King Solomon's proverbs says that stolen waters are sweet and bread eaten in secret is tasty."

Rachel hesitated. This was a question she never thought to hear from her pious sister, a question she'd been afraid to ask herself. Lying with Eudes meant she wouldn't have to suffer those endless months of longing and frustration while her husband was away.

"Maybe . . . if he's skillful." Then Rachel scowled. "But I hate it that I have no choice, that I can't refuse him."

"If you had a choice, then it would be adultery and you wouldn't do it." Miriam's logic was impeccable. "At least you're not a virgin like the high priest's daughter."

Rachel shuddered. "Thank Heaven."

They were still studying Tractate Shabbat when Joheved's family arrived for Hanukkah; yet Rachel had less time to study than before. Thanks to judicious use of black hellebore that Moses haCohen prescribed, Mama had recovered from her fever, but bouts of dizziness continued to plague her. The timing couldn't have been worse. Along with the yeshiva students, numerous foreign merchant scholars also needed to be hosted during the festival. Each of the eight nights of Hanukkah required another banquet, never mind that women were supposed to refrain from work during the holiday, a reward for the high priest's daughter's effort.

It was only when Moses haCohen and Francesca arrived for *souper* one evening that Rachel excused herself to question them in private.

"What gossip have you heard from the court?" she asked anxiously.

Francesca grabbed Rachel's hands. "Count Eudes has a new love, one of his mother's ladies-in-waiting. So it's quite possible he's forgotten about you."

"That's just gossip." Moses frowned. "What I know for certain is that his previous mistress died in childbirth a few weeks ago, and when someone suggested they call in the Jewish midwife, he categorically refused."

Rachel flinched. "So we don't know if the count has actually forgotten about me, or if he's just obeying my wishes." Had Eudes let his lover die rather than risk Rachel learning of her? And how heartless to take a new mistress while his previous one was still warm in her grave.

"It's not mere gossip that he's wooing another lady," Francesca insisted. "He has not been faithful to you."

"I don't think you should hold him to that," Moses warned her.

"Come on, you three. The sun has set already," Eliezer called out from the salon. "We must light the Hanukkah lamp before the stars come out."

The family gathered by the front door, where Grandmamma Leah's large silver menorah sat next to an ornate brass one that Moses had bought in Bavel while studying medicine. Determined to enjoy the time with her husband and children, Rachel beamed as Eliezer held little Rivka on his shoulders to watch as Papa measured out the olive oil and then poured some into four of the silver menorah's little bowls, three next to each other in a line and the fourth above them. After Moses did the same, they said the blessings, lit the upper wick, and then the other three.

Papa's older grandchildren had studied about Hanukkah and waved their hands eagerly as he asked them questions, each appropriate to their age.

For the adolescents—Isaac, Shmuel, and Yom Tov—there were questions whose answers came from Tractate Shabbat.

"Why do we place the menorah near the door?"

"Rava says that this is to publicize the miracle."

"Can we place it on either side of the doorway?"

"Rav Shmuel says that we place it on the left side."

"And why is that?"

"Since the mezuzah hangs on the right side, we will then be surrounded by mitzvot."

To five-year-old Elisha he asked, "How many flames does our menorah have? Count them with me."

"One, two, three, four," Miriam's youngest son counted. Alvina and little Rivka repeated the words after him.

"But what night of Hanukkah is this?"

"The third," Leah and Shemiah, both in their seventh year, called out together.

"So why the extra one?"

Before one of older boys answered again, Hannah spoke up. Just on the cusp of puberty, she was taller than her brother Shmuel and almost as tall as Isaac. "The menorah's flame is to publicize the miracle. We are not allowed to use it for reading or to light our house. So we add an extra flame, whose light we may use."

"We are also forbidden to light from one Hanukkah flame to another," Shmuel added. "So we can use the extra one for this."

Salomon turned to Miriam's middle son, Shimson. "Why is this festival called Hanukkah?"

"Hanukkah is the Hebrew word for dedication," the eight-year-old replied. "After the Hasmoneans defeated the Greeks, they had to rededicate the Temple in Jerusalem, which had been defiled by the enemy."

"And what happened when the Hasmoneans started to rededicate the Temple?" Salomon gestured to Leah and Shemiah.

"There was only enough pure oil for one day," Shemiah burst out, his dark curls bouncing in his excitement. "But a miracle happened and it lasted for eight days."

Leah's face crumpled as her cousin usurped her reply, so Salomon lifted her up on his lap and asked her, "But why did they need the oil to last eight days?"

She smiled up at him. "Because it took eight days to make more oil."

Shmuel was about to speak again, when Salomon interrupted him. "Enough questions. It's time to eat." The Rabbis of the Talmud discussed several reasons for the eight-day holiday, but he would ask about those on another night.

Everyone eagerly headed for the dining table. "I have a question for Mama," Rachel said as the servants began bringing out dishes of food. "Why do we always have goose or duck at Hanukkah? They're so expensive at this time of year."

Despite her dizziness, Rivka had managed to rise from her sickbed to share the holiday meal with her family, and she frowned at her daughter's question. "As you would know if you spent more time in the kitchen, geese and ducks are the fattest of birds, and from them we render the fat to fry with all winter." Cold weather ensured that the stored fat would last until Passover.

"When I was a poor yeshiva student, we couldn't afford to eat goose during Hanukkah." Salomon tried to take the sting out of his wife's rebuke. "Now that our family is more prosperous, I wish to make up for all the good food we missed."

Eliezer chuckled. "If it weren't for goose fat, how would we make all the fried foods we love to eat at this time of year, especially your mother's excellent *grimseli*?" He picked up one of the fried strips of dough, dipped it into strawberry preserves, and licked his lips in anticipation.

"Since we are celebrating the miracle of abundant oil, it is only fitting to enjoy those foods cooked with them." Salomon smiled at Rachel, mumbled a short blessing, and helped himself from a dish containing a mound of walnuts fried with honey. "And I thank you for making the dessert I enjoy above all others."

"Rabbenu Salomon, why did you make a blessing over your dessert?" Moses's daughter Judita asked. "I thought blessing bread is sufficient for everything we eat at a meal."

"You are correct. However, we also bless the wine because it brings us special happiness, and so I say a blessing over these fried nuts because they bring me special happiness." He popped one in his mouth and grinned. "Now that you are betrothed to my Isaac, you must call me Grandpapa."

Judita blushed. "*Oui* . . . Grandpapa."

After the menorah had burned all its oil, the family remained at the table, singing Hanukkah songs and teasing each other with riddles. Rachel tucked her sleepy daughter into bed and hummed a few lullabies, recalling her last view of Eliezer and Shemiah, giggling as they played traditional Hanukkah gambling games with nuts. As she came downstairs to rejoin them, she realized that she had gone nearly a whole evening without worrying about Eudes.

Rachel's respite lasted until Raoul paid his usual post-Hanukkah visit to taste the new vintage. Expecting him on Monday after the festival ended, she left synagogue directly when services were done. The vintage had been a fine one and she anticipated that her current good standing with the count should ensure that Raoul tithed a minimum of it.

Mama and Anna were out shopping when Rachel heard the courtyard gate open. She peeked out the kitchen window and to her horror saw both Eudes and Raoul approaching the front door.

"Your Grace, what a pleasure to see you," she lied.

Eudes' words did nothing to reassure her. "Raoul, stay up here and let me know if anyone approaches." Then he turned to Rachel. "Let's see what delights await me in the cellar."

Her throat tight with fear, Rachel led the count down the steps. No sooner did he reach the bottom than he closed the distance between them and took her hand. "My whole heart's desire is directed toward you. Since you are worthy of a count's love, you must not refrain from loving me in return."

"But your deeds have proven you unworthy of my love. You have given your love elsewhere."

Eudes face darkened and he squeezed her hand painfully. "I have only followed your wish that I behave in such a way that no one should suspect us of evil."

"But you have not kept faith with me. You promised to wait until New Year's Day." Rachel's throat was so choked with fright that she could barely speak, and for the first time in this pregnancy, nausea welled up inside her.

Eudes grabbed her shoulder and forced her to look at him. "Enough of this courtly love charade. It ceases to amuse me. If you cannot willingly render to your sovereign the services that please him, you should be careful not to offend him."

Before Rachel could reply, he pulled her close and fastened his lips on hers. She tried to overcome her revulsion and respond enthusiastically, but Eudes had truly horrific smelling breath. In her queasy state, it was only a moment before she began to gag.

She was saved by Raoul calling down to them, "Your Grace, the vintner's wife and maidservant have returned."

Eudes backed away, while Rachel grasped the nearest cask to steady herself. She had no choice now, no matter how revolting she found his touch. "I have no wish to offend you, Your Grace. If you can be patient until New Year's, when my sickness should subside, I will be your most willing and obedient servant."

"Since I prefer an amenable lover as well as a healthy one, I will wait a few weeks more." His voice hardened. "But willing or not, you will share my bed on New Year's Day."

Outside, crouching next to the half-open cellar window, Eliezer barely managed to restrain his impulse to race to the front door and murder the count. Rachel's odd behavior, so jumpy and secretive, had sent Eliezer to Salomon and Miriam for the cause. What they told him would curdle any husband's blood, and now he had the proof he needed.

Jewish Law permitted a man to kill someone pursuing him, or his family, with evil intent, and it mandated him to do so to prevent the rape of a married woman. So the decision for Eliezer wasn't what to do, but how and, most importantly, when.

ten

t was impossible to shake the loathsome memory of Eudes' lips on hers. That week, each time Rachel reveled in Eliezer's arms she knew she couldn't betray him with their sovereign. Should it come to that, she would rather die than share Eudes' bed. But why should she die when he was the pursuer? Why should she die when, according to the Talmud, lying with the count wasn't even considered a sin?

Papa had said that just as a murder victim should be saved by killing the would-be murderer, so too could a married woman be saved from rape by taking her assailant's life. Hadn't the high priest's daughter killed the Greek commander in similar circumstances?

But how could she just snuff out the life of a man? All he wanted to do was lie with her, not hurt her.

Yet if I don't kill him, I'll have to lie with him—and not just once, but as often as he likes, no matter what horrible things he wants to do. And once people find out, my reputation, my husband's, and even my father's, will be ruined.

When all her reasoning came to an end, Rachel reached her conclusion: If it was no sin to lie with Eudes, it was also no sin to kill him. And she would rather see the count dead than submit to his embraces. With that choice made, she decided to seek help from Moses haCohen.

She forced herself to wait until Judah's monthly bloodletting, when Eliezer would be busy concluding business negotiations as the Cold Fair drew to a close. She fumed with frustration when the doctor stayed to bleed Salomon as well. Being older than fifty, Papa usually had his blood let every other month, as the Talmud recommended, but since the following month, Shevat, was considered inauspicious, he chose to undergo the procedure twice in two months rather than merely once in three. With all the food and wine he'd consumed over Hanukkah, he felt fortified for the procedure.

Just when Rachel thought she'd have Moses to herself, he suggested that Rivka be bled as well, since she no longer rid herself of excess corrupt seed through her menses. Perhaps it would help relieve her dizziness. Rachel paced the courtyard until he stepped outside, and then fell in step with him.

"Moses, I need your advice on an urgent and private matter." Her voice was shaking. "I cannot risk being overheard, and I probably shouldn't be seen entering your house either."

The doctor's right eyebrow rose quizzically. "Nonsense. You have every right to consult me about your mother's illness. We will have all the privacy we need in my salon."

Moses no sooner closed his thick office door than Rachel blurted out, "I have need of a fast-acting, undetectable poison."

The doctor paused and considered her. "Must the victim die immediately, or can he merely be incapacitated and allowed to die later?"

"It matters not, so long as long as he cannot name me his poisoner."

"And when would you need this?"

"By New Year's Day, maybe sooner."

Moses stared up at the ceiling. "I assume this is a case of killing a pursuer who intends you harm. And I assume that you have given this decision very careful thought."

Rachel nodded. "I have thought of little else. I may not need this poison, but I must have it available."

"There are many questions to discuss and much I must explain to you first." So far his face hadn't betrayed the slightest apprehension.

"You will help me?" she whispered.

"Since your situation is so dire."

Rachel sighed with relief. "I thought you might be an expert on poisons."

"I have never assisted a poisoner before." When her face fell he added, "However, while in Bavel I spent several years studying poisons' effects and their antidotes. Poison is the preferred weapon of assassins in the

Levant, and every court physician must be skilled on the subject. Luckily for you, very few people in France have this expertise."

She was indeed fortunate. With the doctor's skills, she stood a far better chance of poisoning Count Eudes without detection. She took a deep breath and began explaining the likely scenario. "I will be alone with a man and able to administer the poison to him personally, probably in the evening."

"So there will be food and wine."

"I will bring wine with me," Rachel said.

"*Oui*, and if there's the slightest inkling of poison, your wine will be the first thing they suspect."

Rachel sighed. "But could we poison the wine and give me the antidote?"

"I would prefer not to," he replied. "Francesca tells me that you're expecting a child."

She nodded. "In the spring."

"It would be better to share your wine with his servants first and then poison his cup. If you poison his food, you'd have to clean the dishes afterward and that would look odd."

"The poison must work right away. If he dies that night, nobody will likely discover the body until the morning."

"We could use pennyroyal oil. Your sister is sure to have some for ending unwanted pregnancies. In that way, we wouldn't need to involve an apothecary." Moses paused to think. "But to kill in one dose causes a great deal of pain, and he might scream so loudly that the household may become alarmed."

"What about arsenic?"

"It's for chronic poisoning, not for what you want," he said. "Let me see. Foxglove, monkshood, and belladonna work fast, but they cause hallucinations and convulsions. You don't want him to injure you."

Rachel thought a moment. "Do you have opium?" It was a common sleeping draught in Maghreb.

"Opium is a possibility. But people might have questions if a healthy young man just fell asleep and didn't wake up."

"Hemlock?" *Will any poison be acceptable to the doctor?*

"*Non*. The arms and legs are paralyzed first, but not the mouth. He'd surely call for help."

"So what else is there?"

"I have it—henbane." Moses nodded in satisfaction. "It's known to have an aphrodisiac effect when added to wine, so nobody would be surprised if a young man with a woman visitor accidentally took too much."

"If I suggested he procure some, I could add a larger dose to his cup." Relief coursed through her. "He'll never suspect that I'm not eager to be with him."

"I suggest you add some of your mother's black hellebore as well," Moses said. "The two together will surely kill him. But Rachel, you must be careful not to drink the wine yourself."

"*Merci, merci.*" Rachel kissed the doctor's palm before leaving. "You're an angel." The Angel of Death to be sure, she thought as she turned for the door, but still an angel.

Rachel's good mood lasted only a week. In the final days of the Cold Fair, she and Eliezer met with Nissim the Clothier. Eliezer, while intrigued by his wife's plan for them to become clothiers, did not share her enthusiasm. There were too many unanswered questions, too many potential pitfalls. Besides, he wasn't sure he wanted to give up his visits to Sepharad. He was, however, willing to keep Rachel content by consulting an expert.

Nissim's hair was more grey than auburn, but he was just as freckled as when Salomon traded him wine for the family's first luxury woolens twenty years earlier. He had been buying the rabbi's wine ever since and never lacked a ready market for it among the Jews of his native Flanders. So he was content to sacrifice a little time now to assist Salomon's attractive youngest daughter.

"Nissim, can you please explain what makes some wool fabrics more valuable than others?" Rachel asked. She needed to understand this if her endeavor were to succeed.

"Let me start at the beginning," Nissim said. "If I come to a subject you're familiar with, we'll move on to the next."

Rachel and Eliezer nodded in agreement, with Rachel eager to hear Nissim's explanation, no matter how familiar.

"Everyone agrees that the quality of the wool itself is paramount," he began. "The best wool for felting comes from sheep with fine, short-fibered, curly hair, while coarser, long, straight fibers are better for worsteds."

Nissim took in their confused expressions and realized he had already assumed too much knowledge. "There are two kinds of wool textiles—worsteds and true woolens, the latter being far more valuable," he said. "All the fabrics I sell are woolens."

"Go on." Eliezer pursed his lips in annoyance. He'd expected Rachel to be more informed before she dragged him into this, and here it seemed she didn't know the first thing about wool.

"In fineness Frankish sheep can't compare to those in Angleterre, so your local product is already at a disadvantage," Nissim continued. "But the spinsters and weavers in Troyes are so skilled that they quite nearly make up for it."

"I thought Joheved's sheep gave fine, short, curly wool." Rachel was mortified at having her ignorance exposed to Eliezer. "At least it seems that way when I spin it."

Nissim pulled out several bolts of cloth that his customers hadn't yet picked up. "The scarlet is woven of pure English wool. These blues are from mixed English and Flemish wool, while those are mixed English and local wool." He waited while they examined the fabrics. "And these red ones are completely local."

"Amazing." Rachel gently stroked the scarlet. "The texture is almost as fine as silk; yet the weight marks it as wool."

Eliezer looked at Nissim skeptically. "But some of the red pieces are clearly superior to the poorer blues."

"So you see that good wool is not the entire story," he said. "I think it's the skilled fuller who's responsible for our finest woolens."

Rachel hated to appear stupid again, but she had no choice. "The fuller?" she asked, ignoring Eliezer's snort of exasperation.

"After woolen cloth is woven, it must be fulled before dyeing," Nissim replied. "Without fulling, the material would soon tear and develop holes, while properly fulled woolens can last a lifetime."

"And what exactly do these fullers do?" Eliezer asked.

"After the cloth comes off the loom, the fullers lower it into a large trough filled with a wash of hot water, fuller's earth, and urine."

"What?" Rachel and Eliezer exclaimed almost simultaneously.

"Fuller's earth is a kind of clay that some call kaolin." Nissim chuckled. "I have no idea why urine is necessary, but once the cloth is covered by the liquid, the fullers climb in and trample the cloth."

Eliezer grimaced. "It sounds like how we make wine from grapes, only worse smelling."

"The stomping part is similar, but luckily a fuller's trough is only filled ankle deep," Nissim said.

"I understand that fulling cleans the cloth, but how can it make it last longer?" Rachel asked.

"Cleaning the cloth is the least of what fulling does. All this stomping in the hot wash forces the fibers to interlock and mat, forming felt. Depending on how warm the weather is, the process can take three to five days, and by that time the cloth has shrunk to half its original size. Then the fulled cloth is attached by tenterhooks to a large frame to dry."

Eliezer scratched his head. "So the fullers spend days shrinking the cloth only to stretch it out again?"

Nissim shrugged. "The cloth needs to be hung up and stretched anyway for the next step."

"There's more?" Rachel's face fell. She'd thought she was close to success with Alette and Albert working for her, but there were still so many other people she would need to hire.

"At this point, any wrinkles that developed in the tank are gone, and the fullers use a teasel to raise the nap so it can be shorn." Nissim didn't wait for their questions, but immediately explained the procedure. "A teasel is a very prickly plant, and pushing it repeatedly over the stretched cloth raises the nap. That is, it lifts up all the straggly loose ends of the wool fibers, which the fuller cuts off with razor-sharp shears."

Eliezer put his arm around Rachel, who was blinking back tears. "It sounds difficult."

"*Oui*. It takes a great deal of skill to nap and shear the cloth repeatedly without damaging it, but when an expert is finished you cannot see the original weave at all." Nissim held up the scarlet woolen. "And the texture is as smooth as silk."

"Does it go to the dyer now?" Rachel asked hopefully. It was no wonder luxury woolens were so expensive—look at all the labor that went into making them.

Nissim nodded and turned to Eliezer. "Here the clothier must make a vital decision—what kind of dye the woolen's quality merits. As a dye merchant, you know that even the finest cloth is worth less than the kermes scarlet required to dye it."

"How did you come to learn all this?" Eliezer asked.

"One of my brothers is a dyer and the other a fuller." Nissim smiled. "I have spent a good deal of time in their vats." Then his expression sobered. "You two are considering an ambitious undertaking, controlling every aspect from raw wool to finished cloth."

"Can it be done?" Rachel made no effort to mask her anxiety. Her future with Eliezer depended on it.

"Possibly." Nissim scratched his head. "While you have an advantage with Joheved supplying the wool and Eliezer the dyestuffs, I'm afraid that the best fullers will prefer to sell to the highest bidder rather than work for you."

"You've given excellent advice, Nissim. Aren't you worried about us putting you out of business?" Eliezer was smiling, but his question was serious.

"Not at all. The supply of luxury woolens doesn't come close to meeting demand. The more high-quality fabric that comes to Troyes, the more people flock here to buy it." Nissim rubbed his hands in anticipation.

Before Rachel could question Nissim further, a customer came up to the stall, forcing her and Eliezer to leave the two men to their private negotiations. Now she would have to endure her husband's justified complaints that she'd acted too quickly.

"I'm sorry I wasted your time this afternoon," she offered, thinking it best to apologize right away and diffuse his anger.

"You didn't. I found Nissim's lecture very interesting." He smiled and took her hand. Now that he knew the extent of what Rachel's plan entailed, Eliezer realized that it would be years before she got the enterprise going, if ever. So he would have years in Córdoba to learn everything there was to know about philosophy and mathematics.

"I shouldn't have asked you to get involved until I knew more about the cloth business." She hadn't planned on crying to get Eliezer's sympathy (although it usually worked), but the tears began to roll down her cheeks.

Eliezer put his arm around her shoulders. "It's all right. I know you would have been more diligent if you weren't distracted by your other worries."

"My other worries?" Rachel fought her rising panic. *Heaven help me if he's learned about Eudes.*

"Your mother's illness." He hugged her closer, wishing there was a way to tell her not to worry about the count. "Naturally it's difficult to think about other things when someone in your family is sick."

"Of course I'm concerned about her, and supervising two households is taxing." She was crying with relief now. *He doesn't know.*

"Especially when one household is the rosh yeshiva's during the fair season," he agreed. "If your mother isn't better by the summer, your father must hire more servants. He can't expect you to keep running everything when you have a new baby." Eliezer gently patted the small bulge in her belly.

"Eliezer, I wish you didn't have to leave next week."

"I promise I'll be back for Passover." He leaned over and kissed her brow. "I intend to be here when this child is born." *And I intend to be as far away from Troyes as possible on New Year's Day.*

Early on Thursday, Tevet 21, known to the Edomites as December 29, Eliezer left Troyes with nearly every other merchant who had come for the Cold Fair. To avoid traveling on the Sabbath or starting a new enterprise on the unlucky days of Monday, Tuesday, and Wednesday, Jews tried to begin their journeys on Thursday or Sunday. But even those who preferred not to leave on Thursday left that day with Eliezer. For the following Sunday was January 1, an inauspicious Egyptian day.

Some said these evil days received their name because the biblical plagues and other ancient calamities occurred in Egypt on those days. Others said that Egyptian astrologers, authorities in this field, identified them as such. Whatever the reason, both Jews and Edomites alike viewed those particular days of the year with dread.

And nobody in Troyes was dreading New Year's Day more than Rachel.

On the final day of the Cold Fair, she veiled herself and, while most men were still in synagogue, paid a visit to an herb dealer whose stall stood at the far end of the fairgrounds. There she purchased a small amount of henbane and black hellebore. To avoid suspicion, she also bought some artemisia, mugwort, and ginger, which Miriam could use in her midwife practice. And when he offered her a good deal on comfrey, she took that as well. Between her children and Miriam's, one of them always seemed to need a healing poultice.

Yet she couldn't keep her hand from shaking as she unlocked the pantry cabinet that held her family's valuable herbs and spices. *Am I actually going to go through with this? Do I have the nerve to poison him?* It was one thing to knife a man who threatened her with his, but to premeditatedly poison his cup?

On the last Friday of the year, Raoul visited Salomon's cellar to requisition additional wine for Countess Adelaide's New Year's feast. Keeping his tone professional, he took Rachel aside and gave her the location where Eudes would meet her on Sunday night—a fashionable address near the St.-Rémy Church, on the far side of the Cordé Canal.

Only two days left. Rachel's stomach churned. Eudes must keep this apartment for assignations with his paramours, away from his mother's and the court's prying eyes. At least she wouldn't be going to the palace or anyplace in the Jewish Quarter.

Maybe I won't have to kill him if we can keep the affair secret.

She could not go on with these feelings gnawing at her. After Raoul concluded his business, Rachel realized that only one thing might calm her nerves. She needed to pray. Leaving the Shabbat *souper* preparations to her mother and Anna, as the sun began to set she accompanied her father to synagogue. Hearing the men chant the special psalms for welcoming the Sabbath (Friday evening being a service that few women attended), she suddenly remembered that Psalm 39 should be recited to thwart an evil design on the part of a king.

Furious for forgetting something so important, she excused herself early from *souper* and sought seclusion in her bedroom, where she recited:

> "I will watch my behavior, that I not sin with my tongue.
> "I will keep my mouth muzzled while the wicked man is near.
> "I was dumb, silent, speechless; and my torment increased.
> "My heart was smoldering inside me, my thoughts burned until I spoke out; Adonai . . .
> "Remove Your scourge from me . . . Adonai, give ear to my cry; do not ignore my tears . . ."

No matter how much trouble the evil this man was causing her, she must neither question nor complain about the Holy One's justice, only pray that He would bring punishment upon the Edomite greater than the affliction the wicked man would inflict on her.

Somehow Rachel expected the room to be more opulent, but there was only a bed, a chest, and a table with two chairs—furnishings similar to those in her parents' house. To her dismay, every dish on the table appeared to contain forbidden food. She recognized bacon immediately, and there were several other meats, all undoubtedly not slaughtered in a kosher manner. The only fish she saw was eel, which Papa said was not a proper fish at all, lacking fins and scales, and therefore was prohibited for Jews to eat.

"Your Grace, I've brought some special wine for you." She tried to smile seductively. "Flavored with henbane."

But instead of returning her smile, Eudes scowled. "You drink some first."

"I can't have very much. Remember I'm enceinte."

He jumped up and seized her around the waist. "I said drink it." He grabbed the flask and held it to her lips.

When she began to struggle he pushed her back against the wall. "You Jewish bitch! You think that I wasn't expecting some treachery, that I didn't know Jews prefer poison over an honest clash of swords."

When she tried to scream, he forced her mouth open and poured the wine down her throat. "If this really does contain henbane, then you and I are in for an exciting night." He began to laugh.

Rachel's eyes flew open, Eudes' cruel laughter still echoing in her head, but the room was silent and completely dark. Drenched in sweat, she groped for the bed curtains and pulled them back. A sliver of light from the waning moon was enough to illuminate her own bedchamber, and she heaved a sigh of relief.

What a horrible dream. She got out of bed, checked that her children were sleeping peacefully, and quickly recited the words recommended in Tractate Berachot:

> "Master of the World, I am Yours and my dreams are Yours . . . Just as You changed wicked Balaam's curse into a blessing, so may You change all my dreams into good."

Shivering with more than the cold, Rachel decided that first thing in the morning she'd have Papa, Miriam, and Judah—surely three of the most pious people in Troyes—annul the dream for her. As Rav Huna said:

> Have him get three people and say to them: "I have seen a good dream." Then they say to him: "It is good and let it be good. May the Merciful One change it for better."

When she told her family that she'd seen a "good dream"—the Talmudic euphemism for a nightmare—Papa, Judah, and Miriam immediately recited the nullifying incantation.

"Just as not all thoughts are true, also not all dreams are true," Papa added, resting his hand on her head.

Hoping her dream wasn't a message from Heaven, Rachel was too upset to eat much for the rest of the day. It was Sunday, New Year's Day, and one thought consumed her. Would this Egyptian day bring calamity to her or to Eudes?

eleven

hen the church bells began tolling, Rachel was in the vineyard with Salomon and Baruch, marking vines that were no longer productive and would need to be replaced.

Baruch shook his head in dismay. "Look how quickly the hours pass on these short winter days. It seems like it was just midday, and now they're chiming None."

"I don't think it's the ninth hour yet." Salomon frowned slightly in concentration. "The bells don't sound like they're chiming the hours either."

Baruch paused to listen. "You're right, they're different."

"They remind me of when Count Thibault died," Salomon said.

Rachel, who hadn't noticed the bells at all, turned her attention to the somber pealing coming from Troyes. "But the countess hasn't been ill."

"I'm sure we'll find out at afternoon services." Baruch returned to the vine he'd been inspecting.

Rachel and Salomon exchanged meaningful glances and her heart began to swell with hope. If Countess Adelaide were dead, surely her son wouldn't be sneaking around the streets of Troyes tonight. And if Eudes were dead . . .

Salomon could see the eager anticipation on his daughter's face. "Rachel, would you mind bringing me another pair of hose from home? One of these has a hole that's irritating my foot."

"Of course, Papa." The look she flashed him was pure adoration. *I'll find out who died, too.*

Thankfully she was in the middle trimester, when a pregnant woman usually feels her best, and her feet flew as she raced back to town. The guards at the Près Gate would have heard what had happened: it was the nearest gate to the castle.

Desperate yet terrified to hear the news, Rachel slowed when she saw the crowd of people clustered there. What if it weren't anyone in Champagne's ruling family? Maybe the bishop had died or King Philip? She cautiously approached the gate, her heart pounding so loudly the others must surely hear it.

"He should have known better than to go hunting on an Egyptian day," a self-righteous voice called out.

"If he'd been a pious man like his brother," another man complained, "he wouldn't have been out hunting on our Lord's Day. Then he'd still be alive."

It has to be Eudes. It has to be.

The next voice confirmed it. "So now we have a seventeen-year-old boy ruling Champagne." He spat in disgust.

"Don't worry. The countess will rule for Hugues just as she did for Eudes."

Rachel, staggered at the unexpected fulfillment of her fervent hopes, broke into sobs of relief, causing a woman nearby to put her arm around Rachel's shoulder and chastise the men. "Shame on you all, standing here complaining about Eudes when you ought to be mourning him."

The crowd soon dispersed, and Rachel hurried back toward the vineyard, only to turn around and head for home when she realized that she had forgotten her father's hose.

She learned more the next day when Guy de Dampierre came for *disner*. The canon, head of Troyes' cathedral school, was a regular guest, timing his visits for Monday or Thursday when the Torah portion was read in synagogue and expounded at Salomon's table. These were also days when clerics were permitted to eat meat.

"Here we are again at the plagues in Egypt." Guy rubbed his hands in anticipation of discussing that week's scriptural passage. "I've been thinking about the problem of God hardening Pharaoh's heart."

"Which problem is that?" Judah poured the cleric some wine. "Our Sages have several difficulties with this text."

"Since it was God who hardened Pharaoh's heart, then what is Pharaoh's sin and why does he deserve to be punished?"

Salomon wagged his finger at Guy. "It does not say 'God hardened his heart' in the first five plagues, only that 'Pharaoh's heart was hardened.' Our sage, Reish Lakish, taught:

> When the Holy One warns a man once, twice, and even a third time, and he still does not repent, only then does the Holy One close his heart against repentance so that He can extract punishment. So it was with wicked Pharaoh. The Holy One sent five plagues to him and he took no notice, so He then said: You have stiffened your neck and hardened your heart, so I will add to your stubbornness."

Judah and Miriam, recognizing the text from Midrash Rabbah, nodded at each other. "Pharaoh ignored five opportunities to repent and free the Israelites," Judah said. "Only then, after Pharaoh proved himself unworthy, did the Holy One intervene."

"That would be an excellent explanation if not for the fact that God tells Moses earlier, 'I will harden Pharaoh's heart, that I may multiply My signs and marvels in the land of Egypt,'" Guy said. "How do your Jewish Sages explain this?"

Miriam's forehead wrinkled. "So the Holy One knew in advance what Pharaoh would do, even hardened his heart to make him do it, and then punished him anyway? It doesn't seem just."

Salomon sighed. "After Pharaoh acted so wickedly it became clear to the Holy One that Pharaoh did not have the spirit to repent with a whole heart," he explained. "It was therefore right that the Holy One hardened Pharaoh's heart in order to multiply His signs so that all would recognize His power."

"Very good, Papa," Judah said. "You should be sure to write that in your Torah commentary."

Thus far Rachel had only partly followed the conversation; her mind was too preoccupied with Eudes' untimely death and her near-miraculous escape from his clutches. Still, she wanted to be sure she understood Papa properly. "So if repentance is not possible, the Holy One is justified to use this person as a tool to benefit those who can repent, such as Israel."

Salomon nodded and turned to Guy. "What do you think?"

The canon smiled. "On this matter, we agree. In our scriptures, it is written:

> Shall we say is God unjust? Heaven forbid. For scripture says to Pharaoh: 'I enthroned you for this purpose, that I might display My power in you and that My name might be proclaimed in all the earth.' Thus God has mercy on whom He wants to have mercy, and He hardens whom He wants to harden. You may say to Me: 'Then why does God still blame us? For who can resist His will?' But who are you, O man, to question God? Shall what is formed ask Him who formed it, 'Why did you make me like this?' Does not the potter have the right to make out of the same lump of clay some pottery for noble purposes and some for common use?"

Papa looked so pleased that Rachel hesitated asking what happens with ordinary people. Since God knows before a man is born how he will behave during his life, how can a man like Eudes be blamed and punished for his sinful acts or one like Papa praised and rewarded for his virtue?

She was about to ask when Miriam turned to Guy and changed the subject. "Could you please express our community's deepest condolences to the Countess Adelaide?"

Guy sobered. "Of course." Then his eyes began to twinkle. "There seems to be some question about how Count Eudes died."

Rachel gulped. "We heard it was a hunting accident."

"When his body was found on the ground with a fatal head wound, it was *assumed* that he'd been thrown from his horse and hit his head." Guy raised his eyebrows and everyone at the table leaned in closer.

"And you think this assumption may be wrong?" Salomon asked.

"I don't know." Guy said, helping himself to more cake. "But I heard that the wound looked more like one from an attack than one received in an accident. If he was dazed by his fall, it would be easy to take a branch or rock and finish the job."

"But who would want him dead?" Rachel asked. *Besides me.*

Guy shrugged. "The number is too great to count: the father or brothers of his previous mistress who died in childbirth, other nobility who covet his land, members of his court who prefer his brother Hugues, or Heaven knows how many who seek revenge for some perceived injury or insult."

"Or perhaps it wasn't murder at all," Miriam said. "If his horse was so spooked as to throw him, perhaps the animal kicked him as well."

"In all probability you are correct." Guy sighed. "However, people much prefer to discuss the possibility of foul deeds."

Guy returned to Salomon's a week later. "It is audacious of me to ask you for a favor that will only waste your time, but I have come to think that to truly understand scripture, I must ascertain the *Hebraica veritas* from the original Hebrew."

Cheered by Eudes' death, Rachel couldn't resist teasing him. "You just realized that the Bible wasn't given in Latin?"

He smiled and took his customary seat at the table. "I grant that many of my colleagues seem unaware of that fact."

"If you wish to read Hebrew, someone will need to teach you." Salomon stroked his beard in thought. "And that someone should be a Jew, although I cannot in good conscience ask any of my students to take time away from their studies."

To everyone's surprise, Joheved's son Shmuel spoke up. "I'll tutor him, Grandpapa . . . if he teaches me Latin in return."

Before Salomon could protest, Miriam also volunteered. "I'd be happy to teach him." She looked at Guy questioningly. "If he doesn't mind learning along with my children."

"I'm sure both of you would be excellent instructors," Guy said. "And I'd consider it an honor to teach Shmuel Latin. I've heard excellent reports of his scholarship."

When Salomon consented, Guy arranged a study schedule with his new teachers and bid them adieu.

When the canon was out of hearing, Judah turned to his nephew in astonishment. "What possessed you to agree to teach Hebrew to the Notzrim?"

"So I can learn Latin." Shmuel glared at Guy closing the courtyard gate behind him. "The *minim* misuse our Torah to prove their heresies, and I want to know what their scripture says so I can refute them."

"Amen," Salomon said.

* * *

On an unseasonably warm day in early March, Shmuel and Guy were sitting in Salomon's courtyard as the cleric tried to explain a rule of Latin grammar by comparing it to French. They were too engrossed in their discussion to hear the gate open and close, until an elderly, yet commanding, voice interrupted them.

"If you want your student to truly understand grammar, Guy de Dampierre, you should have him study Priscian's *Institutiones grammaticae*."

Shmuel spun around to take in the two black-robed monks standing before them. The elder, grey-haired and gaunt, whose arm was supported by his companion, looked to be the oldest man Shmuel had ever seen. The younger monk's tonsure was completely brown, and Shmuel judged him to be around forty.

Guy looked at the two in astonishment before jumping up to embrace the old monk, the man who had admonished him. But before he could say anything, Salomon burst out of the kitchen door.

"Robert, what brings you here?" Salomon must have realized how rude he sounded because he quickly said, "I'm delighted to see you, of course, but why aren't you in Molesme?"

The monk sighed. "It's a long story."

Now Rivka, Judah, Miriam, and Rachel were outside, eyeing the new arrivals with apprehension.

"Please, come in and tell it."

Salomon waved everyone toward the house, while Rivka called to her daughters, "Rachel and Miriam, bring some free-press wine from Montier-la-Celle for your father's guests."

Salomon chuckled and turned to the elderly monk, "You picked a good time to visit, Robert. The vintage from your old abbey is one of the finest in years."

"Robert was prior of Montier-la-Celle in the days when we first began using its grapes for our wine," Miriam explained to Rachel as they filled jugs in the cellar. "Then, when you were still little, he founded his own monastery at Molesme."

"I remember how upset Papa was when he left. They used to study together." Maybe that was why Papa liked Guy's visits.

"I've never seen the other monk before," Miriam said.

The younger cleric was Étienne, a fellow member of Robert's abbey. Over bread, wine, and cheese, they learned that he was born in Angleterre, studied in Paris and Rome, and was returning from the latter city when he stopped in at Molesme.

"I was so impressed with Robert's piety that I joined his community," Étienne explained in heavily accented French. "So when he decided to leave Molesme on account of its laxity, I came with him."

The salon was filled with questions directed at Robert.

"Molesme lax?" Salomon shook his head. "Surely strict discipline was one of your hallmarks."

Judah couldn't understand how a monastery could become lax, since men entered it to devote themselves to the Almighty. Guy didn't see how Robert could just leave Molesme when he was the abbot. Wouldn't the pope make him return?

Over bread and cheese, which Rivka pushed on the slender monks, Robert explained that the trouble started ten years ago, when the canon Bruno of Reims became a monk and Molesme began to attract rich benefactors. Ultimately their reputation not only brought unwanted wealth but also unsuitable new members: younger sons forced on them by their noble patrons.

Robert blamed himself. "If I'd been a better abbot, a firm disciplinarian, and if I'd had strength to reject unfit candidates the nobility foisted on us and rally my monks to strict dedication to Benedict's rule—then I would be worthy to lead Molesme. But I can neither bear the slackers nor reform them."

"Then what do you intend to do?" Salomon asked.

"I plan to found a new house," the abbot replied. "But first I must get Étienne settled in Troyes. Here, I am confident, he can continue his excellent education."

Étienne blushed at the compliment. "Guy wrote to Abbot Robert about the importance of learning Hebrew, and he thought it was a shame that, despite my years of study, there remains a subject of which I am ignorant. We agreed that I should not leave the scholar's world for the monastic one until I have mastered *Hebraica veritas*."

Robert gazed hopefully at Salomon, "I want Étienne to learn Hebrew from true scholars, so I must again ask for your help. Will you teach him?"

Salomon paused to stroke his beard, and Rivka whispered to him, "We'd finally have a chance to repay our debt to him for sharing Montier-la-Celle's grapes with us."

Salomon turned to Robert and nodded.

Guy broke into a grin. "So, Shmuel, are you ready for another student? And you, Miriam?"

Shmuel shrugged. "It should be no more difficult to teach two than one. And with another teacher, I can learn Latin faster."

"I will gladly add Étienne to our little class," Miriam said to Guy with a smile. "It will be good for you to have a study partner more at your level."

Rachel didn't think Guy or Étienne took their vows of chastity lightly; nevertheless she preferred to avoid the men. But as the final months of Joheved's pregnancy arrived, Miriam announced her intention of helping with the lambing in Ramerupt until the baby came, leaving Rachel to reluctantly assume her sister's teaching responsibilities.

But Guy's usual levity was dampened by Étienne's severity, and Étienne was so devoted to his studies, ignoring her gender, that at first Rachel thought he was a Ganymede. But she soon saw that his passion for learning had replaced carnal desire and, with a sudden insight, realized that the same thing had probably happened to Papa. *No wonder Mama hasn't been happy with him.*

Rachel was starting to enjoy their studies when Lent intervened, forcing Guy and Étienne to suspend their lessons. Then no sooner was Easter past than Joheved gave birth to another boy, sending Salomon's entire household to Ramerupt to await the brit milah. Now for the third time, Joheved and Meir named a newborn son Salomon, again depriving Rachel of the opportunity to honor their father that way.

Rachel and Miriam were riding at the rear as their families returned to Troyes after the brit milah, when Miriam motioned Rachel to come along side her. "I'm worried about Joheved: she shouldn't be bleeding this much after eight days."

"Surely you can do something to help her," Rachel said.

"I'm giving her mugwort juice mixed with sage, pennyroyal, and willow seed plus mallow and beet soups," Miriam replied. "But they cannot be effective unless she is well rested."

"She'll be getting plenty of rest now that everyone's gone home." Rachel couldn't see why Miriam was telling her this.

"Joheved will not rest if we celebrate Passover at Ramerupt. No matter how much I caution her, she will insist on supervising the preparations."

"So one of us will do it instead."

Miriam shook her head and, using her midwife's voice of authority, declared, "The only way to prevent Joheved from rising from her bed is to celebrate Passover at Troyes, not Ramerupt, with Joheved a guest rather than the hostess."

Rachel, who'd been anticipating a pleasant holiday week in Ramerupt with Eliezer, burned with resentment. "So even though I'm pregnant, I have no choice but to ready my house for the festival too?"

"Joheved's life depends on it," Miriam said sternly. "And don't expect much help from me or Mama. We'll be busy doing the same thing at our homes."

"But you've done this before, while I've gone to Ramerupt every Passover since I've been married." Rachel grimaced at the enormous amount of work necessary to remove every trace of leaven that had accumulated in her home during those nine years.

Every dish had to be washed with soap, rinsed in boiling water then cold water, and finally dipped in hot water again. Every pot needed to be scrubbed with salt stone then rinsed in boiling water, all metal items (like spits and tripods) passed through fire in the hearth, and wooden boards for cutting and kneading cleaned until not a speck of *hametz* could be seen.

Rushes would have to be taken up and discarded—no easy task—then the floors carefully swept and freshly cut rushes put down. Papa's students slept in the attic, and undoubtedly took bread or pastries up there on occasion, so all the old straw had to be removed and the floor cleaned before new straw was brought up.

"Stop acting like a spoiled child, Rachel," Miriam hissed. "Passover will be here in a few weeks whether you like it or not, and our homes must be ready. Be thankful for all those years when Joheved did the work for you!"

Rachel had never seen Miriam so angry, and she blushed with shame. *Am I really such a spoiled child? I suppose I must be, to whine about doing the same work that every other Jewish woman in Troyes has to do, when the important thing is my sister's health.* She looked over at Miriam, whose mask of fury had been replaced with one of sorrow.

"Miriam, do you really think Joheved is in danger?"

"I'm afraid so, although I pray that she is not."

When they arrived home, Rachel joined her servants in thoroughly cleaning her house in preparation for Passover. The dung collector's cart acquired a new purpose as he hauled the dirty straw and rushes to Papa's vineyard for mulch. Along with other Jewish housewives in Troyes, Rachel anxiously awaited a rainy day when she could empty the waste pits in her kitchen. As soon as sufficient rain turned the Jewish Quarter's streets into fast-flowing rivulets, every bit of garbage amassed in those pits would be dumped into the roads.

But before this happened, Mama suffered a relapse of dizziness and took to her bed, leaving her younger daughters responsible for cleaning her house as well as their own. With Miriam riding back and forth to Ramerupt several times a week to check on Joheved—who, may the Holy One protect her, was regaining her strength and would probably be well enough to attend Papa's seder—this labor fell on Rachel's shoulders, who seethed with resentment at the vagaries of life.

To make matters worse, they discovered that the privy's cesspit was nearing its capacity. Lined with stones to let the liquid escape and so deep that a man who fell in would drown, a cesspit took years to fill—so many years that Rachel couldn't remember when theirs had been emptied. Though the nausea of pregnancy was behind her, as the dung collector and his sons lowered buckets into the privy's vile contents and dumped them into his cart, the stench that permeated the courtyard—nay, the entire block—was overpowering.

Her relief came only when the men carted the disgusting muck off to fertilize the vineyard. It took several days of effort before the cesspit was finally clean, during which Rachel swallowed her envy whenever Miriam rode off to Ramerupt. She wavered between sympathy and guilty satisfaction at the thought of Mama, who had bequeathed her all this extra work, confined to bed and thus suffering the evil smell even more than Rachel, who at least left home to attend synagogue. But mostly she was too busy and too tired to feel much of anything.

When Eliezer arrived in Troyes three days before the start of Passover, he entered through the rarely used Chapes Gate and made for a nearby tavern on the outskirts of town. The place was as disreputable as its clientele, and he waved off a couple of whores heading in his direction. As eager as Eliezer was to see his family again, he walked past the dice players to a table in the back, where he sat down and opened his accounts ledger.

He moved numbers from one column to another, added a little here and subtracted a little there. Finally, when the church bells chimed None, he was satisfied. True, if Rachel looked carefully she might notice some merchandise he'd sold for less than usual or bought for more, but he was confident that he had hidden the discrepancy of forty dinars. Twenty dinars to repay what he'd borrowed at the Cold Fair and twenty more now to complete payment to the man he was waiting for.

The short man entered as the echo of bells disappeared, his hat pulled low over his face, a cloak wrapped around his body. After a furtive glance around the room, he made a beeline toward Eliezer. When he sat down, Eliezer silently passed him a heavy purse under the table and then rose to leave.

But the man motioned Eliezer to sit down again. He seemed to struggle inwardly before finally speaking. "I don't deserve this." He slipped the purse back into Eliezer's hand.

"Why not?" Eliezer whispered. "He's dead, exactly as we planned."

twelve

he man pulled out some cards and dealt a few to Eliezer. "I took the monkshood to the stables, but as I hid in the shadows to be sure no one was around, another man came in." He paused and laid down a card. "I could tell immediately that he was up to no good, and sure enough, he snuck over to the horse's feed trough and mixed something into the grain."

Eliezer picked up the man's card and randomly put one down from his hand. "Who was he? Did he see you?"

"He was another stable hand. I waited until he'd gone, and a little more time after that to be sure, and then left another way. I was careful that nobody saw me."

"So you didn't tamper with the horse's fodder at all?"

The man shook his head. "I didn't dare add your poison to what he'd put there; if the horse was obviously ill in the morning, Eudes would ride another."

"You deserve to be paid. You took the same risk, did the same work."

"I did nothing except watch another do the job instead of me, so what you paid me in December is more than enough."

Eliezer's mouth dropped in astonishment. *An honest criminal?* "So we each have an extra twenty dinars and a clear conscience."

Their business concluded, the man collected his cards. "With any luck, we won't meet again."

By the time Eliezer stepped into the street, the stable hand had disappeared into one of the many alleys off rue du Cloître St.-Estienne. Whistling a merry tune, Eliezer headed toward the Jewish Quarter.

His pace quickened as he approached Salomon's courtyard gate. *Don't expect her to be there; she's probably still in the vineyard.* But there she was, sitting under the apple tree with their son, Miriam's two younger boys, Guy de Dampierre, and some strange monk. His heart swelled with pride to see Shemiah reading from a manuscript while the others listened intently.

He let the gate slam behind him, and as Rachel struggled to stand up, Shemiah thrust the book at his cousin and raced into Eliezer's open arms. Rachel took longer to reach him, and clung to him fiercely as he embraced her.

Guy and the black-robed monk paused as they walked past. "I see our lesson for today is finished," Guy said with a smile. "Shall we return when your festival is over?"

Rachel nodded. "*Oui*, after Passover would be best."

The unknown monk looked disappointed, but he didn't challenge this and the two men left together.

"Oh, Eliezer," Rachel said breathlessly once they were inside. "I'm so glad you're home. It's been a nightmare since you left. Mama is sick again, Joheved is too ill to have Passover in Ramerupt, and I've had to do everything all by myself." *Thank Heaven my worst nightmare died in January.*

"But the children are well?"

"You can see for yourself how Shemiah is." She didn't dare tempt the Evil Eye again by praising the children. "When little Rivka wakes from her nap, you'll see how she's doing."

"How's the cloth business coming?" Eliezer asked, surprised that she hadn't told him about it immediately.

"I've had no time to look for fullers."

Rachel's angry voice made him change the subject. "Where's Judah? I have some information for him."

"You found Aaron's family?"

"*Oui*, but he won't like what I learned."

"Tell me," she whispered.

Just before Eliezer left for Córdoba, Judah asked for help in locating his deceased study partner's family there. Judah was particularly concerned that Aaron's widow, without proof of her husband's death, would become an *agunah*, chained to him and unable to remarry. That was why Rachel, like other Jewish women in Ashkenaz, received a conditional *get* when her husband began to travel. But Judah wasn't sure that women in Córdoba had the same protection.

He took her arm and guided her to the nearest bench. "Judah was right to have me search them out. Aaron's family had no idea he was dead. They thought he'd remained in Ashkenaz to study Talmud." He hesitated a moment. "Apparently there were rumors about him and other men, so they weren't surprised that he'd decided against returning home, especially with travel around Córdoba becoming so dangerous."

Rachel's throat tightened. "You've been going there for two years and never mentioned any danger."

"Until this year I thought merchants were safe, but then the Berbers returned, captured Seville, and threatened Córdoba. Many Jews are heading north for Toledo, where King Alfonso has promised that all Jewish persons and property will be secure."

"It doesn't make sense. Why would the Berbers attack their fellow Saracens instead of the Spaniards?" And after years of the opposite situation, Rachel wondered, how could Jews in Sepharad be persecuted by the Moors and find refuge with the Notzrim?

"The Berbers are fanatics." Eliezer frowned in disapproval. "Who oppose the Moors' lack of religious fervor, which they say causes the Moors to tolerate synagogues and churches in their cities, share bathhouses with infidels, and marry Jewish and Edomite women—along with other objectionable behavior. They razed Granada's entire Jewish Quarter."

"What are you going to do?" Rachel asked anxiously. Until they became clothiers, Eliezer would have to keep traveling.

"I've had enough of southern Sepharad. I'm moving my operations to Toledo."

"Will you be safe there?"

"Alfonso has promised to respect Toledo's diverse communities, and other than his new bishop transforming the main mosque into a cathedral, things remain as they were under the Moors." He smiled. "Toledo is a city with very cold winters. Now that it houses the court of the wealthiest king in Sepharad, its inhabitants will be in need of fine furs and luxury woolens."

"Despite the danger, I'm glad you went to Córdoba and gave Aaron's family the news. Now his wife can remarry."

"She already has." Eliezer's tone was heavy with disgust.

"But Judah was so sure that Aaron hadn't given her a conditional *get*."

"He hadn't." He held up his hand to stop Rachel's question. "Aaron's wife converted to Islam and obtained a divorce from their court."

Rachel stared in shocked silence as his words sunk in. "In order to marry a Moor, of course." She shivered.

"You're ill." He put his arm around her.

"I'm fine." She squeezed his arm in return. "And definitely better for seeing you again." She had been feeling unwell but put it down to all the work and worry she'd suffered. Now that Eliezer was home, she'd be back to normal in no time—undoubtedly that very night.

But Rachel felt worse as the days passed, with a chill in her bones that never dissipated and a growing discomfort beneath her navel. After the second seder, when she realized that she had not felt her child move recently, she consulted Miriam.

"Think carefully," her sister asked. "When was the last time you felt life?"

The fear welled up and threatened to choke her. "I don't remember exactly . . . I was so busy getting ready for Passover that I didn't notice."

"A few days?" Miriam asked. "A week? A month?"

"Possibly one week." *Surely not a whole month.*

"Have you had any evil dreams, especially of dead people?"

Rachel shuddered. "*Oui*." She had dreamt of Eudes the night before Eliezer came home.

"Lie on your back and let me examine you." Miriam knew it was useless to pray that the child be alive; if it were dead she couldn't bring it back to life, and if it were alive her prayers were unnecessary. Yet she prayed anyway.

But Rachel's breasts were slack rather than swollen, and the putrid smell that emanated from between her legs served only to confirm the dread diagnosis. Even so, Miriam wet her hand in warm water and rubbed it over her sister's belly, feeling in vain for the slightest stirring within. As she did, she could smell in Rachel's breath the same foul odor as below.

There could be no doubt—the baby was dead. Now she needed to learn how long ago it had succumbed, for a woman carrying a dead child in her womb was in grave danger herself. And the longer the corpse remained there, the greater that danger.

"Eliezer," she asked him in private after giving them the sad news. "When you first . . . uh, returned, did Rachel smell different than usual?" Surely they couldn't have had relations without him noticing the stink.

He nodded. "I thought she'd been too busy to bathe." And he'd been too eager to use the bed to care.

Miriam had no choice but to confirm her sister's fears. The baby had been dead at least a week, probably longer if the smell was there when Eliezer got home. Now its body must be removed as soon as possible.

"I want you to fast today," Miriam told Rachel, who was still in shock. "Then tonight and tomorrow morning, I'll give you a nasty-tasting drink to make your womb expel its contents."

"Will it hurt?" Rachel's eyes were wide with fright.

"Probably not as much as real labor." Miriam wasn't sure about someone as sensitive to pain as her little sister.

She had considered several potions that midwives used in these cases and decided that a mixture of rue, mugwort, wormwood, and iris, ground up and boiled in wine, might be the easiest to try first. There was another, one that the Edomite midwife Elizabeth recommended, which involved boiling a blind young puppy in vervain juice with mint and lady's mantle, but it would take too long to prepare. And Miriam didn't want to go searching for a newborn puppy when she already had the ingredients for the first potion, never mind that she found the procedure revolting.

But two days later, though Rachel complained of cramps and blood was draining from her womb, its contents remained inside. So Miriam consulted Elizabeth about using a pessary smeared with pennyroyal, hyssop, and dittany.

"These, and your previous potion, work well when there is a live child within," the more experienced midwife said. "However, a dead one requires stronger medicine, since he lacks any motion to strengthen his mother's labor."

"A stronger potion could kill my sister. She's already ill."

Elizabeth shook her head sadly. "Then you must draw forth the child yourself, either with your hand or with hooks."

Miriam gasped. "Aunt Sarah left me hooks in her midwife kit, but I've never used them."

"Then I'll come and explain what to do." She looked down and added, "It's a good thing you have small hands."

Miriam didn't mention the hooks, only telling Rachel that she would prefer to extract the child manually rather than use stronger medicine. She took advantage of her mother and Joheved's illnesses to exclude them from the lying-in room, leaving her and Elizabeth alone with Rachel. Sure that the pain would be too much for her sensitive sister, Miriam took the precaution of dosing her with opium. The procedure would be difficult enough without Rachel screaming and thrashing about.

Recalling how she helped deliver many babies, including the current count of Champagne, Miriam dipped her hand in olive oil and then reached up into her sister's womb. Her heart sank when she felt the opening blocked by the baby's arm. Rachel, barely conscious, groaned softly but remained still as Miriam ascertained the child's position.

"One arm and shoulder are in the birth canal, but the head is stuck inside." There was silence while she tried some maneuvering and then, "I can't push the arm back in to bring the baby into a better position."

"Tie this ribbon around the hand and give the end to me," Elizabeth said. "Then you know what to do."

Miriam nodded. With Elizabeth grasping the ribbon in one hand and holding Rachel's torso immobile with the other, Miriam grasped the knife she used for cutting a newborn's chord. The blade was razor sharp; yet somehow Miriam had to insert it into Rachel's womb and cut off the child's arm without injuring her sister or herself. Seeing no other way, she shielded the blade with her palm as she pushed her hand back up the canal, trying not to flinch as it cut into her. Thank Heaven Rachel was too sedated to move.

She took a deep breath, reached up as far as she could, and with her *mohelet*'s speed and precision, sliced the arm from its shoulder. "You can pull now," she told Elizabeth as she carefully slipped the knife back out.

Miriam examined her own minor wounds as she washed her hands, averting her eyes from the tiny decomposing arm that Elizabeth wrapped in linen cloth. Then she bathed Rachel's birth canal with clean oil. "I don't think I cut my sister much. I don't see any fresh blood." The child had been dead so long that severing its arm didn't cause it to bleed.

"Good," Elizabeth said. "Now let's hope you can push the shoulder up so the head will come into position."

Miriam was able to do this without difficulty and, repulsed by the feel of what she knew was the child's rotting flesh, hurriedly pulled out her hand.

Elizabeth took in Miriam's distressed visage. "Only a little longer and it will be over. I would do this next part myself if my hand would fit."

Miriam straightened up tall. "Let's get it over with then."

Elizabeth handed her two hooks, each attached to the end of a silk cord. "Try for an eye socket or under the chin. If you can't find those, use the roof of the mouth or one of the shoulders."

Miriam managed to attach the two hooks and, as she withdrew her hand, handed the silk cords to Elizabeth. Now her part was done, and she paced the room as her colleague gently tugged on the cords, slowly pulling the child's body along with them.

When Rachel regained full consciousness, her womb was empty and Miriam was pressing her to drink some ale mixed with nutmeg and feverfew.

"She must drink a cup of this every hour, including during the night," she told Eliezer.

"Was it a girl or a boy?" he asked.

"It was a boy, but even so you must not resume relations until two weeks after she's stopped bleeding," Miriam warned him. "It doesn't matter that the blood of childbirth is pure. Rachel needs time to heal."

Miriam hadn't wanted to look at what remained of the baby, but she'd forced herself to check the gender. After seeing that it was male, she kept from gagging just long enough to circumcise him. Then she waited for Rachel to wake up.

As soon as the opium wore off, Rachel asked Miriam what causes a child to die in the womb.

"Many things, but usually we don't know for sure."

"What things?" Rachel insisted.

"Want of nutrients and a corrupt diet, as during a famine," Miriam said. "Although that certainly can't be the case here. Just as it doesn't seem possible that your child died because you ate too much and choked him."

"What do you see as a likely cause?" Rachel had to know.

"If the mother suffers from sudden fears, extreme joy, or sorrow, or much trouble of mind, these strong emotions can keep blood from reaching the womb to nourish the child."

Rachel gulped. From the moment Eudes first approached her in the wine cellar, she'd been buffeted by strong emotions. Fear that he would seduce her, followed by anxiety that Eliezer would learn of their liaison, then terror as she plotted to kill him, followed by joy and relief when he died first.

"But I had strong emotions when Eliezer's father and brother died before Shemiah was born."

"Shemiah was fully formed by then, but with this one, your mind was troubled for much of the pregnancy." Miriam took Rachel's hand and lowered her voice. "What happened is probably for the best. I hate to imagine how the child would have been influenced by you thinking about that evil man so much."

Sitting on her porch with her feet elevated, Rachel savored the last hour of warmth before the sun set; she'd felt so cold while she was ill. Everyone else was at synagogue on this eighth and final day of Passover. There were no seders to end Passover, but the last two days, like the first two, were holidays. Even Joheved and her new baby were attending afternoon services, while Rachel prayed at home.

Miriam had insisted that Rachel stay home and rest for seven days, exactly as she would have done following a normal birth. The feverfew had done its job, and each day Rachel felt her health improve. Yet she did not feel well: at times a heaviness in her heart and tightness in her chest made it difficult to breathe. Her emotions fluctuated randomly between listlessness, melancholy, and anger. Thank Heaven there were no important decisions she needed to make, as it was difficult to concentrate on what people were saying.

Eliezer was more solicitous than ever; yet she oddly felt little grief for their stillborn son, only emptiness. Definitely not the agony she'd experienced last year when baby Asher died.

Somehow this child's demise was tied in with Eudes, and a part of her wanted to forget about both of them as soon as possible. Miriam said her emotional numbness could come from being dosed with opium, but Rachel still found her lack of overt sorrow bewildering.

Her reflections were interrupted by the gate squeaking open. Who could it be when everyone is supposed to be at services?

Guy de Dampierre who, of course, wouldn't be in synagogue today, lumbered up the path with a smile. Too lethargic to stand up, Rachel waited for Guy to come to her. But before he reached the well, Mama stepped out of the kitchen door and waved to him.

Rachel's contemplative mood evaporated. Mama must have had one of her dizzy spells again; that's why she's home on the holiday. Rachel knew it was wrong to feel this way, but her resentment bubbled up anyway. It couldn't be coincidence that Mama always felt dizzy when it meant extra work for Rachel, the daughter Papa loved the most, maybe more than he loved Mama.

If it weren't for Mama's dizziness, I wouldn't have been so busy cleaning two houses for Passover, and I might have noticed that my baby had stopped moving in time for Miriam to save it.

Immediately Rachel felt overwhelmed with guilt. A Jewish daughter should respect and honor her mother, be grateful for everything her mother does for her. Mama had born her and raised her, cared for her and her children when they were sick, worried ceaselessly over their health and welfare. Mama had never raised a hand against her.

Even so, Rachel found her bile rising whenever Mama complained of dizziness. But she had no time to dwell on this. Mama and Guy were approaching, and they looked upset.

"It is true that you cannot accept my eggs, bread, and cakes tonight?" Guy's voice rose with annoyance. "I thought today was the last day of your Festival of Unleavened Bread."

"We can accept them later, once Passover is finished," Rachel replied. "But we cannot take them yet."

"The baker's assistant is outside in the street with a full cart," Guy said. "Can't he at least come inside and wait?"

Mama looked at Rachel hopefully, but Rachel shook her head. "Jews are forbidden to have any leaven in our homes or in our possession during Passover."

Guy turned around and was heading for the gate when Mama called out, "Wait. I'll go get my husband."

Rachel didn't know which made her angrier—that Mama didn't accept her knowledge of Jewish Law or that Mama would interrupt Papa at synagogue.

Guy calmed at this and turned back to Rachel. "So if you can't have any leaven in your possession during Passover, what does a Jewish wheat merchant do?"

"He finds a trustworthy non-Jew who buys it from him before the festival and sells it back afterward at a small profit."

"And if the non-Jew refuses to sell back the grain or asks for a larger profit?"

"That's why the non-Jew has to be trustworthy."

Rachel had barely scratched the surface of the complex laws of Passover when the gate banged open and there was Papa. "I told them that we couldn't accept his gift until after sunset," she said. "But Mama insisted on getting you."

Salomon looked at the nearly setting sun and stroked his beard. Finally he turned to Guy. "My daughter is right about the leavened food. I thank you for thinking of us kindly, for realizing how we much would appreciate the taste of bread and cakes after a week of matzah, and for not wanting us to wait."

He took in his wife's frowning visage and sighed. "The lad can bring in the eggs and put them in that shady corner, and when the proper time has passed we can use them. But I cannot take the bread and cakes."

"I'll leave them next door then," Guy suggested. Not all of Salomon's neighbors were Jews.

"Even if you leave them with a non-Jew, as long as they are designated for me, they will come into my possession," Salomon said. "And that would make them forbidden to me, or to any Jew."

Guy rolled his eyes in exasperation. "Very well. I will send the cart back to the bakery and tell the boy to return later."

"*Merci*, Guy. He can come when he sees three stars in the sky," Salomon added.

Rachel's strength slowly returned, and when Joheved's son Isaac married Moses haCohen's daughter Judita one month later on Lag b'Omer, Rachel managed to dance at the wedding and the seven celebratory banquets that followed. After that Miriam agreed that she might be sufficiently strong to work in the vineyard again. Eliezer worried that it would be too much for her, all that standing in the sun to train the shoots properly. But Rachel reminded him that this had to be done by someone with experience, that the angle at which the branch is made to grow is critical for its productivity.

Rachel felt drawn to the vineyard. There she was spared the condolences and sympathetic glances that follow a stillbirth, and no opportunities arose for comparisons between Joheved's robust infant and her own empty arms. She had held her head up high at Isaac's wedding, dancing even when she felt weak, never letting a tear stain her face, but she knew what everyone was saying—words of pity that merely covered their relief that it was her loss and not theirs. In the vineyard she suffered no awkward moments when someone tried to comfort her but instead rubbed salt into her wound.

With summer approaching, the grape vines were finally safe from a sudden late frost, and Papa's relief translated into voluble explanations of Torah for the students who helped him trim the vine's canopy of leaves to achieve the correct exposure of the grape buds to sunlight. By early afternoon, with a warm haze rising from the freshly hoed soil, the clean and tidy vineyard was a joy to behold—its vine props standing to attention, the first small buds venturing timidly along the branches.

After all her worries about Eudes and about Eliezer's travels, as well as the baby she'd lost because of them, Rachel just wanted to sit outdoors, surrounded by new growth, and soak up the silent sunshine. She'd start looking for fullers and dyers to hire once the Hot Fair was over. By then she'd likely be pregnant again, and the oh-so-compassionate tongues would stop wagging about poor Rachel.

But neither of her assumptions came to pass. The Hot Fair had scarcely begun when her flowers returned, and eleven days later she accompanied Miriam at sunset to a secluded pool where a small stream fed into the Seine. There the two sisters immersed in the *mayim chaim*, the "living waters," which made this a natural *mikvah*. One month later they repeated the process, and again a month after that.

While she was waiting to be permitted to Eliezer again, word came that Érard of Brienne had attacked, and then overrun, one of the Count of Champagne's more remote castles. Eudes' successor, his youngest brother, Hugues, had most of his men occupied patrolling the fairgrounds or guarding the roads leading to Troyes, and thus Érard's knights easily overcame the castle's small squadron.

As usual Salomon's household received the latest, and most correct, information from Guy de Dampierre.

"I don't understand why Érard would risk a war over such a small fief," Meir said at *disner*.

"And why now?" Joheved asked. "There's been peace in Champagne for years."

"Érard is testing our new young count," Guy replied. "He's hoping that either Hugues will not consider the castle worth fighting over or will prove unable to retake it."

Salomon took a ladleful of stew and passed the bowl around the table. "Érard deliberately chose a time when Hugues was at a disadvantage."

Guy nodded. "Hugues will have to wait until the Hot Fair is over before he can marshal a force large enough to attack Brienne. That gives some other baron, thinking similarly, an opportunity to assault another of Hugues' castles."

"What if King Philip or the Duke of Burgundy decides to test him?" Miriam voiced the worry they all felt.

"We must pray that they do not," Eliezer replied. "Such an attack would entangle Count Stephen of Blois and perhaps even the king of Angleterre."

"Don't worry. Countess Adelaide is too wise and experienced to let that happen." Guy smiled conspiratorially. "I've heard that she's arranged for Hugues to marry Princess Constance, so we probably needn't worry about King Philip."

Rachel listened in silence, her dismay growing. Most woolen merchants wouldn't share Guy's knowledge or confidence, so they might not be keen on entering a risky new venture with her and Eliezer until the trouble with Brienne was settled. And if Hugues were as inept a leader as Érard hoped, that could be years away.

More disappointing, her flowers started again the day before Selichot, the Saturday preceding Rosh Hashanah, and she feared that getting pregnant again might not be so easy as before. Then to make matters worse, that afternoon the sun was almost totally eclipsed.

Mon Dieu, hasn't this year been bad enough? What great disasters are You sending us in the coming year?

Part Two

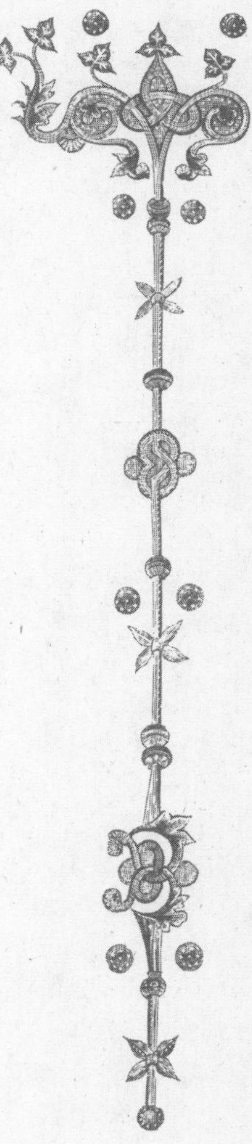

thirteen

Toledo, Sepharad
Winter 4854 (1094 C.E.)

fter following the Tagus River for several days, Eliezer gazed at last on the distant walls of Toledo and felt a surge of eagerness, followed immediately by a stab of guilt. The cloth enterprise was going to take longer to establish than Rachel had anticipated, and to ensure sufficient time for him to launch his business in Toledo in the meantime Rachel unhappily agreed not to expect his return to Troyes until summer.

Eliezer's heart swelled with compassion for his lovely, sad, and overworked wife. Her mother's health had declined precipitously after Yom Kippur, and when he returned from Mayence for the Cold Fair, the old woman was bedridden. Rachel had always enjoyed being Salomon's favorite daughter, but now, in addition to her other duties, she was suddenly responsible for hosting yeshiva students and visiting scholars. Not that Miriam wouldn't share the burden of running his household, but Salomon always asked for Rachel, who couldn't bring herself to refuse him.

It seemed to Eliezer that his wife had changed after the stillbirth. Most men would be pleased if their wives stopped arguing with them, but now that she no longer teased or challenged him, Eliezer realized how much spice their verbal battles had added to their marriage.

Its loss only exacerbated the decline in their marital relations. Rachel still wasn't pregnant when the Hot Fair closed, which had meant that for each of the next six months they were permitted to use the bed only during the two weeks between her immersions in the *mikvah* and when she became *niddah* again. According to Tractate Niddah, this was supposed to increase their desire for each other.

> Rabbi Meir said, "Why does the Torah make the *niddah* forbidden to her husband for seven days? Because, if not, he would be with her frequently and become repulsed by her. So the Torah said—let her be impure for seven days and then she will be as desirable to her husband as under the bridal canopy."

Indeed Salomon taught that if a husband can have his wife whenever he wants, he will lose his desire for her; while the forced abstinence makes him as eager for her as on their wedding night. But this wasn't the case for Eliezer. Since *niddah* made Rachel more desperate to be pregnant with each ensuing month, their coupling became more an obligation than a pleasure.

When she flowered again just after the Hot Fair ended, he'd considered leaving immediately. But he followed the Talmud's admonition that a man must "visit" his wife before he leaves for a journey and waited the necessary days until she was clean again.

As it was, he arrived in Mayence so late that many of the best pelts were already sold. Thank Heaven for Samson, uncle to Salomon's servant Anna. Samson had saved some for him, because Eliezer had taken on an additional task that only added to his delay.

Anna's husband, Baruch, had written to Samson, pouring out his frustration at not finding a bride for their son, Pesach. Baruch originally asked Salomon to approach merchants who frequented the Troyes fairs, hinting that Pesach would accept a bride with a few defects, but to no avail. Despite Pesach's piety and Talmud knowledge, no Jewish father wanted his daughter to marry a vineyard laborer—no matter how exalted his master. It didn't help that Pesach's parents were converts and originally pagan slaves.

With all the young mothers who died giving birth, there were far more unmarried men than women. So in desperation, Anna begged her uncle Samson to allow his oldest daughter, Dulcie, to marry Pesach.

Thus Eliezer had been charged with bringing Pesach to Mayence with him, where the young couple would meet and, assuming all went well, become betrothed. It was the least he could do to repay Samson, who'd not only risked life and limb to bring news of the death of Eliezer's father and brother but also accompanied him all the way to Prague to retrieve their personal effects.

Regretfully, young Pesach was somewhat poor company. The surly adolescent spent much of the journey vacillating between worries that Dulcie would find him no better husband material than other potential brides had, and fear that she must have some flaw that repulsed other suitors, so that he'd be stuck with the choice between a defective bride and none at all.

To distract him from these worries, Eliezer made Pesach concentrate on the Talmud he would need to teach at the *erusin* banquet. Samson's acquaintances were unlikely to be learned, so Eliezer offered to share some of his learning as well. Pesach kept muttering "what *erusin* banquet?" but when he finally saw his intended, tall and slim with a crown of reddish blond braids, there was no more talk of defective brides. Thank Heaven Dulcie did not refuse the match, and the next day Eliezer was buying Pesach new clothes for the ceremony, something nobody in Troyes had remembered to do.

Samson and his wife, Catharina, looked ready to burst with pride as their courtyard filled with scholars who were curious to find out if Salomon ben Isaac's third son-in-law was as much a *talmid chacham* as the other two. And Pesach, who hadn't grown up in a yeshiva without learning something, was able to acquit himself well enough that Dulcie began looking at him with interest instead of apprehension.

Thus with a sufficient supply of beaver, ermine, and sable, and his debt to Samson repaid, Eliezer left Mayence with the promise that he and Pesach would return next year for the wedding. The two men's mood was celebratory on the journey home, and Eliezer began to hope that his luck had changed—perhaps he would even arrive home to find Rachel pregnant.

But she had been *niddah*. Again.

Eliezer sighed with regret, and then sat up straight in his saddle. Toledo loomed larger as he approached the city, and he was determined to banish all but optimistic thoughts. Unlike his first trip to Sepharad, this time he had an introduction to a prominent Jewish merchant in town, Dunash, whom Hasdai had written last spring.

Eliezer couldn't help but smile as he recalled his great haste to reach Córdoba the previous year, eager for knowledge and new ideas to replace all thoughts of Count Eudes' premature demise. Eliezer felt no remorse for his actions, and his decision had been immediate, as was his need to leave Troyes as soon as the Cold Fair ended. He'd looked forward to hiding in Hasdai's library for six months, studying Philo. Here, at last, was a Jew among the ancient philosophers, who was determined to reconcile Torah with their beliefs, yet not afraid to reject the great Aristotle on the crucial subject of Creation.

Eliezer was convinced that once he understood Philo he would no longer be ashamed to open his mouth at a gathering of Sephardic Jews. But as he delved deeper into Philo's works, he realized that he still had much learning to do. For Philo insisted that the highest perception of truth is possible only after a thorough study of the sciences, which meant that Eliezer would have to find a mathematics tutor after all.

Months later, he'd returned from one of his lessons and was disconcerted to see Hasdai sitting alone at the dining table. The boys and their mother ate separately except on Shabbat, but usually there were guests in attendance.

Hasdai handed Eliezer the platter filled with dried fruits, the customary first course. "I hear that you're an excellent mathematics student, that you can solve al-Khwarīzmī's most difficult equations. What are you going to study next?"

"I thought I'd follow Philo's advice and study more science." Eliezer was surprised by his host's interest in his studies.

"I have some advice for you," Hasdai said. "As much as I enjoy your visits, Córdoba grows too risky for Jews. If you wish to continue doing business in Sepharad, I suggest shifting your efforts to someplace safer . . . like Toledo."

"Why not Barcelona?" Trying to hide his dismay at having to start over in a new Sephardic city, Eliezer casually helped himself to the second course, fish with lettuce and carrots.

"While there are many communities in the north where a Jewish merchant may prosper, in Toledo you will be able to study astronomy."

"Astronomy?" Al-Khwarīzmī's writings on astronomy were intriguing, but Eliezer didn't want to spend so much effort learning something only sailors needed to know. Better to study philosophy and impress the merchants he would meet in his new place of business.

"Wouldn't you like to learn how the stars move in the heavens and determine the future?"

"Even if a man understood how to do this, the calculations would be impossibly difficult," Eliezer replied. Salomon taught that these kinds of studies were forbidden, like asking about what came before Creation or after death. Yet here in Córdoba, Creation was one of the Jews' favorite topics.

Hasdai chuckled. "Some think that memorizing and understanding the entire Talmud is impossibly difficult."

"Supposing that I did want to study astronomy, why should I do so in Toledo?"

"Al-Zarqālī of Toledo was the finest mathematician and astronomer of our time. His death a few years ago was a great loss, but his students carry on his work." Hasdai sighed. "Ah, the discoveries they must be making at his observatory . . ."

Eliezer could hear the longing in Hasdai's voice, and his curiosity was stirred. What would it be like to learn among the best astronomers in the world, to study subjects that most men couldn't fathom? Maybe in Toledo they could discover the secrets of the stars, comprehend the mystery of Creation. And if he were among them, he'd have knowledge that only a few men shared.

"The Jews of Toledo must be rich now that Alfonso has made their city his capital," Eliezer said.

"Not just the Jews," Hasdai encouraged him. "Should you decide to visit Toledo, I'll write you an introduction to several families there. You will have no difficulty finding lodging—and business opportunities."

Thus it was decided. On Eliezer's final day in Córdoba, as he loaded his goods onto the pack animals, Hasdai directed a manservant to add another chest to the pile.

"No astronomer can tell me if our city will be standing next year," Hasdai said. "Or if I will ever have great-grandsons to enjoy my books."

Eliezer suddenly realized what treasure Hasdai's chest contained and, with tears in his eyes, he'd embraced the old man. They would probably never meet again.

That chest was sitting in his cart now, a year later, hidden under rolls of woolens and furs, as he passed through Toledo's city gate. Along with volumes of Philo, Aristotle, and al-Khwarīzmī was a pouch containing some magnificent diamond jewelry. Rachel told him a dubious story about Count Eudes' mistress pawning them and then dying before she could redeem them, which is why they couldn't be sold in Troyes.

Eliezer shrugged. Eudes was the one who was dead, and if he'd given Rachel diamonds, then that was just payment for all the aggravation he'd put their family through.

Joheved put her hands on her hips and scowled at her little sister. "I don't care how busy you are, Rachel, you're coming to the bathhouse with me and Miriam. I haven't had a hot bath since the Cold Fair, and after two months delivering lambs in the sheepfold, I am more than ready for one."

"We're not prepared for Purim yet." As much as Rachel loved hot baths, she wasn't going to let Joheved order her around.

"Joheved and I will help you, and so will Zipporah and Judita." Miriam tried to diffuse the tension between her sisters. "By the way, Zipporah was so useful with the lambing that I've decided to train her as my apprentice."

"You're going to make a mohel out of her? Shemayah will be furious." Joheved said this with a great deal of pleasure. Negotiating Zipporah and Shmuel's betrothal agreement with the man had been infuriating.

"You'll have to find your own way to punish Shemayah for how he mistreats his wife and daughter. I'm only teaching Zipporah to be a midwife," Miriam replied. "But if she wants to become a mohel later, that's her decision."

"Considering her family's curse, I can't imagine that she'll want to perform circumcisions," Rachel said.

Along with the other women in her family, Zipporah's mother, Brunetta, was cursed. If their sons were cut, the bleeding sometimes didn't stop. Enough of their baby boys had died after being circumcised that Salomon exempted them from the rite, and Shemayah had never stopped blaming Brunetta for only giving him daughters.

Joheved reached out and ran her fingers through Rachel's stringy curls. "Can you even remember the last time you washed your hair? Your husband being away is no excuse."

Joheved was appalled by her sister's wan appearance. Rachel had always been the beautiful one, but now her once lustrous hair hung limply like burnt straw. Her creamy skin had lost its glow and in the sunlight looked decidedly sallow. It seemed impossible, but even Rachel's gorgeous green eyes seemed changed, more like murky ponds than emeralds.

"When I washed my hair last is none of your business."

Before Joheved could say something even more argumentative, Miriam grabbed her and Rachel's hands. "Now that I'm back in Troyes I need to immerse in the *mikvah*, and it would be nice if both my sisters came with me to bathe." Rachel would surely respond better to her plea than to Joheved's criticism.

"All right, I'll come with you." The thought of her sisters luxuriating in hot water while she cleaned the courtyard made Rachel even more irritated. "But if Mama complains, it will be both your faults."

Seated in the large bathtub, clouds of steam surrounding them, Rachel allowed herself to relax, while Joheved and Miriam exchanged glances and nodded.

"Now that Joheved has recovered her full health, we've decided that our family should continue to celebrate Passover in Ramerupt," Miriam said.

Before Rachel could speak, Joheved explained, "Then you and Miriam won't have to expend all that effort preparing for the festival, and I can invite Zipporah and Judita's families without making more work for you."

"What about Mama?" Rachel stared at them in astonishment. Their mother had been bedridden for months.

"If Mama can sit in a chair, she can sit in a cart." Miriam felt guilty for harboring such thoughts about her own mother, but she sometimes wondered if Mama's symptoms were exaggerated in order to thwart Rachel.

Rachel reached for a handful of soft soap and began lathering her hair. "Have you talked to Papa?"

"Not yet," Joheved replied. "We thought it best if the three of us approached him together."

The three of them bathing together, planning to present a united front to Papa, created an intimacy Rachel had never felt with her sisters.

"Do you mind if I ask you something first?"

Joheved handed Rachel a bucket of clean water for rinsing her hair. "Not at all."

Rachel took a deep breath. "Does it bother you very much that I'm Papa's favorite?" There, she'd actually said it.

Miriam spoke first. "Before you came along, Joheved was Papa's favorite, so things didn't change for me. And once I became a mother, I made sure to keep my preference to myself."

"You have a favorite?" Rachel had no idea; her sister seemed the perfect mother.

"When a woman has many sons and one daughter . . ." Miriam shrugged, her cheeks redder than from the steam alone.

They turned to Joheved, who looked down at the water for some time before speaking. "I admit that I did resent you for some time." Joheved's chin began to quiver. "But then we both lost babies to Shibeta."

Now, after Rachel's stillbirth and subsequent barrenness, Joheved's jealousy had been replaced by sympathy. Not that she would hurt her little sister further by reminding her of these.

"If I'm Mama's least favorite child," Rachel posited, "who do you think she prefers?"

"Not me," Joheved replied immediately. "I've given her far too much aggravation by studying Talmud and wearing tefillin."

They both looked at Miriam, who shook her head. "I don't think any of us has replaced the boy Shibeta took from her."

There was an awkward silence until Joheved turned to Rachel. "So will you talk to Papa with us?"

"Of course. He can't possibly refuse all of us together."

Miriam broke into a smile. "I told you she'd agree." Then she turned from Joheved back to Rachel. "We've also decided that you and your children should go back to Ramerupt with Joheved after Purim. The country air will be good for you."

"But . . ." Rachel began to protest.

"My alewife has more daughters than she knows what to do with," Joheved said. "So I offered to take two of them off her hands and bring them to Troyes, where they can help Anna look after Mama and Papa."

"And all the yeshiva students." Rachel's mood brightened further. "Papa should have hired more servants long ago."

"Sending those two girls to Troyes will solve another of Joheved's problems," Miriam said. "Then they won't be chasing after Milo and he can get his work done."

"Oy, Milo." Joheved sighed. "I don't know what to do about him."

"What's the matter with him?" Rachel asked. "I thought he was a better steward than old Étienne."

"He's an excellent steward; that's part of the problem. If he were at all unsatisfactory, we could just replace him."

Rachel squinted at her sister in confusion. "But why do you want to replace him if he's so good at his job?"

Joheved blushed and looked away. "Milo says that he's so sick with love for me that if I don't return it he'll die. It's all nonsense of course, and I can't imagine how he came up with such an idea. But the more I tell him the whole thing is impossible, that I will never love him, the more determined he becomes."

"Milo didn't invent this idea of knights suffering from love for their ladies." Rachel had no choice but to explain the subject, despite the unpleasant memories it evoked. "It's called courtly love, and it seems to be the fashion in French courts. The knight expects his love to be unrequited, at least at the beginning."

"I'm a married woman and I'll soon be a grandmother," Joheved declared. "His love will remain unrequited forever."

"But according to the rules of courtly love, the more you reject him, the more you insist that he will never win your love, the more determined he becomes to have it. What you're doing now only encourages him."

"Joheved, now you see," Miriam said. "Rachel knows all about these things."

Rachel's eyes flashed. "You told Joheved about—" She stopped in time to avoid naming the count in the public bath.

"Joheved needs your help." Miriam remained calm. "How long do you think this can go one before Meir or someone else becomes suspicious and your sister's reputation is damaged? Besides, you know about Joheved and Meir and their magic mirror, and about Judah and Aaron. Why should you be the only one with secrets?"

"That's why you're so eager for me to go to Ramerupt," Rachel accused them.

"I want you to come to Ramerupt for your health," Joheved said softly. "And if you can help me find a way to disabuse Milo of his ridiculous courtly love notion while you're there, I would greatly appreciate it."

As Rachel rode with Joheved through the mostly leafless forest, her daughter snuggled in her lap, she felt at peace for the first time in months. When the fields of sheep and lambs came into view, causing Rivka to squeal with delight, Rachel had to smile as well.

"How is your plan to become a clothier coming?" Joheved asked. "Are you going to need our wool this spring?"

Rachel's spirits fell abruptly. "I found some weavers who've agreed to work for me, and Simon the Dyer has colleagues who will gladly dye any fabric we bring them if we provide the dye and alum. But . . ." How could she tell Joheved the truth without insulting her?

"But what?"

"I still need a fuller, preferably more than one." Rachel stared at the sheep, avoiding her sister's gaze. "But that's only a matter of money. The bigger problem is the quality of your wool. The expensive dyes Eliezer imports would be wasted on anything less than the finest woolens, and everyone says that the best wool comes from English sheep."

"Oh." Joheved sounded disappointed, not upset. "Importing English wool would cut into your profits."

"Unfortunate, but true."

They rode silently until they rounded a bend, where Rachel was startled to see a man riding toward them. He waved his arm in greeting and Joheved groaned.

"It's Milo. I keep telling him not to, but he always rides out to meet me. He says a lady should have an entourage of knights to escort her home, but since he's the only knight available on our estate, he comes alone."

Rachel observed carefully as Milo rode closer. No wonder the alewife's daughters needed to be sent away: this was a very attractive fellow. But the smile he flashed while welcoming Joheved, and the way his face lit up as she addressed him, filled Rachel with trepidation. Meir was as fine a husband as a woman could want, but how long could he compete with this young Adonis? How long could any normal woman remain unaffected by

Milo's offers of love? Rachel had no idea how she would dissuade him if Joheved couldn't, but she resolved that at least she would not leave the two of them alone.

Rachel soon found that this was unnecessary. Joheved was meticulous in ensuring that someone was present whenever she met with Milo. The two might have a private conversation while sitting at the dining table and going over the estate's accounts, but they did so in full view of the household.

Suspecting that Joheved was not as forceful in her denials as she could have been, Rachel decided to speak with Milo herself. After all, she'd kept Count Eudes at bay for months and would surely have been successful in rejecting him if he hadn't been her sovereign. Here the situation was reversed. Joheved was lady of the manor and Milo a lowly knight. If Rachel could convince him how hopeless his situation was, he might turn his attentions toward a woman who'd welcome them.

She asked him to show her the new vineyard, hoping for an excuse to ask about his feelings for Joheved. "Milo, the fields look different from the last time I was here for Passover."

"That was two years ago." Milo paused to think. "The land that was planted in wheat back then lay fallow last year, so now it's growing spring crops like peas or barley, and the land that was fallow then—"

"I understand the three-field rotation." Rachel cut him off. "But before the spring crop was oats. Now I realize what's different: there are scarcely any oats now."

"Remember the eclipse last fall."

Rachel nodded.

"Such a sign portends disaster in the coming year. With the mild winter we just had, I thought that if the trend continued we'd have a hot, dry summer and a poor wheat harvest." An expression of pride appeared on Milo's face. "When I discussed this with Lady Joheved, she decided to plant the spring fields with food crops for people rather than for horses."

The mention of Joheved's name was what Rachel was waiting for. "Speaking of Joheved . . . Milo, I don't know how best to approach this." She cleared her throat while Milo looked at her expectantly. "My sister tells me that you have become greatly enamored of her, and despite her every effort to dissuade you, you keep trying to win her love."

Milo blushed crimson, and to Rachel's surprise, tears came to his eyes. "I was smitten with Lady Joheved not long after arriving here, and I have tried with all my might to conceal my wound. Yet the more I tried to hide it, the more my pain increased, until I could no longer remain silent."

"Milo. You must not imagine for an instant that my sister can love you." Rachel was saddened by Milo's passion and by his blindness to its futility. "It would be sinful for her to enjoy the embraces of another man, especially when she has such an excellent husband. Meir loves her with his whole heart, and she is equally devoted to him."

"My lord is most blessed to be worthy of the joy of embracing her." Milo's eyes narrowed with defiance. "But you misapply the word *love* to the marital affections that spouses are expected to feel for each other. I am my lady's true lover."

"What you call love is merely lustful desire," Rachel shot back.

"*Non.* I wish only to serve her, to prove my devotion."

Rachel took a deep breath to calm herself. "You condemn love between husband and wife because they embrace without fear of anyone objecting. But this is the best kind of love, practiced without sin and encouraged by the security of continual embraces."

"Anyone touched by love knows that love cannot exist without jealousy," Milo said with confidence. "But a husband may not suspect his wife without thinking her capable of shameful conduct, and if he believes this of her, then his love ceases. Therefore true love cannot exist between husband and wife."

It was clear they were talking at cross-purposes. It seemed Milo would never accept that Joheved and Meir loved each other, and since every woman deserves love, who better to love her than Milo? Rachel bowed her head and they rode on in silence.

"Rachel," Joheved asked her later, "do you believe that Milo's love for me isn't carnal? That he wishes only to serve me?"

"Not for a moment," Rachel replied. "Although he may have convinced himself of it."

"So you don't believe I can dissuade him?"

"*Non*, I'm afraid not. Not if he stays in Ramerupt."

"But he's too good a steward to dismiss," Joheved said. "Besides, we couldn't ask him to leave without people suspecting that I'm the cause. Milo is right about one thing: it would be scandalous for a husband to display any jealousy of his wife. It would be tantamount to an accusation of adultery."

Rachel smiled as an idea occurred to her. "These courtly lovers are supposed to prove their devotion by performing heroic deeds, the more difficult the better."

"*Oui*." Joheved's eyebrows rose with suspicion.

"English wool is the best, but I can't afford to import it. So send Milo to Angleterre to buy a fine English ram and bring it back to father next year's lambs."

Joheved's face lit with understanding. "He'll need to be gone many months, during which time he may lose his love for me. Or perhaps he won't find a good enough ram, which will give me an excuse to repudiate him."

When Joheved told Milo of her request, insisting that eighteen-year-old Isaac needed to try his hand at managing the estate himself, Milo wavered between despair at being sent away and exultation at the knowledge that she was asking for his help. If he succeeded, he might be deserving of her love. Rachel hoped he'd bring back the best ram in Angleterre to bolster her chances of becoming a clothier—no matter that then Joheved would have to deal with an even more ardent suitor.

None of them, however, realized that Meir was also trying to find a solution to the problem.

fourteen

alomon's forehead creased with apprehension. "If you think Joheved is in danger of sinning with your steward, you must send him away immediately."

"I can't do that." Meir proceeded to give the same explanation Joheved had given Rachel. "Ideally a lord should act flattered by a knight's affection for his lady, displaying perfect confidence in her virtue. If I can't do that, I must at least appear to ignore it."

"But the situation is too risky. No woman can withstand such continual temptation. Not even my daughter."

"That's what I'm afraid of, especially with me being away in Troyes so often."

As they passed the convent of Notre-Dame-aux-Nonnaines, Meir was suddenly reminded of another spring afternoon, twenty years ago, when he and Salomon had wandered the streets of Troyes discussing Joheved's unruly *yetzer hara*.

He'd been worried then too. "Sometimes I think of staying away longer, giving them the chance, and seeing what she'd do."

Salomon grabbed Meir's arm. "Absolutely not. Don't even think of such a thing."

"Papa, why are you so upset? Nothing's happened yet."

Salomon stopped to adjust his hose. "Tell me about Beruria, the daughter of Rabbi Hananiah ben Tradion."

Meir was sure his father-in-law had a good reason for this seemingly incongruous request, so he replied, "She was the wife of Rabbi Meir, and such an excellent scholar herself that she studied three hundred laws of Talmud every day. She was impatient with those students she considered fools; yet she was compassionate in consoling Meir after their two sons died. When her father continued to teach Torah in defiance of the Romans, they executed him and her mother, and forced her sister into a brothel."

"What is the last thing it says about Beruria in the first chapter of Tractate Avodah Zarah?"

Meir searched his memory for the obscure text.

> Beruria said to Meir, "It is shameful that my sister sits in a brothel." So he took three dinars and went to Rome, thinking, if she has done nothing forbidden, a miracle will occur. He disguised himself as a cavalryman and told her, "Submit to me." She replied, "I am menstruating." He said, "I do not care," and she said, "But there are many more beautiful than I." He thought, clearly she has not done what is forbidden. She says this to whoever comes here.
>
> He went to her guard and said, "Give her to me." The man replied, "I fear the government." Meir said to him, "Take these three dinars. Use half for bribes and keep half" . . . So the guard released her. The authorities learned of the matter . . . they carved the likeness of Rabbi Meir on the gates and declared that whoever sees his face should arrest him . . . Meir fled to Bavel. Some say because of this; others say because of the Beruria incident.

Meir eyed Salomon with trepidation. "The Beruria incident?"

Salomon closed his eyes and sighed. "I learned this from my teachers in Mayence. It has never been written down:

> One time Beruria mocked what the sages said about women being flighty. Meir said to her, 'By your life! You will eventually accept their words.' He instructed one of his disciples to tempt her to infidelity. The disciple urged her for many days, until she finally consented. When the matter became known, she strangled herself, while Rabbi Meir fled because of the disgrace."

Meir shuddered. What could have possessed Rabbi Meir to do such a thing? No wonder this piece of Talmud wasn't written down. He could feel Salomon's gaze and knew he must demonstrate what he'd learned from the ignominious tale.

"I must not be like my namesake and tempt my wife to sin."

Salomon nodded, and they began walking again.

Meir usually prided himself on the parallels between himself and the Talmudic Rabbi Meir, especially when it came to them both having very learned wives. But now their similarity frightened him.

Meir thought of how hard he fought to hide his outrage whenever he observed Milo staring at Joheved with adulation, and his heart overflowed with sadness for Rabbi Meir and Beruria, that the scholar's jealousy had brought about such terrible consequences. He had no choice but to trust Joheved and pray that their story wouldn't end in tragedy.

Eliezer unhitched his pack animals and watched from the bridge as they lumbered to the riverbank. The gushing waterway he'd crossed on the way to Toledo had shrunk upon his return to a small stream, but at least there was some water flowing. The previous two creeks were dry. The horses drank eagerly as he scanned the cloudless sky. It hadn't rained at all on his trip to Troyes, which normally would be a blessing, but as the passing wheat fields looked increasingly stunted and parched, Eliezer began buying grain from any estate with a surplus.

Once he reached the borders of Champagne, there was none to be had, and the covetous looks his bulging grain sacks drew made him grateful for the count's men patrolling the roads. On his last night outside Troyes, Eliezer regretfully packed away the book he brought to read on the journey—an Arabic translation of Ptolemy's *Great Treatise*. Until he left Troyes once more, the only languages he'd be reading would be Hebrew and Aramaic.

Thinking of Rachel, Eliezer sighed. Would she welcome him with an eager smile, or would some disaster have befallen his family while he was gone? Even if all was well otherwise, she might have her flowers. Or worse. He grimaced as he remembered the Talmudic curse, "May you return from a journey and find your wife an uncertain *niddah*."

With some anxiety, he entered Salomon's courtyard, where Anna was showing some new maidservants how to do laundry. That was a good sign—now Rachel wouldn't be so burdened by housework.

Anna hurried to greet him. "Rachel and the others are still in the vineyard, but they should be home soon. Are you hungry? I can get you some bread and cheese."

"I can wait for *souper*." He lowered his voice to a whisper and asked, "My mother-in-law?"

"Rivka is much the same." Anna's expression sobered. "But Judah's mother is very ill. He, Miriam, and the children left for Paris a month ago."

"Any more news I should be aware of?"

She broke into a smile. "Your children and Rachel are well—may the Holy One protect them. Just two days ago, she and Joheved went swimming together."

Eliezer grinned back at her. Things were better than he'd expected. Together they unloaded his merchandise, giving him plenty of time to get his animals settled at the stables before afternoon services. And whom should he meet there but Judah's old study partner, Elisha.

"So you too have just arrived in Troyes." Eliezer greeted him with a quick embrace. "Where's Giuseppe?"

"He's trying to find us some new lodgings," Elisha said as they stepped into the now well-swept streets. "The inn we were assigned to is dreadful."

Elisha and Giuseppe were business partners, the former from Worms and the latter from Genoa. According to Rachel, who seemed to know all the Ganymedes, their relationship was carnal as well as professional. She'd also told him that Judah had once been the object of Elisha's affection.

That reminded him. "Judah and his family are in Paris with his sick mother. You two can stay with us until they return."

"I appreciate it, although it's disappointing not to see Judah until the Cold Fair." Elisha began waving furiously, and a few moments later Giuseppe joined them.

"What merchandise did you bring from Sepharad?" Giuseppe draped his arm around Elisha's shoulder. "Perhaps we can take it off your hands."

"The usual—dyestuffs, pepper, other spices. I can give you a good deal on cinnamon and cumin. And I picked up some grain on my way back."

Elisha's jaw dropped. "You have wheat? In Worms it's worth almost as much as pepper."

"I have some wheat, but mostly I have peas and barley from the spring harvest."

"It doesn't matter. Unless it rains soon, you'll make an obscene profit on all of them." Elisha shook his head sadly. "It hasn't rained in the Rhineland for over six months and . . ."

"This spring was the hottest anyone can remember." Giuseppe completed Elisha's sentence. "People are worried about famine."

"Surely there will be other merchants here with wheat."

"Not if the drought is widespread," Elisha said.

Eliezer recalled the eclipse last fall. The sun had only been partially hidden in Troyes, but in Allemagne the eclipse was total. "We should find out where wheat is plentiful and send buyers there immediately. If it's so far away that we can't bring the grain here by the end of the Hot Fair, at least we'll have some to sell at the Cold Fair."

"Giuseppe and I won't have money to invest until the fair ends," Elisha said. "But if you put up the capital, we can find the wheat."

"Then we can split the profits," Giuseppe added.

"Agreed."

Eliezer's spirits soared when he saw Rachel standing at the gate, apparently waiting for him. His gait quickened as she began walking toward him, and by the time he reached her they were both running.

"I missed you so much," Rachel whispered between kisses.

"How much time do we have before afternoon services?"

"I'm sure there's enough time left." Rachel pulled him toward the stairs. "Joheved is watching the children."

As soon as he closed their bedroom door, Rachel was in his arms, simultaneously kissing him and removing his clothes. She had already loosened her *bliaut* and chemise, which were lying on the floor moments later. Eliezer didn't bother to take off his hose before diving onto their bed and pulling the curtains closed.

Rachel was equally eager that night, the next morning, and every day until her flowers began, two weeks later. Eliezer braced himself for the return of her dark moods, but she remained uncharacteristically cheerful.

"You're remarkably happy for someone who has to sleep in her own linens," he said as she made a point of slowly pulling up her hose as they dressed in the morning.

She blew him a kiss across the room. "Miriam has made being *niddah* much less unpleasant for me."

"How so?"

"First of all, I don't have to immerse in the synagogue's disgusting dark *mikvah*. At least not most months." When he looked at her with concern, as she knew he would, she continued, "Miriam showed me a lovely pond in the forest. It's secluded, with a sandy bank, and after Papa said it was a kosher *mikvah*, lots of us go there to immerse when it's not too cold."

"You'll have to show me the place." He did a mental calculation and grinned at her. "Maybe we can use it together at Rosh Hashanah."

"Maybe," she replied. "Miriam also showed me how to use a *mokh* when I have my flowers. It's less messy than wearing a *sinar* alone."

"I suppose it would be." Eliezer's flirtatious mood evaporated at this mention of his wife's menstrual apparatus.

"I think it was Joheved's idea, since she had all that extra wool. But she wasn't sure it would be allowed on Shabbat, since it might be considered carrying instead of wearing. So she discussed it with Papa."

Carrying items from one domain to another was forbidden work on the Sabbath, but wearing something was, of course, permitted. Since a *mokh* went into a woman's womb, Eliezer could understand how it could be acceptable, despite the fact that it was a new innovation. "If it makes being *niddah* less onerous for women, I think we should be lenient," he said.

"Not that Joheved cares anymore," Rachel said. "She hasn't been *niddah* since little Salomon was born. I guess he'll be her final child."

Eliezer gave silent thanks to his sister-in-law. Last summer Rachel went to bed early when she was *niddah*, but now she and Joheved stayed up studying together until he and Meir returned from the late-night Talmud sessions. Now that he thought of it, something seemed to be bothering Meir; he occasionally asked Eliezer what the last speaker had said, and his young students sometimes had to repeat their questions for him.

"I'm also happy because Milo will soon return with a new English ram for Joheved," she continued. "He has to be back soon or it will be too late for the rutting season in September."

"That's an odd thing to make you happy," he said.

Rachel proceeded to explain the situation in Ramerupt. "I know we won't have better wool immediately, but we can keep the male lambs with the finest wool for breeding, and eventually we'll have wool that's worth dyeing with kermes and indigo."

Eliezer sighed. *So that's what was distracting Meir from Talmud.* "What's Joheved going to do when Milo returns, as you're so sure he will?"

"Oh, I have an idea how to solve that." Rachel grinned at him but said nothing more.

Eliezer smiled at her confidence. Even in the unlikely event that Milo did bring back a ram that met Rachel's expectations, it would still take several years for her scheme to work. And that was assuming she found a competent fuller—which meant he was in no danger of having to give up his astronomy studies in Toledo.

He was a student in al-Zarqālī's school now—a novice astronomer to be sure, but Eliezer knew he would quickly rise in the ranks. For his study partner, and good friend, was Abraham bar Hiyya, son of the Nasi in Barcelona. When it came to astronomy and mathematics, Abraham was brilliant. Slightly younger than Eliezer, he too had little patience for those with less intellect. But because he understood that Eliezer's ignorance was due to lack of exposure to the subject, and because he saw how quickly Eliezer learned the material, Abraham was willing to study with him. Normally Eliezer would have chafed under such an unequal partnership, but Abraham was even more ignorant of Talmud than Eliezer was of astronomy.

Abraham had studied Jewish Law with Rabbi Isaac Alfasi, author of the great legal code *Sefer ha-Halachot.* Eliezer was horrified to learn that instead of having his students study the Talmud itself, Alfasi had transcribed the Talmud's halachic conclusions verbatim, without the surrounding deliberations.

Eliezer and Abraham almost came to blows early on, when Abraham declared Talmud study unnecessary because Alfasi's work contained all the essential decisions and laws. But once Eliezer quoted a few choice sections of Talmud for him, and showed him the importance of somebody knowing enough Talmud to make new laws, Abraham laughingly agreed that the French and German Jews could concentrate on Talmud exclusively. He intended to study the stars.

Eliezer was still smiling when Rachel finished dressing and went downstairs with Shemiah and little Rivka. One girl and one boy. Now that he'd fulfilled the mitzvah of procreation, he didn't need to father any more children. Rachel might be eager for another baby, but he found that he wasn't. No more pregnancies meant that Rachel would be able to travel with him again. Half the year in Troyes, for the fairs, and half in Toledo—that would be perfect.

Suddenly another thought cheered him. Milo would surely notice how well wheat was growing in the lands he passed through on his way back from Angleterre.

Looking forward to immersing that evening and resuming relations with Eliezer, Rachel returned from the vineyard early to find the courtyard bustling with more unexpected guests. She recognized Samson from Mayence: no one could forget that redheaded giant. But the group included three veiled women, a young man, and several children.

Joheved rushed up as soon as Rachel closed the gate. "Can you find room for Samson's family in your house?"

Rachel groaned inwardly. She could put them in the children's bedroom, but then Shemiah and Rivka would have to share hers. "But I'm going to the river tonight to immerse, remember. Isn't there anyplace else they can stay?"

"Everyplace else is full of yeshiva students. And thanks to your husband, Elisha and Giuseppe are at Miriam's." Joheved paused to think. "What if your children sleep with mine?"

"I suppose so." Rachel's pout changed to curiosity. "What's Samson's family doing in Troyes?"

"They're here for Pesach's wedding." Joheved saw Rachel's startled expression and held up her hand to forestall any questions. "There's a severe shortage of wheat in Worms, so Samson decided to have the wedding here. I'm so happy to see Catharina again."

"I thought she wasn't to come back here," Rachel whispered. Catharina, the parchment maker's daughter, and Joheved were girlhood friends. But Catharina had moved to Mayence after she converted to Judaism and married Samson.

"Her brother and everyone who worked in his shop died a few years ago. Some of their sheepskins carried a pestilence." Joheved shuddered. "Thank Heaven it wasn't from any of ours. Besides, it's been over fifteen years since she left Troyes. No one will remember her."

Within a week, Rachel was grateful for Catharina's visit. Except to attend services, Catharina never stepped outside Salomon's courtyard. Anna and Miriam's cook did the shopping, but Catharina insisted on helping with the other household chores. Her daughters and daughter-in-law pitched in as well, leaving Rachel free to concentrate on the vineyard and her jewelry clients.

Baruch and Samson agreed to postpone the wedding for a month, hoping that Judah and Miriam would return by then. But regardless, it seemed that Samson preferred to stay in Troyes as long as possible, should more grain merchants arrive. Samson clearly had the credit to buy wheat at the outrageous price the dealers asked.

"He does very well in the fur business," Eliezer explained to Rachel. "With his size and expertise in arms, he needn't hire mercenaries for protection. He speaks the Slavic language, so his old countrymen trust him. And I've never seen anyone who could drink more and still remain sober."

She laughed. "Quite an advantage in negotiating prices."

Rachel had just slid her jewelry case behind one of the wine casks in her cellar when a noise on the stairs startled her. She peered up to see who'd been watching her, but it was only Joheved.

"There you are." Joheved sighed with relief as she hurried down the stairs. "I've been looking all over for you."

"What's the matter? Is Judita in labor?"

"Not yet." Joheved looked at her with dread. "Milo is home. And he's brought back two of the finest rams I've ever seen. Whatever am I to do?"

If not for her sister's anxiety, Rachel would have hugged Joheved in exultation. "Don't worry. I'll explain what to do when we get to Ramerupt. I want to see these rams."

Two hectic weeks passed, however, before Rachel found an opportunity to visit the new livestock. Miriam's family returned from sitting shiva for Judah's mother just before Shabbat. Their arrival was fortuitous, because three days later Judita went into labor, giving birth to a baby boy. Zipporah performed the midwife's job perfectly, while Miriam supervised.

Joheved wouldn't leave Troyes until after her grandson's brit milah, which Miriam reluctantly agreed to do. She'd been doing circumcisions for seven years, but she'd never grown accustomed to the hostile stares that greeted her presence on the *bima* with her mohel's kit. Miriam didn't want her actions to challenge her community; she just wanted to fulfill the mitzvah. So unless the mother asked for her specifically, or the baby boy was family, Miriam left the rites during fair times to Avram the Goldsmith, the mohel who'd trained her.

Samson and Baruch scheduled their children's wedding for Tuesday, while the moon was still waxing. Rachel was so impatient to see those rams that, when she became *niddah* again, she convinced Eliezer to relinquish their large four-poster bed to the newlyweds for the nuptial week. After the ceremony, she and Joheved would go to Ramerupt.

Eliezer needed no convincing. As anticipated, Milo had reported passing lush fields of wheat in Picardy, near the Flemish border, which Eliezer was determined to reach at harvest time. Elisha and Giuseppe had already left for the area, their funds augmented by Samson and Miriam. Talmudic skills were required to renegotiate Eliezer's original simple partnership with Elisha to the five parties' satisfaction; it was necessary to take into account the different amount of capital supplied by each investor, that the men buying wheat would likely not bring back equal quality or quantities, and that the ones traveling west to procure the grain were not those who'd be selling it in the Rhineland.

"Are you sure you don't want to sell your share in Troyes?" Eliezer asked Miriam.

"I can wait for the higher prices in Mayence and Worms. And I'd rather our wheat goes where people really need it."

"Do you want me to bring back your profit or buy more furs with it?"

"I suppose I should invest in your furs." She shook her head in amazement. "This is becoming a complicated process."

Eliezer laughed. "It's nothing compared to the contracts I arranged in Maghreb. There we negotiate with dozens of partners and have contingencies for circumstances such as the boat sinking in a storm, being attacked by pirates, the traveling partners having to be ransomed, or if an opportunity for additional profit presents itself on the journey."

"I can understand why Talmud scholars make the best merchants."

Joheved had sent no word that she was coming, but Milo still rode out to meet them. He looked so happy to see her, and so proud of himself, that Rachel couldn't help but feel sorry for him. Once Joheved followed her advice, this would be the last time he'd be riding with his ladylove.

At Rachel's insistence, they stopped where the rams were pastured. "They are indeed magnificent creatures," she said after stroking their wool. "Are you sure they're not related?"

"That would be very unlikely," Milo replied. "One comes from the Welsh marches and the other from the Midlands."

Rachel had no idea where these places were, but she accepted Milo's assurance. "You have done my sister a great service. I'm sure she will wish to reward you."

"I deserve no reward other than the knowledge that I have served my lady well."

Joheved's face blanched as she raised the slightest brow at Rachel, who could barely wait for her scheme to come to fruition.

"How could you tell Milo that I'm going to reward him?" Joheved demanded, as they dressed for the evening meal. "What have you gotten me into?"

"Tonight at *souper*, will it be just the three of us at the high board and all the servants below?" Rachel asked.

"*Oui*."

"So they won't be able to hear us, but we'll be in clear view all the time?"

"*Oui*."

"Then we will give Milo the supreme test. Prepare him by saying that if his face betrays a hint of his feelings at what I say to him, you will deem him unworthy of your affection." Rachel patted his sister's hand. "Trust me."

Joheved wanted to object, but she had no choice but to remain silent as Milo escorted them to the table.

"Follow my lead," Rachel whispered in her sister's ear.

It was a struggle but Milo managed to maintain a bland expression when Joheved repeated Rachel's earlier words.

"You have another trial for me?" he asked.

"My sister will explain it to you," Joheved said. "So I can carefully observe your responses."

Rachel was impressed at Joheved's quick-wittedness. "Milo, we all know that if a man easily gets what he desires, he holds it cheaply."

Milo brightened with hope and then abruptly calmed himself.

"*Oui* . . . just as when the possession of some good thing is postponed by the difficulty of getting it, we desire it more strongly and put forth greater effort to keep it."

"We understand each other well," Rachel said. "My sister absolutely forbade you to love her; yet you persisted. To test you, she gave you an exceedingly difficult task, and now she must admit that you performed it twice beyond her satisfaction."

"Give me another task, even more arduous."

Rachel was pleased to see that, despite the passion of Milo's words, he appeared to be saying something mundane. It looked like her idea might succeed. "In order to obtain my sister's love, you must promise that you will always obey her commands."

"I gladly make such a promise," he answered.

"And if you violate your word, you will lose her love completely," Rachel warned him.

"Heaven forbid that I should ever do such a thing."

"Then if you truly love my sister, and wish to protect her from shame, you must cease all talk of love, all demonstrations of tenderness. You must display not the slightest hint of affection other than the loyalty she expects of all servants."

He turned to Joheved and blinked back tears. "Is this truly what you wish of me?"

If Joheved felt any sympathy for Milo, she hid it well. "I command you to make no visible effort to gain my love," she said sternly. "And indeed to give all appearances of having lost your love for me."

"What you ask is a heavy burden; yet I will bear it patiently and obey."

Rachel held her breath, hoping against hope that Joheved would show some sign of fondness for Milo, something that would give him the strength to keep his promise. And her sister surpassed her expectations.

"In gratitude for your excellent service," Joheved extended her arm, "you may kiss my hand."

Milo dropped to his knees and took her hand in his. Perhaps his lips lingered on her palm a trifle too long, but for the most part he acted as if he'd been asked to kiss any other noble lady's hand. He didn't react at all when Joheved gently squeezed his hand in return.

fifteen

liezer was determined to talk to Meir before he left for Picardy. His brother-in-law was more distracted than ever now that Milo had returned, but Eliezer was sure he had a cure for Meir's distress—if only the man would confide in him.

Luckily the evening study sessions grew longer as the Hot Fair came to a close, and one night Eliezer suggested they stop at a tavern on the way home.

"What's the point in hurrying home to our empty beds?" He poured Meir some ale.

Meir drank it in one long gulp and looked forlornly at the empty cup. "My bed may be empty, but I wonder if my wife's is."

Eliezer refilled Meir's cup. This was going to be easy. "Neither of our wives sleeps in an empty bed tonight." He smiled at Meir's confusion. "They are surely sharing a bed together in Ramerupt."

"Your wife is so beautiful and you're away so much. Don't you worry about her?"

"About her taking a lover? Never," Eliezer lied.

"Never?" Meir looked doubtful.

"And not just because my wife is a pious, God-fearing woman." Eliezer leaned forward and whispered, "I keep her so happy in bed that I know she will never desire another man."

"I used to feel that way when I was younger, but I'm almost forty. Now I have to worry about men half my age."

"Your new steward?"

Meir nodded glumly and shared the advice that Salomon had given him. Had that been Rabbi Meir's fear? That he'd grown too old to satisfy Beruria?

"Our father-in-law is a wise man, but not, I think, in the ways of giving women pleasure." Eliezer gave Meir a wicked grin. "I can teach you things that aren't in Tractate Kallah. And once Joheved experiences them, you can be sure she'll never even think about another man."

The new rams proved so vigorous with the ewes that Joheved told her daughters that the old one would be slaughtered. With so many people celebrating the New Year at Salomon's, it would take a large animal to feed them all.

"Are we going to eat the ram's head, Mama?" Leah asked.

"It's good luck to eat the head of an animal: its *rosh* at Rosh Hashanah," Joheved replied.

"And we eat sheep to remember the sacrifice of Isaac, which the Holy One prevented by sending a ram in Isaac's place." Hannah scolded her little sister. "Don't you remember reading that part of Torah on the second day?"

"I know very well that we read about Abraham and Isaac on the second day of Rosh Hashanah and about Hagar and Ishmael on the first," Leah said. "Just as I know that we eat lamb on Rosh Hashanah and chicken for Yom Kippur. I just wanted to know if we're going to eat the whole head, with the horns attached."

Joheved paused to think. They hadn't cooked a ram in years. "It would look impressive, wouldn't it?" The old ram had long and curvy horns.

"But won't cooking the horn ruin it as a shofar?" Hannah asked anxiously.

"What do we need another shofar for? We have plenty," Leah said. "And Papa blows the same old one every year."

"You're right, Hannah, cooking might ruin it as a shofar. But we could cook the head without them and then tie them on when we serve it." Joheved turned to her younger daughter. "Someday your brothers and cousins will want their own, Leah."

"Can I have one, Mama?" Hannah's voice was timid. "Please."

Joheved gulped and gazed into her daughter's pleading eyes, brown like Meir's rather than blue like her own (much to his disappointment).

Hannah was now taller than she was; when did that happen? Joheved surreptitiously surveyed her daughters. Although their similar features marked them as sisters, Leah was still a child while Hannah was on the verge of womanhood.

"Why do you want a shofar?"

"To blow it," Hannah whispered.

"You should hear her, Mama," Leah said. "She blows it really loud. Not like Shmuel, who always makes it sound like he's blowing his nose. She's even better than Papa."

Hannah shot her sister a look that should have silenced her, but Leah continued, "She is. I've heard her lots of times."

Joheved took in the shock and fear on Hannah's face, and was transported back in time to the moment when her mother had caught her wearing Papa's tefillin. She had been in her twelfth year, the same age as Hannah. She shook her head in resignation.

"Since it's Elul and your father isn't here today to blow the shofar, do you think you could blow it for us?"

Hannah remained rooted to the spot, so Joheved headed toward a storage cabinet in the main hall. "Do you prefer one in particular or do you blow them all?" She beckoned her daughter to follow.

When Hannah remained silent, Leah answered for her. "She blows all of them. Each one sounds different."

"How about this one?" Joheved selected a shofar at random.

Joheved wasn't sure Hannah would take it, but eventually her daughter grasped the ram's horn, holding it as if it were full of liquid that might spill. Leah hopped excitedly from one foot to the other as they waited for Hannah to slowly raise the shofar to her mouth. Joheved held her breath and prayed: *Please, mon Dieu, let her make a clear, strong sound.*

The noise was tentative at first, a cough followed by a sputter. Then Hannah took a deep breath and tried again. This time the shofar blasted a clarion call that echoed from the rafters, a clear, sweet tone that brought tears to Joheved's eyes.

Servants poured out of the kitchen, looking around wildly for the sound's source. Milo bolted through the front door and walked swiftly to Joheved's side. "What was that?"

Before she could answer, Rachel called from the stairs. "That was amazing. I didn't know you could blow the shofar, Joheved."

"I can't. It was Hannah."

"Blow it again," Rachel demanded.

Leah raced to the cabinet and returned with a longer ram's horn. "Blow this one."

The roomful of people exhaled in awe as another perfect note, deeper than the first, sounded and then slowly faded away.

"Go get the others, Leah." Rachel's eyes twinkled with anticipation. "Let's hear them all."

Hannah looked questioningly at Joheved, who smiled and nodded at Leah, already halfway to the cabinet. Each new shofar tone drew soft oohs and aahs from Hannah's audience, until Milo finally waved the servants toward the doors and declared, "Everyone return to your work. The entertainment is finished."

Joheved gave Hannah a big hug. "Whichever shofar you want, it is yours. Even one of the new ones."

"I can't wait for Meir and Papa to hear her," Rachel said.

"She's better than anyone else in our family."

"Hannah should blow it in synagogue." Leah clapped her hands with excitement.

"Only a man may blow the shofar in synagogue." Joheved's voice was emotionless.

Leah's face fell. "But why, Mama? She's better than the man who blows it there."

"*Oui*, Joheved," Rachel said with a saucy grin. "Tell her why?"

It was Hannah who answered her sister. "Don't you remember the Mishnah we studied? Where it says that women, children and slaves are exempt from the mitzvah of shofar?"

"But it says that children can blow it, to practice," Leah protested.

"Only boy children, because they will have to fulfill the commandment when they grow up." Joheved looked at Rachel, a small smile playing on her lips. "Maybe we can study what else the Talmud says about the commandments women are exempt from."

Rachel returned Joheved's smile. "What section did you have in mind?" There were several such discussions.

"Let's go to the source and study Tractate Kiddushin."

"Do you think your daughters are ready for such a complicated *sugia*?"

"Please, Mama, let us study Gemara with you and Aunt Rachel." Hannah tugged on her mother's sleeve. "We're ready."

"Miriam and I were about that age when Papa started teaching us, and it was hard," Joheved said. "But the girls can probably follow along if you and I study it together."

"I learned it years ago with Eliezer, but I think I can remember what Papa's *kuntres* says." Rachel nodded. "It will be interesting, and different, to study this with a woman."

"You won't need to remember Papa's *kuntres*. I have a copy," Joheved said proudly. "He gave it to me when I moved to Ramerupt so I wouldn't forget my learning."

"Let's start by reviewing the seventh Mishnah of the first chapter," Rachel said, her eyes shining with eagerness.

> "All time-bound positive mitzvot, men are obligated and women are exempt. All positive mitzvot that are not time-bound, men and women are both obligated. All negative mitzvot, time-bound or not, both men and women are obligated."

She turned to her nieces. "What questions do you have about this Mishnah?"

Hannah's hand shot up. "The Torah never mentions such a thing as time-bound positive mitzvot. So why should women be exempt from them?"

She was about to say more when Rachel stopped her. "Let Leah ask her question too."

"What is a time-bound positive mitzvah anyway?"

"Very good, Leah. That is the very first question our Rabbis asked," Joheved replied. "A time-bound positive mitzvah is one that must be done at a specific time. For instance . . ." She waited for her daughters to give examples.

"Blowing the shofar," Hannah said immediately. "We blow it at Rosh Hashanah. And sitting in the sukkah, and lighting the Hanukkah menorah—"

"Every mitzvah we do at holidays," Leah interrupted.

"But women aren't exempt from Passover," Rachel pointed out. "Or Shabbat for that matter." How would her nieces react to the contradiction?

The girls looked uncertain, and Joheved opened her father's *kuntres*. "Let's see how the Gemara answers your questions. Rachel and I will read it, but stop us if you have questions." She smiled at Leah. "See, the first thing here is your question:

> What are time-bound positive mitzvot? Sukkah . . . shofar . . . and tefillin."

"But tefillin aren't worn at any specific time," Hannah objected.

"Tefillin are only worn in the daytime," Rachel explained. "So they are considered time bound." When the girls nodded, albeit unenthusiastically, she said, "Now we'll see that the Gemara finds a problem with this:

> But is this rule always true? For we have matzah [at Passover] and rejoicing [on the three festivals] which are mitzvot done at a specific time and women are obligated. And there is Torah study . . . not time bound, yet women are exempt.

"In fact there are more time-bound positive mitzvot that women must perform today—eating matzah and drinking four cups of wine on Pesach, reading the Megillah at Purim, lighting the Hanukkah lamp, and observing Shabbat—than those we're exempt from," Rachel declared with a smile, recalling how vigorously she and Eliezer had debated this *sugia*.

"So how can it be a rule that women are exempt from them?" Leah asked.

Joheved showed them what Salomon had written: "Though the Mishnah teaches that women are generally exempt from time-bound positive mitzvot and obligated to perform those that are not time bound, it did not intend to make this law absolute."

Rachel nodded. "Now the Gemara is going to ask your question, Hannah.

> From where do we know this? [that women are exempt from time-bound positive mitzvot]. It is derived from tefillin. Because women are exempt from tefillin, they are also exempt from all time-bound positive mitzvot."

Rachel chuckled as both nieces started to object. "I see you have important questions, but let's finish the passage first.

> The exemption from tefillin is derived from Torah study. Because women are exempt from Torah study, so they are also exempt from tefillin.

"We know this because the verse in Deuteronomy commanding men to teach their sons, *benaichem*, Torah, but not their daughters, is immediately followed by the verse about tefillin. So our Sages link them."

"Grandpapa says that we have to translate *benaichem* as sons and not children," Hannah said bitterly. "But it's not fair. Not only are we exempt from studying Torah, we're exempt from all these other mitzvot too."

"Just because you're exempt doesn't mean you can't do them." Joheved tried to sound encouraging. "You're just not obligated to do them."

"Wait until we read further, Hannah," Rachel said. "You'll see that the Gemara tries very hard to make women obligated for time-bound positive mitzvot."

Sure enough, the next Sage rejected the Torah study/tefillin connection and argued that tefillin could just as well be compared to mezuzah, since the verse about mezuzah immediately follows the one about tefillin.

"That would make women obligated for tefillin like they're obligated for mezuzah," Hannah said triumphantly.

"Or it might make a woman exempt from mezuzah, and maybe all positive commandments," Rachel suggested, curious how her nieces would react to this disturbing idea.

Hannah and Leah's faces clouded, and Joheved shook her finger at Rachel. "Papa says it's impossible that women should be exempt from mezuzah, which prolongs our lives," Joheved explained. "He asks how anybody could even think that women don't need life as much as men do."

Rachel chuckled. "If Papa is right, then women should be obligated to study Torah, because it also gives us life and length of days."

Joheved rolled her eyes. "You and Papa can debate this until the Messiah comes." She turned to her daughters and said, "You two memorize what we studied today, and we'll do more tomorrow."

It took a week for Salomon's daughters and granddaughters to wade through the complicated debate of over thirty objections and responses. They were heartened as the Gemara's anonymous voice seemed determined to overturn the rule that exempted women from time-bound positive mitzvot.

It demanded proof that women were indeed exempt from sukkah, which it compared to Passover, and then argued that instead of deriving an exemption from "tefillin," you could instead derive an obligation to perform time-bound positive mitzvot from "rejoicing at festivals." Each time one of its contentions was rejected, along came another.

It was almost time for everyone to return to Troyes for Rosh Hashanah, when they abruptly came back to the Mishnah:

> All negative mitzvot, whether time-bound or not, both men and women are obligated.

Hannah and Leah looked at each other in surprise. Apparently the discussion of women and time-bound positive mitzvot was finished.

"So despite a great effort to demolish it, our Mishnah still stands," Joheved concluded. "Thus women are considered exempt from time-bound positive mitzvot."

"Yet we may perform them if we wish." Hannah's voice was firm. This year she would blow the shofar, not for her little sister in the forest, but for all her family to hear, in Troyes.

However, by the time Joheved's family arrived in Salomon's courtyard, the old ram tied behind Meir's horse, Hannah's determination had wavered. Samson's relatives were still there, as was Cousin Samuel and his father, Simcha. Judita's parents were constantly dropping by to see their new grandson and check how Rivka was feeling, and often Zipporah and her mother, Brunetta, visited as well. Hannah soon realized that all these people would be dining there on Rosh Hashanah, making the audience for her shofar blasts larger than she intended.

So she said nothing about the shofar when the midday meal was served—sheep stew with squash and leeks, pickled beets, whole fish fried with the heads still attached, followed by the magnificent ram's head, with its severed horns tied on.

Salomon explained that their menu was partly dictated by the Talmud, which said in two different tractates:

> At the beginning of the year one should prepare himself to eat squash, fenugreek, leek, beets, and dates.

"Just as some of these are sweet and some grow quickly, so too may we enjoy a sweet year when our possessions and luck grow."

But his dour expression belied his hopeful words, for Rivka was now too weak to dine at the table, even on a festival.

"We don't have dates," Miriam said. "So for sweetness we have raspberry preserves, apple tarts, and honey."

When the meal was finished, Meir stood up and Joheved handed him the ram's horn that had adorned their main dish earlier. With Rivka too ill to attend services, Joheved asked Meir to blow the shofar for her.

"Mama always looked forward to hearing it."

Skeptical of the unfamiliar ram's horn, Meir examined it carefully before saying the blessing, "*Baruch ata Adonai* . . . Who has commanded us to hear the sound of the shofar."

He took a sip of wine before bringing it to his lips. But unused to a different ram's horn, he sounded more like a donkey than a call for repentance. He cleared his throat and licked his lips to try again, but the result was no better.

"I guess I'll keep my old shofar." He handed the curly new one to Shmuel.

Shmuel tried his luck, but Rachel had to admit that even at his best, her nephew did sound like he was blowing his nose. She caught Joheved's eye and tilted her head in Hannah's direction. It was both frustrating and disappointing to endure such poor attempts when an expert was sitting at their table. Besides, since Mama was exempt from the mitzvah of shofar, it shouldn't matter if a girl sounded it.

When Joheved hesitated, Rachel's impatience flared. She grabbed the shofar from Shmuel and thrust it at her niece. "Hannah, let's hear how you blow it."

Hannah blushed to the roots of her hair and turned to Meir. "May I, Papa?"

Meir looked at Joheved, and when she nodded, he did so as well. But before she had the shofar halfway to her mouth, Salomon stood and addressed her. "You may blow the shofar if you wish, but don't make the blessing."

Joheved stood to face him. "But how can she perform the mitzvah without saying the blessing?"

"You know very well that women are exempt from shofar," he scolded her. "And since she is not commanded to do it, it would be a lie for her to say 'commanded us' when she does."

Hannah's chin began to quiver and Meir, faced with the choice of supporting his teacher against his wife and daughter, sided with the latter. "But Michal, the wife of King David, made the blessing when she wore tefillin."

Shmuel, to no one's surprise, supported Salomon. He was at the age when his parents were always wrong. "If she's not commanded, it's a useless blessing, which is prohibited."

"Yet if there's no Levi in the congregation, the Cohen who did the first blessing over the Torah reading blesses again." Judah's was the calmest voice so far. When Torah was read in synagogue, the first readings were reserved for Cohens and Levis, descendants of the ancient temple priesthood.

"If there's doubt about saying the Holy One's name unnecessarily, don't we learn in Tractate Berachot that if you're in the middle of Tefillah and you're not sure if you said all the blessings, you must go back to the beginning and repeat the prayer?" Rachel asked.

To see nearly his entire family, including his favorite daughter, aligned against him, was the last straw for Salomon. He slammed his fist down on the table, sending everyone to steady their dishes. "It is worse than a useless blessing for a woman to say 'commanded us'—it is *hilchul hashem*, a desecration of God's name."

The room was silent until Miriam said softly, "It's Rosh Hashanah. Surely fighting with one another is not how we want the Heavenly Court to fill the coming year."

Everyone exchanged guilty looks until Eliezer raised his wine cup. "I can think of nothing better than for our family to spend the next year arguing Torah together."

While the others offered similar toasts, Rachel leaned over and whispered to Miriam. "Why is Papa so upset? We've been laying tefillin for years and saying the blessing."

"How can you be so blind?" Miriam hissed. "The wine harvest was a disaster and Mama has been sick for over a year. Of course he's upset."

Rachel sat back as though her sister had punched her. Gazing across the table, where her father sat trembling, trying to control his rage, she was overcome with shame. Of course the heat and drought that made wheat so scarce had decimated the vineyard, leaving more raisins than grapes. And Mama's illness was getting worse.

She walked to his seat and hugged him. "Don't worry, Papa. Miriam and I will have more than enough profit from our wheat sales to make up for the poor vintage." Then she addressed the company. "There's no need for Hannah to make the shofar blessing. Meir has already said it."

Salomon patted her hand and sighed. "Though women are permitted to perform these time-bound mitzvot, and may certainly hear the shofar, blowing it is a man's responsibility, just as a man should be the one to do circumcisions."

"But Papa," Miriam began to protest.

"Obviously a woman may, indeed must, perform a brit milah when no competent man is available," Salomon continued. "But that's not the case with blowing a shofar; many men here are capable."

Rachel kept her arm around him and whispered, "Poor Papa. It must be difficult having daughters, and now granddaughters, who refuse to leave all the men's mitzvot to men."

His only response was a long sigh.

She prayed that despite all this tumult, Hannah would have the *kavanah* to blow this unfamiliar shofar well. And whether Rachel's prayer was answered or unnecessary, Hannah sounded the new shofar beautifully. Her listeners sighed with awe when she finished the complicated series of Rosh Hashanah blasts and the last long, clear note finally faded away.

Leave it to Shmuel to complain. "I understand that a woman is permitted to blow the shofar for another woman, but what if a man heard her from the street? He'd assume it was a man and think he'd fulfilled the mitzvah."

"And what if he heard a donkey braying and assumed it was you blowing the shofar?" Hannah shot back. "He'd also think he'd fulfilled the mitzvah."

When everyone stopped laughing, they launched into a discussion over what constituted fulfilling a mitzvah, who could perform one on another's behalf, and whether intent was necessary. This time nobody lost their temper, and the afternoon passed quite pleasantly.

That night Salomon's three daughters happily retired to bed with their husbands. According to the Rabbis, Rosh Hashanah was when the barren Sarah conceived Isaac and when the loved but barren wife Hannah conceived the prophet Samuel—which was why their stories from scripture were read in synagogue that day. Thus using the bed was considered a special mitzvah.

Miriam and Judah hadn't been intimate since her nearly lethal pregnancy with Alvina. But she wasn't *niddah*, so she was able to snuggle with Judah and, pleasurably anticipating the New Year, fall asleep in his arms. After years of teaching Hebrew to children and Notzrim, Miriam had acquired her first women pupils. During midwife training, Zipporah asked if Miriam would continue the Torah studies Joheved started with her. Of course Miriam agreed, and soon Brunetta, Francesca, and several other women joined them.

Rachel too was in a fine humor. Not only had Eliezer diffused a difficult situation to allow Hannah to blow the shofar, but Papa had shared a letter he'd received about Adam of Roanne, the drunken merchant who'd set the Evil Eye on her son Asher. The rogue had gone on one of his typical forays, following Duke Odo's raids and buying his men's pillaged items, but failed to return. There were no witnesses to his demise, but rumors abounded that he'd been killed either at the hands of those who goods were looted or by a greedy knight demanding a higher price than Adam was willing to pay.

The question to Salomon was from Adam's wife, claiming that she was now a widow with the right to remarry and to receive her *ketubah* from his estate. Obviously his captor would be demanding ransom if he were still alive.

"How did you answer her, Papa?" Rachel asked.

"Normally I'm sympathetic to a woman's plight if her husband died without witnesses. If there is only one witness, even a woman, I will accept that testimony and free the wife to remarry."

"But if a man were in a battle and didn't come back or wasn't captured, he must be dead," Rachel said. Surely Adam had finally gotten the end he deserved, and with his death, the curse he'd put on Salomon's family might be lifted.

"Adam had many enemies, so perhaps he disappeared in order to avoid them," Salomon replied. "Under the circumstances, I cannot accept his death without a witness."

"But what about his widow—I mean, his wife?"

"She enjoyed his ill-gotten gains for many years, and if she disapproved of his behavior and wished to dissociate herself from him, she had time to initiate a divorce." Salomon's voice was stern. "So now she must suffer the consequences."

Rachel appreciated her father's answer, but she thought Adam was likely dead, killed on the battleground. It gave her pleasure to imagine his corpse trampled by Odo's warhorses and buried ignominiously in some field, just retribution for the deaths of her and Joheved's little boys. But she said no more. This was not the time of year to boast about how unforgiving she was.

sixteen

oheved's feelings at the New Year were both happy and sad. Just before bedtime, she checked Mama's sickroom and was pleasantly surprised to find her mother awake. One would expect someone who ate as little as Mama to be thin; yet her chemise clung tightly around her swollen body.

"*L'shana tova*, Mama." Joheved bent down to kiss her. "How are you feeling?"

"I'm tired, always tired." Rivka took Joheved's hand with her puffy fingers. "I think this will be the last year I hear the shofar. I'm glad Meir blew it so beautifully; I could almost imagine the angels blowing it to welcome me to Gan Eden."

Joheved fought back tears and sat down at Mama's bedside. Should she divulge that it was Hannah? Mama was always so unhappy about her daughters wearing tefillin and studying Talmud; why upset her now? "I'm pleased you got to hear it."

Mama gave her a wan smile. "Don't tell your father I said so, but I think it's wrong that women are exempt from hearing the shofar. It doesn't take much time, nearly all of us are in synagogue anyway that day, and women also need to be remembered for life at Rosh Hashanah, not just men."

"I agree." Joheved recalled so many years spent upstairs with the women: how they cried and prayed during the shofar service for the Merciful One to remember them and their children, and for the New Year to be one of peace and prosperity.

"I may not get another chance, so I want to ask your forgiveness before Yom Kippur," Mama said between labored breaths.

"Of course I forgive you."

"But you haven't heard what you should forgive me for." Mama squeezed Joheved's hand tighter. "I'm sorry I fought you and your sister so hard over studying Talmud. You're good girls and it hasn't done you any harm. Maybe your learning even protected you from Lillit."

Joheved wiped away the tears running down her cheeks. Mama hadn't been this alert in months. "Maybe it did."

"So, do you forgive me?"

Joheved threw her arms around her mother. "I forgive you. And I ask your forgiveness for all the trouble and grief I caused you."

"Children are supposed to give their mother trouble and grief, especially daughters. But I forgive you . . . And tell your sisters that I forgive them too."

Joheved made her decision. She couldn't let Mama die thinking Meir had blown that shofar. "Mama, it wasn't Meir blowing the shofar for you. It was Hannah."

Mama chuckled softly. "Your father must have gotten angry."

"*Oui*, he did. But he calmed down eventually, like always."

"Thank Heaven for that. Otherwise I never could have lived with him."

Mama closed her eyes and lapsed into silence. Joheved watched her chest slowly rise and fall, and then quietly left the room. Meir was waiting in the hall.

He smiled and whispered, "After hearing about the new rams, I decided to pay them a visit and see for myself. I thought I'd revitalize your special mirror while I was there."

Twenty years earlier, Joheved's magic mirror had saved their marriage and led to the birth of their first child. She looked up at him and smiled. He was gazing at her with the expression that still, years later, could kindle her desire.

She blushed and whispered back, "I don't think you need any magic to strengthen your *yetzer hara*, but then again it couldn't hurt."

That night it seemed as though Meir had just returned from a journey, so quickly did he and Joheved rid themselves of their clothes and wrap their arms around each other. Meir half caressed, half massaged her naked back as they kissed hungrily. Soon his hands slipped around to her breasts, tweaking her nipples as her tongue fenced with his.

Though she was expecting it, the first flush of desire made her whimper, and when he continued to toy with her hardening nipples, her moans of pleasure grew stronger. Now his lips were on her neck, and the surging fire below made her squirm in his embrace.

Joheved's sensuous movements so close to his groin, coupled with thoughts of what he'd be doing next, soon had Meir fully aroused. He lifted her onto the bed and lay down beside her, his kisses forcing her head against the sheets, his hand fondling her breasts.

Joheved couldn't wait a moment longer. She pulled his hand down her belly, the ache below desperate for attention. Meir replaced his fingers on her nipple with his mouth, while his hand spread her thighs, stroking her gently. She rewarded him with more groans of delight.

Meir continued caressing her opening until his fingers were wet. But instead of entering immediately when her passion flared, he searched until he found the small knob where he knew she would be most sensitive. He drew slow circles around it with his index finger, noting with satisfaction as Joheved's breathing quickened and her hips thrust against his hand.

When he finally pulled his hand away, he knew she was expecting him to enter, and he smiled at her surprise when he stood up and pulled her sideways on the bed, her derriere at the edge. Then he knelt and rested her legs on his shoulders.

Joheved raised herself on her elbows. "Meir! What are you doing?"

"Just let me pleasure you." He began stroking the inside of her thighs as she fell back.

With her legs spread wide before him, Meir gently massaged her lower lips, bending closer so his tongue could reach that sensitive spot his fingers had so recently caressed. Eliezer said that it might be difficult to find, but Joheved's sudden squeals made it clear that Meir had found his goal.

Careful not to overstimulate her, he varied his technique. Circling with his tongue, moving from side to side, strongly and then more gently, he listened as Joheved gasped and moaned, trying to ascertain what she enjoyed the most. All the while his fingers were busy inside her damp passage, probing its depths, as his senses reveled in her intimate flavor and aroma.

For her part, Joheved was helpless to do anything except revel in the spiraling delight Meir's mouth was creating. Who could have imagined that her body was capable of such feelings? Ripples of exquisite sensation passed through her as Meir modified his efforts. Just when she thought she was going to explode with passion, he would pause and begin something new. She desperately wanted both the ultimate climax and for him to never stop.

Meir sensed that her release was near. Her secret place had grown round and hard, like a pearl, under his lashing tongue. Her lower lips were swollen and full, much like her nipples after he'd fondled them. He pressed his hand hard against the muscles inside her womb, waiting for her contractions.

Abruptly Joheved's cries reached a crescendo, as wave after wave of the ecstasy coursed through her. Mindless with rapture, she grabbed Meir's arms and squeezed them convulsively, while he forced his mouth to remain in position, leaning back only after she finally jerked her body away.

When Meir opened his eyes, he was glad they had forgotten to extinguish the lamp. He gazed in awe at Joheved's most private parts, glistening and plump like segments of apple dripping with honey. He'd never seen anything so erotic and exciting, and his loins responded immediately. He began lightly caressing her thighs, then kissing her flesh closer and closer to the crease where her leg met her torso.

Joheved lay exhausted, her heart pounding, focused on the receding spasms of pleasure. She was sure she wouldn't be able to move for hours. Her breasts and *ervah* were still pulsing when she felt Meir's lips on her leg, so gentle at first that she might have imagined it. But as the sensation moved up her thigh, her desire flared so intensely that before she knew it she'd dragged Meir up on top of her.

More delights awaited her. Meir had barely entered before she was at the zenith once again, urging him to move faster and deeper. As she reached a new climax, he found that, for the first time, he was able to restrain himself while her womb convulsed around him. When he began moving within her again, he allowed himself to fully savor the sensation, confident that when his passion was about to overwhelm him, his vigorous thrusts would force Joheved to emit her seed as well.

Finally it was over and Joheved lay limp in his arms, her heart beating wildly and her body damp with sweat. How was it possible that after twenty years of marriage, they should discover something so new and wonderful?

She somehow found the strength to reach over and brush his lips with hers. "*Merci beaucoup*. That was magnificent."

Meir chuckled and replied, "My pleasure."

As Rachel forecast, when Eliezer returned to Troyes for the Cold Fair, he brought back sufficient grain profits to more than offset Salomon's dismal vintage.

"I was lucky to get out of Mayence without injury," he told her that night. "Wheat was so scarce that we could name our price, but buyers resented having to pay that much for it."

"They should have been grateful you had any wheat at all. If not for your shipments, the famine would have been worse."

"Most didn't see it that way. They were angry that we took advantage of their suffering to make more money."

Rachel's curls shook with exasperation. "They probably think you should have donated the wheat out of charity, never mind all your trouble and expense procuring it."

"Logic had nothing to do with it," he replied. "There was such rancor over Jews profiteering while 'good Christians' went hungry that I came through Worms on my way back from Prague rather than face anyone in Mayence again."

"The bishop was probably charging just as much for his wheat."

"Of course he was, but nobody's going to complain about the bishop—at least not out loud."

When Rachel remained silent, Eliezer saw his chance to say what he'd been thinking about the entire ride home. He pulled her close and dropped his voice seductively. "Belle, I hate being away from you. Come with me to Toledo."

Rachel's heart leapt with joy. "What about the children?"

"Shemiah should remain to continue his studies, but we can bring little Rivka if you'd like."

Rachel thought back to their early journeys, how inhibited she'd felt with Shemiah sharing their room and often occupying their bed. And yet the one season she'd left Shemiah with Eliezer's mother, he hadn't recognized her when they returned.

"I don't know," she said slowly.

"You'll only be gone a few months." He pulled her close. "Let Miriam take care of your clients and help in the vineyard. After all, you shouldered her responsibilities last summer while she was in Paris."

"I didn't mean I don't know about going with you." She gazed up at him and smiled. "I miss you so much when we're separated; I just don't know whether we should take Rivka or not."

"You can decide that when it's time to leave." He bent down to kiss her.

But Rachel had already made up her mind. If she weren't enceinte by the end of Hanukkah, she would leave her daughter with Miriam and accompany her husband the following week when the Cold Fair closed. Little Rivka was almost four years old; she wouldn't forget her mother so easily.

To avoid the Evil Eye, Rachel divulged her plans to Miriam alone.

"Of course your children will stay with me. Alvina would be lost without Rivka to play with," Miriam said. "While you're away, I can begin teaching her how to read and write."

Rachel threw her arms around Miriam. "*Merci*, you are the most wonderful sister." Though they were alone, she lowered her voice and added, "Maybe Adam's curse won't reach as far away as Toledo, and I'll get pregnant."

Miriam smiled conspiratorially. "It's either broken or it didn't reach to Ramerupt. Joheved's expecting another child this summer," she whispered.

"So that's why she goes to bed early rather than study Talmud with us," Rachel said. "But are you sure? I thought her flowers had stopped."

"I'm a midwife; I can tell. But just to be safe, don't speak of it to anyone, please."

Meir knew very well that his wife was with child. When Joheved greeted the first week of Troyes Cold Fair by throwing up each morning and then eating a hearty *disner*, he calculated that their new son should arrive shortly after Shavuot.

Of course they would have a son. Joheved had emitted her seed first every time. And if, as the Talmud taught, a child's quality reflected the quality of the act that conceived him, this boy would surely grow to be a *talmid chacham*. But Meir said nothing of this, keeping the blissful knowledge inside, where it warmed him better than any hearth during those chilly autumn days.

Each night, as she kindled another wick in their Hanukkah menorah, Rachel grew increasingly uneasy about going to Toledo. Eight years had passed, but she recalled her previous visit well. Isolated at home like the Sephardic women, her only companion had been little Shemiah. True, Eliezer shared her bed at night, which was a mighty consolation, and she had no nagging anxieties about his safety in some faraway place. The price she would pay for enjoying those pleasures this time would be her constant worries about Papa and Mama's health, no Talmud study with her sisters, and missing her children for six months.

But when her flowers arrived the day before their departure, Rachel put her concerns aside and packed her things. That night she slept with little Rivka, holding her daughter securely in her arms, and the next morning at dawn she was overcome with guilt at her daughter's tears and wails of protest as she and Eliezer joined a band of Jewish merchants heading southwest.

Their caravan was enlarged by pilgrims on their way to Santiago de Compostela, which gave Rachel the company of enough women that she no longer felt like an oddity. They had just passed through the Pyrenees, thankfully without experiencing a blizzard, when she realized that her seven clean days were finished. But it was too cold for her to immerse in the local rivers, so she and Eliezer abandoned the others and made for Saragossa. The large Jewish community there was sure to have a *mikvah*.

Luxuriating in the sumptuous bathhouse that housed the *mikvah*, while a masseuse kneaded the muscles that ached from too many long days on horseback, Rachel began to anticipate her six months in Sepharad. Perhaps it wouldn't be so bad after all. Papa had given her a copy of Tractate Nedarim, one of the few he hadn't written a commentary on, with instructions to go through each page and jot down anything he ought to address. Surely that would keep her occupied during the day.

The Jewish Quarter was overflowing with refugees fleeing Berber attacks in the south, but Eliezer's old host Dunash still had space in his house, located just off Calle del Ángel, the main thoroughfare. Like other homes in Toledo, the whitewashed walls facing the street had no windows, and the entry door opened into a hallway that immediately turned right, thus presenting any curious passersby with a blank wall.

Standing in the tiled entry hall, Rachel knew that the austere exterior was a facade, and that the interior rooms would open onto a central courtyard. But Dunash's beautiful patio was quite unlike Papa's utilitarian outdoor space in Troyes. Its walls were covered with flowering vines, and a path wandered among bushes and fruit trees to the well in the center, which fed a fountain surrounded by a shallow pool. Benches sat scattered along the path, and Rachel imagined herself studying Tractate Nedarim on one of them, while the fountain gurgled pleasantly in the background.

She held her breath, waiting to see their chambers, hoping there would at least be a view of the garden. The apartment was small, just two rooms off one of the lesser salons. The tiny bedroom had no windows, but the sitting room did open onto the courtyard. Rachel sighed with relief; they could enter and exit their quarters without walking through the main house.

The next few days were heavenly. Daily downpours, for February was the height of Toledo's rainy season, prevented her from studying outside, but Eliezer arrived home shortly after sunset, and they spent much of the long nights in bed. But that was one of the few things they did together. Except on Shabbat, men and women dined separately, and at synagogue they entered through different doors. Once inside, the women's pews were hidden behind a wall with only a small grill looking into the sanctuary.

On their first Shabbat in Toledo, the afternoon skies cleared sufficiently that Eliezer took her to see one of the town's most prized sites, al-Zarqālī's water clock. Located in a wide plaza on the waterfront, the clock was fashioned out of marble and decorated with life-sized paintings of men and elephants. Rachel had to admit that it looked impressive shining in the sunlight.

"See those two basins?" Eliezer pointed to the large vessels, which were marked with many parallel lines. "Al-Zarqālī designed the clock so they fill and empty according to the waxing or waning of the moon."

"So?" Rachel saw nothing extraordinary happening.

"Pipes underneath the plaza lead to the river. At the moment the new moon appears on the horizon, water flows into the empty basins at a rate carefully calculated so that at dawn each basin contains one-fourth of a seventh part, and at sunset one-half a seventh part of the water required to fill them. The water continues to flow in this manner until a week has passed." He paused and looked at her questioningly.

"At which time both basins will be half full," Rachel said in awe, realizing that the clock's unseen mechanism was actually more impressive than its appearance.

"Over the next seven days and nights, this process continues until the two basins fill completely when the moon is at its fullest." Eliezer's voice became more animated. "Then on the fifteenth night of the month, just as the moon wanes, the basins begin to lose one-half of a seventh part of their water each day until . . ."

Rachel continued, "Until they are half empty on the twenty-first of the month and completely empty when the moon reaches her twenty-ninth night."

Eliezer led her to another, smaller, device nearby. "And this clock, by means of cleverly designed valves and pumps, fills and empties over the course of a day, so that by comparing the water level to the marks painted on it, we can see what hour it is." He pointed to the vessels, which were almost empty. "See, we have slightly more than two hours left until sunset."

"And only five more days until the full moon," Rachel added. She stopped and stared at Eliezer. Her flowers, which usually came on the tenth of the month, hadn't arrived.

She said nothing of this and asked instead, "These water clocks are remarkable devices, but why were they made?"

Eliezer, thinking she'd asked how they were made, began explaining, "The clock is constructed so that water drips out at a constant rate, and its mechanism is then calibrated so that it measures how much time has passed."

"I realize that." She cut him off. "What I want to know is why someone would go to all this effort to tell what hour it is when we can just wait for the church bells to chime."

"But they only chime every three hours."

"Why do I need to know when it's one hour past noon?" She glanced over at the clock's display. "Or two hours until sunset? And if for some reason I did, what's wrong with using a sundial?"

As if in reply, the sun disappeared behind a cloud and Eliezer looked at her triumphantly. "With a water clock you can tell the hour even on a cloudy day or at night."

Rachel still didn't see any great urgency to know the time so precisely, but clearly Eliezer thought this was important. "But why create the big one? Surely they have calendars here."

"The Saracens declare a new month when they see the new moon, but if it's overcast, they can rely on al-Zarqālī's water clock." The clouds were darkening precipitously, so he took her arm, adding, "We'd better head back."

She tried to remember how they'd reached the plaza, and though she recognized the landmarks they passed, the twisting, mazelike streets thwarted her efforts. The only route she could negotiate on her own was the short distance from the main road to their lodgings. How long would she have to live in Toledo before she wouldn't feel so lost?

Raindrops began splattering on the cobblestones, causing Eliezer to increase their pace. But Rachel's mind was still in the plaza. "Why do you care so much what time it is?"

"For those of us studying at al-Zarqālī's observatory, charting how stars move, we must have the ability to measure time precisely. We have clocks there that are accurate to the smallest portion of an hour."

For a moment Rachel was too shocked to speak. "You're studying astronomy? What happened to your Talmud studies?"

"Here in Sepharad, Talmud expertise is not sufficient for a man to be considered learned," he defended himself. "Unless a man also knows philosophy, mathematics, and astronomy, the Spaniards judge him ignorant."

"But everything a man needs to know is in the Talmud; secular subjects take time away from Torah study." *What have these people done to my husband, replacing his Torah knowledge with astronomy?*

Eliezer shook his head. "*Non*, in the seventh chapter of Tractate Shabbat, Rabbi Shimon ben Pazzi said in the name of Rabbi Yehoshua ben Levi:

> He who knows how to calculate the solstices and planetary motions, but does not, of him it is written: They regard not the work of the Eternal, neither have they considered the work of His hands. Rabbi Samuel ben Nahmani said in the name of Rabbi Yohanan: Where do we know that it is a mitzvah for a person to calculate the solstices and planetary motions? Because it is written: For this is wisdom and understanding in the sight of the people. And what wisdom and understanding is in the sight of the people? It is the science of calculating the solstices and planetary motions."

But Rachel only saw Eliezer's Torah knowledge draining away, like the water in al-Zarqālī's clock, to be replaced with foreign philosophy, mathematics, and astronomy.

Eliezer could tell that she was unconvinced. "Belle, I'm not giving up Talmud. As Rabbi Elazar ben Chisma said in Pirke Avot:

> The laws of bird offerings and *niddah* are essential halachah. Astronomy and geometry are the spices of wisdom.

Torah is like bread—you must have it. But people like me need spices with their bread."

"Yet if you only eat spices, you will starve."

Their argument came to an abrupt halt when the skies opened and they had to race home to escape the downpour. Even so, their clothes were soaked when they got indoors, and after quickly disrobing, conversation gave way to a more pleasant way to pass what remained of the stormy afternoon.

Rachel attempted to explore her surroundings the next day, but twice she had to pay a boy on the street to return her to Calle del Ángel. After accidentally venturing onto streets where women weren't welcome, she discovered that the best way to escape her neighborhood was to attend funerals. Death, regretfully, made no distinction between men and women.

The Jewish cemetery was located outside the city, and consequently most funerals proceeded along Calle del Ángel on their way to Jews' Gate, Toledo's northernmost exit. Rachel could hear the wailing and chanting of psalms as a funeral party drew near, enabling her to throw on a black cloak and follow them. Then, when the rite was finished, it was a simple matter to join someone heading back in her direction.

It seemed odd that mourners dressed in black: she couldn't help but imagine a procession of monks and nuns. Nowhere else did people wear special clothes to a funeral. But that was the custom in Toledo, and with a Jewish population of five thousand, there were enough funerals to make owning a black outfit a necessity.

Strange also was Toledo's custom of burying the dead in their shrouds, eschewing coffins. The first time Rachel saw a funeral procession, the corpse carried high above it, she'd stopped and stared in horror. A light drizzle caused the woman's body to be clearly outlined under the damp shroud. But more upsetting were all the precious objects deposited in the grave. She didn't know which was worse—women buried with jewelry or men entombed with their books. It was clear that the Jews of Toledo needed to study fewer secular subjects and more Talmud; the Sages strongly objected to such a wasteful practice.

On the day of the full moon, with a sky so clear she didn't need al-Zarqālī's clock to advise her of the date, her flowers began. That night Eliezer didn't return until it was almost dawn, and the next day, Friday, he reminded her that women in Sepharad didn't attend synagogue while they were *niddah*.

Rachel was outraged. "Even on Shabbat?" There was no point in asking why—the reason wouldn't matter anyway.

"That's the tradition here."

"But I'm a stranger." She smiled slyly. "How will they know I'm *niddah*?"

"If you go to services every week, without eventually appearing pregnant, someone will notice. Besides, you and I would know, and we have no right to violate their rules."

Eliezer's tone of voice made it clear that he would not allow her to accompany him the next morning. So Rachel pretended to acquiesce and stayed in bed until he left for services. Once the house was quiet, she dressed and hurried to Calle del Ángel, where she didn't have to wait long before a group of well-dressed women and children passed her, heading up the hill. None looked familiar, so she followed them.

Toledo had at least a dozen synagogues; she could go to a different one each Shabbat when she was *niddah*, and no one would be the wiser—so long as she returned home before Eliezer.

Rachel had counted on the women returning the same way after services, but when they turned to walk farther up the hill instead, she realized her mistake. They were likely dining elsewhere and wouldn't be coming home for hours. In a panic Rachel hurried downhill, hoping against hope that she'd find her way. Confident that the women would lead her back to Calle del Ángel, she'd paid little attention to their route. And since it was the Sabbath, she carried no coins with which to pay a guide.

It was past noon when she finally reached her lodgings, and she desperately needed to change her *mokh* and the wool in her *sinar*. Eliezer had to be home already, and he'd know she was lying if she said she'd merely been taking a walk.

She stood in the courtyard and steeled herself for another argument with her husband. But before she felt composed, two figures stood up from one of the benches and walked in her direction. One of them was Eliezer, but the other was . . .

Mon Dieu. What is Milo doing here?

seventeen

ilo stepped forward, his features etched with sympathy. "My lady Joheved sent me. Mistress Rachel, your mother is very ill and wants to see you . . . before she dies."

Rachel staggered backward. Milo took a moment to realize that Eliezer wasn't going to steady her, and then reached for her arm. "Are you able to leave tomorrow?"

Tears filling her eyes, Rachel gave Eliezer a questioning look. It would be a week until she could immerse, too long to delay. Unless he left with her, she wouldn't even be able to hug him good-bye.

"I must stay in Toledo." Eliezer gazed at her pleadingly. "The winter caravan from Maghreb hasn't arrived yet."

Rachel nodded weakly. Of course she had to return to Troyes, no matter how much she preferred to stay with her husband.

Eliezer turned to Milo. "You'll have to escort my wife for me, but I don't see how you can stay at any inns if you are to protect both her person and her reputation." It was unthinkable that Milo should share Rachel's room; yet it would not be safe for her to sleep alone either.

"My lady's father prepared me for that eventuality. He recommended several Jewish communities on our return route where we may obtain hospitality, especially on the Sabbath, and I have a list of convents as well."

"Convents?" Rachel's eyebrows rose in surprise.

"*Oui*. Most have guest quarters for ladies. Since all good Christians are fasting from meat for Lent, you needn't worry about forbidden foods."

"I see your return was carefully planned," Eliezer said, buffeted with conflicting feelings.

While he didn't like his wife traveling alone with the handsome young steward, he consoled himself that Milo was too smitten with Joheved to attempt to seduce her sister. And though he would greatly miss Rachel's sweet company, he felt a guilty relief at being able to spend clear nights at the observatory without feeling he was neglecting his wife. Now when Shavuot arrived and he finally had to leave, he and Abraham bar Hiyya might have sufficient results from their surveillance of the heavens to prove that Ptolemy's planetary orbits were incorrect.

Bundled in furs, Rachel left with Milo early the next morning. The palfrey Eudes bequeathed her had no trouble keeping up with Milo's mount, and the two travelers covered far more ground each day than Rachel and Eliezer had done in the other direction. There was no difficulty finding Jews to house them in Sepharad and Provence, but as they rode further into Aquitaine, Rachel found herself sleeping with nuns as well.

Oddly enough there were more clerics than Jews on the road, so many that often every table at a roadside inn was occupied when Rachel and Milo arrived for *disner*. Between the stink of cooked fish and a roomful of men who never bathed, Rachel was in no mood to tarry.

"In all my travels, I've never seen such a multitude of churchmen, and their retainers, on the move," Rachel complained when they were finally seated.

"It was just as crowded on my way to Toledo," he said. "Pope Urban has called a church council to meet at Piacenza in early March."

"It must be important."

Milo shrugged. "I've shared all my meals with men going to Piacenza, clerics and laymen, and none expect anything unusual—King Henry's wife will complain about his affairs, various heresies will be condemned, the false pope Clement and his supporters will be denounced, and Urban will again prohibit any payment to priests for baptisms or burials. The most interesting item on the agenda should be the ambassadors from King Philip, who will attempt to appeal his excommunication for marrying Bertrade."

Rachel didn't find these topics remotely interesting. She helped herself to more stew and retreated into her own thoughts. Joheved wouldn't have sent Milo all this distance unless Mama was seriously ill. Or was this just another task to take Milo away from Ramerupt? *What if the Angel of Death comes for Mama before I get home?*

Rachel was pondering whether she'd be more relieved or disappointed to miss her mother's funeral, when Milo stood up. "It's starting to snow," he said. "We'd better leave if we want our horses saddled without delay."

They watched the sky anxiously as they rode north, dreading the sudden darkening that would be a blizzard's first warning. "Perhaps we should head for Limoges instead of Clermont?" Milo suggested.

"Absolutely not." Rachel shuddered. "When some evil liar of a monk accused the Jews there of plotting with Saracens to destroy some church in Jerusalem, the bishop of Limoges insisted his Jews convert, and then expelled them when they wouldn't."

"The convent of Aubeterre is just outside Clermont," Milo said. "We'll stop there if we can't make the city before dark."

He wisely said nothing of the rumors surrounding the Church of the Holy Sepulchre's destruction. Saracens had physically razed the structure, but some believed that Frankish Jews had instigated it. Milo had heard that the Jews of Orléans were responsible. But that was over fifty years ago. The Church of the Holy Sepulchre had been rebuilt and pilgrims continued to worship there.

"Milo, I appreciate your efforts on my behalf, coming all the way to Toledo to bring me home safely." Rachel was glad to change the topic. "You have done my sister another great service."

His expression became wary. "I am your sister's steward: it is my responsibility to fulfill her requests."

"We both know your devotion goes beyond mere service."

"If you are trying to trick me into breaking my vow, you won't succeed." He gave her an icy stare.

"I'm sorry, Milo. I had no intention of testing you." She was instantly contrite. "I was so worried about my mother that I forgot."

To ease his concerns, she dropped the subject. "I hope it doesn't snow too heavily." Tomorrow was Friday and she'd rather not spend the Sabbath in a nunnery.

* * *

Neither rain nor snow fell as they headed north, but the slush and mud slowed the horses sufficiently that Rachel had no choice but to stop in Chapes the following Friday afternoon. There she seethed with frustration at being so close to Troyes yet unable to reach the city until Sunday.

But Milo wasn't bound by Jewish Law.

"Your horse is stronger than mine," she urged him. "You must ride on to Troyes and let my family know I'm almost home."

"I'll get there as fast as I can," he promised. "And then I'll hurry back to bring you the news."

Rachel fretted out an anxious Shabbat, consoled only by the knowledge that her mare would be well rested for the final leg of the journey. Her hosts were lighting the lamps when she heard the sound of horse's hooves outside. She took one step toward the door when it opened, and Milo's relieved visage was illuminated.

He addressed Rachel before she could ask the dreaded question. "Your mother is very weak, but she still lives."

Rachel sank back into her seat, tears of gratitude spilling down her cheeks. The next morning she ate hastily but refused to rush her morning prayers, including a lengthy plea for her mother's health. She and Milo were halfway to Troyes when rain began to fall and the horses' pace slowed on the muddy road. It seemed like hours before she could hear the city's bells chiming noon in the distance, and her stomach growled in complaint at the meal she was missing.

It was still raining when they entered the city, so Rachel was not alarmed to find her family's courtyard uninhabited. She trudged into her parents' kitchen and threw off her dripping cloak.

"*Mon Dieu!*" one of the new maidservants shrieked, staring at Rachel as if she'd seen a ghost.

The other girl grabbed Rachel's sleeve to prevent her from leaving the kitchen. "What a time to return," she muttered.

Rachel shook her off and, terrified of what she would find there, bolted for her mother's sickroom—which was empty.

"Where is she?" Rachel screamed at the cowering maids.

Milo handed Rachel her cloak. "The servants say she is being buried as we speak. If you hurry you can reach the cemetery in time. I must return to Ramerupt to manage things while my lord and lady are mourning here."

Rachel was too numb with shock to protest as Milo propelled her outside. Mama dead? It wasn't possible. Didn't Milo see her alive yesterday? Rachel railed at the heavens: couldn't the Angel of Death have waited just one more day?

The streets in the Jewish Quarter were empty, every shutter closed. It couldn't be the rain; they must be at Mama's funeral. Mama, who had no money to finance trading journeys or make large donations to charity; who didn't curry favor with the wealthy and powerful women in the community. Quiet, pious Mama who never left home except to attend services and shop for food. Yet where else could everyone have gone?

Rachel splashed through the muddy streets, grateful she was wearing her traveling clothes. *Mon Dieu*—her clothes. She must do *kriah* and tear them as a sign of her grief. Papa taught that a mourner who doesn't do *kriah* is punished with death. She ducked into a doorway, trying to remember the Baraita from Tractate Moed Katan that explained how a woman did *kriah* for a parent.

> For all dead, even if he has ten shirts on, he tears only the outer one. For his father and mother, he does *kriah* on them all . . . both a man and a woman. Rabbi Shimon ben Elazar says: A woman tears her chemise first and turns it backwards; then she tears her outer garment.

Outdoors in the rain, Rachel had no intention of following Shimon ben Elazar, especially since the Sages in Moed Katan also taught:

> For all the dead, he may baste the tear after shiva and sew completely after *sheloshim*; but for his father and mother, he may baste after *sheloshim*, but may never sew it completely. However, a woman may baste immediately (after the burial) for her modesty.

Clearly this disagreed with Shimon ben Elazar, because a woman whose torn chemise was hidden wouldn't need to baste her clothes immediately to protect her modesty. It was also clear that Rachel couldn't arrive at her mother's burial with her clothes intact. She was already standing, the posture Jewish Law required for performing *kriah*, so she reached for her *bliaut*'s neckline, took a deep breath, and ripped it down as far as she could.

The noise shocked her with its destruction, and Rachel staggered at the knowledge that, just as this cloth had been torn apart and would never be repaired, so had her mother been torn forever from her life. Tears spilling down her cheeks, she tore her chemise, then wrapped her cloak tightly around her and raced up rue de la Cité toward the Près Gate that led to the Jewish cemetery.

Her shoes and hose were soaked by the time she reached the crowd, and she sobbed with relief that they were still praying. Her cries were loud enough that those in the back twisted around in curiosity, and immediately a passage formed for her. Between her tears and the rain, she could hardly see, and the next thing she knew her son, Shemiah, was leading her to the graveside.

Her arrival interrupted the heart of the funeral service, the Justification of Judgment. The hazzan hesitated in confusion and remained silent as she sank weeping into her father's arms, Miriam and Joheved quickly joining the embrace. The four of them wept together until Papa finally looked up and realized everyone was waiting.

With the newcomer one of the three principle mourners, the hazzan nodded in unspoken understanding and started over. He turned to face Jerusalem, and Rachel choked back sobs to join him, her family, and all the community in reciting the verses from Deuteronomy that affirmed the rightness of the Creator's disposition of humanity.

> He is our Rock, His work is perfect; for all His ways are judgment; a God of truth and without iniquity, right and just is He . . . Great in counsel and mighty in deeds, Your eyes are open to all the ways of men . . .

The mourners would say this prayer three times a day during shiva, the first seven days of mourning.

As the funeral cortege prepared to exit the cemetery, Rachel reached down, snatched a handful of mud and grass, inhaled its earthy odor, and threw it over her shoulders while reciting the words from Psalms:

"They shall flourish like grass of the field.
Remember that we are dust."

When everyone attending the funeral had done the same, Mama's soul would be permitted to leave her body yet prevented from returning home with the mourners. According to Tractate Sanhedrin, those buried during a rainstorm are assured atonement, and thus Rachel felt confident that Mama, who had few sins to atone for, would quickly find peace in Gan Eden.

Inside the courtyard, bowls of water were set out for the community to wash their hands, another precaution against *ruchot* entering the house. Mourners were forbidden to wear shoes, and Rachel thankfully left her muddy boots at the door next to her sisters'. She may have missed being there when Mama took her last breath, but at least she had made it back for the burial.

It seemed impossible that everyone attending the funeral could fit in the house, but no one dared return home directly from the cemetery, because of the *ruchot* that would follow them. So the visitors squeezed into Salomon's to eat and stay a while, waiting for the *ruchot* to give up and leave. They watched in silence as Rivka's daughters ate their meal of consolation, dishes prepared by the community since mourners are forbidden to eat their own food.

Rachel hadn't eaten since breakfast, but she had no appetite. Still she emulated Joheved and Miriam when each took one of the boiled eggs. Papa once explained that mourners eat eggs after a funeral because eggs are round and have no mouth—round just as everything comes around in life, and no mouth just as mourners are quiet, accepting the Holy One's judgment.

Rachel struggled to choke down her egg, after which Miriam reached over to embrace her. "I'm so glad you are home." Jews learn from Job that no one addresses mourners until they speak first, so this was the signal the community was waiting for. Now words of consolation flowed.

It was well past sunset, with her children tucked into bed, before Rachel was finally able to be alone with her sisters. Upstairs in their old bedroom, Rivka's three daughters were not quite ready to share their feelings about her death, but there were other, less-difficult, subjects to talk about.

"I left the very day Milo found me in Toledo." Tears of frustration trailed down Rachel's cheeks. "But I still couldn't get here before Mama died. The roads were terrible, and of course I couldn't travel on Shabbat."

"We understand," Miriam said soothingly. "Milo told us."

Rachel turned to her older sister. "You must do something to reward him, Joheved. Eliezer wasn't happy about me traveling alone with him, but despite all his opportunities Milo never attempted any advances on my person. And he always found us a safe place to stay."

"I'm sure he doesn't expect a reward, but I can speak to Meir about it."

"We were worried that he wouldn't be able to find you," Miriam said. "And that you wouldn't get home in time."

"Did Mama have any pain at the end?" Rachel asked, afraid of the answer. She felt shame both for missing Mama's deathbed and for feeling relief at having avoided it.

"*Non*," Joheved replied. "She was barely conscious these last few weeks."

"But when Milo returned, she woke up enough to leave you a message." Miriam turned to Rachel, who stared back with trepidation. "Mama's last words were for you to take care of Papa."

Rachel gulped. "Surely she asked you both the same thing."

Joheved shook her head. "She asked me to interrupt my mourning to celebrate this baby's birth, and if it's a boy, Meir and I must prepare banquets for his brit milah no less sumptuous than for her other grandsons."

"She told me not to delay Yom Tov's betrothal on her account," Miriam said.

"Yom Tov's betrothal?" Rachel stared at her sister in bewilderment. What else had happened while she was gone?

"When we were in Paris last summer, several families approached us," Miriam replied. "Judah's brother, Azariel, did some investigating and then invited Yom Tov to spend Passover week with him, so he can meet potential brides."

"Shmuel is going with him," Joheved said. "They can accompany our wine casks and ensure their kosher status." Her face fell slightly and she sighed. "It will be my first Passover without all the children."

Rachel exchanged a furtive glance with Miriam, who had to be remembering that terrible Passover she'd spent without her children, sick with the pox in Paris. But Miriam was thinking of their mother.

"We have to expect our children to grow up and leave us eventually." Miriam's chin began to quiver. "It will be our first Passover without Mama."

"It will be Papa's first Passover without her since they were married," Rachel said, overwhelmed that Mama had singled her out to care for him. Had Mama finally accepted Rachel's special place in Papa's heart? She couldn't have worried that Joheved and Miriam would neglect him. Rachel sighed. Probably Mama wanted to guarantee that she wouldn't return to Toledo after *sheloshim* but would stay in Troyes with Papa.

Joheved yawned. "If you don't mind, Rachel, I need to go to sleep. Miriam and I were up all night, guarding Mama's body."

Rachel felt another stab of guilt and quickly let her sisters prepare for bed. Tired as she was, Rachel had to see how Papa was doing first. Downstairs, he seemed well comforted by Judah, Yom Tov, and Shmuel, while Meir was deep in conversation with Samuel and Simcha de Vitry. When she heard Talmud mentioned, she stopped to listen. Anything to delay going to bed and wondering what was behind Mama's haunting last words.

"Did you know that the Justification of Judgment prayer comes from the Talmud?" Meir asked.

"Isn't it from Deuteronomy?" his nephew responded.

"The beginning is, but the reason we recite it at funerals and during mourning comes from Tractate Avodah Zarah."

After Salomon told him of Rabbi Meir and Beruria's tragic fate, Meir had read a page earlier in the Gemara and learned how Beruria's parents had suffered their deaths.

Simcha leaned forward. "Teach it to us . . . if it isn't too long."

"Of course," Meir said.

> "They (the Roman tribunal) brought in Rabbi Hanina ben Tradion and asked him: Why have you occupied yourself with Torah? He replied [quoting Deuteronomy]: 'Thus Adonai, my God commanded

> me.' At once they sentenced him to be burnt, his wife to be slain, and his daughter to a brothel.

"Not Beruria, Rabbi Meir's wife, but Rabbi Hanina's other daughter," Meir quickly explained when he saw their shocked expressions.

> "As the three went out, they declared the righteousness of Divine judgment. Hanina recited: *The Rock, His work is perfect, for all His ways are just.* His wife continued: *A God of truth and without iniquity, true and upright is He.* And the daughter quoted: *Wondrous in purpose and mighty in deed, Your eyes observe all the ways of men . . .* Rebbi said: How great were these righteous ones, in that these three verses, acknowledging submission to Divine justice, occurred to them exactly at the appropriate moment."

Simcha and Samuel, both of whom had lost beloved wives in childbirth, sighed sadly at the inscrutability of the Holy One's ways. Rachel trudged upstairs to try to acknowledge her own loses.

One week later, at the end of shiva, Rachel wasn't at all sure that Papa needed to be taken care of. Rivka's grandchildren lamented her loss more than he did, and if he shed any tears, she hadn't seen them. His grief was clearly not great enough to stop him from teaching Talmud.

"Thirty days is too long for my students to remain idle," he declared. "However, since this is a house of mourning we will refrain from whatever makes one rejoice, including the study of Torah, because the Nineteenth Psalm reads:

> The precepts of Adonai are right, rejoicing the heart."

His students stared in confusion, and Salomon continued, "Thus our Sages allow a mourner to study the sorrowful sacred texts—the books of Job, Lamentations, and Jeremiah, or those passages of Talmud dealing with mourning in Tractate Moed Katan and the Temple's destruction in Tractate Gittin."

Salomon picked a nonmourner, the orphan Samson ben Joseph, to read a Mishnah from the third chapter of Moed Katan.

> "These are prohibited to a mourner: He is forbidden to work, to bathe, to perfume himself, to have marital relations, and to wear shoes."

Salomon looked around the room. "Does this Mishnah give rise to any questions?" Several hands rose and Salomon called on his oldest student.

"Who precisely is a mourner?" Simcha de Vitry asked. "I recall that there was a question about Meir mourning his sister."

Salomon nodded and addressed the room. "Will one of our younger students please recite from Leviticus what the Holy One said to Moses concerning the dead that priests may defile themselves for?"

Before a boy could speak, Hannah answered confidently,

> "Speak to the priests, the sons of Aaron, and say to them: None shall defile himself for the dead among his people except for his kin that are near to him—his mother, his father, his son, his daughter, and his brother; also for a virgin sister that is near to him and has no husband."

Salomon may not have expected to hear a feminine voice, but he displayed no displeasure and nodded again. "These are the relatives we must mourn by refraining from the activities our Mishnah prohibits."

Several of Salomon's pupils looked questioningly at him, who was mourning his wife though Moses had not mentioned a spouse. So he addressed their concerns.

"The Sages interpret 'his kin' to denote his wife, and they also include a married sister if she has not moved to a distant location."

When Salomon said no more, Meir added, "We also mourn for those whom our relatives are mourning. Thus because a man is required to mourn for his wife and she for her parents, he also mourns his in-laws."

"The most severe restrictions apply to those who mourn a parent," Salomon continued. "As we also learn in Moed Katan:

> For all the dead, he may remove his shoes or not; for his father or mother, he removes his shoes . . . For all the dead, he may cut his hair after *sheloshim*; for his father and mother, only after his friends complain how he looks. For all the dead, he may attend a celebration after *sheloshim*; for his father or mother, only after twelve months."

Everyone looked at Joheved, who would hopefully need to celebrate a brit milah in several months. She, along with Miriam and Rachel, had agreed to the stringency of not participating in the Talmud discussion, except as observers.

"The Sages disagree on whether this includes banquets accompanying a mitzvah like a marriage or circumcision," Judah said. "Some permit mourners to attend and some prohibit this."

"In my wife's case . . ." Salomon paused, and Rachel saw tears glistening in his eyes. "She specifically requested that our daughters celebrate any such mitzvah that occurs in our family."

Her father's grief brought only a mist of sympathetic moisture to Rachel's eyes. She was overwhelmed with contradictory feelings over Mama's death: grief, guilt, resentment, relief. But uppermost in her thoughts was whether Mama meant to reward her or punish her by making Papa's care her responsibility.

eighteen

achel couldn't tell if the tapping noise that woke her was coming from her bedroom door or somewhere outside, so she lay still in bed, her senses poised to hear it again. Her daughter Rivka and niece Alvina, inseparable at night as well as by day, lay beside her, their chests rising and falling in gentle unison, and Rachel couldn't resist the urge to drop a kiss on her child's forehead.

Tap, tap—this time she knew it was her door. She was slipping on her chemise when Papa whispered from the hall, "Rachel, wake up."

"What's the matter, Papa?"

Mama had been dead almost three months, and Rachel had yet to see an indication that Papa had any special need of her. After spending Passover in Ramerupt, she decided to stay in her old room at Papa's until Eliezer came home, which thank Heaven would be very soon.

"Nothing's the matter . . . I think." Salomon's voice became more urgent. "Put on your mantle and come outside."

Rachel couldn't imagine what her father found so interesting outdoors on this moonless night, but she followed him downstairs and onto the porch. Baruch and Anna were already there, staring at the sky, and it seemed that others were standing outside Miriam's house.

When Papa looked up, Rachel followed his gaze and gasped with wonder as a shooting star bolted across the sky. "*Baruch ata Adonai* . . . Whose strength and power fill the world," she recited the Talmudic blessing said upon seeing *zikim*.

Immediately the meteor was followed by others, then the heavens remained stationary for a short while until another abruptly appeared and disappeared. She found that she could not count to five before a new shooting star burst into view, and sometimes there were several in the sky simultaneously.

She could barely tear herself away from the spectacle overhead when the bells chimed Matins, but the sky was more incredible the following night. By the third night, all the yeshiva students as well as her children were outside at midnight to gape in awe at the stars falling.

"What does it mean?" everyone was asking, for this was surely a sign portending the future.

Judah shrugged his shoulders. "In Berachot the sages ask:

> What do *zikim* mean? Shmuel said: the paths of Heaven are as known to me as the streets of Nehardea [where he lived] except for shooting stars; of these I am ignorant.

"So if the great Babylonian astronomer Shmuel didn't understand them, I don't see how we can."

"When Rabbi Hiyya died, fiery stones came down from the sky," Salomon said. "So they may accompany the death of a scholar, an event we cannot ascertain in advance."

"My father told me he saw such stars when Guillaume the Bastard invaded Angleterre," a student from Normandy said.

"So was that a good omen for the Normans or an evil one for the English they defeated?" Miriam asked him.

"Perhaps it foretold the great battle."

"We learn some omens from Tractate Sukkah," Salomon said.

> "At the time the sun is eclipsed, it is a bad omen for the Edomites; when the moon is eclipsed, it is a bad omen for Israel. For Israel's calendar follows the moon and the Edomites' the sun."

"But how can stars suddenly move like that?" Rachel asked. Knowing that Eliezer was studying astronomy, she'd searched the Talmud for the subject. "Surely they're fixed in place, as it is taught in Pesachim:

> Jewish Sages say the sphere is fixed and the constellations rotate, but other sages say the sphere rotates and the constellations are fixed on it.

Thus the position of individual stars doesn't change within their constellations, no matter which sages are correct."

"Perhaps it is as Rav Huna says," Judah suggested.

> "*Zikim* are seen when the innermost firmament is torn and light of the upper level appears through the slit."

No one watching the sky could imagine how the firmament might tear, but surely such a thing was more likely to bode evil than well.

Salomon tried to end their discussion with words of comfort. "Don't worry. Our Sages also teach in Tractate Sukkah:

> When Israel does the Holy One's will, they have no fear of these omens; as it is written [in Jeremiah], 'Do not be dismayed by the Heavenly portents—let other nations be dismayed by them.' "

When Guy de Dampierre dined with Salomon that Thursday, the topic was scripture rather than shooting stars. Having mastered the simpler Hebrew texts, Guy and Étienne were eager to attempt the prophetic words of Isaiah.

Rachel exchanged a surreptitious look with her father, who subtly shook his head. "Isaiah is one of the most difficult Hebrew prophets," Salomon told Guy. "Besides many obscure words, Isaiah is filled with allegory. I'd prefer that you studied it with Shmuel, once his Latin is equal to the task."

Isaiah was the prophet whose words were often twisted by the Notzrim to justify their worship of the Hanged One, so Rachel was sure Papa wouldn't want anyone but an expert discussing the subject with Guy or Étienne. Indeed, Papa excused himself to return to his students and left Guy in her hands.

"Perhaps I can help you learn Psalms," Rachel offered as she headed toward the cellar to inventory the wine remaining after Passover. Heaven forbid that Guy or Étienne should be offended. "The poetic Hebrew in Psalms can be tricky, but no other text can match its beauty."

Guy brightened immediately. "Then I shall be sure to bring my Psalter to our next lesson."

"Learning Psalms while anticipating Isaiah should be worth the wait," Rachel said. "My nephews are still in Paris and won't return until the Mai Faire de Provins, when many merchants are on the road. In the meantime Shmuel has been studying with some of your scholars in Paris."

"Then he'll be learning Latin from the best." Guy followed Rachel down the cellar stairs. "It's wise to travel with a caravan these days: the roads around Paris are infested with highwaymen, those with noble blood among the worst."

"Can nothing be done to enforce the pope's truce?"

"Perhaps. Complaints at Piacenza have encouraged Pope Urban to call for another council in Clermont, in the fall."

Rachel paused to mark an empty cask. "Another church council so soon?"

"Urban has given Philip six months to rid himself of Bertrade, and if the king does so, his excommunication will be lifted at Clermont. Also, ambassadors from Emperor Alexius want Urban's help in fighting the Turks who threaten Byzantium."

"If the pope can persuade some of our rapacious barons to exchange local battlefields for those in the east, he would do both France and Alexius a service." Yet Rachel doubted that even the pope could make this happen.

"Perhaps that will be the great event those shooting stars portend."

"You're an optimist, Guy. Most fear a catastrophe."

"Let people think what they will, but I recall that the birth of our Savior was heralded by a bright new star." Guy turned to grin at Rachel. "Maybe one of the meteors is for your family: a great scholar to be born here."

Rachel frowned. "I know you're joking, but even a jest might bring the Evil Eye on my family."

"Of course. I'm sorry." He headed for the cellar door. "Is there any particular psalm you want me to start with? Or should I commence with the first one?"

"Pick your favorites, and we'll begin with those."

While it was reassuring to believe that Joheved and Meir's baby might be a great scholar the meteors heralded, most Jews would pessimistically agree that such a massive shower of shooting stars could only forebode disaster. Rachel was sure of one thing however: Eliezer was studying with Sepharad's finest astronomers, more learned than the great Shmuel of Nehardea, and if they understood the meaning, he would tell her.

Joheved calculated that her baby was due in mid-June, but Miriam took no chances and insisted her older sister move to Troyes early in the month. This turned out to be a wise decision, as less than a week elapsed before Joheved gave birth to her sixth child, a fourth son. Despite her advanced age, she did so with less pain and bleeding than while bearing her previous children.

Rachel couldn't help but remember poor Milo, who would be desperately anxious for news of Joheved's health. "The weather is so fine today that I think I'll ride to Ramerupt," she told her sister. "I'd like to see how the new lambs' wool compares to last year's."

Joheved understood her concern. "*Merci.* Then Milo will be able to concentrate on supervising the sheep shearing."

"Don't worry if I'm not back until sunset. I don't expect Eliezer just yet, but since my clean days are finished, I may as well immerse in that nice pond you have."

"It's too bad it's so far to ride." Joheved paused to expertly rouse her sleepy newborn and shift him to her other breast. "I'd rather immerse there when my seven days of childbirth impurity are finished."

"At least it's warm enough to use the Seine," Rachel said. "Miriam and I can show you some quiet streams nearby, not as nice as in Ramerupt, but fine nevertheless."

Despite the many *mazikim* reputed to dwell in rivers, and cognizant that no demon could endure the pure water of the synagogue's *mikvah*, Rachel, her sisters, and indeed most of the Jewish women of Troyes still preferred to perform their first immersion after childbirth upstream from town. Luckily most tended to give birth when the weather was warm.

Rachel set out immediately after *disner*, and as she rode through the forest, she couldn't decide whether she should deliver the good news immediately or tease Milo by asking about the sheep first and only later announce Joheved's new son. She still hadn't made up her mind when she heard the sound of approaching horses.

Milo had ridden out to meet her, and before she could speak, he called out, "What news do you bring of my lady Joheved?"

She had no choice but to reply, "Just this morning my sister was safely delivered of another son—may the Holy One protect them both."

The joyous relief on Milo's face made Rachel ashamed that she had thought to delay telling him. But he quickly recovered his equanimity and asked, "Is there anything I can do for you? Would you like some refreshments?"

"Not right now," she replied. "If possible I would like to see the wool that the new lambs produced."

"The sheep are being sheared as we speak, and I would be pleased to show you our different grades of wool." He blushed slightly with pride. "You can see for yourself the superiority of the wool we got from the new rams' offspring."

He wheeled his horse around and led her to a field where the stream had been dammed to create a large, shallow pool, now full of unhappy sheep. At the water's edge, women rubbed the sheep well with the greasy brown soft soap that Joheved's estate made every winter from ashes and rendered fat. Then they forced the sheep into the stream, where the men were waiting.

There the men rinsed out the dirty suds while pushing the sheep toward the deeper water, forcing the animals to swim to the other side. Slowly the clean sheep dried in the sun, looking to Rachel like a field of giant dandelion puffs. One by one they were led to the shearers, who made quick work of separating them from their wool. It was a noisy enterprise, what with sheep bleating and workers yelling to each other.

"It takes more time to wash the sheep first," Milo shouted to be heard over the din. "But a clean fleece brings a better price than a dirty one."

They rode to a shed piled high with rolls of fleeces. Rachel examined the various grades, where despite her inexperience, the difference between wool of this and last year's lambs was clear.

"I've marked the females that each ram sired, so I can ensure that they are not bred to their fathers," he said.

She nodded. "Milo, this is truly wonderful. Next year we can expect even finer quality."

* * *

Rachel watched the sheep shearing a while longer—the process was almost hypnotic, until a bead of sweat trickling down her face reminded her that she still wanted to immerse. She asked Joheved's maidservant to lead her to the place and keep guard while she bathed. By the time they reached the secluded pool with its soft mossy bank, Rachel was perspiring heavily, and she waited only until the girl moved out of sight before doffing her clothes and wading into the water.

"Aah." She sighed with contentment after her first immersion. Joheved had found the perfect location.

She paddled around the pond to prove to herself that she still remembered how to swim, and then immersed for the second time. When she came up, she floated on her back, listening to the birds while gazing at the patterns the leafy branches made against the sky.

Suddenly the birds went silent, and Rachel had the feeling that someone was watching her. Covering her breasts with her arms, she stood up and listened attentively, but there was no sound or movement. Still she waited a few cautious moments before performing her final immersion.

She had just surfaced and was shaking the water from her curls when the pond erupted with a loud splash. Somebody had jumped in with her—and that somebody was a man.

Panicked, she backed away as rapidly as she could, at the same time calling for the maidservant. But the man was faster as he reached out to grab her hand. She splashed and struggled but he was too strong for her, pulling her around to face him.

Eliezer!

"Wha . . . What are you doing here?" She stammered in surprise. She didn't know which she wanted to do more, hit him or kiss him. "I nearly died of fright."

He closed the distance between them and cradled her in his arms. "I couldn't wait to see you. I wanted to surprise you."

"You certainly did." She splashed water at him.

"A pleasant surprise, I hope."

When he grinned at her like that, Rachel couldn't help but smile back. "Most definitely." She pulled his head down and kissed him.

Despite the cool water, Rachel could feel his heat against her, and the passion of his embrace quickly evoked an equal response. She clung to him as his hands caressed her breasts and then moved down between her thighs. Soon they were racing to the water's edge where they sank down into the velvety moss.

Later Rachel pulled herself up on an elbow and lovingly surveyed her husband dozing beside her. She had never seen Eliezer naked in the daytime. She admired his body, so shapely and well fleshed; his legs in particular were nicely formed. Was it her imagination or was there more hair on his chest than when they married? Rachel reached out her hand to stroke the soft down and then hesitated. He'd probably ridden long and hard today, she reminded herself, and decided to let him rest a while longer.

Was it like this for Adam and Eve in Gan Eden? she wondered, as she watched the clouds float by and listened to the birds' renewed songs. Eliezer stirred and she looked down to find him smiling.

"How long were you watching me?" Rachel demanded.

"I got here shortly after you did. The maid recognized me and agreed not to warn you." His grin widened. "It was all I could do to keep from jumping in earlier: you were so tempting."

"Did you see all those *zikim* just after Passover? For almost a week our skies were ablaze with them."

"We saw some for a couple of nights, but nothing extraordinary."

"You're studying astronomy," she accused him. "What does it mean to have so many shooting stars like that?"

"Unlike eclipses and movement of the planets, we cannot predict *zikim.*" He was about to say that consequently no one can determine what they forebode, but Rachel looked so disappointed that he replied instead, "But surely they portend something momentous, although for good or evil we don't know."

She thought of the Normans conquering Angleterre. "Perhaps good for some and evil for others."

"Exactly."

Eliezer was clearly in a fine mood, and their surroundings encouraged intimacy, so Rachel dared ask him about a subject that was increasingly bothering her. "Would you be disappointed if I can't have more children?"

His eyes widened in surprise. "Not at all. I've fulfilled the mitzvah of procreation with Shemiah and Rivka."

"You're sure?" "You don't envy Meir?"

"Joheved almost died from childbirth." His voice became serious. "And look at poor Simcha, his son Samuel, and countless other widowed men." He tilted up her chin and locked eyes with her. "I will never suffer that tragedy."

His expression was so sincere that Rachel was quite unable to speak. But lying outdoors, naked together, it was impossible to stay sad. Eliezer lazily ran his hand along her torso.

"I will also never cease to appreciate your beauty, because repeated pregnancies won't mar it." And he proceeded to appreciate her beauty with more than just his eyes.

Miriam's joy at Joheved's easy labor was followed by her relief at performing the boy's brit milah well before the community was overrun with foreign merchants. She was contentedly weeding her herb garden when a small boy hesitantly entered the courtyard leading a pregnant cow on a rope.

"Is this the home of Salomon the Scholar?" he asked her.

"*Oui*, I'm his daughter." Miriam looked back and forth from the cow to the boy, wondering what he could possibly want with Papa. "He's in the vineyard right now; can I help you?"

"This cow is a gift of thanks from Guy de Dampierre, for all the help Master Salomon's family has given him."

Anna, who had poked her head out the kitchen door when the gate slammed shut, walked out to join them. "A cow for Master Salomon?"

When Miriam and the boy nodded, her face lit up. "I used to be a milkmaid when I was a girl in Romania." Anna pulled up a clump of grass and offered it to the animal. "I would be happy to take charge of this one."

Thus, soon after, it was Anna who innocently alerted Salomon to his imminent problem. "This cow doesn't have any milk yet," she informed the household. Observing their disappointment and suspicion, she added, "There's nothing wrong with her. She's young and pregnant for the first time. Guy has given you a doubly valuable gift: a cow and a calf."

"This cow has never been pregnant before?" Salomon's brows furrowed. "Are you sure?"

"I believe so, but we can ask the cowherd."

When the boy confirmed Anna's statement, Salomon's face clouded and he began to stroke his beard.

"The problem is that, according to the Torah, all firstborn males are consecrated to the Creator," Miriam explained. "But since we can't sacrifice firstborn male animals at the Temple anymore, they must be destroyed."

Rachel turned to Meir. "You must have this problem every year with some of the lambs. Do you just kill them?"

Meir shook his head. "We sell Milo a share of every ewe that's pregnant for the first time. Not being Jewish, he's not subject to the law of firstlings. When we sell the male lambs among them, he receives a share of the price."

"I could also sell a share of the cow herself," Salomon said. "Because if a non-Jew owns any part of the mother, the male firstling is not consecrated."

This is how Elizabeth the Midwife became half owner of the new cow. When the animal did eventually give birth to a bull calf, she gladly sold her share in the mother back to Salomon in exchange for the offspring. Owning their own cow brought a new benefit to Salomon's household. Besides fresh milk for the children at breakfast, Anna used the afternoon milking to make a sweet creamy cheese that tasted wonderful on freshly baked bread. Plus the cow's dung was excellent for the garden.

Though Eliezer had assured her that he was content with their two children, Rachel, whenever she saw Anna milking the cow or Joheved feeding little Jacob, named for Meir's grandfather, thought longingly of the comfort she'd received from nursing little Rivka again after baby Asher died. Surely she'd have gotten pregnant by now if she were able. But if she were barren, she'd have to appreciate the children she had.

Past her first taste of Torah study, Rivka now eagerly pestered everyone in the family with questions, especially her older brother, Shemiah. Sometimes he showed off his knowledge with erudite answers, especially when Rachel or Eliezer were present. But usually he ignored her, preferring to discuss Mishnah with Shimson. Rachel tried not to intervene in her children's squabbles and gave thanks that, even if they didn't have siblings of the same gender, their cousins provided plenty of companionship.

* * *

Despite endless speculation over the shooting stars' meaning, one forecast that did come true in the next six months had nothing to do with the heavens. As Guy predicted, Pope Urban presided over a Church council at Clermont that fall, during the third week of November. But Troyes' attention was focused elsewhere. In the middle of the Cold Fair, on November 28, Count Hugues married Princess Constance of France with all the pomp a royal wedding demanded. His daughter's marriage was exactly the excuse King Philip needed to ignore events in Clermont, where, since he'd made no effort to separate from Bertrade, the pope reaffirmed his excommunication.

The first warning Salomon's household received about other events in Clermont came from Guy when he unexpectedly joined them for *souper* during the final week of the Cold Fair.

"Eliezer." Guy's ominous tone chilled Rachel's heart. "I urge you in the strongest terms to delay your departure from Troyes."

Everyone within hearing turned to Guy as Eliezer asked, "Why? What happened?"

"His last day at Clermont, standing in an open field before nobility and clerics, Pope Urban gave an extraordinary speech." Guy fell silent, his expression full of wonder. "First he chastised the knights for breaking the Truce of God by wantonly attacking pilgrims, clerics, women, and merchants. He accused them of waging unjust wars on each other, to their mutual destruction, for no other reason than covetousness and pride, and said they were deserving of eternal damnation."

Rachel stared at Guy with curiosity. The pope had long rebuked men of arms for such crimes, but Guy's awed voice showed that something new was involved. "Then he began speaking of Jerusalem, the navel of the world, of how the accursed Turks invaded her confines and depopulated them by sword, pillage, and fire. He described how her holy altars were destroyed and Christians subjected to unspeakable degradation and servitude. He urged the knights, most valiant soldiers and descendants of invincible ancestors, to be not degenerate, but to recall the valor of their progenitors."

"What did he want from them?" Salomon asked, his voice heavy with dread.

"To let their quarrels and wars cease as they entered upon the road to the Holy Sepulchre, to wrest the Holy Land from that wicked race of infidels and make it subject to them," Guy replied. "Pope Urban further proclaimed that they should not let their possessions, nor solicitude for their families, keep them from undertaking this holy pilgrimage, for which they would receive remission of their sins and assurance of the Kingdom of Heaven's glory."

Guy shook his head in amazement. "With that, the crowd cried out as one, 'It is God's will! It is God's will!' The pope then told those who would undertake this holy war to sew crosses on their chests for all to see, and within moments men began tearing at their clothes to produce crosses."

"That was a month ago," Eliezer said. "What has happened since?"

"The pope has been preaching throughout France, staying clear of the king's lands while Philip remains excommunicated. In addition, itinerant preachers have appeared, attracting flocks of pilgrims as well as bands of less-innocent folk."

"But you said the pope's appeal was to knights." Meir wondered which, if any, of Count André of Ramerupt's men would participate.

"That was Pope Urban's intent, but the enterprise has spiraled out of his hands, so that we now see poor townsfolk and villeins selling their possessions to provision themselves for the journey. My uncle is besieged by men, and women, asking for their bishop's blessing."

Joheved exchanged anxious glances with Meir. "I hope these preachers don't seduce too many of our villeins to leave. The villagers know nothing of warfare; they would never survive."

"The pope has promised eternal salvation to those who die on pilgrimage," Guy said. "And as further inducement, whoever undertakes this holy war is exempt from repayment of debts."

"Their debts are discharged?" Rachel asked with dismay, thinking of the women who owed her money.

"For the duration of their pilgrimage, *oui*," Guy said. "And more than that: those vowed to retake Jerusalem may substitute the journey for all penance."

"So all kinds of scoundrels will join them," Eliezer said, recognizing the danger such undisciplined mobs would pose.

"The officially sanctioned group of knights and foot soldiers is to begin its journey in August, continuing to Constantinople, where it will meet up with Alexius's troops," Guy explained. "But these impatient preachers have urged their followers to start immediately, and I fear that thousands, perhaps tens of thousands, of Frankish pilgrims will be heading in our direction."

"What will we do?" Miriam whispered in horror.

"I believe I will delay my departure for Toledo until after these pilgrims have passed through Champagne into the east," Eliezer declared.

Rachel squeezed his hand under the table and sighed with relief. But along with the rest of her family, she could not find the appetite to finish *souper.*

nineteen

"How long before these pilgrims finally leave?" Eliezer pounded the table in frustration. "For months they've been milling around Troyes, living off our lands, terrifying the women and children. Let them go to Jerusalem already. I've had enough."

"There's nothing we can do about them, so let's just continue our Talmud discussion." Judah was determined to force Eliezer to accept his interpretation of Tractate Kiddushin. The text was complicated and hopefully could distract them from their worries. "You cannot derive a woman's obligation to eat matzah at Passover from the law in Deuteronomy that obligates her to assemble every year to hear the king read the Torah. Therefore women should be exempt from time-bound positive mitzvot."

Eliezer refused to capitulate. "I say a woman's obligation to assemble is derived from her obligation to eat matzah." He turned Judah's argument around. "For without the verses about matzah, we would say that a boy's obligation is stronger than a woman's, since he will eventually grow to perform the mitzvah. Yet a woman is commanded to eat matzah while a child is not."

"Then you agree with me. Since women are obligated to eat matzah while children are not, then if minors must attend the assembly, surely a woman, who is treated more strictly, must do so as well," Judah said. "But even so, these two mitzvot don't teach that women are commanded to perform the other time-bound positive mitzvot."

Eliezer sighed with exasperation. "While they certainly show that women are not exempt from them, at the moment I cannot think of a better argument."

Judah looked at his study partner with alarm. For Eliezer to acquiesce so easily was proof of how stressful life was for the Jews of Troyes. "I admit that I also cannot think of another refutation." Even Talmud study couldn't divert their minds from the threat outside the city walls.

Their Talmud debate finished, Eliezer cradled his head in his hands. Over two months had elapsed since Guy convinced him to remain behind when other merchants left at year's end, and there was nothing to suggest that he'd be leaving any time soon. For two months some crazy preacher from Amiens, Peter the Hermit they called him, had been urging the Notzrim to come with him to free Jerusalem from the infidels, convincing them that the Holy Spirit was with them, God's own army.

Crowds gathered around Troyes, camping in field and forest, the lucky ones sheltering in barns. So far the pilgrims had done no harm, but that was only because Countess Adelaide, partly out of Christian charity and partly fearing they'd pillage the city otherwise, provided provisions.

But every Jew in town knew that a mob of so-called pilgrims had attacked the Jewish community of Rouen, shouting, "Here we are, going off to attack God's enemies in the East, having to travel great distances, when before our eyes are the Jews, more hostile to God than any other race."

Thus Eliezer hadn't been able to study astronomy for months, a situation that became almost unbearable when February brought an eclipse of the moon and no way to measure its passage. Yet how could he leave when the countryside was infested with armed idiots who believed in such things as Peter the Hermit's talking donkey?

Anna's urgent whisper interrupted his indignant thoughts. "Eliezer, there's a man here who says you know him."

He took in her frightened features, but before he could ask what the fellow looked like, she added, "He's one of those pilgrims."

Eliezer and Judah jumped up to follow her outside where Baruch and Pesach were keeping a close watch on the fellow.

"Call off your guards. I won't hurt anyone," he said, eyeing Salomon's two menservants with trepidation. "Master Eliezer, it's me, Jehan, from the forest in Burgundy."

"Jehan, it's good to see you again." Eliezer never would have recognized him. The young man looked better fed than before and a bit taller as well. "What are you doing here?"

"I'm going to Jerusalem. All of Geoffrey's men are."

"I mean, how did you get in the city?" Eliezer asked.

"At first the guards wouldn't let me past the city gate. They don't let anyone in who doesn't have money to shop with, and even those only come in a few at a time."

"But they did let you in," Judah pointed out.

"Only because Geoffrey came with me, and they could see that he was a knight."

Eliezer nodded, waiting to hear what Jehan wanted with him.

"Geoffrey, all of us actually, need your help," Jehan said. "He's waiting just outside the Près Gate."

Judah reached for his mantle. "I'll go with you."

"So will I," Baruch said, grabbing a length of wood that could be used as both a walking stick and a weapon.

Eliezer had a suspicion of what Geoffrey wanted, but he waited patiently as his old captor explained how he'd repented of his former banditry and turned to offering safety, for a fee, to those who crossed the Forest of Burgundy.

"But my men aren't cut out to be toll takers," Geoffrey said. "They long for their former lives as men of action."

Eliezer nodded. "So you've joined Peter's army."

"What could be more ideal?" Geoffrey grinned. "Instead of being condemned for fighting, we'll be rewarded, both materially and spiritually."

"When we reach Jerusalem, the booty will be greater than a man can imagine." Jehan's eyes shone with enthusiasm. "And those who die in the attempt will instantly ascend to Heaven."

Geoffrey's brow furrowed. "But we have a long road ahead, and most of Peter's pilgrims scarcely have food to eat each day, never mind enough for a journey to Constantinople."

"Of course not," Eliezer said soothingly. "Not with so many peasants among you."

"Peter wants everyone to participate." Geoffrey's tone made it clear that he disagreed with this view.

"What if more supplies can be arranged?" Eliezer asked. "Will Peter start on his way?"

"I believe so, but you must talk to him about it first."

Eliezer looked questioningly at Judah, who nodded in return. "Can you set up a meeting between us, as soon as possible? Once we understand his needs, the leaders in our community will discuss how to provide for them."

Salomon, Bonfils haParnas, and the other Jewish leaders avidly endorsed Eliezer's efforts to bribe Peter into leaving.

"The sooner these people are gone, the better," Bonfils said. "Trade in town is terrible. Half the shopkeepers shutter their doors out of fear, and the other half have no goods to sell because so little traffic enters the city."

"You're not telling us something we don't know," Avram the Mohel said. "The question is how much to offer."

"As little as possible," interrupted Leontin.

"Yet not so little as to anger him," Moses haCohen said.

"Should we offer only money?" Salomon asked. "Or provisions like food, blankets, or animals?"

"If any stables have old horses or carts they'd like to be rid of, this would be the perfect time to do so," Leontin said. He, like the other men, recognized that few of the pilgrims would ever reach Jerusalem, and even fewer would return.

"As well as any worn clothes or blankets," Avram agreed.

"Before we offer anything, we should see what they want." Bonfils was an experienced merchant, famous for never naming the first price. "It may be less than we are willing to pay."

"With your permission, my son-in-law will handle the negotiations," Salomon said, causing the others to nod vigorously. "He's an able trader and the pilgrims trust him."

"Plus he has an ally in their camp," Moses said. He left unsaid what they were all thinking—whoever negotiated with Peter was risking his life to do so, and Eliezer would have Geoffrey's small cadre of soldiers for protection.

Safe astride her horse, Rachel gaped at the teeming crowd of pilgrims. Tents and carts were scattered as far as she could see, while children played in the dirt among the horses and oxen.

"What are children doing on a pilgrimage to Jerusalem?" she muttered to Miriam, riding next to her. "The Saracens will slaughter them—those they don't take as slaves."

Miriam frowned. "Notzrim believe that even children are tainted by original sin."

As usual in late winter, Miriam was staying in Ramerupt to help with the lambing. Once Rachel learned that Meir had a secret route through the forest to Troyes, which avoided the pilgrims, she used it regularly to visit her sisters. With each trip, she grew more curious to see the charismatic hermit and his camp, maybe glimpse the famous donkey whose tail hairs fetched incredible sums in town. Eliezer had been there many times as his parleys with their leader continued, but he never let her accompany him. It wasn't safe for a woman, he said, while at the same time asserting that it was perfectly safe for him.

So as the lambing slowed and Miriam had time to spare, Rachel cajoled her to come see the pilgrims. Such a historic sight was not to be missed, and they'd be safe on horseback together. Besides, Eliezer said there were plenty of women pilgrims, and nothing bad happened to them. He also told her that negotiations were nearly complete, that the fields would hopefully be empty again by Purim.

"Look," Rachel pointed to an opening in the trees. "Those children are as black as soot."

"Their parents are charcoal burners." Miriam's heart caught in her throat as she watched them, the poorest of the poor, approach the field with armfuls of charcoal to sell. "Meir allows several families to earn a living in the forest."

"Charcoal burners would make good pilgrims. They have nothing to lose, and their lives couldn't get worse."

Miriam gave her sister a withering look and turned her horse toward the children. When she'd encountered youngsters like these years before, Count André's servants had prevented her from helping them. But nobody would stop her today.

"Miriam, where are you going? Wait," Rachel called out.

But it was too late. Miriam had reached the children, taken her purse from her sleeve, and begun distributing coins.

"Stop. Don't give them anything," Rachel shouted, but Miriam ignored her. "Once you start giving alms, every child in a hundred cubits will want some."

Indeed within moments the sisters were surrounded by a sea of pinched faces and outstretched arms. It was impossible to move the horses without trampling the nearest ones, and soon the smaller children were being pushed aside by older, more threatening youths. Rachel would gladly have ridden over them, but she couldn't leave Miriam, who seemed paralyzed with fear.

Suddenly a masculine voice was shouting, "Hey! What's going on there? Step aside. Make way."

The mob of beggars melted away, leaving Rachel and Miriam staring gratefully at a grizzled knight on horseback.

"I told her not to do it," Rachel insisted.

But the knight was staring at Miriam and scratching his head. "I know you," he said slowly. "You're Lady Joheved's sister. This is the second time I've come to your rescue."

"Flaubert," Miriam whispered. She looked like she'd seen a ghost. "I can't thank you enough."

"You must be the third sister," he addressed Rachel with a scowl. "What devil possessed you two Jewesses to ride out among these good pilgrims today? Have you no idea the trouble you could cause?"

Rachel remained silent, burning with shame, but Miriam questioned him in return. "I see you wear a cross on your shoulder. Have you joined Peter, or are you going with the other knights later?"

"I'm with Peter." Flaubert's ire was replaced with awe. "I've never met anyone so filled with the Holy Spirit. People shower him with gifts but he gives everything to the poor. He eats only fish and wine, like our Savior did, and he dresses in a simple woolen shirt with bare arms and feet. And when Peter preaches it's as if Our Savior is speaking through him." His face shone at the memory.

"You will be a great help to him." Rachel wanted to make amends for her earlier folly. "He doesn't have many knights, I hear."

"Nothing would give me more satisfaction that to die in his service."

"Most others want wealth and glory," Miriam said.

Her sympathetic tone must have touched something in the old warrior, because his eyes filled with tears. "Years ago I wanted a woman in my lord's court, a woman with hair the color of fire." He sighed. "But I had no land and insufficient skill to make my fortune at tournaments. I knew we could never marry; yet thinking only of my selfish pleasure I seduced her."

Miriam's eyebrows rose with dawning understanding. He'd been Rosaline's lover. But she said only, "And that sin is deserving of death?"

"I got her with child and then abandoned her." Flaubert blinked back tears. "I learned later that she died trying to rid herself of the pregnancy."

"I'm so sorry." There was nothing else Miriam could say. It was years ago, but she could still recall her frustration and despair after being called to Rosaline's sickbed and finding the young woman beyond help.

Flaubert sat up straight in his saddle. "No other penance can remove this stain from my soul. Before, the best I could hope for was thousands of years in purgatory instead of eternity in hell. But Peter assured me that those joining this holy war to cleanse Jerusalem of the infidels who pollute her may substitute their pilgrimage for all penance, both in this world and the next. And those who die on the journey will attain immediate salvation."

Perhaps realizing he'd said too much, Flaubert offered to accompany them to Ramerupt. However, once they were no longer in view of the field, Miriam insisted that she and Rachel could continue on their own. Then, once the knight disappeared, she told Rosaline's sad story to Rachel, who shuddered in disgust.

"So according to their beliefs, Flaubert, cause of all this suffering, dies in a battle on the way to Jerusalem instead of in some local brawl, and goes straight to Heaven," Rachel spat out the words. "While poor Rosaline spends perpetuity in hell."

The Jews of Troyes celebrated Purim that year with more relief than joy, Peter and his followers having vacated the environs just days before the festival. Rachel suddenly found herself the owner of several looms, including Albert's horizontal model, as he and other local weavers sold their possessions to join the pilgrimage. She similarly purchased some fullers' equipment, although she had no idea yet of where she'd find the skilled labor to use either of these.

Milo, on the other hand, declined taking the cross. He didn't like what he saw of the pilgrims and refused to leave his lord's family unprotected.

Meir happened to notice Milo admiring one of the more attractive maidservants and, furious at his own stupidity for not thinking of it sooner, realized that with one action he could both reward his faithful steward and lessen the man's passion for Joheved. He promptly told Milo to consult his father, investigate the ladies-in-waiting in the courts of Ramerupt and Troyes—do whatever it took to acquire an appropriate bride before the year was out. Milo was fervent with gratitude, for Meir's command meant that, once married, Milo would remain the estate's steward until age or infirmity forced his retirement.

When Peter finally left for Allemagne, far richer than when he'd arrived thanks to the Champagnois Jews' munificence, he carried a letter for the Jews in the Rhineland. Besides urging them to be equally generous, the letter warned of danger from so many fanatical pilgrims eager to kill infidels.

Rachel watched Eliezer pack for Toledo with mixed feelings. While it was good for them financially that he had time to complete the trip, she still wished he were staying in Troyes. But Eliezer couldn't wait to leave the pilgrims far behind.

"While I was able to come and go among them undisturbed," he shivered at the memory, "there was an undercurrent of animosity, mutterings about why these Jews should walk the earth freely after murdering the Hanged One."

"You were very brave to handle the negotiations so they could leave. I'm proud of you."

"I had no idea so many Franks felt this way," he said. "Thank Heaven the Spaniards don't share these views."

"Yet they've been fighting the Saracens for years." She was also surprised by the recent turn of events.

"I fear for the Jewish communities in Ashkenaz," Salomon said as they watched Eliezer ride away. "And for those in Sepharad."

But the Jews of Mayence weren't afraid. They wrote back, "We have done our part and decreed a fast, for we are deeply fearful for you. We, however, have less reason to fear for ourselves, since we have not even heard a rumor of this armed pilgrimage."

Salomon scowled at his colleagues' ignorance and announced that his students should study Tractate Taanit, which dealt with fast days. Perhaps their efforts would help their German brethren.

For her part, Rachel began praying Psalm 88 at night, the incantation to save a city or community. She couldn't imagine how this text was fitting for such a purpose, for the psalmist's words were frightening, and seemed more a curse on the Jews than a prayer on their behalf.

> Let my prayer come before You; incline Your ear to my cry.
>
> My soul is filled with troubles . . . Because of You my friends shun me; You make me loathsome to them . . . Why reject me, Adonai? Why hide Your face from me? . . . Your terrors have reduced me to silence. All day they surge round like a flood; from every side they close in on me.

Salomon's anxiety increased as, instead of heading for Jerusalem immediately, Peter began preaching throughout the Rhineland, climaxing with a rally in Cologne on Easter. But the hermit did not stay to organize his new recruits. That task fell to other, less-peaceable men, who instead of following the hermit south when they reached the Danube, unaccountably headed north, back down the Rhine.

Throughout Speyer's Jewish Quarter, the rumors multiplied like flies on dung:

"Just pay them off, like the Jews of Trier did with Peter the Hermit—serve the king of Bavel and live."

"But they say that anyone who kills even one Jew will have all his sins pardoned."

"Bishop Johann won't let that happen. He'll protect us."

"Against so many of them? I heard they killed over thirty Jews in Metz. Nobody was expecting them, so the community was taken by surprise; that won't happen here."

"They'll be in Speyer within a week. They just want money for bread; if we give it to them, they'll leave us in peace."

"No, they're just waiting for the Sabbath, when we'll be in synagogue; they want to capture us all together, to kidnap our children, and raise them as heretics."

Salomon's nephew Elazar, son of Rivka's sister, didn't know what tale to believe, if any. But he was a prudent man. So when Rabbi Moses told the Jews to pray early on Shabbat and quickly return to their homes, Elazar was one of the first to finish his prayers and leave.

When the other men who lived in the dwellings around his courtyard returned (the women had prayed at home), they locked and barricaded the gate, their doors, and their windows. The sun had barely risen above the courtyard walls when Elazar's chanting of psalms was interrupted by angry shouts in the distance. Their enemies had discovered the synagogue empty and, enraged, were rioting in the street.

Terrified, Elazar's family huddled together and prayed.

Though they saw nothing but ebbing shadows, they could hear the changing tenor of the battle outside. Soon new voices, full of authority and shouting commands, mixed with the mob's cries of fury. This was followed by the clash of steel against steel and screams of pain. Through it all, Elazar waited in dread for the assault on his gate, for the sound of cracking wood.

But his courtyard remained undisturbed, and eventually the fighting diminished. Yet night brought no sleep for Elazar and his wife, who dared not go outside even to get water. Only with the silence of dawn did he open his door to admit his wife's brother, whose family shared the courtyard with them.

First he embraced his sister, then Elazar. "Praised be the Holy One. Our enemies are scattered. Bishop Johann's men beat them back."

Elazar's wife wept with relief. "Praised be His Holy Name."

"But eleven Jews didn't get home in time and were killed," he said. "The bishop was outraged. He arrested the worst offenders and cut off their hands as a warning that he would not tolerate violence against any of his townspeople."

"The mobs are gone?" Elazar whispered, not quite believing what he'd just heard.

"When they saw that they could not prevail against Johann's army, they rode off."

"Which way did they go?" A horrible thought occurred to Elazar, whose son was studying at the yeshiva in Worms.

Fear clouded the man's face. "To the north."

Elazar threw on his mantle and grabbed his sword. "If I stay off the King's Highway, I can ride to Worms without being seen, warn the community, and bring my son home."

* * *

As the screams outside his courtyard grew louder, Elisha wished with all his heart to be in Troyes with Giuseppe and Judah, anywhere but Worms.

He'd made a terrible mistake. When news came of the deaths in Speyer, the Jews of Worms couldn't decide what to do. Some wanted to remain barricaded at home and let the authorities protect them. Others said they should accept the bishop's offer of sanctuary in his palace. And thus the Jewish community divided into two groups.

That was my first error, Elisha thought bitterly. His family should have gone with the bishop. Then came the second, trusting the burghers. His Edomite neighbors had sounded confident, assuring him that they would protect his family—once he'd left his valuables with them, for safekeeping. Oh what hollow, deceitful promises.

Soon the marauders were at the city gates, thousands of them, more than anyone expected. They carried a corpse through the city shouting, "See what the Jews did to our fellow. They boiled him and poured the water in our wells to poison us."

When the burghers heard this, anyone capable of wearing a sword gathered, bellowing in outrage, "It is time to avenge our Savior, whom their ancestors killed. Let not one of them escape, not even a suckling in its crib!"

Now, with the enemy at Elisha's gate, the neighbors who swore to safeguard his family had disappeared. Elisha had no doubt what would happen next; he'd peeked out an upstairs window once and that was enough. Transfixed by the sight, he watched in anguish as a young family across the road was slain in its own home. First the husband's body, blood flowing from multiple wounds, was thrown into the dirt. Then his wife was dragged out by her hair, her screams cut short by a sword driven into her chest. Last came their two children, impaled together on a spear, their small limbs still twitching. But there was another horror to be endured as the murderers proceeded to strip the bodies naked and drag them away. Elisha closed his eyes and staggered away from the shutters. Cries reverberated in his ears from other streets as he vomited into the chamber pot.

Elisha fought back his nausea and stood up, fortitude coursing through him. His family wasn't going to be slaughtered like sheep. "Better we should die by the Holy One's hand rather than by the hands of His enemies," he told his terrified wife.

"Please, Elisha, not that," she begged him, shaking with fright. "Tell the heretics that we'll accept the Crucified One. Then they'll leave us in peace."

"What?" he shouted. "Exchange the Holy One's unity for a degraded idol? Deny Him and dishonor His Divine Name? How can you consider such a sin when one stroke will ensure our place in Gan Eden?"

His wife shrank back and began to weep. "Then kill me first. I cannot bear to see our children slain."

They shut the two older children in another room. Then Elisha chose the largest, strongest knife from the kitchen and, tears streaming down his cheeks, began to sharpen it. A knife for kosher slaughter must have no nicks or imperfections that might delay the animal's death. His wife never took her eyes off him, her mouth moving in silent prayer. Finally he was satisfied that the blade was perfectly honed. He looked up at his wife and they stared into each other's eyes, gathering the strength they needed. Finally she nodded imperceptibly.

"Please forgive the sin I'm about to commit against you, as well as the sins I've committed against you in the past." He sniffed back tears. "I could have been a better husband."

"I forgive all your sins against me," she whispered, her voice so hoarse he could barely hear her. "You were a fine husband."

She walked over and kissed his forehead, after which she continued to the cradle and picked up their infant son. "I would like to die with the baby in my arms."

Then she laid her head on the kitchen table and pulled her hair back, exposing her neck. They stared silently at each other for what seemed like hours; then she closed her eyes and, very slowly and deliberately, said the Shema. "Hear O Israel, Adonai is our God, Adonai is One."

Elisha knew what she wanted him to do, and as she drew out the final word, he forced his trembling hand to steady and slit her throat; then, before the baby could slip to the floor, he took the knife to his son's throat as well.

As if in a dream, Elisha watched his wife's and child's blood pool on the floor. His senses seemed extraordinarily acute: he felt his heart pounding like thunder inside him, tasted the tears and sweat mingling on his lips, and inhaled the sour stink of vomit that clung to his sleeve. Outside, the shouts and screams were reaching a crescendo.

Smash! The clamor at his front door brought Elisha out of his trance. Quickly, he must get to his children before the door gave way. He grabbed the knife, wiped it on his sleeve and checked the edge. Thank Heaven it was still perfect.

With a final glance at his wife and child, he entered the room where young Judah and little Miriam cowered in the corner.

"Papa." The girl rushed into his arms. "What's happening? Why are you crying?"

What possible explanation could he give? "It's time for us to join our saintly ancestors in Gan Eden."

And which child to sacrifice first?

Nine-year-old Judah must have realized what was going on, because he hurriedly pushed a chest against the closed door. "I understand, Papa. I won't cry."

"Hurry now. Help me with your sister." Elisha kept the knife hidden behind his back.

"Close your eyes, Miriam, and say your bedtime Shema," Judah urged her. "Going to Gan Eden is like going to sleep."

To Elisha's relief, his daughter complied after he kissed her good night. When she lay bleeding on the sheets, he turned to his son, who was staring with wide eyes and quaking with fear. Judah was big for his age, and if he bolted, Elisha would never be able to catch him in time.

"Come sit with me, Judah, and we'll say the Shema together," he said gently. He was suddenly very tired.

Judah looked franticly around the room, desperate for an escape, but then he took a deep breath and stepped toward his father. Halfway there, his knees buckled and Elisha rushed to keep him from falling. They stood together, arms supporting each other, until Elisha heard the unmistakable sounds of wood splintering in the outer room.

Trembling violently, Judah climbed onto the bed next to his sister and tried to hold his head steady over the edge as he recited the Shema.

Elisha silenced his son's final "one" with a quick, sure cut, and sank down beside him.

As ax blades shattered the door in front of him, Elisha quailed at the grief his beloved Giuseppe would suffer. "Don't worry, dear Giuseppe. We'll see each other again in Gan Eden." Then he affirmed his faith in the One Eternal God and plunged the bloody blade into his chest.

twenty

is voice shaking, Samson turned to Rabbi Kalonymus, leader of Mayence's Jewish community. "Rabbenu, I was not born into the House of Jacob. If I die sanctifying the Holy Name, what will be my lot?" Trapped inside Bishop Rothard's palace with his family and other Jews fleeing Count Emicho's bloodthirsty minions, Samson gripped the sword at his belt.

The rabbi laid his hand on Samson's arm. "You shall sit with us and the rest of the true converts in our circle in Gan Eden, along with Abraham Avinu, the first convert."

Upon hearing this, Samson slammed his fist against the stone wall, cracking the mortar in several places. "I will not stretch out my neck and be slaughtered like an ox. I intend to die like my namesake, taking the enemy along with me."

There were murmurs of approval until one of the elders shouted, "That's fine for you, a man trained in arms. But what about the rest of us? The bishop may have intended to shelter us in his stronghold, but now there are thousands of defiant soldiers and burghers attacking his gate. The Holy One has decreed against us; we cannot be saved."

"Oh, Almighty One!" a woman cried out. "Where are all Your miracles our fathers told us about? Did You not bring us up from Egypt?" She broke down weeping. "And now You leave us in the power of our enemies, that they may destroy us."

The crowd quieted as Rabbi Kalonymus began to speak. "Despite the bribes we paid, the burghers have betrayed us and opened the city gates for Count Emicho and his army, numerous as sand on the seashore. Yet we will wholeheartedly defend, to the death if necessary, the Holy Awesome Name. Don your shields and gird your weapons, young and old, and join me in battle."

"Papa, why do the burghers hate us so?" Jacob asked Samson, his voice barely audible over the clanking swords being drawn.

Samson, still mystified at the anger directed at him and Eliezer when they brought grain for the starving townsfolk, shook his head sadly. "I don't know."

The Italian rabbi Amnon, visiting his sister for Shavuot, raised his sword high. "Have courage. Our enemies kill us for merely a moment, and with the sword, the easiest of the four deaths. Then we will dwell in Gan Eden forever."

Emicho's men broke through into the palace courtyard on the Third of Sivan, the date that long ago Moses told the Children of Israel, "Be ready for the third day," so they would be pure to receive the Ten Commandments. Bishop Rothard's soldiers gaped at the advancing mob and fled.

Crying out in one voice, "Hear O Israel, Adonai is our God; Adonai is One!" the Jews rushed their attackers. The courtyard echoed with the clang of metal against metal, shouts of battle lust, and, soon, shrieks of the dying and wounded.

"Protect Catharina and the children," Samson called to his son Jacob. Then he tucked his shield into position and, his heart racing, looked eagerly to where he could inflict the greatest injury.

Most of the older Jews, plus some of the women, had not hung back but flung themselves at the marauders. Armed only with knives, they did what damage they could, but even if each managed to bring down several of the enemy before he fell, there would still be thousands outside to replace them.

Hacking his way through the melee, Samson worked his way toward the gate. Once he found a fortified position, he could cut down his foes as they entered. A trail of bodies followed in his wake, as his long arm severed limbs of those imprudent enough to raise a sword against him. Blood surged through his veins as his memory was flooded with battles fought against the Mongols in his youth. Then too he had been one against many.

Stay back, he reminded himself. *Don't continue assaulting one man until he's dead, disable him quickly and move on to the next.*

The piles of twitching, moaning bodies grew around him, and still the enemy poured through the gate, too many out of reach of his deadly sword. There seemed no end to the devils. He looked up, thanking his lucky stars for the height that allowed him to see over everyone else.

There were still pockets of fighting, but much of the courtyard resembled a slaughterhouse. Corpses lay everywhere, clouds of flies buzzing around those killed first. Samson felt a triumphant thrill that many were Emicho's soldiers, but his heart sank as he recognized the women and children among them.

Catharina! Where was Catharina?

He spotted his tall redheaded son among those still engaged in battle, near the far wall. Catharina and the children stood behind him, knives held ready. Slashing his way through the mob, trying not to slip on the blood-soaked stones, Samson finally reached his family.

"Hurry everyone." Rabbi Kalonymus somehow made his voice heard above the tumult. "Follow me inside."

Suddenly there was an open door, and with Samson, Jacob, and the few remaining Jews wielding swords to defend the rear, the survivors of Emicho's initial attack escaped into the palace. Following the rabbi though a maze of rooms and halls, they reached the bishop's fortified treasury storeroom. Samson slammed the heavy door behind him and threw down the drop bars.

They were safe—for the moment.

Catharina flew into Samson's arms as the room's beleaguered inhabitants heaved great sighs of relief. But when they gazed around and realized who was missing, their tears began to flow. Their number had been reduced to less than one tenth of those originally in the courtyard. They wept silently, restraining their anguish and praying that the enemy would remain ignorant of their hiding place.

The next morning, before dawn, one of the priests in charge of the treasury whispered through a small window, "Kalonymus, are you there? I've come with water. You must be thirsty."

The rabbi recognized the voice as one he could trust, but the vessel was too wide to fit between the window's narrow bars. They improvised a tube to drink through, thus temporarily slaking their thirst. And so the remnant of the once great Jewish community, terrified and weak with hunger, hid in the storeroom until evening. After dark the priest came again with water, but this time there was also a message from the bishop.

"Rothard wishes to save you, but he was forced to flee himself and no longer has sufficient strength to assist you," the priest said. "Your God has abandoned you. Either accept baptism or bear the sins of your ancestors."

"The verdict against us has been decreed and we cannot be saved." Kalonymus slumped against the wall. "Give us until tomorrow to respond."

But the rabbi didn't need to ask his followers what to do. Rabbi Amnon eloquently spoke for all when he said, "We cannot ponder the Holy One's ways. He gave us His Torah and therein commanded that we allow ourselves to be slain for the Sanctification of His Holy Name. How fortunate is the one to do His will. Not only does he merit eternal life, sitting among the righteous, but he exchanges a world of darkness for one of light, a world of trouble for one of joy, a fleeting world for one that endures forever." Then Amnon sat down at one of the desks, found parchment and quill, and began to write.

Catharina gazed around the locked room, its air heavy with the stench of the latrine they'd improvised in a corner, and her heart sank. They were trapped: fish in a net. It was too late for her, or any of them, to accept the bishop's offer. None of them would leave this place alive.

The following morning, it wasn't the friendly priest at the window but, to their horror, one of Emicho's men. Soon there were heavy footsteps on the roof, and those who remained of the once mighty Jewish community stared at each other, defiance burning in their eyes. The end had come, but it would be on their terms.

The women screamed curses out the window, abusing and insulting the enemy.

"In whom do you trust, a trodden corpse?" Catharina taunted them.

"The disgraced, disgusting son of adultery," her neighbor yelled.

Rabbi Amnon's sister was not to be outdone. "We will never exchange the Holy One for a hanged, crucified, dirty, abominable Nazarene, disgusting even in his own generation, a bastard, the son of a menstruant."

The women cheered when this last blasphemy drew bellows of rage from the soldiers outside.

"We cannot delay! Our foes are approaching!" A yeshiva student named Asher bared his neck. "Let us act like Abraham Avinu with his son Isaac, offering ourselves to the Holy One in Heaven. Whoever has a knife, come sacrifice me."

When everyone stepped back in shock, Amnon looked pleadingly at Kalonymus, who slowly nodded his approval. The Italian rabbi examined his sword, saw that its edge was perfect, and recited the blessing for ritual slaughter. Then, as all except Samson averted their eyes, he slit Asher's throat and threw himself on his sword.

They were still transfixed by the blood gushing from the two dying men when the sudden crash of falling ceiling tiles made them look up into a rain of arrows. Samson jumped onto a table, shield held high to protect those below. He slashed wildly at the enemy on the roof, forcing the archers back.

Rabbi Amnon's sister begged those with knives, "Do not spare our children, for the uncircumcised ones will capture them and raise them with their foul heresy."

In an instant she was surrounded by a frenzy of killing as husband slaughtered wife, parents sacrificed sons and daughters, and friend killed friend, their blood mingling on the floor.

Catharina gazed at her children, standing silent as statues, and marveled that her family had survived until now. Suddenly Jacob fell at her feet, grasping at an arrow in his shoulder. She looked up at her husband, arrow shafts protruding from his body, and let out a bitter wail. "Will You bear this, Oh, Holy One, and keep silent at our extreme suffering? May Your servants' spilt blood be speedily avenged!"

She quickly ended Jacob's agony, then her view shifted to a hole in the roof where light flooded in. "Oh, Angels in Heaven, has there ever been so great a sacrifice, even since the time of Abraham?"

Her heart heavy as lead, she slit one child's throat after another. Finally she clutched little Salomon to her breast and ended the life that had so recently filled hers with joy. Then as her youngest son slumped in her arms, she collapsed atop her children's corpses, an arrow in her back.

Samson felt only a sting when the first arrow lodged in his thigh. The second arrow tore through his side, but he ignored the searing pain and fought on, determined to uphold his shield until no Jew remained who needed his protection. A third arrow grazed his cheek, but then another struck his calf and his leg buckled.

"What sons of adultery you are, believing in one born of adultery!" he goaded his attackers. "But I believe in the One God who lives forever. In Him I have trusted until this day, and in Him I shall trust until my soul leaves me. If you kill me, my soul will rest in the Garden of Eden, whereas you will descend into the very pit of hell."

Arrow after arrow slammed into him, forcing him down and pinning him to the wooden floorboards. Agony threatened to overwhelm him until the torment abruptly disappeared and the room around him shone with incredible light. Dressed in white, brightness radiating from her body, Catharina beckoned to him. Smiling behind her, also in white, were their children, his old master Jacob, and, in the back, Abraham Avinu himself. They were all calling him, welcoming him, encouraging him to join them.

Samson let the sword drop from his hand.

Returning to Troyes with spices and dyestuffs from Toledo, Eliezer sensed something amiss as soon as he entered the Auxerre Gate. Normally excitement and eager anticipation were palpable as the Hot Fair approached. But there were no cheerful greetings from the guards, and the fairgrounds, while tidy and festooned, were too quiet. And shouldn't there be more merchants around? The Cloth Fair was due to open at the week's end.

Could rumors of attacks on the Jews of Speyer and Worms be true? Eliezer shook his head in disbelief. Even if so, riots in Rouen last winter hadn't disturbed the Cold Fair. Still, he hurried his pace. It was nearly time for *disner*, and those at Salomon's table would have the latest news.

His anxiety heightened when Rachel ran out to greet him, clinging to him with relief instead of passion.

"Oh, Eliezer, thank Heaven you're home." Tears spilled down her cheeks. "I've been so worried."

Before he could ask why, Salomon and Judah were bearing down on them, and Eliezer knew something dreadful had happened. It was difficult to say which man looked more miserable; both had lost weight and there were dark circles under their swollen eyes. Judah hadn't looked this desolate since learning of Aaron's death, and Salomon appeared worse than when Rivka died. Refusing to let go, Rachel kept her arm around Eliezer as he washed. Desperate for information, yet afraid of what her family would tell him, he silently accompanied them into Salomon's salon.

Miriam spoke first, apparently the only one who could do so without breaking into tears. "We just received the most distressing letter from Cousin Elazar."

Eliezer looked at her blankly, until she added, "Aunt Sarah's son in Speyer."

Eliezer relaxed slightly. Cousin Elazar was obviously well enough to write about the situation.

"He says that a horde of fanatical pilgrims, led by Count Emicho of Lorraine, may his bones be ground to dust, attacked the Jewish Quarter in Speyer on the eighth of Iyar," Miriam began. "Bishop Johann's men were able to protect most of his Jews, so the evil ones headed for Worms."

Judah was trembling, and she reached for his hand. "Cousin Elazar tells us the Jews there weren't so fortunate. In the few days it took the wicked Emicho to reach Worms, he attracted every villain in the vicinity, promising plunder and guaranteeing that whoever killed a Jew would have his sins pardoned."

Judah began to weep, and Miriam paused to comfort him, leaving Rachel to continue. "Apparently half the Jewish community remained in their homes, while the rest took refuge in the bishop's castle. When our cousin wrote this, he'd heard only that those at home were murdered. He had no word on the fate of those who sheltered with the bishop." Her expression held more fear than hope.

"When is the letter dated?" Eliezer asked.

"The twentieth of Iyar. Almost a month ago." Rachel's face crumpled. "But no merchants from Worms have yet arrived in Troyes, and none from Speyer or Mayence either."

Eliezer stared at Judah and Salomon, both of whom had barely touched their food. *No wonder they're so distraught.*

"Giuseppe was here when we received the letter," Miriam said. "No one could keep him from riding to Worms immediately."

"Just because merchants from the Rhineland aren't here yet doesn't mean that a disaster has occurred there," Eliezer said. "Surely none will dare to set out with Emicho's men roaming the countryside; just as I wouldn't leave Troyes until Peter's pilgrims were gone."

"That's true." Salomon sighed with relief and reached for a piece of bread. "And we did write to warn them of the danger."

"Even so, I'm fasting on Monday and Thursday until Giuseppe returns." Judah crossed his arms over his chest.

Rachel doubted that she'd see Giuseppe or her horse again, but she said nothing of her fears. Nor of the fact that there had been an eclipse of the moon only four months ago. Helpless to save their brethren in the Rhineland, she and her sisters threw themselves into their study of Tractate Taanit, which taught about fasts decreed to avert drought or other disasters. But this only increased her fright over the German Jews' fate.

They soon reached the sixth Mishnah of chapter 4, which explained the two darkest fasts in the Jewish calendar: fasts the Jews of Troyes would be observing in a few weeks. Each commemorated a series of calamities befalling Israel.

> Five events befell our fathers on the Seventeenth of Tammuz and five on Tishah b'Av [the Ninth of Av]. On the Seventeenth of Tammuz, the Tablets were broken, the daily offering ceased, the city [Jerusalem] walls were breached, Apostumos burned the Torah, and an idol was set up in the Temple. On Tishah b'Av, it was decreed that our fathers should not enter the land, the Temple was destroyed the first and second time, Bethar was captured, and the city was plowed up. When Av arrives, gladness is diminished.

For the benefit of Hannah and Leah, who listened to their mother's Talmud study whenever possible, Joheved read from Salomon's *kuntres* to clarify these tragic events, which eerily threatened to reflect those in Worms.

"It was on the Seventeenth of Tammuz that Moses came down from Sinai and saw Israel sinning with the golden calf, which caused him to smash the Ten Commandments."

Leah looked at her mother in confusion. "How do the Rabbis know what day Moses broke the Tablets?" She was too young to understand why all the adults were so sad, and Joheved hoped to keep it that way.

"Listen to how the Gemara explains it," Miriam said.

> "The Law was given on Shavuot, the Sixth of Sivan, and Moses climbed Mount Sinai on the seventh, as it is written [in Exodus]: 'He called to Moses on the seventh day.' It is further written: 'Moses was on the mountain for forty days and forty nights'—the last twenty-four days of Sivan and the first sixteen of Tammuz. Thus Moses came down and broke the Tablets on the Seventeenth of Tammuz."

"The Rabbis also deduce that the spies returned to Moses with their dire assessment on Tishah b'Av," Rachel added. "Causing the Almighty to decree that the Children of Israel must wander in the desert for forty years before entering Eretz Israel."

"Papa says that Bethar was one of the largest Jewish cities remaining after the Romans destroyed Jerusalem," Joheved said. "They fought for fifty years before it fell."

Rachel flinched as she mentally compared Bethar to Worms or Mayence, cities that would fall in days, not years.

It was Hannah, clearly not ignorant of the events in the Rhineland, who asked the question that occupied her elders' thoughts as well: "Why do all these terrible things keep happening to us?"

As the monstrous news from the east trickled into Troyes, the fairgrounds grew subdued. By the Seventeenth of Tammuz, many Jews of Troyes were mourning relatives from the Rhineland, and when Giuseppe returned, throwing himself into Judah's arms and bawling like a child, most already knew the worst. Cousin Elazar's community in Speyer was the only one to withstand Emicho's marauders. In Worms the bishop had been as unsuccessful at saving the Jews hiding in his castle as in protecting those hidden in their homes.

"I went to Elisha's, may his merit protect us." Giuseppe trembled as he told Salomon's distraught household, "The courtyard had been ransacked."

"Perhaps his family escaped," Judah said in desperation.

Giuseppe's chin began to quiver so he could scarcely speak. "There were bloodstains on the floor . . . several of them."

"*Mon Dieu.*" Miriam began to cry.

"I located one of the survivors." Giuseppe forced himself to continue. "A few Jews from the castle agreed to sully themselves with the heretics' smelly waters in order to bury those lying naked in the streets. Two weeks later they returned to bury the rest of them."

The color drained from Salomon's face. "Our people in Worms, the yeshiva, my colleagues there—all destroyed."

"You're sure Elisha is dead?" Judah couldn't give up hope. "Perhaps he was away from home."

"He was home for Shavuot." Giuseppe put his arm around Judah for support. "I spoke with the man who buried him."

"Is it true what they're saying about Mayence?" Eliezer asked, hoping against hope that the rumors were false.

Giuseppe blinked back tears and nodded. "The entire community of Mayence . . . over one thousand pious souls . . . massacred. The last I heard, the evil ones were approaching Cologne."

"Adonai our God! You are wiping out the remnant of Israel," Salomon cried out, quoting the prophet Ezekiel. "All the great yeshivot are gone." He buried his face in his hands and wept.

Rachel put her hand on his shoulder. "Not all of them, Papa. Your yeshiva is still here."

The day before Tishah b'Av, Salomon's household sat silently on the floor to eat their final frugal meal, the enormity of their grief heavy upon them. Like mourners, Rachel and Eliezer ate boiled eggs for their one cooked dish and vegetables and fruit served without sauces. Salomon and Judah ate only bread, water, and salt.

Its rituals were the same, but this year's Tishah b'Av observance was nothing like those before the calamity in the Rhineland. In previous years most Jews worked at their occupations, acting out a mourning they did not deeply feel. After all, life in Troyes was good and the Temple had been destroyed almost a thousand years ago. Some tears were shed, and by mid-afternoon everyone was weak with thirst after fasting through the long hot day, but business negotiations continued even if no money changed hands.

This year, when Rachel entered the synagogue that evening and saw it stripped of adornment, even the ark shorn of its decorative curtains, she shrank back, envisioning the plundered German synagogues and their murdered occupants. Taking off her shoes, reclining on the floor, and gazing at the bare feet around her, Rachel could not dispel the horrible image of naked Jewish bodies lying on the synagogue floors of Allemagne.

When prayers were finished and the service leader began chanting Lamentations—not the hazzan because he sang too beautifully—it was impossible to hear the verses describing Jerusalem's destruction and not mourn for Worms and Mayence. In a low voice, Joheved translated the text for the women, words that Rachel never imagined would describe a city in Ashkenaz.

> Alas, lonely sits the city once great with people.
> She has become like a widow . . .
> All her friends betrayed her; they became her enemies . . .
> When her people fell by enemy hands, with none to help her . . .
> When enemies looked on and gloated over her downfall . . .
> For these things I weep, my eyes overflow with tears . . .

Wails of grief issued from men and women alike, threatening to drown out the readers' voices, and both Joheved and her male counterpart below had to pause when their own sadness overcame them. Rachel wept as she hadn't done since baby Asher died. Yet the dreadful text of Lamentations continued:

> Outside the sword deals bereavement, inside like death . . .
> Prostrate in the streets lie both young and old.
> My maidens and youths have fallen by the sword . . .
> None survived or escaped . . . Our enemies loudly rail against us.
>   Panic and pitfall are our lot, death and destruction.
> My eyes shed streams of tears over the ruin of my people.

The final verses of comfort, urging the Holy One to take His people back and renew their days, were overshadowed by a series of *kinot*, dirges and somber poems, each more melancholy than the last. When the final doleful note was chanted, the red-eyed congregants slowly stood and, heads down, made their way to the street. Then, without a word of greeting, they trudged home.

The next morning at services, Rachel's bereavement was even stronger after praying at home stripped of her tefillin. Again the shoes came off and everyone sat on the floor; again the seemingly endless *kinot*, composed for the express purpose of searing the heart and grieving the soul, and again the congregation's tears flowed copiously as they mourned the destruction of Jerusalem and the martyrdom of Mayence and Worms.

When the closing dirge was done, the Jews of Troyes headed, not to their homes, but to the cemetery, where they would remain until it was time for the afternoon service. Salomon's family gathered around Rivka's grave, where he taught from his *kuntres* on Lamentations and Jeremiah. Like at a house of mourning, this was the only Torah study permitted on Tishah b'Av. But the tradition of not ending a study session with an unhappy text was too entrenched to violate, even on such a black day.

So when he explained the first verse of Lamentations, "She has become like a widow," he emphasized the word "like." "This doesn't mean a true widow. Rather she is a woman whose husband has gone abroad on a journey, and he intends to return to her."

Neither his words, nor those of the prophet Isaiah, whose consolations were read each Shabbat between Tishah b'Av and Rosh Hashanah, provided any comfort for Rachel. The Sages taught that Jerusalem was destroyed because of the Jews' sins, their needless hatred for each other. *But what sins had the pious Jews of Worms and Mayence committed?*

Her dread only heightened when the Fifteenth of Av brought, instead of the day of great happiness described at the close of Tractate Taanit, another eclipse of the moon.

twenty-one

alomon's yeshiva received an unusually large infusion of new students at the start of the Cold Fair, many of them older youths who'd previously studied in Mayence or Worms and who, by fortuitous providence, were away celebrating Shavuot when Emicho's marauders descended on those cities. But many of them, filled with grief and rage, found their studies difficult, and instead of a source of pride for Salomon, the increased number of students was a heartrending reminder of his people's loss.

Even more depressing, merchants brought responsa questions from communities that had never written to him before.

"What's wrong, Papa," Rachel inquired gently when she observed him weeping while reading one of these missives.

"This letter comes from Rome." Salomon cradled his head in his hands.

"But it's an honor for Jews so far away to recognize your wisdom and seek your advice."

"*Ma fille*, I have no more wisdom now than last year." He brushed away his tears. "They consult me only because the more knowledgeable scholars are dead."

Rachel sighed and placed her hand on his shoulder. She, better than most, should know how devastating a loss Judaism had sustained.

Eliezer and Pesach had just returned from their autumn trip east for furs. At Dulcie's insistence, they stopped in Mayence to ascertain what, if anything, remained of her family's home.

"The Jewish Quarter was plundered." Eliezer couldn't hide his outrage. "The only thing Pesach brought back for Dulcie was a letter written by one of the martyrs who died in the bishop's castle along with her parents and siblings."

"Are there any Jews left in Mayence?" Rachel asked in dismay. She still could not accept the enormity of the community's destruction.

"Only a few *anusim* who said they'd had no choice but to abandon the faith."

"So the Talmud academy won't be rebuilt."

He shook his head. "Probably not in Worms either."

"Oh, Eliezer." Her chin began to quiver. "So many yeshivot have disappeared."

The once great Babylonian Talmud academies were emptied by the Turks, Bedouins had destroyed Kairouan's Jewish district, and the few schools left in Andalusia were closing as the Berbers forced the Jews to flee.

But Salomon and the Jews of Troyes were too troubled by their own quarrels to consider the fate of foreign communities. Cursing the marauders, now far away, was a poor outlet for their rage over the destruction of Rhineland Jewry, and none would publicly vent their frustration that God had let it happen. So their feelings were displaced onto arguments about how to deal with those Jews who'd apostatized when confronted with the choice of baptism or death. With the threat over, many *anusim* were eager to return to Judaism, and some were desirous of enrolling their sons in Salomon's yeshiva.

Yet not everyone was eager to accept them.

Salomon's daughters and their husbands mirrored every side of the vehement debate in Ashkenaz—should a Jew die rather than violate the Torah prohibition against idolatry? To his growing irritation, they argued continuously for the three weeks it took the grapes to ferment into wine in his courtyard.

Joheved was adamant that death was the only acceptable alternative to apostasy, and that the Rhineland Jews should be praised for refusing to violate Jewish Law. "It says so clearly in the eighth chapter of Tractate Sanhedrin:

> All transgressions in the Torah—if they tell a man to sin and then he will not be killed, he should sin and not let himself be killed. Except for the sins of idolatry, forbidden sexual relations, and murder."

She stamped her foot into the fizzing must, sending waves of half wine toward her daughters in the vat.

"If that were the case, there'd be no Jews left alive, and Judaism would cease to exist." Rachel wasn't about to let Joheved lecture her about Talmud. "For Sanhedrin also says:

> Is this true that he dies rather than worship idols? But Rabbi Yishmael taught: if they tell a man to worship idols and thus he will not be killed, where do we learn that he should worship them and not be killed? From Leviticus, where it is written, 'You shall keep My laws, by which man shall live.' This means live, not die."

Meir, treading grapes with their sons in the vat next to his wife, supported her by quoting more of the text, while Shmuel stamped his feet in approval.

> "You might think this means even in public, but it is also written in Leviticus, 'You shall not profane my Holy Name, that I will be sanctified among Israel.' This is in agreement with Rabbi Eleazar.

Thus a Jew should die sanctifying the Holy Name rather than publicly forsake the Laws of Moses, as did the martyrs of Worms and Mayence—may their merit protect us."

Eliezer, sharing a wine vat with Judah, quickly turned over his paddle of grapes so he could lean out to refute Joheved. "You tell us that a man should die rather than commit murder. If so, how do you justify what happened in Mayence and Worms, where Jews killed themselves and their children rather than pretend to worship the Hanged One?"

"Their children would be raised as heretics if they were captured," Joheved retorted.

"That's no call to murder them." Rachel stomped down into the tangled raft of grapes and stems, sending ripples through the vat she shared with Miriam.

Miriam was torn between her sisters' views. While she would rather die than see her children abandon Judaism, she couldn't imagine killing them to prevent it. "But if your children were captured, wouldn't it be prudent to submit to the heretics while secretly remaining loyal to the Holy One?" she asked. "Then you could bring them up yourself and see that they followed the Laws of Moses."

"Rabbi Yishmael's view may be appropriate for most Jews." Judah also took the middle ground. "However, a scholar, who sets an example for the people, should be held to Rabbi Eleazar's higher standard."

Yet who was he to give such advice? Hadn't he, a *talmid chacham*, been ready, eager even, to engage in a forbidden sexual relationship when he should have been willing to die instead?

"That's absurd." Eliezer's voice rose in ire. "If all the scholars are dead, who will teach Torah when other Jews repent?"

"Yet if scholars worship the Hanged One in public, even if only pretending to do so," Joheved shook her paddle at him, "then less-educated Jews will believe that they truly committed idolatry and may follow their example."

Meir's eyes flashed with anger. "No true *chacham* would publicly desecrate the Holy Name in such a manner. He would die first like Rabbi Akiva."

Salomon's students and neighbors in the other vats found his family's acrimony heartrending. Normally, treading the vintage was a jolly effort, with much singing and joking, and this harvest, after the first year of ample rainfall in some time, had looked to be a cause of celebration.

"Don't you see that by choosing martyrdom, the German scholars have allowed their Torah knowledge to die with them?" Rachel heaved her grapes in Meir's direction and trod on them. "Rather than follow Rabbi Akiva's example, we should be like Rabbi Yohanan ben Zakai, who escaped Jerusalem and negotiated with the Roman enemy to save his yeshiva in Yavneh."

"It's not as if the *anusim* can't return to Judaism." Miriam stirred the contents of her vat to calm the stormy fermentation, hoping her gentle words would have the same effect on her family. "Once they move where the Church won't find them, they can repent their idolatry."

Judah said aloud what many Jews in Troyes were thinking. "Yet how can we welcome these *anusim* back without penalty, when they cravenly sullied themselves in the heretic's evil waters while their brethren died sanctifying the Holy Name?"

All this time Salomon said nothing, his face growing redder by the moment. Finally he slammed his paddle down hard on the vat's edge, cracking the wood. "Enough! None of us know what he would do if, Heaven forbid, the sword were at his throat. None of us may judge what another Jew should do under such duress."

He stared furiously around the now silent courtyard, bending everyone to his will. "A Jew who sins, no matter how grievously, remains a Jew," he declared. "One who shows sincere remorse and genuine repentance is received back to his former status."

He locked eyes with each family member in turn. "You all know that it is forbidden to remind a penitent of his previous sins. I will not tolerate anyone in my community doing so."

Even Salomon's pronouncement didn't stop the fighting; it merely moved out of his presence or found another subject.

His daughters now argued over how many of the astringent stalks to leave in the vats for added flavor and bite, followed by disputes over when to remove the new wine from the lees. The vintner should wait long enough for the flavor to gain complexity, but too long gives the wine an unpleasant yeasty taste. They disagreed over how many whipped egg whites to pour through the wine to clarify it sufficiently without detracting from its character. And no sooner did one daughter open the cellar windows to prevent the rising temperature from speeding the fermentation, than another closed them to keep the fermentation from stopping in the cold.

When Eliezer returned to Troyes for the Cold Fair, variations of the opinions he'd heard in the wine vats were being bandied around the fairgrounds and whispered in the synagogues. Salomon must have remembered Meir's condemnation of forced converts, because he gave Judah the responsibility of interviewing prospective students from the Rhineland. Judah was showing Eliezer what texts Salomon intended to teach that winter when a balding middle-aged man and teenage youth hesitantly entered his salon. There was something familiar about the pair; yet Judah was sure he'd never met them before.

"This is my son, Gedaliah ben Daniel." The man spoke Hebrew with a German accent. "We resided in Cologne for many years, but I'm not sure we will live there much longer. In the meantime, I'd like him to stay in Troyes and study at your yeshiva."

Eliezer observed the pair with interest. They were likely survivors of the massacres, possibly even *anusim.*

Judah reacted with astonishment. His first study partner, Daniel ben Gedaliah, had hailed from that city. Judah stared at the man's thin hair and slack jowls, trying to find some hint of the youth he'd studied with, and loved so desperately, in Worms.

"We're always eager for more students." Judah reached out and clasped Daniel's hand. "I'm Judah ben Natan, the rosh yeshiva's son-in-law." He carefully observed the man's reaction.

Daniel squinted at Judah and scratched his head. Then his jaw dropped. "Judah ben Natan of Paris? A student in Worms about twenty years ago? Is it really you?"

Judah smiled and held out his arms.

"I don't deserve a warm welcome." Daniel's eyes lowered in remorse. "Especially from a *talmid chacham* like you. I have committed too great a sin."

Judah waved everyone to the table. "Sit down and have some wine." He brought a flask and cups from the kitchen.

Eliezer was impressed that, instead of pouring the wine himself, Judah deliberately handed the flask to Daniel and busied himself with wiping some imaginary dirt from one of the cups. Jewish Law prohibited Jews from drinking wine handled by non-Jews, which was why Salomon employed Jewish servants. Without a word, Judah demonstrated to Daniel that, whatever the man's sin, Judah considered him a Jew.

"Thank you." Daniel's voice conveyed his gratitude for more than a cup of wine. "The last six months have been a nightmare."

Before Daniel could continue, the front door opened to admit Miriam and Rachel, home from vineyard, where they'd spent the afternoon pulling out the vine props and stacking them between rows. All that tugging and bending was arduous work that had to be completed before the vines could be pruned.

The two women collapsed onto benches while Judah made the introductions and Eliezer got more cups.

"I'm mortified by my transgression," Daniel said. "Yet I feel a great need to explain what happened to us in Cologne."

"You will find us a most compassionate audience." Miriam's voice was warm in its sincerity.

The others nodded and pulled their benches closer; at last they would hear an eyewitness report instead of rumors.

"On the eve of Shavuot we learned that the communities of Worms and Mayence had been decimated." Daniel's voice betrayed no emotion. "So we fled to our Notzrim acquaintances and hid as the enemy looted our homes, destroyed the synagogue, and desecrated the Torah scrolls." He took a deep breath. "But we were still alive."

"We heard that Cologne suffered the same fate as Worms and Mayence," Rachel said without thinking.

"Not at this juncture it hadn't." Daniel proceeded to describe how the archbishop divided the community and sent them to seven of his most fortified towns.

"We hid in the countryside for almost a month," Gedaliah said.

Daniel began to tremble, sending Judah to stand beside him and pat his shoulder. "One day the priest came running to us, yelling that Emicho's men were coming, that we should follow him to a new hiding place. The rest of the townsfolk were with him, urging us to come with them, that they would protect us."

He put his head in his hands and fell silent.

Gedaliah continued his father's tale. "The people surrounded us, herding us like sheep toward the river. Before we realized it, we were standing in the water while the priest said something in Latin and made his evil sign over us."

Daniel's eyes begged for mercy. "When the enemy arrived, we were huddled together on the riverbank, shivering like wet dogs. The priest told Emicho, may his bones be ground between iron millstones, to leave us in peace, that he had baptized us."

"His men didn't harm you?" Rachel asked in astonishment.

He shook his head. "So we returned to Cologne. There we heard that most of the other Jews had thrown themselves into the Rhine . . . including my brother."

Daniel paused to control his feelings. "He and his study partner loved each other greatly, such that neither could bear to see the other die. They climbed a high tower, kissed and embraced, and jumped into the river, clasped in each other's arms."

Judah gasped and Miriam took his hand in sympathy. Daniel's brother had chosen to die in another man's arms and received admiration for his act, not condemnation.

Gedaliah concluded, "Of the seven towns the archbishop sent us to, only Kerpen was able to protect its Jews."

"Your town saved its Jews," Rachel said. "Everyone sent there from Cologne survived."

"We desecrated the Holy Name; we deserved to die." Daniel's face was a mask of pain. "How could He leave such unworthy ones as us alive and let the pious Jews be killed?"

"None of us can fathom the Holy One's ways," Eliezer declared. "It is not for us to question who is worthy or not."

"Surely your community returned to the Law of Moses after the enemy left?" Miriam asked. "And repented at Yom Kippur?"

"My family did." Daniel brightened at their support.

"Sending Gedaliah to yeshiva is proof of your loyalty to the Law of Moses." Judah gave Daniel a hug. "It's almost time for afternoon services. Please come worship with us."

Rachel and Eliezer hung back from the others as they walked. "I don't understand the heretics," she whispered. "One instant Jews are despised infidels who killed the Hanged One and the next, with no change in our beliefs, merely being dunked in water, we are welcomed into the fold."

"Emicho may not have attacked the *anusim*, but I doubt that his men warmly embraced them." Eliezer grimaced. "And I suspect that no matter how hard the *anusim* try to prove they've abandoned their old faith, someone in the Church will always be distrusting them, checking on them, spying on them."

"So they'll never be safe. What a terrible way to live."

Eliezer nodded. Right now his family was secure in Troyes. But who knows for how long? He had no doubts that if Emicho's army had attacked Troyes' Jewish community, the inexperienced Count Hugues would have offered little protection. Maybe it would be a good thing if Rachel's aspirations to be a clothier were never realized. Then they could all move to Toledo and be safe.

Rachel tallied her accounts in late November and despaired of ever putting her woolen business into operation. Joheved's sheep would soon start giving high-quality wool, but who would Rachel find to weave it? The two horizontal looms still sat unused in the cellar. Yet she had to succeed: with all these armed pilgrims on the road, Eliezer's travels would only grow more dangerous.

Alette the Spinster had come to borrow money at the start of the Cold Fair, promising to pay it when the fair closed, and Rachel had lent it to her, although the wool Alette spun would never bring in the income they'd earned from Albert's weaving. Indeed a month later Alette was back, and judging by her stooped posture as she crept through the courtyard she would be needing another loan rather than paying off the last one.

"Oh, Mistress Rachel, I don't know what to do," Alette whined as Rachel mentally calculated how much she could spare for the weaver. "Albert came back yesterday, but he's in a terrible state."

Albert—back in Troyes already? "How is that possible?" No one could get to Constantinople and back that fast, never mind Jerusalem.

"I don't know. He has refused to speak since his return. I am wondering if he is able. He just went straight to bed. And he was limping something awful."

"Let me see him." Rachel jumped up and grabbed her mantle. They hurried down the chilly street, Rachel only half listening to Alette's anxious voice. What difference did it make if Albert remained mute? The important question was could he weave.

Alette called out and opened the door slowly when they arrived, careful not to startle her brother.

Albert sat by the hearth, staring at the fire, and he neither turned nor greeted his sister when they entered. "I've brought you a visitor," Alette announced in an artificially cheerful tone. "Mistress Rachel."

Albert turned around, but his expression was blank.

Rachel took in the gaunt lined face, the listless eyes, and knew he'd undergone some trauma on his pilgrimage. "I'm glad to see that you've come back to us. Alette tells me that you hurt your leg."

To her surprise, Albert stretched out his leg and pulled up his pants. It was obvious what ailed him—just below the knee his leg was bent at an odd angle. But the break must have happened early on his journey; his skin wasn't discolored.

"Oh, Albert," Alette cried out. "Does it hurt much? Let me fetch the doctor."

Albert shook his head vigorously, although the poorly healed break must be painful.

Rachel gave a sigh of relief that Albert was capable of some communication. "Do you think you can work the foot pedals of a loom again?" she asked him. "If not, you must allow the doctor to help you. Your family will starve unless you start weaving again."

Albert gingerly pumped his injured foot up and down a few times, grimacing slightly.

"Your loom is in my cellar. Do you want to try it there?" Rachel suggested.

He shook his head and pointed to the empty space where the loom used to sit. Alette looked at him doubtfully and asked, "You just got back. Maybe you should wait to regain your strength."

Albert scowled, shook his head again, and pointed several times to the empty area in his sister's salon. She turned to Rachel and shrugged in acquiescence.

"I'll have a carter bring it over," Rachel said. Maybe exercising his hurt leg would help it heal. Perhaps it was just as well that he didn't speak. After hearing the Jews' horror stories, she wasn't sure she could listen to his.

Alette, however, didn't think there was anything horrific behind her brother's sudden dumbness. "Clearly he broke his leg at the beginning," she said after the loom was delivered. "Since he could no longer keep up with the other pilgrims, they left him behind to heal. When he ended up lame, it became impossible to catch up with them, so he returned home."

But Albert didn't nod or show any sign of agreement with his sister's wishful explanation. Rather he clenched his jaw and worked the loom even faster.

The first inkling of what befell Albert and others who'd followed Peter the Hermit came when another refugee turned up at Rachel's door during the week before Hanukkah. She was preparing the children for bed, and Eliezer was about to return to the Old Synagogue for Salomon's evening Talmud session. He'd just stepped out of the privy when Baruch called to him from the open courtyard gate.

"Eliezer, I'm glad you haven't left yet. That pilgrim fellow who was here last spring—he's back. Do you want to see him or shall I give him *souper* and send him on his way?"

"Please, Master Eliezer, please help me." The panicky voice belonged to Jehan. "You're the only person left in the world I know. Geoffrey, my brother, all the others—they're dead."

Eliezer's jaw dropped, and he stopped in his tracks. What the devil was Jehan doing back in Troyes? Eliezer realized he couldn't turn the miserable fellow away. Jehan had made his captivity bearable, possibly saving his life. And if the youth was the only survivor of the horde that had camped outside Troyes last spring, Eliezer had to hear what happened.

"It's all right, Baruch. He can stay in the attic for the time being." Eliezer put his arm around Jehan, noting that the youth was little more than skin and bones, and led him indoors.

Rachel came downstairs as soon as she heard the strange man's voice, and one look at Jehan's torn clothes and long stringy hair sent her rushing to the kitchen for a loaf of bread and large bowl of stew. Eliezer, torn between his studies and impatience to hear Jehan's story, decided to delay until the youth had filled his stomach. At the rate Jehan was wolfing down his food, the wait wouldn't be long.

On Rachel's part, she couldn't help but feel both eagerness and trepidation. When she heard Jehan's last sentence, hope welled within her that the evil ones responsible for the destruction of Rhineland Jewry had themselves been annihilated. Whatever caused Albert's silence had not affected Jehan: the youth's tale spilled out as quickly as mouthfuls of stew disappeared.

"Master Eliezer . . . you can't imagine . . . what disasters I've endured." Jehan tried to eat and speak simultaneously. "I've lost track . . . of all the times . . . I was sure I'd be killed."

"Please start from the beginning." Rachel refilled his cup of wine. "There's no need to gulp down your *souper*. You wouldn't want to survive all these dangers only to choke on a piece of meat now that you are safe."

"Safe." Jehan gazed around the room in awe. "I'm finally safe." Then he gazed into the hearth as if he were looking at something far away.

twenty-two

"hings started well." Jehan looked longingly at the bread and Rachel cut him a large piece. "We had plenty of provisions and Peter had money to buy more. The villages we passed on our way to the Danube were generous, and we attracted more pilgrims the farther we traveled. Soon we were too many for most towns to feed, and there were reports of theft in the camp along with looting the countryside."

Rachel and Eliezer exchanged anxious glances.

"When we reached Prague, Peter's money was gone. Some of the Teutons wanted to attack the Jews there, but Geoffrey would have none of it. Which was just as well because, instead of easy pickings, the Teutons found themselves facing five hundred armed Jews along with a thousand of the duke's soldiers."

Jehan shook his head at the memory, while Rachel was filled with pride at knowing that in one place, at least, the Jews had fought back and vanquished their enemies.

"We left Prague in a hurry, empty handed. As we headed into the Balkans, it became more difficult to beg food from the country folk or live off the land. Most towns were closed tight against us, and to make matters worse the mountain passes were infested with bandits who eagerly picked off the stragglers."

He sighed heavily. "I stayed near the front with Geoffrey and the other knights, and thus I was one of the first to arrive at Belgrade. Word of our numbers and desperation must have reached them, because the place was deserted. Most of us hadn't had a good meal in weeks, so when bands formed to plunder the town, my only excuse for what I did was my hunger," he said, his eyelids lowering in embarrassment.

"Belgrade's storehouses were empty, and in our fury we burned the city. I still can't believe I was capable of such a despicable act." Jehan looked up at his hosts, his eyes begging their forgiveness. "We'd escaped repercussions thus far, despite the damage we'd caused, so we felt above the law. That ended at Nis, where a battalion of the emperor's soldiers was waiting to escort us to Constantinople. The commander distributed food, but the Teutons started pillaging again anyway."

Jehan let out a deep breath. "A few days later, I was foraging for nuts and berries when I heard a sound like thunder in the distance; yet there were no clouds in the sky. I rode to the forest's edge, where I saw pilgrims yelling and snatching up their possessions and running back the way we'd come. Suddenly the entire garrison of Nis was bearing down on us, and before I knew it, my horse was racing into the woods with me holding on for dear life."

Jehan stared into the hearth. "The next morning I retraced my steps, but there was no camp, only a battlefield. Corpses were everywhere—men, women, children, livestock—with jackals and vultures picking at them. Every cart had been demolished, every dish smashed, every container of foodstuff ripped open and spoiled. Slowly other survivors appeared from the forest, including Geoffrey and Peter the Hermit. I wanted to go home more than anything, but I had sworn the pilgrim's oath."

"What happened to your brother?" Eliezer asked. "And the rest of Geoffrey's men?"

"I couldn't find my brother's body, but I never saw him again." Jehan sniffed back tears. "Those of us left, and there weren't many, collected whatever we could find that was still edible and made our way to Sofia, where the emperor gave us shelter. Eventually other pilgrims joined us from France and Italy, but we heard that most of the Germans had been killed by the Hungarian army."

Rachel and Eliezer exchanged excited looks. Had the Almighty already exacted vengeance for the slaughter of His people? "Did you learn the names of any of the German leaders?" she asked. "Was one of them a Count Emicho?"

"I'm pretty sure that was one of them." Jehan scratched his head in thought. "Also a priest, Folkmar, and a monk, Gottschalk, I think, but there may have been others."

"What happened next?" Rachel asked. A surge of anger against the German pilgrims vied with her eagerness to hear how they had been defeated.

"Emperor Alexius wanted us to wait until the main body of knights arrived, but Peter refused to delay. The French and Germans were quarreling over who should be the leader and how to divide the booty, so they weren't about to wait for more knights to share it with."

Jehan shook his head in disgust. "So all of us, maybe eighty thousand strong, crossed the Bosporus and headed for Nicaea. We were camped a day's ride away when we heard a rumor that the Germans and Italians had taken Nicaea and were looting it. The French were outraged and began a mad dash to the city, followed by the Germans and Italians who thought the French were trying to obtain the spoils first."

"And?" Eliezer asked when Jehan hesitated.

"The rumor had been started by the Turks, whose army was waiting to ambush us on the road to Nicaea." Jehan paused, his forehead creased in pain. "It was a rout. The Turks slew the men, sparing only those who surrendered and converted to Islam. The women and children in camp were captured and taken as slaves—those who didn't drown themselves in the sea first. I managed to escape on horseback to a nearby castle, along with Geoffrey and a few others."

Jehan's eyes grew wide with horror. "We had no food or water, and the Turks immediately lay siege. After three days in the heat—you have no idea how hot it gets there in August, worse than an oven—we were so thirsty that we drank our own piss and bled the horses to drink their blood. The last thing I remember is lying in the shade, waiting to die. I was unconscious when the emperor's soldiers finally rescued us."

Jehan sighed and regarded his hosts with resignation. "When I woke up in Constantinople, our pilgrimage was over. Emperor Alexius made the few survivors sell their arms and return home. I thought of Troyes, such a prosperous city, and that if I lived there for a year I'd be a free man, not a runaway villein."

Rachel stared at Eliezer in shock at the enormity of Jehan's tale. Not only had ten thousand Jews died in the Rhineland, but apparently over a hundred thousand pilgrims had lost their lives on this fool's errand.

"Now that you've reached Troyes, what do you intend to do?" Eliezer asked Jehan.

"I'll find work," he replied. "With all the men gone on pilgrimage who will never return, there must be jobs that need doing."

The solution came to Rachel in an instant, and she couldn't help but smile seductively. "Would you like to learn to weave?"

The next morning Jehan accompanied her to Alette's, where Rachel was gratified to hear the big horizontal loom working as she knocked on the door. Alette was surprised to see her again so soon and frowned at the skinny youth in dirty clothes (at least Rachel had made Jehan wash his hands and face) at her patron's side.

Albert's reaction was astonishing. He began trembling violently as he and Jehan stared wide-eyed at each other. Finally Jehan sputtered, "I never thought I'd see you again."

Albert closed his mouth, which had dropped open, and swallowed hard. Then he whispered, "What are you doing here?"

Alette wept as Jehan retold his story. Albert had turned back at Belgrade, after breaking his leg in the stampede of pilgrims fleeing Nis's soldiers. He'd dragged himself into the woods, where Jehan found him.

With gentle questioning by Rachel, Albert confirmed that Emicho's undisciplined men had been easy prey for the Hungarian army. He had passed the battlefield on his return and seen the Germans' plundered bodies himself. The horrific memories still gave him nightmares.

Rachel murmured something sympathetic, but inside she wanted to shout with triumph. To make her satisfaction complete, Albert was pleased to accept Jehan as an apprentice weaver after learning that Rachel had an additional loom for the youth to use.

"Should we tell anyone that Emicho and his men have received their punishment?" Rachel asked Eliezer later that night. "Or wait for better witnesses?"

"Say nothing yet. If Jehan and Albert's tale is true, the news will reach Troyes soon enough."

She sighed. "I wish I could tell Papa. He's been terribly melancholy over all those Rhineland Jews dying."

Eliezer hesitated, lost in thought. "Nobody will talk about it, but I don't understand what sin of theirs was so great that the Almighty averted His eyes and consigned them to the sword."

At first Rachel was shocked into silence. The pious martyrs of Worms and Mayence couldn't possibly have committed sins worthy of such punishment; it was scandalous to think so. Yet hadn't Jerusalem been destroyed because of its inhabitants' sins, baseless hatred in particular?

"Papa complained sometimes that they erected too many fences around the Torah, prohibited what was permitted, and made Judaism onerous for the people," she said. Could that be such a terrible sin?

Eliezer nodded. "I've often heard him say that any idiot can prohibit out of ignorance, while it takes a true *talmid chacham* who knows the law to rule leniently."

"He wrote that into his *kuntres*." Rachel struggled with her conflicted feelings; no wonder everyone avoided the subject. "It is difficult to believe that they deserved to be slaughtered on that account; yet the Holy One is a righteous judge and therefore they must be to blame."

"I heard Meir and Shmuel say the pious ones of the Rhineland were blameless, that they were granted the privilege of sanctifying the Holy Name to prove to the world that we were as willing to die for the true faith as the pilgrims were for their heresy."

"What did you say in return?" Rachel asked with apprehension. She was sure his response would provoke them.

"I didn't say anything. Pesach was there and he shared the letter we got in Mayence, the one written by a martyr who died with Samson and Catharina." Eliezer blinked back tears. "Nobody could say much after that."

"What was in it?"

"Wait while I recall the words properly. They were very powerful." He collected his thoughts, and then recited slowly,

> "Let me relate the power of this holy day, awesome and full of dread;
> today Your Kingship will be exalted. The angels are dismayed, seized

by fear and trembling as they proclaim: Behold the Day of Judgment! On Rosh Hashanah it was inscribed and on Yom Kippur it was sealed:

How many shall pass away and how many shall be born; who shall live and who shall die, who at his predestined time and who before his time; who by fire and who by water; who by sword and who by beast; who by hunger and who by thirst; who by storm and who by plague; who by strangulation and who by stoning; who shall rest and who shall wander; who shall be tranquil and who shall be afflicted; who shall be at peace and who shall be tormented; who shall be impoverished and who shall be rich; who shall be brought low and who shall be exalted."

He stopped and took a deep breath. "There was more but I can't remember it exactly."

Rachel swallowed hard, too awed to speak. Eventually she whispered, "You don't need to remember more, that was plenty."

"The letter is signed Rabbi Amnon, but Dulcie said she doesn't recall any Amnon living in Mayence."

"It's an Italian name, maybe he was there for Shavuot." Suddenly a terrible thought occurred to her. "I hope Papa wasn't there when you read this. He's melancholy enough already."

"He was not only there, but he made a copy of it."

"I suppose it would be difficult to keep such compelling words from him." She sighed.

Eliezer took Rachel's hand. "Your father wasn't unhappy about it. He told us he'd heard of a prayer like that, except its concluding line was, 'But repentance, prayer, and charity avert the severe decree.' "

"Surely the German Jews did all those things," Rachel said.

"Then perhaps Meir and Shmuel are correct."

"Oh, Eliezer, I don't want to be here when the other pilgrims come back," she cried out. "I don't want to die by the sword." Was that what the August eclipse of the moon warned of?

"Then you and the children must come to Toledo with me." Eliezer took her in his arms. "Your father can manage without your care for a few months."

She snuggled up to him. "I hope so." What a relief to escape from all this talk of pilgrims, massacres, and *anusim*.

The second night of Hanukkah was on Saturday, and as had been the tradition in Troyes for generations, Salomon the Vintner's family celebrated by tasting the new vintage for the first time. Further confounding the pilgrims, who had deserted lands devastated by years of drought, rains that summer had been abundant and the resulting harvests bountiful. Salomon's community expected a fine product from his vineyard, and they eagerly congregated in his courtyard to sample it.

Salomon took a sip of the new wine and grimaced.

"What's the matter, Papa?" Rachel looked anxiously at her sisters. Had all their arguing somehow ruined the vintage?

Salomon shook his head as if to clear it. "There's nothing wrong with the wine. It's just that suddenly I have a headache." He reached out to support himself on her shoulder. "And I feel a bit dizzy."

"The last six months have been difficult," Miriam said soothingly. "No wonder you're exhausted."

"You don't have to stay up and celebrate," Joheved said. "We'll keep the guests entertained so you can go to bed early."

"Perhaps I am overtired," he replied slowly. "I definitely don't feel well."

Rachel took his arm. "I'll help you upstairs, Papa."

He stumbled a little on the steps, but made it into bed without falling. "*Merci, ma fille*. You take good care of me."

Rachel felt a stab of guilt for deciding to spend the next six months in Sepharad with Eliezer. "*Bonne nuit*, Papa. Sleep well." She leaned over to kiss his brow.

As she drew near, Salomon saw her visage separate into two. He blinked several times to dispel the double image, but there were still twin Rachels in front of him. He closed his eyes to escape the strange sight, and when he opened them again it was dark. Rachel had blown out the lamp.

She came downstairs to great commotion. People were talking loudly, with occasional cheers or shrill laughter. She followed the tumult to its source, where Guy de Dampierre was standing next to Judah, fielding questions from the crowd. *Whatever possessed Guy to attend our Hanukkah party?*

She knew the answer as soon as he spoke. "The report I received is from a most trustworthy source," he insisted. "There can be no doubt as to its veracity."

"You're sure Count Emicho didn't get away?" a doubtful voice called out.

"He and his followers were destroyed." Guy had to shout to be heard over the musicians. "A few men may have escaped, but we would have heard if Emicho had survived."

"When did this happen?"

"Late summer, I believe."

Murmurs of astonishment spread through the crowd and Meir began chanting from Moses's Song at the Sea, which the Israelites sang after Pharaoh's army drowned.

> "Your right hand, Adonai, glorious in power
> Your right hand, Adonai, shatters the enemy
> In Your great Excellency, You overthrow Your foes."

When Guy recognized the Hebrew, he declared, "Thus the hand of the Lord was raised against these false pilgrims, who sinned by their impiety when they slaughtered the Jews and whose guilt was manifest by their failure. For our Lord is a just judge and orders no one unwillingly to bear the yoke of Christian faith."

Rachel hurried back upstairs to tell Papa the incredible news. He would be thrilled to hear that his commentary on those verses from Exodus had actually come to pass.

"When the Almighty raises His right arm with great Excellency, He will overthrow all enemies," Papa had taught. "And who are His foes? The ones who rise up against Israel."

"Papa," she whispered. "Guy de Dampierre is here to see you. He has some incredible news."

The only response from Salomon's bed was his continued snoring. Reluctant to wake him from a deep sleep, Rachel returned to the courtyard.

Salomon bounded up the glistening marble steps. *Hopefully the wealthy benefactor of this yeshiva has attracted students whose knowledge shines as brightly as the exterior.*

Waving at him from the top of the stairs was Shimon ben Yochai, his friend from the days when the Troyes yeshiva was established. Ben Yochai wore a gold crown with pearls. "Salomon, I've been waiting for you. At last I can teach you all the secrets of the hidden Torah."

Before Salomon could respond, another man came out to join them, and Salomon gasped for joy. It was Jacob ben Yakar, his very first Talmud teacher in Worms, wearing a gold crown set with sparkling jewels. Somehow Salomon did not find it odd that both these men had been dead at least twenty years.

Jacob ben Yakar took Salomon's arm. "Let our new arrival meet the others first, Shimon," he told ben Yochai.

Salomon's two colleagues accompanied him through an arched canopy woven of golden grapevines, its grape clusters a mass of pearls. They came to a large garden, heady with the scent of hundreds of rose bushes. There were fruit trees of every kind, including many Salomon had never seen before, and under each tree men with crowns sat at golden tables, studying Torah. One tree had fruit that twinkled like stars, and though he'd never met them, Salomon knew that the men under it included the martyrs Amnon and Kalonymus of Mayence.

They came to a large table under a magnificent flowering almond tree, where Salomon recognized his old teacher from Mayence, Eliezer haLevi, and Rivka's brother, Isaac ben Judah. They greeted him with pleasure and waved him to an empty bench between them.

As Salomon took his seat, the other scholars introduced themselves: Hai Gaon of Bavel, Elijah ben Joseph haCohen of Eretz Israel, Elhanan ben Hushiel of Kairouan, Samuel haNagid of Granada, and, as Salomon gaped in awe, Rabbenu Gershom ben Judah. These men did not appear quite so happy, and Salomon suddenly realized that all of them headed Talmud academies that had been destroyed in the last hundred years.

As awesome as Salomon found everything in this heavenly yeshiva, for that is surely where he was, the most amazing thing was that, in front of everyone at the table, lay a copy of his own *kuntres*. As they prepared to return to their studies, Rabbenu Gershom looked up with attention, as if someone had spoken to him. The other men grew silent as well, listening intently to something Salomon couldn't hear.

Finally Hai Gaon stood up and addressed Salomon. "Your vineyard is too recently planted; it still requires an experienced vintner to thrive. You must return to tend it."

Elhanan ben Hushiel, who Salomon recognized as also having written a Talmud commentary, added, "You must finish your *kuntres*, revise them so that students in other yeshivot can learn from them, not merely your own."

"But there are no other yeshivot." Tears spilled from Salomon's eyes, mourning both the lost knowledge and having to leave this beautiful place.

Rabbenu Gershom's smile and final words lifted Salomon's soul. "After you succeed, there will be."

The next morning, Rachel was awakened by Joheved banging at her door. "Wake up. There's something terribly wrong with Papa," she screamed. "He can't talk and he can't sit up."

Rachel bolted outside just as Miriam did. They raced together across the courtyard, with Judah and Eliezer moments behind them. They found Salomon propped up in bed, his eyes unfocused, and Rachel gave a quick prayer of thanks that he wasn't completely senseless.

But her heart sank when she took his hand in hers, for his arm was like a dead weight. And though he tried to talk, only garbled sounds resulted. It seemed like hours before Baruch returned with Moses haCohen, and another eternity while Salomon's family waited in the kitchen for the result of the doctor's examination.

Moses's face was grave when he came downstairs. "A powerful demon has attacked him, and it is beyond my skill to know who will win the battle."

Rachel burst into tears as the doctor continued, "Your father's right side is paralyzed and his speech is confused. There is little I can do except bleed him, to correct any imbalance of humors that aids the demon." No matter how sick the patient, Moses always gave some encouragement. "But it is a good sign that he still lives—may the Holy One protect him."

Their expressions grim yet determined, Salomon's daughters and sons-in-law gazed around the room at each other. They knew how to fight demons: had they not prevailed when Joheved suffered from childbed fever?

"Can we move Papa into my room?" Joheved asked. "Its doorpost has the mezuzah Papa wrote when I was ill."

The doctor shook his head. "Not so soon."

"Thank Heaven Mordecai the Scribe won't be leaving until the Cold Fair closes," Miriam said. "On Monday morning, I will have him prepare a new mezuzah for Papa's room." There were only two hours in the week when a mezuzah may be written: Monday during the fifth hour after sunrise and Thursday in the fourth.

"Papa must never be left alone," Judah reminded them. "Two of us must accompany him at all times, studying or praying."

"On my travels, a scholar of the secret Torah taught me that each of the psalms has a protective purpose," Eliezer said as everyone turned to him expectantly. "Obviously whoever is guarding Salomon must pray the Ninety-first Psalm against demons, but as I recall, the Third and Thirteenth Psalms are used specifically to drive them out. Isn't that right, Rachel?"

Rachel, tears streaming down her cheeks, could only nod. *The demons must want Papa to die without finishing his kuntres.*

To counteract that possibility, she immediately recited the Third Psalm, which was also effective against headaches.

> "Many are those who attack me . . .
> But You, O Adonai, are a shield around me . . .
> I lie down and sleep and wake again for Adonai sustains me
> I have no fear of the myriad foes arrayed against me."

Meir put on his cloak. "I'll bring a Torah scroll from the synagogue."

"You said I was too young to fast when Mama was ill," Shmuel said. "But nobody will prevent me from fasting from meat for Grandpapa, even in Paris."

Joheved gave her son a hug. "There will be no meat at this table, except on Shabbat, until Papa can eat it with us."

Rachel had acted as mistress of Salomon's household since Rivka died, but she was too distressed by a new thought to challenge her older sister usurping the role. *What if Papa's death is the evil event the lunar eclipse portended for the Jews?* Terrified, she switched to the Thirteenth Psalm, which more accurately reflected her mind.

"How long will my enemy have the upper hand?
Look at me, answer me, O Adonai, my God.
Restore the luster to my eyes lest I sleep the sleep of death . . . lest
my foes exult when I fall.
Yet I trust in Your faithfulness,
My heart will exult in Your deliverance."

She'd gone to Sepharad when Mama was ill, and Mama had died. Rachel's heart froze as she recalled her mother's deathbed wish—for her to take good care of Papa. As much as Rachel trusted in the Almighty's faithfulness, as much as she longed to be with Eliezer in Toledo, she could not, would not, leave Papa's side until he recovered completely.

She could feel Eliezer staring at her, and when their eyes met, she knew he'd come to the same unhappy conclusion.

Part Three

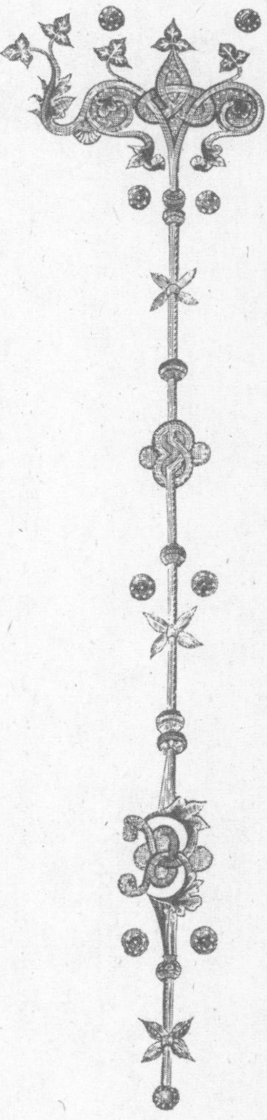

twenty-three

Toledo, Sepharad
Spring 4859 (1099 C.E.)

he gentle spring breeze should have been a warm caress, but Eliezer shivered as he cradled Rachel's two letters in his hands. It had been over three months since he'd seen her. *Which one did she write last?*

He never thought he'd be grateful for Pope Urban stirring up pilgrimage fervor among the faithful. But with war blocking the route to Jerusalem, while the false pope Clement's supporters fought Urban's in Rome, Santiago de Compostela in Galicia was now the pilgrims' destination of choice.

Eliezer's journeys to and from Sepharad had grown safer with the increased traffic. He also appreciated the mail that pilgrims brought to Toledo as they stopped by to admire the magnificent cathedral King Alfonso had built from a mosque. A letter usually came from Rachel before Pâques, a popular time for pilgrims, and sometimes another in late May. But today two letters were waiting at the synagogue for him.

Eliezer gaped at them, dreading the bad news that would have forced Rachel to write twice in such a short time. One was less travel worn than the other, and, guessing it was written more recently, Eliezer ran his knife under the seal.

"Dearest husband, do not worry," it began, filling Eliezer with trepidation. "I am in Paris for Yom Tov's wedding. A traveler is going to Toledo, and I hurry to write this before he leaves. Papa's health is much improved, enabling us to spend Passover here with Judah's family. Perhaps this demon was less powerful than the one who attacked Papa two years ago or the new mezuzah provides better protection, but Papa's speech recovered faster this time. His right hand remains weak, so Simcha and I write his responsa for him. His *kuntres* he dictates to Judah and Miriam, while Meir and Shemayah manage the yeshiva."

Eliezer scanned the page, but there was nothing else of importance. Rachel had investigated the Parisian woolen markets and found that Troyes indeed boasted the finest cloth. The letter ended with hopes that their business was prospering, Eliezer was well, and that she would soon see his beloved face again.

Eliezer sighed. How he longed to behold her beloved face, and the rest of her body as well. He opened the second letter, which had been written months before the first.

"Dearest husband, I write with trembling hand and heavy heart. As last month's lunar eclipse portended, Papa was attacked by another demon, or perhaps the same one, for his symptoms are similar. He has lost all progress he made in regaining his speech, and he cannot move his right arm or leg. But after witnessing his earlier miraculous recovery, we pray that his health and strength will return. May the Holy One heal and protect him. As for the heretic who gave Papa the Evil Eye, may his bones be ground by millstones."

Here the writing began again with a different quill, for the new letters were slightly smaller. "There are few travelers this early in the season, so I have waited in hopes of giving you better news of Papa's health. But there is as yet little improvement. I despair that he will be unable to attend Yom Tov's wedding in Paris after Purim, even if we wait until the lambing is finished in Ramerupt to travel with Joheved's family."

Eliezer wrinkled his brow. What was this about a heretic bringing trouble down on Salomon? Hadn't he always gotten on well with the Edomites? Eliezer would have to wait to find out. As for Rachel's conviction that the recent lunar eclipse foretold a threat to her father, Eliezer felt sure the future catastrophe would take place in Eretz Israel. Thus far the Frankish knights, too quarrelsome to unite under one leader, had gotten bogged down besieging Antioch. Unfortunately Eliezer had seen enough of the Levant to know that the Turks, Fatimids, and local Saracens would each stand back and expect the other to battle the pilgrim army. Thus Jerusalem would fall to Edom, a certain disaster for the Jews.

Eliezer shook his head and went back to Rachel's letter.

"Moses haCohen says that Papa is strong and should soon be better—

may the Holy One protect him," it continued. "Moses has also approached me about a match between Shemiah and his younger daughter, Glorietta. I have no objections, as Shemiah seems to fancy the girl, but the decision will wait until your return. In the meantime, I have allowed our children to travel to Paris with Miriam.

"Joheved is disappointed that Shmuel will stay there until summer to study with the monk Victor after Zipporah returns to Troyes. My sister hoped that Shmuel would give up his Edomite studies when Robert and Étienne founded their new abbey in Cîteaux last spring. I understand how a Talmud student might leave his wife at home, but I cannot fathom what Shmuel finds so interesting in the Edomite's teachings or why Papa and Meir permit him to delay the mitzvah of procreation to study them. I also don't understand why Meir allows his younger daughter to be betrothed before the elder, yet Samson ben Joseph, our old *parnas*'s grandson, will be marrying Leah, not Hannah."

Rachel concluded by urging him pray the Third, Thirteenth, and Ninety-first Psalms against demons, with Papa in mind, and finally ended with prayers for his good health and success in business, and assurances of her eagerness to see him again.

Eliezer reread the two letters, his spirits sinking. For the last three years Rachel's efforts to find a competent fuller had been fruitless, and each year Eliezer grew more hopeful that she would finally accept the necessity of their spending part of the year together in Troyes and part in Toledo.

But Rachel wouldn't leave Troyes until Salomon recovered his health, and how likely was that after this recent setback? Yet Eliezer couldn't imagine living without his wife: he missed her terribly for the six months they spent apart. Was there nothing he could do except wait until Salomon died?

As for Rachel's complaint about Shmuel's studies in Paris, Eliezer understood well the attraction of secular knowledge. It had taken four years, but he'd finally mastered Ptolemy and Aristotle sufficiently to understand how their systems of astronomy differed. Now, after so many observations and calculations, he was coming to agree with Abraham bar Hiyya that both ancient scholars might be wrong.

Aristotle, believing that creation must be as perfect as the Creator, declared that the cosmos consisted of a series of perfect spheres with the earth at its center, and that the sun, moon, fixed stars, and planets move at uniform speed around the motionless earth. Unlike Aristotle, Ptolemy painstakingly observed the motion of the heavens and thus determined that they did not follow Aristotle's model.

Both agreed that fixed stars were firmly attached to their celestial sphere, which lay beyond that of Saturn, the furthermost planet. But Ptolemy postulated his own model for the planets' movements. Loath to abandon Aristotle's system of perfect circles and spheres, Ptolemy explained that each planet orbited a point on a small circle, called an epicycle, which in turn traveled in a large circle around the earth. The moon's motion was more complicated, requiring a three-orb system.

Eliezer had a feeling there must be another, simpler explanation. While he admired Aristotle and Ptolemy's vast erudition, he lacked the other astronomy students' absolute belief in the ancient scholars' pronouncements. He had the Talmud to thank for that skepticism, for in the ninth chapter of Tractate Pesachim there was a Baraita that taught:

> The learned of Israel say the sphere is fixed and the stars revolve; the learned of the nations say the sphere moves and the stars are fixed on it . . . Rav Acha bar Yaakov objected: Perhaps the spheres move [independently] like a door and lintel.

Eliezer had so many questions. What if both Rav Acha and the Sages were correct? What if stars and planets moved independently, each revolving in their own sphere? What kind of observations and calculations would he need to prove, or disprove, his idea? Every winter Eliezer arrived in Toledo determined that this year he'd discover the answers.

Yet without continual practice, mathematics and astronomy were soon lost. Each time Eliezer returned, he wasted precious weeks relearning material he'd previously understood before he could begin examining what Abraham had done in his absence. And only after meticulously checking Abraham's work could Eliezer ascertain what to try next. Then finally, just when he felt on the verge of formulating a new description of how the planets and fixed stars moved, it was time to return to Troyes.

If only he didn't have to spend so much time away. Pesach now dealt with Samson's old trading partners so successfully that Eliezer didn't need to travel to Prague or Kiev for furs anymore. Pesach liked to travel and preferred a merchant's status to that of a vineyard worker; it would be easy for the youth to bring furs to Toledo and return with spices and dyes supplied by Eliezer. Shemiah was almost fifteen now and would soon be old enough to travel with Pesach. Eliezer had no doubt that his clever son would easily learn everything he knew and eventually take over his role entirely. Then Eliezer could devote his full attention to astronomy.

A lovely plan—except that Rachel wouldn't leave Troyes.

"Excuse me, Eliezer." The voice belonged to his host, Dunash. "Is there bad news from home?"

Eliezer realized that his unhappy expression had made Dunash suspect the worst. "Not at all. My father-in-law was ill, but now he's better. It's just that my wife's letters remind me how much I miss her."

"As long as we're on the subject of women . . ." Dunash hesitated and cleared his throat. "It damages your reputation that you frequent brothels. People are gossiping."

Eliezer fought the urge to say that people should concern themselves with their own behavior. "What would they have me do? Live like a monk?"

"Take another wife," Dunash replied. "Or a concubine."

"Rabbi Gershom has forbidden a man from having more than one wife." *And Rachel would never agree.*

"Rabbi Gershom's laws apply only in Ashkenaz. Men here commonly have several wives." Dunash smiled at Eliezer's skeptical expression. "Perhaps not several wives, then, but often a concubine or two."

"That is more acceptable than going to a brothel?" Eliezer protested. A harlot relieved his needs and it was over. A wife expected attention and emotional attachment, responsibilities he was not eager to undertake. Rachel's complaints about his journeys were bad enough; he didn't need another wife in Toledo, whining that he spent too much time in Troyes.

Dunash nodded. "Since your wife is back in France, you wouldn't have to worry about the two women getting along."

"Assuming, just assuming, that I wanted to acquire a concubine," Eliezer said slowly, his mind turning over that option. A concubine wouldn't require the same level of commitment as a wife, and Rachel wouldn't be so upset. Not that he intended to ask her permission. What his wife didn't know wouldn't hurt her. "Do I buy one at the slave market like any other servant?"

"First see if any of my current maidservants appeal to you," Dunash suggested. "They are excellent workers and my wife already trusts them in our home."

Eliezer's *yetzer hara* immediately provided him with a mental picture of Gazelle. A Nubian beauty with a cheerful disposition, she was assigned to clean Eliezer's rooms. Having a concubine at home, available whenever he wanted, would certainly be more convenient than hiring harlots. And if Rachel should visit, Gazelle could go back to being a housemaid.

"Now that you mention it, one of your slave girls does interest me." Eliezer hoped his flushed face wasn't obvious. The idea of having two women was growing quite attractive.

Dunash chuckled. "Let me guess—Gazelle."

"How did you know?"

"My wife was not pleased when I bought her last year, and she made it clear that she would not tolerate a concubine under her roof," he replied. "But Gazelle is such a good worker that my wife is loath to sell her. So she sent Gazelle to serve you, hoping you would find her attractive."

"I can't take a woman you acquired for yourself."

Dunash sighed. "Gazelle was an old man's passing fancy, and after considering the matter, I prefer peace in my house. A wife in Toledo and concubine in Valencia are plenty for me."

Eliezer raised an eyebrow in curiosity. He knew the man held some position in Alfonso's court (favoring neither Christians nor Muslims, Spanish Jews used their neutral status to gain employment as diplomats and courtiers), but Dunash seldom spoke of his official duties.

"How does Valencia fare under El Cid?" Eliezer tried to sound nonchalant. Valencia was a costal city that ought to be a safe port while the Berbers were attacking Granada. "Is he truly the hero that the stories paint him to be?"

"Usually these great warriors are poor administrators, but El Cid rules Valencia competently, attracting both Edomites and Moors to serve in his administration." Dunash cleared his throat. "Officially, of course, he governs in Alfonso's name, but El Cid has always been his own man. I have enjoyed negotiating with him."

"You don't sound like these negotiations will continue."

"El Cid is almost sixty. Who knows who will rule after him?" Dunash said. "But enough of politics. Shall I send Gazelle to you tonight?"

"Let me think about it," Eliezer replied. But his *yetzer hara* knew that, if not tonight, Gazelle would share his bed soon enough. After all, why should he suffer when it was Rachel's decision to remain in Troyes instead of joining him in Toledo?

Unaware of the threat to her own marriage, Rachel looked up in annoyance as the calm in Miriam's cellar was shattered by the furious marital argument outside between Shemayah and Brunetta. Miriam and Zipporah paused from sorting their medicinal herbs, and Zipporah blanched as she recognized her parents' voices. Shemayah was shouting his insistence that Brunetta leave their daughter's house, where she'd been staying since Zipporah's miscarriage several months earlier.

None of Brunetta's words reached the cellar, but she obviously refused his demand, for the quarrel continued.

"Mama won't go back to him, even though I've been fine for weeks," Zipporah said. "She's finally had enough."

Shemayah's anger grew, filling the air with curses, until he was interrupted by Brunetta shrieking, "You can't curse me, you foul dog. I'm already cursed."

Epithets flew back and forth until Brunetta taunted her husband, "Divorce me then; write me a *get*. I dare you."

"And give you the pleasure, you witch—never!" This was followed by a brief silence, which ended with the gate slamming as Brunetta stumbled down the cellar steps into their midst. Tears running down her face, she fell into her daughter's outstretched arms.

Miriam scowled. "To think that a *talmid chacham* like Shemayah would refuse his wife a divorce so as to increase her suffering."

"That's not why he won't give me a *get*." Brunetta's voice was bitter. "He has no intention of paying my *ketubah*. That's what I get for marrying a poor man." If a man died or divorced his wife, she received a *ketubah* of two hundred dinars before any creditor, even before his children.

"But, Mama," Zipporah said. "What need do you have for your *ketubah*? Papa has already provided my dowry, and you still have money your father gave you."

Rachel faced Brunetta squarely, her hands on her hips. "If you don't mind forfeiting your *ketubah*, you can initiate the divorce. Then the *beit din* will compel him to write you a *get*."

"Nobody can make that man do anything, not even a court of seventy judges."

Miriam smiled with assurance. "Your husband will do it when the *beit din* threatens him with *herem*. If he's excommunicated, Shemayah will never be able to teach Torah again or even enter a synagogue. No Jew will speak with him or tolerate his presence."

"I don't know if I'm strong enough to face him in front of the court," Brunetta replied. "And what will people say?"

"People will say you should have done it long ago," Zipporah said firmly. Then her voice softened. "Don't worry, Mama. You'll always have a home with Shmuel and me. Who else would watch our children when I'm out delivering babies?"

"Of course you'll be strong enough," Miriam said. "Look how long you've been studying Torah with me; surely that has given you a great deal of strength."

"And you won't have to face the *beit din* alone." Rachel added her support. "We'll go with you."

The following Thursday, the *beit din* of Troyes met without its eminent head or his sons-in-law, who were prohibited from judging cases involving relatives. But there was no need for their superior knowledge: the case was clear.

"Why do you seek a divorce from your husband?" a judge asked Brunetta, his expression kindly.

She forced her voice to remain steady and replied with the reason all women used, "I find this man repulsive. I can no longer live with him."

The other two judges nodded. The temporary head judge stared at Shemayah, who frowned back at him, and declared, "No one should have to share a basket with a snake. This court demands Shemayah to write his wife Brunetta a *get* and deliver it into her hand."

Rachel exchanged anxious glances with Joheved, who was in town to watch the proceedings. Shemayah had been Meir's study partner for years, but Joheved still disliked him as much as the day they'd met, when he'd declared his disapproval of women who studied Torah. The cruelty he'd inflicted on Brunetta for not giving him a son, as if the poor woman hadn't suffered enough watching her baby boys die, only infuriated Joheved further.

But Shemayah smiled triumphantly. "As she has surrendered her *ketubah* claim, I will write it immediately, with this court as witnesses." He produced a sheet of parchment, a quill, and a vial of ink.

The scribe took the items only after one of the judges ascertained that the parchment and ink truly belonged to Shemayah and were not merely loaned for the occasion. The scribe dutifully etched twelve parallel lines, as well as the date, names of witnesses, plus the place where the *get* was written, where Brunetta lived, and where Shemayah lived.

Then he, along with everyone in the room, waited for Shemayah to make the required statements out loud. "This *get* is from me to Brunetta of Troyes, formerly of Provins . . ." Finally the scribe indicated that he was ready to write again, and Shemayah turned to the soon-to-be divorcée and spat out the words *harei at muteret lekol adam*, meaning "may you be permitted to all men."

Meir closely inspected the finished parchment after the witnesses signed it, and then gave it to Judah for further examination. Even the smallest irregularity could invalidate a *get,* and though he hated to believe his best friend and study partner was capable of such evil, Meir knew Joheved suspected that Shemayah hated Brunetta sufficiently to use his expertise in Jewish Law to make a tiny, yet significant, error—one that left her believing she was divorced when she wasn't. Then, if Brunetta married again, she would commit the sin of adultery.

But Meir could find no errors, and neither could Judah. They returned the document to the judges, one of who gently dropped it into Brunetta's outstretched hands. Joheved, Miriam, and Rachel simultaneously let out their breath. Zipporah's sigh of relief had to be audible to her father, but he pointedly ignored the group of females hugging his ex-wife and strode out of the courtroom.

* * *

A week later he was gone, his house rented out along with all its furnishings except his books, and Shmuel was recalled from Paris to help his father in the yeshiva. A month later, Meir received a letter from Orléans: Shemayah was its new rosh yeshiva and had betrothed a new wife on Lag b'Omer.

"Yum, that smells wonderful." Rachel sniffed the air appreciatively. "Is someone baking a cake for Leah's betrothal?"

"Of course not, silly," Hannah answered. Since Papa became friends with Guy de Dampierre, the bishop's bakery provided their pastries. "I'm baking special cakes for my brother Shlomo's first day of school on Shavuot; they have to be baked by a virgin."

"What?" Rachel burst out. Despite her years of Talmud study, she'd never heard of this tradition.

"I didn't know about it myself until Meir suggested that Shlomo go to school in town." Joheved sighed heavily. "I wish I could teach our son myself, but between running the manor, planning for Leah's betrothal banquet next week, plus caring for Judita's children and little Jacob, I'm exhausted."

Judita had begun to bleed midway through this, her third pregnancy, so Miriam had confined her to bed.

"Of course you are, Joheved," Miriam said. "Most forty-year-old women are finished getting up with babies at night."

"Meir insists that I make time for my own studies with Hannah and Leah," Joheved said proudly. "But I worry that Shlomo's too young to be separated from the family."

"It will be nice for Shlomo to have friends his own age in town," Rachel said.

"It's a good thing I don't have my flowers, since whoever bakes the Shavuot cakes is supposed to be *tahor* (ritually clean)." Hannah was eager to educate her aunts.

Rachel's expression clouded. She too was between menses, but that meant she would likely be *niddah* when Eliezer returned in a couple of weeks. To hide her dismay, she thoughtlessly asked Hannah, "Since you've already flowered, why is it that your little sister will soon have a husband, and you don't?"

Hannah's face flamed, and Miriam quickly spoke before Joheved could vent her outrage. "There's no need to be rude, Rachel. We've known for years that Joseph's dying wish was for Samson to marry one of Papa's granddaughters. Since Leah took a liking to the boy, she may as well marry him."

"And if Hannah doesn't like any of the suitors offered to her, she can remain unwed." Joheved's tone made it clear how unhappy she was about the situation.

Rachel couldn't resist baiting her sister. "Perhaps your daughter refused all these suitors because she's waiting for the one she wants to present himself."

To Rachel's astonishment, Hannah's eyes filled with tears and her face turned an even brighter red. Joheved's mouth dropped as she realized that Rachel had inadvertently hit upon the truth, while Miriam reached out to hug her distraught niece.

"Is he one of Papa's students?" Miriam asked gently. Surely he wasn't one of the merchants.

When Hannah nodded, Joheved's anger melted. "Don't worry. We will let this shy fellow know that we welcome him into our family." Surely any of Salomon's students would jump at a chance to marry his granddaughter.

"He already is one of our family," Hannah whispered.

Rachel squinted at Miriam. Could Hannah have set her heart on Yom Tov, only to see him wed to another in Paris?

Joheved smiled. "You mean your cousin Samuel ben Simcha?"

Hannah gave a shy smile and nodded again.

"Of course he hasn't asked for her," Miriam said. "He's already lost two wives, one in childbirth and the other in a fire, so he's probably afraid that Meir would object to his daughter being the third."

Rachel gave Miriam a knowing look. "Which only proves that Hannah must be his *bashert*." A Baraita in Tractate Taanit taught that women, and men, died early in marriage because their spouses were ordained in Heaven for others.

Joheved hurried to Hannah's side and hugged her tight. "Meir will be thrilled to see his sister's line continue through you." Joheved smiled broadly. "I can't wait to tell him."

"I can't wait to see Samuel's face." Rachel grinned at her red-faced niece. "I remember how he looked at you when you blew the shofar."

"*Mon Dieu*, the cakes." Hannah dashed to a pot on the hearth and poked the cake inside it with a straw.

Miriam took this opportunity to spare her niece further embarrassment. "Besides being baked by a *tahor* virgin, Hannah, what else is special about these cakes?"

"As I kneaded the dough, I recited a prayer, saying, 'I am making these cakes for Shlomo, son of Joheved. May it be Your will, the Eternal One in Heaven, that he be open to the study of Torah and not forget anything he learns.' "

Joheved beamed with pleasure, imagining one daughter betrothed at the Hot Fair and the other at the Cold Fair. Both would be married in six months, while avoiding the bad luck that arose when two sisters married within the same year.

"Before I put the cakes on the fire, which must be made with wood from grape vines, I took grape juice and wrote the holy names Arimas and Avrimas on top and 'sweet as honey' below." Proud of her knowledge, and thrilled at her sudden good fortune, Hannah smiled at her elders. "You remember, from the third chapter of Ezekiel."

"It's a good thing we grow grapes," Joheved said, her eyes twinkling. Samuel ben Simcha was quite competent in the vineyard and thus a useful worker to have in Ramerupt.

"When does Shlomo get to eat these special cakes?" Rachel asked. "I assume he does get to eat them." She knew that little boys started their formal Jewish education at Shavuot, but without a brother who'd undergone this initiation rite, she was only familiar with the holiday's universal rituals.

Shavuot was the holiday when Jews commemorated receiving the Torah at Mount Sinai. It was one of the three pilgrimage festivals celebrated in Jerusalem when the Holy Temple still stood. But observing Shavuot wasn't as complicated as the other two: Passover with its elaborate seder and complicated dietary restrictions and Sukkot with the diversion of building booths and dwelling in them for a week.

Shavuot, celebrated for two days, seemed more like an extended Sabbath highlighted by a recitation of the Ten Commandments during the festival service. Even so, most yeshiva students went home for the brief holiday, which was often immediately followed by a wedding or betrothal. Because of a plague among Rabbi Akiva's students, Jews avoided celebrations between Passover and Shavuot, a tradition reinforced by the recent tragedies in the Rhineland during the same months. Thus there were usually couples ready to be married immediately after the period of semi-mourning was over.

This year Leah and Samson would be among them.

twenty-four

havuot came so late that year that Eliezer would have to celebrate the holiday on his return trip to Troyes. But he was determined not to forget his astronomy, no matter how Salomon's family might object to secular studies. He carefully packed his new astrolabe, his feelings wavering between eagerness to make observations of the night sky above Troyes and trepidation over how Rachel would react when she saw the instrument he'd spent much of their profits on. Ibrahim ibn Said al-Wazzân, creator of the finest astrolabes in the world, had crafted it.

Advanced astronomy was impossible without an astrolabe, a model of the celestial sphere consisting of two circular brass plates that rotated independently around each other. One was engraved with gradations of time and the other with a detailed map of the zodiac that identified the most important stars. An experienced astronomer could accurately measure the time of night or year, as well as the position of celestial objects, and thus compute what part of the sky was visible at any time. He could also determine the altitude of any object over the horizon as well as his own current latitude.

Abraham bar Hiyya was delighted with Eliezer's decision. Most astronomical observations had been made within a narrow range of latitudes around the Great Sea, and measurements of the sky as far north as Troyes should add significantly to their store of knowledge.

"I want you to take careful note of the planets' movements," he told Eliezer. "Especially Mercury and Venus."

"Why?" Eliezer asked. Abraham had that smug secretive look. "Will it help you predict the Messiah's coming?" Most rabbis prohibited such speculation, but that didn't stop Abraham.

"Perhaps, but that's not my main motivation."

Eliezer raised an eyebrow. "Do you think you'll finally be able to discern if the earth rotates, rather than the celestial sphere?" This was another of his friend's special projects.

Abraham smiled but shook his head. "Ptolémy admits that the heavens' motion would appear the same no matter whether the earth or the sphere rotated."

"There must be some way to determine the truth."

"One day you and I may discover it," Abraham said. "But we will not need Mercury and Venus to do so."

"You hope that observing their positions from a different latitude will enable you to determine if they orbit the sun." Eliezer grinned triumphantly.

Abraham nodded. "Every astronomer in Toledo has noticed that these inner planets sometimes appear to move behind the sun, an impossibility if their spheres lie closer to the earth," He clasped Eliezer by the shoulder. "Have a safe journey, my friend. And pay particular attention to the planets' positions at the *tekufot*."

Eliezer was left to ponder why their positions at the *tekufot*, the turning points of the sun, were so important. He would be in Troyes for three of them, the autumnal equinox plus the summer and winter solstices. Hopefully there would be no clouds on those nights.

On Sunday morning, the first day of Shavuot, three generations of Salomon's family eagerly got up when the church bells chimed Prime. It was a beautiful spring day, perfect for showing off one's holiday clothes. Despite the warm weather, Meir wrapped Shlomo in a large cloak and carried him to the synagogue.

"He can't walk by himself like usual," Rivka solemnly informed Rachel. "Because he might see a dog or pig on the way." Her daughter's low voice made it clear that this would be a very bad thing.

One young boy was waiting at the synagogue with his family and another soon joined them. Last to arrive was their teacher, Master Levi, whom Rachel recognized as one of the local undistinguished scholars Eliezer complained about. Levi led his new pupils to a small room, where, one by one, he took each on his lap and held up a wax tablet with the

Hebrew alphabet written on it. When it was Shlomo's turn, his family craned their necks to watch.

First the teacher read the alphabet forward, with Shlomo repeating each letter aloud; then they recited the letters backward, and finally various letters in paired combinations. After Shlomo finished, Levi smeared the tablet with honey for the boy to lick off. Cakes and eggs were distributed next, and after the teacher recited the words written on them, the three boys imitated him before eating their second sweet reward.

Finally the teacher made the boys repeat after him, "I adjure you, Potach, Prince of Forgetfulness, to remove from me a foolish heart and throw it far away on a high mountain, in the holy names of Arimas, Avrimas, Arimimas."

These words proved more difficult than those on the cakes, but when each pupil successfully made the incantation, Levi distributed nuts and dried fruits while explaining how being brought to school for the first time by their fathers was like Moses receiving the Torah at Mount Sinai. After this speech, he dismissed everyone to rejoin the congregation, now beginning Shavuot services in the sanctuary. Shlomo proudly accompanied Meir and their male relatives downstairs.

Only young Jacob now sat upstairs with the women. A shy child who rarely spoke, his siblings and cousins called him Jacob Tam, Jacob the Simple, just as the biblical Jacob was described. Of course they never said this when Meir or Joheved might hear, but Rachel knew that the other children considered him a simpleton. Miriam said this condition was more common if a baby came when his mother was old, which gave Rachel some compensation for having stopped bearing while she was young.

She wanted to go home to check on the Shavuot feast after synagogue, but Shlomo's initiation wasn't over. Levi now led his new pupils' families to the banks of the Seine, where he explained that, like the river's continually rushing water, a man's study of Torah would never stop. Rachel felt a pang of sadness for her nephew as she realized that, from this day forward, Shlomo would be expected to spend every daylight hour in the schoolroom. No lessons in the vineyard for him.

Because *niddah* lasted twelve days a month, Eliezer knew the odds were almost even that Rachel would be forbidden to him at any particular time. Even so, he couldn't hide his disappointment when he arrived in Troyes and she reluctantly stood her ground instead of rushing into his arms. He looked at her questioningly; perhaps she was nearing the end of her clean days and he wasn't too unlucky.

But when they were alone together upstairs, she sadly disclosed that they still had over a week to wait. Her next announcement was even more disturbing.

"We need you to teach in the yeshiva this summer." Her eyes pleaded with him. "Papa's speech is still difficult for strangers to understand, and he doesn't have the strength to teach day and night during the Hot Fair."

"What happened to him? You wrote that a demon attacked him and that a heretic gave him the Evil Eye."

Rachel pursed her lips. "I know it helps Papa's wine sell for more than I think it's worth, but ever since Moses haCohen used Jewish wine to cure that sick nobleman, too many Edomites want to buy some when they can't afford it."

Eliezer rolled his eyes and waited for her to continue. This was an old complaint.

"A baron from Sens bought a cask and promised to pay for it at the Cold Fair, after he'd sold his livestock," she said. "But when the time came, the liar claimed that he'd only agreed to pay last year's price, which of course was lower."

"And people took his word over your father's?" For Salomon to have lost the Edomites' respect was an alarming development.

"Papa was convinced that the fellow would never agree and required him to take an oath." Rachel shook her head in disgust. "Papa even led him to the church door, where we expected him to back down and admit the truth."

"And?" he asked anxiously.

"When the priest brought a relic before him, the swindler laid down a silver coin and began to swear," she said. "Of course Papa immediately desisted."

"And allowed the heretic to pay the lower price?"

"Papa was so angry I thought he'd explode." She shuddered at the memory. "He resolved to never again deal with *minim* in a situation where they could be forced to give money to benefit the Church."

Eliezer nodded. "It also might look as though he gave some validity to the man's heresy if he accepted an oath based on it. That's why we learn in Tractate Sanhedrin:

> One should not vow in the name of an idol or cause others to vow in its name . . . It is forbidden to make a partnership with an idolater, lest the idolater become obligated to swear to him by the idol."

"Papa doesn't consider Notzrim to be idolaters."

"Perhaps we should when it comes to vows," he said. "But wait a moment. Why would the heretic give your father the Evil Eye if he won the case?"

"I don't know. All I know is that Papa was upset for weeks, and once the Cold Fair ended and the cheater left, Papa was attacked. Who else could have enmity for him?"

"No one. Look how the Notzrim scholars respect him." The last thing Eliezer wanted on his first day home was an angry wife. "Speaking of scholars, why do you need me to teach at the yeshiva? I thought Meir and Shemayah were in charge."

She shook her head. "Meir was thrown from his horse after Shavuot and injured his back. The doctor says he needs to stay in bed for at least another month."

"What happened to Shemayah?" This wasn't fair. The last thing he wanted was to become the acting rosh yeshiva.

Rachel explained about Brunetta's divorce.

"I don't suppose there's any chance of Judah taking over," Eliezer said, resignation creeping into his voice.

"Judah will never challenge his *yetzer hara* by assuming a place of authority over the students," she reminded him. "Besides, Judah must help Papa finish his *kuntres*; he's one of the few who understands what Papa says."

"How can I teach this summer and conduct my own business too? Never mind negotiating a betrothal agreement with Moses." Eliezer felt his frustration mounting. When would he have time to accomplish his astronomical research?

"I'll handle Moses. I'll tell him that you accept the match between

Shemiah and Glorietta, but that we'll work out the actual agreement later. And Shmuel can help at the yeshiva. He's such a *talmid chacham* that he could probably run it himself, except that nobody would accept a rosh yeshiva who was only nineteen."

"I need to think about it," he muttered. "And I'll want to talk to your father first." Was Salomon really as debilitated as Rachel said? Or was this another of his wife's ploys to keep him in Troyes?

"Nobody's chosen the curriculum yet, Eliezer." Her voice was as sweet as honey. "You could teach whatever tractate you want."

The next day Eliezer sadly discovered that Rachel had not misled him or exaggerated any of the problems. A short visit with Meir was enough to verify his brother-in-law's incapacity. The poor bedridden fellow was in agony no matter what position he assumed, subjecting Eliezer to more profanity in a half hour than he normally heard in a month of traveling. And after a meal with Salomon, during which he was lucky to decipher one word out of three, Eliezer sadly realized that foreign merchants would find the scholar incomprehensible.

The only good thing was that Rachel was so eager to appease him that she not only refrained from complaints about his buying an astrolabe, but she displayed interest in his astronomical studies or at least convincingly pretended to.

"There must be a way to ascertain whether the celestial sphere rotates and the earth is motionless," Rachel said slowly, trying to envision the situation. "Or if it's the reverse."

"The sky would look identical in either case," Eliezer pointed out, curious as to how she would respond.

She paused to think. "Surely it would be easier for the earth to rotate than for the stars to race so quickly across the heavens."

He had to admit that this made sense. Still he followed with some objections he'd heard. "Wouldn't people and animals fly off a revolving earth? And if the earth were constantly moving, wouldn't an arrow shot up into the sky come down some distance behind the archer?"

She shot him a withering look. "People and animals don't fly off a moving boat, and if you throw something in the air while traveling by boat it falls at your feet."

Eliezer's eyes widened with respect. "But if the earth revolved, shouldn't all the stars and planets, plus the sun and the moon, appear to move at the same speed in the sky?"

"Not necessarily. Didn't Rav Acha bar Yaakov suggest that each planet moves independently?" Rachel's voice betrayed her frustration. Why was Eliezer asking all these questions?

"So how do you show that he's right? What evidence would prove that the earth rotates rather than the stars?"

"I'm not an astronomer." She'd had enough of this subject. "You tell me."

"That's it." Eliezer almost grabbed her shoulder in excitement, but caught himself just in time. "I'm going to teach astronomy in the yeshiva this summer."

Rachel's jaw dropped. *Mon Dieu*, what had she started?

"I'm going to teach from the first chapter of Rosh Hashanah, the Sanctification of the New Moon," he said. "When the Hot Fair is over, your father's students will know how the sun moves, how the moon moves, and all the secrets of calculating the calendar."

Her trepidation transformed into enthusiasm; now it was Rachel's turn to refrain from physical contact. "Oh, Eliezer. I've always wanted to know how the calendar is determined. Even Papa doesn't know the secret calculations; he's always relied on tables from Mayence."

Their excitement dampened at the memory of that ruined community and Eliezer sighed. "In that case, it's even more important that I explain them."

Each afternoon, ostensibly to benefit his injured brother-in-law, but more for his wife and her sisters, Eliezer summarized his lectures at the yeshiva. Rachel and Joheved kept busy with distaff and spindle while Miriam, the only decent embroiderer among them, worked on decorating the sleeves and necklines of Leah's betrothal outfit.

Eliezer waited until the women were settled with their handiwork. "According to Rabbenu Salomon, the Holy One created the calendar, as it is written [in Genesis]:

> The Eternal said—let there be lights in the heavens to divide between day and night; and they shall be for signs and for appointed seasons, and for days and years."

Rachel nodded. "Papa says that 'seasons' mean our festivals, which occur on certain dates of a month," she said. "So if there were days, years, and months at Creation, clearly the calendar began then."

"I think the four components listed in this verse refer to the four celestial creations," Meir said. "Signs are eclipses, brought by the sun, while seasons or festivals rely on the moon's cycle. Days last from one appearance of the stars until the next, and a complete cycle of the four *tekufot* constitutes a year."

"Quite possibly," Eliezer replied. "While everyone agrees that a month lasts from one new moon to the next, the Rabbis disagree over what constitutes a year." He continued, "As we study in the first chapter of Tractate Sanhedrin:

> Rebbi says for a full year [of rent] he counts 365 days, the number of days in a solar year. But the Sages say he counts twelve months, and if the year was intercalated, it is lengthened [a month] for him."

Miriam paused to thread her needle with a new color. "Then what does constitute a year? Which of them is correct?"

"Both are." Eliezer smiled. "The solar year, the time for the *tekufot* to complete their cycle, is 365 days, as Rebbi says." He turned to Rachel and asked her to explain when the four *tekufot* occur, at what times of year the sun turns in its path.

"Nissan's *tekufah* occurs in the spring, just before Passover, and Sivan's in the summer, at the beginning of the Hot Fair," she said. "The other two are at Sukkot, in the fall, and in winter." She refused to say that the heretics celebrated the birth of the Hanged One at the winter solstice.

"Excellent. A lunar year is also the time from the first day of Nissan, the first month, until Nissan comes again. As the Sages teach, a year contains twelve months—each corresponding to one of the constellations of the zodiac."

Rachel surprised him by saying, "Papa once taught us that Nissan's constellation is the Lamb, for the Passover sacrifice, and that Tishri's is the Scales, for the judgment we receive on Yom Kippur that month."

Before they could digress into discussing the other constellations, Eliezer asked, "So how long is a month?"

Joheved raised an eyebrow at his seemingly simple question. "Sometimes twenty-nine days and sometimes thirty. As it says in our Gemara,

> If the *Beit Din* wishes, it makes a month twenty-nine days; if it wishes, thirty days."

"That is because a month, the time between one new moon and the next, is actually twenty-nine days and twelve hours," Eliezer explained. "But our Rabbis decreed that we cannot have half a day in one month and half in another."

When nobody asked any questions, Eliezer continued, "In a lunar calendar, the moon will be in the same phase on the same day of the month, which is why Passover, the Fourteenth of Nissan, always occurs at the full moon. But 12 lunar months only add up to 354 days, which means the holidays occur 11 days earlier in the seasons each year."

"But if that were the case," Rachel protested, "after ten years Passover would be in the winter."

"And the Torah says that Passover must be in the spring," Joheved reminded them.

"That's why we sometimes have two months of Adar," Meir said. "To keep Nissan in the spring." Adar was the month before Nissan.

"Exactly," Eliezer saluted his brother-in-law. "Our Sages require that if the sun will not reach its spring *tekufah,* the vernal equinox, by the sixteenth day in the month following Adar, then that month is declared Adar II instead of Nissan."

The others knew this from the Talmud and waited for him to continue. "After the Holy Temple was destroyed, the intercalation rules were secretly established by a council of seven rabbis, the Sod ha-Ibur," Eliezer explained. "Even so, the *beit din* waited for witnesses before declaring the new moon."

"Our Gemara says they calculated the calendar to be sure the witnesses were correct," Rachel said, adding raw wool to her distaff. She could spin almost as quickly as Joheved, who had taken more wool a few moments before.

Eliezer waited until they'd finished the first chapter of Tractate Rosh Hashanah before sharing the calendar's secret. "Eventually the Edomites made it too dangerous to send messengers from Eretz Israel to the Diaspora to announce the new month. That's when Hillel II allowed the rules of intercalation to be publicized."

His audience sat up straight, their attention rapt as he continued, "There are four criteria to determine the calendar."

"I know two of them," Meir said, shifting awkwardly in his seat as he attempted to find a less-painful position. "Passover must be in the spring, and a month must begin at the new moon."

"Meir is correct. The calendar must combine both solar and lunar aspects," Eliezer replied. "Since the solar year is 365 days and a month is 29½ days, we need a cycle that contains both a whole number of years and a whole number of months. Long ago, astronomers in Bavel established a workable cycle of 19 years, or 235 months. They found that if you alternate months of 29 and 30 days, a month will always begin with the new moon."

"That's why Elul is twenty-nine days and Tishri is thirty," Miriam said. "And why, when we have two Adars, the first is full and the second deficient."

"I assume the Sod ha-Ibur calculated where in the nineteen-year cycle these extra months should go," Joheved speculated.

"*Oui*. We add a second Adar seven times during the nineteen years," Eliezer said. "In years three, six, eight, eleven, fourteen, seventeen, and nineteen."

Miriam leaned forward eagerly. "What year are we in now?"

"We're in year fourteen, so there were two Adars."

Rachel had sat silently, deep in thought, when suddenly she frowned and looked her husband in the eye. "You said the months alternate between twenty-nine and thirty days, but this year both Heshvan and Kislev were full."

"And next year they'll both be deficient," he challenged her in return. "That brings us to our third and fourth rules."

The room grew quiet with anticipation. Many Jews knew about the nineteen-year cycle and how to add an extra Adar, but now they'd come to the more complicated rules, the secret ones.

"As Miriam reminded us, Elul is always a deficient month, with twenty-nine days," Eliezer began. "However, our Gemara mentions the *beit din* making Elul full, thirty days, as a favor.

> What is the favor? To separate Shabbat from yom tov [holiday] for the vegetables. Rabbi Acha bar Chanina said: to separate Shabbat from Yom Kippur for the dead."

Meir explained, "This means they arranged for a day between Shabbat and Rosh Hashanah, when fresh food could be prepared for the holiday, or between Shabbat and Yom Kippur so those who died in the preceding afternoon would not remain unburied for two days."

"Thus we manipulate the calendar so that neither Rosh Hashanah nor Yom Kippur falls on Friday or Sunday," Eliezer said.

"I see," Rachel nodded with understanding. "If either Holy Day fell the day before or the day after Shabbat, we would have two days in a row when you couldn't cook or hold a funeral."

"Which would be a hardship for the people." Eliezer finished his wife's thought. "But instead of changing the length of Elul as the *beit din* did, today we change Heshvan or Kislev, sometimes adding an extra day to Heshvan, making it full instead of deficient, and sometimes by shortening Kislev from thirty days to twenty-nine."

"What is the fourth rule?" Rachel asked. Surely the other three were sufficient.

"It is based on the section of our Gemara that discusses the *molad*." Eliezer took a deep breath before continuing. He'd saved the most complicated rule for last.

"Oy," groaned Meir. "Understanding the *molad* is more aggravating than my bad back.

A *molad*, the birth of the new moon, was the exact moment when the sun and moon were in conjunction. However, due to the sun's brightness, the moon is invisible at that time, which complicates determining when a new month begins. The subject was abstruse even for the Talmud, necessitating one of Salomon's longest commentaries.

"It's not that difficult," Eliezer insisted. "Let's go back to our Gemara, where Rav Zeira says:

> The moon [near *molad*] is not visible for twenty-four hours . . . six hours of the new moon and eighteen of the old moon in Eretz Israel."

Eliezer tried to curb his impatience when four confused faces stared at him blankly. "Imagine the sky at sunset on Rosh Hashanah. Since the new moon trails behind the sun, the first sliver of the new moon will be observed immediately after the sun sets, as the sky darkens; but only for a brief time until the moon itself sets."

No one challenged this so he continued. "Remember, the new moon cannot be seen in Jerusalem until at least six hours have passed since *molad* . . ." He paused for them to consider this. "So for any *molad* that occurs at noon or later, no one will be able to see the moon until the following day."

Miriam was quick to demonstrate her understanding. "Because six hours later the moon has already set."

"Exactly." He smiled with relief as the others nodded their agreement. "Since Rosh Hashanah may begin only after the new moon of Tishri is sighted in Jerusalem, we delay *yom tov* a day if the *molad* occurs after midday."

"And if that day is Sunday, Wednesday, or Friday, we must delay another day," Meir added. "Otherwise Rosh Hashanah or Yom Kippur would occur immediately before or after Shabbat."

"This coming year the *molad* will occur on Shabbat, at two hours past noon, so the fourth rule postpones Rosh Hashanah to the next day." Eliezer waited to see who would continue his reasoning.

It was Joheved who spoke. "But the third rule says that Rosh Hashanah may not fall on Sunday, so we delay an additional day to Monday." She smiled at the others. By this time everyone knew that the upcoming New Year would be celebrated on the last Monday of September.

"That's why Heshvan and Kislev will both be deficient this coming year, to make up the two days that Rosh Hashanah was delayed," Rachel said, proud of her comprehension.

That evening, after Eliezer showed her how to determine the *molad* anywhere with the astrolabe, she asked him, "You're an astronomer; tell me how accurate is this cycle? Did the Sod ha-Ibur make any mistakes?"

He grinned and nodded. "The lunar part is very accurate; after six hundred years the calculated *molad* will only be an hour off from true conjunction." Then he sighed. "But the solar calendar gains a day every 224 years."

"Don't worry." Rachel laughed seductively. "It will take ten thousand years to be off a month and there's sure to be a new Sanhedrin in Jerusalem before then to fix it."

He pulled her into his arms. His wife had immersed in the Seine three days ago, and he didn't care what would happen in ten thousand years. Abraham bar Hiyya had determined that the Messiah would come long before then.

twenty-five

eavy autumn rains pelted the windows, and outside the wind howled, but Salomon's cellar was warm and sweet smelling from the new vintage's fermentation. Rachel give silent thanks that the storm had delayed its attack until after Sukkot, saving her family the unhappy choice of dwelling in a wet *sukkah* or not performing the mitzvah. When the weather cleared, she and her sisters would return to the vineyard to collect straw ties and vine props, but today they did indoor chores, cleaning the winemaking equipment and sharpening pruning knives.

"What's bothering you, Joheved?" Miriam asked as she handed a knife back to her older sister. "This is the third blade you've sharpened that still has a significant burr."

Curious how Joheved would respond, Rachel restrained her pique that Miriam had returned her poorly sharpened knives without the slightest concern that something might be bothering her. Not that Rachel wanted to share how discouraged she felt that the fuller Albert recommended had turned out to be less competent than she expected—or her frustration that Eliezer would spend yet another winter and spring in Toledo.

Joheved sighed. "I don't know what to do about Shlomo. He doesn't want to go to school."

"He doesn't want to study Torah?" Rachel blurted out, almost dropping her knife. "Papa's namesake?"

"I'm so ashamed." Joheved blinked back tears.

"Maybe it's the school itself Shlomo doesn't like . . . or his teacher." Miriam glared at Rachel. "Judah hated his when he was young, yet he became a *talmid chacham*."

"Perhaps he misses his family," Rachel suggested, trying to be more helpful. "Or he resents being sent away while his brothers and cousins study at home."

"Of course he'd prefer to study at home," Joheved replied. "But Meir is occupied with the new yeshiva, and I have even less time now that all those boys are boarding with us."

Meir's back had continued to plague him, preventing his regular rides between Ramerupt and Troyes. So Salomon chose to split the yeshiva: the younger students to study in Ramerupt with Meir while the older ones remained in Troyes.

"I'd love to teach Shlomo, but I'm already teaching all the women I can handle." Miriam held up her knife to inspect the blade, and then, satisfied, took up another. "I had no idea my Torah class would be so popular."

"Why can't Hannah teach him? She's not getting married until Hanukkah," Rachel suggested. "And if Hannah gets pregnant right away, Leah can take over."

To Rachel's surprise, Miriam supported her. "Shlomo's only beginning Torah study, Joheved. Surely your daughters are competent to teach him."

"I suppose we can try it and see if he likes his studies better." But there was more doubt than hope in Joheved's voice.

A few weeks later, Joheved burst into her father's kitchen shortly before *disner*, her face brimming with excitement. She headed straight for Rachel, who was tasting a pot of stew, and embraced her. "I owe you a debt of gratitude for suggesting that Hannah teach Shlomo."

Rachel put down the spoon and grinned. "So he no longer hates his studies?"

"*Oui*, that's true. He's doing quite well now," Joheved replied. "But that's not why I'm here. It's about Jacob."

"What about Jacob?" Concern etched Salomon's face.

"He's talking. And not just a few words but whole sentences." Smiling broadly, Joheved began speaking faster. "He's been sitting with Hannah and Shlomo as they study, and one day when Shlomo stumbled over a verse Jacob corrected him. When I asked Jacob, I discovered that he's not only understood the weekly Torah portion for some time now but he's memorized nearly every verse."

Her audience stared at her in amazement.

"That's not all," Joheved continued proudly. "You should hear his questions. Last week when Hannah taught about Noah's Ark, Jacob asked why Noah didn't have any children when he was young, like normal people do, but only after he was five hundred years old."

"Meir must be relieved," Miriam said.

"Meir never had the slightest doubt about our son's abilities." Inexplicably Joheved blushed.

She had become pregnant with Jacob shortly after Meir began "kissing that place" as a prelude to using the bed. With the Talmud teaching that the quality of a child is proportional to the quality of the act that conceives him, Meir assured her that the boy would outshine their older children. Despite the phenomenal pleasure Joheved experienced, she hadn't quite shared her husband's confidence. Now he'd been vindicated.

She noticed that the stew was almost boiling over and picked up a spoon from the table to stir it down.

"Wait, Joheved." Too late Rachel grabbed for her sister's arm. "That's a milk spoon—the one Anna uses to make cheese."

"Oh no." Her face flaming, Joheved snatched the errant spoon from the stew and threw it in a pan of soapy water. She turned to her father. "Papa, what are we going to do?"

Rachel frowned. "Don't tell me we have to throw the stew out?" When was Joheved going to realize that Rachel was in charge of Papa's kitchen?

Salomon stroked his beard. Jewish Law demanded a strict separation of milk and meat. Dairy and meat dishes were never served at the same meal, and a plate or utensil used for one could not be used for the other without washing it in between. His daughters gazed at him anxiously, awaiting his decision.

"When did Anna last use the milk spoon?" he asked.

"I think it was yesterday morning," Miriam said. "Or maybe the day before."

Salomon nodded. "In that case I will permit the stew, the spoon, and the pot because . . ." He paused to let his daughters come to their own conclusions first. "Most important, there is more than sixty times as much meat in the pot as milk on the spoon. Also the spoon has not been used for over twenty-four hours." He smiled at Joheved. "And we cannot say that you used the spoon to give the stew a better taste."

When Rachel hugged him with relief, he added, "But to avoid further problems, wash the spoon in hot water before anyone uses it again."

Embarrassed at her negligence, Joheved brought the subject back to her son. "This week, with the binding of Isaac, Jacob asked us why Abraham didn't tell Sarah about sacrificing their son, and if that's why she died afterward."

"So my youngest grandson is indeed Jacob Tam." Salomon's eyes twinkled with pleasure as he made a mental note to answer Jacob's questions in his Torah commentary. Yet his voice held a chilly warning.

A child this brilliant would inflame the demons' jealousy. Better everyone should continue to call the boy Jacob the Simple to fool the evil spirits, protecting him from their enmity.

Joheved clamped her hand over her mouth, her eyes widening in fear at how she'd just endangered her son. "Never mind, it's nothing important," she stammered. "Let's go eat."

"I always welcome news of my little nephews, Shlomo and Jacob Tam." Rachel carried the bread into the dining room. "May the Holy One protect them."

Joheved gazed around the unusually empty table, where only Simcha and his son Samuel sat at the men's end. "Where's Shmuel? And the other students?"

"They're at my house," Miriam said. "Your son and Judah got into quite a debate this morning about Creation, and the students are keen to hear the outcome."

The family had barely finished blessing the bread when the air was split with the clanging of church bells. Salomon's family exchanged looks of surprised curiosity; the noon hour had already chimed. Eventually all the churches in Troyes had their say, and as the final echo melted away, Guy de Dampierre stood in the doorway, his expression more ecstatic than Joheved's was earlier.

"We've received marvelous news." The canon paused to catch his breath. "The Franks have defeated the Turks and taken Jerusalem. Pope Urban's great quest has been successful."

It seemed an eternity before Miriam broke the stunned silence. "So that's why all the bells are ringing."

He nodded and turned to Salomon, eager for the Jewish scholar's opinion.

"What a shame that Urban died before he could celebrate the event." Salomon's bland statement was crafted to hide his true opinion while not antagonizing the cleric.

Guy was too thrilled to notice his audience's dismay. "*Oui*. He died a mere fourteen days after Jerusalem fell, but I'm sure he celebrated the joyous tidings in Heaven."

Rachel had no choice but to set a place for Guy, who babbled on excitedly, "Who could imagine the pilgrims succeeding, especially when Count Étienne returned after fleeing the siege of Antioch? And who would believe that Raymond de Toulouse and Godfrey de Bouillon both rejected sovereignty over Jerusalem, refusing to rule the city where Jesus suffered?"

Salomon passed Guy a dish of pickled leeks. "That doesn't sound like the Godfrey de Bouillon I'm familiar with."

"Godfrey declared that he wouldn't wear a crown of gold where Christ had worn a crown of thorns."

Rachel flinched at the mention of Christ. The word meant "Messiah," so Jews avoided using it.

"So who rules Jerusalem now?" Joheved asked only to be polite.

Guy flashed the grin the sisters recognized as one preceding the dissemination of gossip. "Apparently Raymond's refusal was merely a feint, a show of piety he expected would make the other nobles insist he take the throne. But they turned to Godfrey instead, who took leadership not as king, but as 'Defender of the Holy Sepulchre.' Furious, Raymond removed his army and laid siege to Tripoli."

"Count Étienne must be mortified at the news." Rachel refilled Guy's bowl of stew.

"I hear that Adèle is making his life miserable with accusations of cowardice," Guy said. "Despite Étienne spending three years on pilgrimage and going all the way to Antioch."

"Unlike his brother Hugues, who never stepped foot out of Champagne," Joheved pointed out.

Miriam turned to Guy. "Do you think Hugues should have gone?"

Countess Adelaide's second son, Philip, had recently died after a lengthy illness, and any mother would prefer that her last living son not embark on such a dangerous enterprise. "Who would rule Champagne if he died there?"

"I suppose Adelaide was right to keep him home; one brother on pilgrimage was enough. But that won't stop people from calling Thibault's sons craven."

Rachel nodded. Whatever feelings the Jews of Troyes might have about the fall of Jerusalem, they would share their sovereign's shame when he was mocked as a coward.

Guy, his enthusiasm somewhat deflated, drained his cup of wine and found an excuse to leave.

As soon as Rachel heard the courtyard gate close, she turned to her father. Salomon seemed frozen, lost in thought. Sure that Guy's visit had plunged him back into despair over the Rhineland's lost yeshivot, she racked her brain for something to distract him. "Papa, Eliezer heard a rumor that Godfrey de Bouillon once consulted you. Is it true?"

All heads turned toward Salomon, who let out a sigh. "Actually it was his envoy, Godfrey de Esch-sur-Sûre, not the duke himself."

"What did he want?" Simcha asked.

"He wanted me to travel to Lorraine, to write a letter urging its Jewish communities to generously provision him and his knights for their pilgrimage." Salomon was unable to keep the bitterness from his voice.

"But you never left Troyes," Miriam pointed out.

Salomon shook his head. "After I heard that Godfrey's messenger was looking for me, I absented myself whenever he came around, until eventually he left me in peace." He sighed again. "Not that it made any difference. Godfrey was perfectly capable of extorting money himself, including a chest of silver from the *parnas* of Mayence."

"You defied Godfrey de Bouillon without evil consequences." Samuel looked at Salomon with awe. "Weren't you afraid?"

"I didn't think the duke would come into Troyes to chastise me," Salomon replied. "Count Hugues would never have allowed such a violation of his territory. Look how he fought Érard of Brienne for five years over one small castle."

"Thank Heaven that war is finally over without Ramerupt getting dragged into it," Joheved said.

"In any case, I don't have to worry about Godfrey chastising me now," Salomon said. "As sovereign of Jerusalem, he's unlikely to return to France."

While the others speculated over whether the Edomites would prove better rulers of Jerusalem than the Turks, how long it would be until the Saracens ousted them, and what it all meant for the Jews, Salomon sat silently stroking his beard.

It was Samuel who naively asked, "Rabbenu, what do you think of all this?"

"Pardon me." Salomon looked embarrassed, as if he'd been caught napping in synagogue.

Samuel repeated his question, and, to Rachel's surprise, her father replied, "I was thinking of Judah and Shmuel arguing over Creation. And how I'll need to revise my Torah commentary."

"Revise it?" Miriam asked. "But why?" It was his Talmud commentary that wasn't finished.

Before he could answer, Judah and Shmuel rushed in, followed by their students. "You're going to rewrite your Torah commentary? Again?" Judah stared at him, aghast.

"But you've been pushing to finish your *kuntres* before . . ." Shmuel began. Joheved loudly cleared her throat, and her son's words trailed off before he could mention how little time Salomon might have to live.

"I know I haven't many years left." Salomon's stern visage silenced any protests. "But Miriam, the *minim* will use conquest of Jerusalem as proof that the Holy One has abandoned us and proof that He has made a covenant with them, the new Israel."

The room erupted in angry murmurs. "Never."

"I must give our people tools to answer the heretics who base their apostasy on the Torah," Salomon continued. "Not all *anusim* will repent, especially not after this, and those who knew Judaism and rejected it will become even more difficult to convince."

"All the more so when the *minim* justify their corrupt faith with our Torah," Joheved said, her eyes flashing.

"Your Torah commentary must concentrate on the plain, literal sense of the text," Shmuel insisted, now keen on the project. "The heretics may dismiss our Midrash, but they can't ignore the clear meaning of the Holy One's words."

Salomon locked eyes with his grandson. "Shmuel, you've been studying with the *minim* for several years, both here and in Paris. If any Jew understands their claims and can help me refute them, you are the one."

Then he turned to Rachel. "And you, *ma fille*, have taught Hebrew to both Guy and Étienne Harding. You can't help but have heard their interpretations of scripture. Let your sisters focus on Tractate Nedarim while you assist me."

Finally his gaze settled on his son-in-law. "Judah, you must continue editing my Talmud *kuntres*. We cannot allow that endeavor to cease."

"You don't need to revise your entire Torah commentary," Shmuel said. "Genesis should be your priority, because in Creation the *minim* find justification for their most basic heresies: original sin, the Trinity, the fall of the angels."

Rachel nodded. "Isaiah also needs to be addressed, and we mustn't forget Psalms. The heretics imagine and invent more references to the Hanged One in these two books than in all the others combined."

When Eliezer returned from his autumn trip buying furs with Pesach, Rachel tried to convince him how important it was for Papa to spend his time revising his Torah commentaries, but nothing would induce Eliezer to teach at the Cold Fair. It seemed to him only a matter of time until Talmud study in Ashkenaz was supplanted by the production of codes, as had happened in Sepharad. Salomon's small yeshiva would never be able to replace all the learning lost in the Rhineland.

"This summer I missed precious commercial opportunities by taking your father's place," he declared. "And I can't afford to repeat the loss." He had also been unable to keep up his astronomical calculations, and now he'd have to waste time relearning them.

Normally Rachel would have interpreted this as more grumbling about how her grand scheme to produce woolens in Troyes had come to naught. But there was something about his tone, an undercurrent of despair mixed in with anger and resentment, that gave her pause. His business in the east had been successful, she wasn't *niddah* when he got home, and there was Hannah's wedding to celebrate. Yet his happiness was muted.

And when Judah suggested that Elisha and Rivka would make a good match, she had seen a flicker of fear in Eliezer's eyes before he and Judah embraced in apparent joy.

"Eliezer, is anything wrong?" she asked as they lay in bed together. Usually he fell asleep immediately after the holy deed, even in the winter when nights were long and they went to bed early. But his swift shallow breathing confirmed that he was still awake. He was agitated about something.

"You've got to come back to Toledo with me." His entreaty sounded more urgent than previously. "The children too."

"But I have to help Papa with Psalms. And Shemiah is just starting to understand Gemara. You can't interrupt our son's studies now." Her voice rose with alarm. "Something happened on your trip. What was it?"

"The Edomites captured Jerusalem."

"And what does that have to do with us going to Toledo?"

Eliezer leaned up on an elbow to face her. "Rachel, the great bloodshed wasn't an aberration. Underneath their pleasantries, the Edomites hate us, and it's only a matter of time until what happened in Mayence and Worms happens in Troyes and Ramerupt."

"How can you believe such a thing?" Yet he had to be serious if he was calling her Rachel, not Belle. "Both the Church and King Henry strongly condemned the marauders. And everyone agreed that they received the punishment they deserved when the Hungarian army slaughtered them."

He sighed. "At first I thought it was my imagination, that grief and anger were affecting my interpretation of events. But other Jews agree that the change I've experienced in Ashkenaz, while subtle, is real."

"What's so different?"

"It used to be that each October when I traveled east, particularly after a hard winter and crop failures, local merchants welcomed me, were eager to buy my grain and sell me their furs in return. They didn't seem to care that I was Jewish and I didn't care if they weren't."

"And now, because the Turks no longer rule Jerusalem and people are hungry, suddenly everyone hates you?"

He paused to consider when and how things began to change. "It's been happening slowly, ever since the great bloodshed, and not just to me but to other merchants as well. There are burghers who now look at Jews with suspicion and loathing. They can't understand how any normal person could kill himself and his children rather than worship the Hanged One. In Mayence there are rumors that we're demons or in league with the devil, which is one of the reasons I won't go there anymore."

Rachel's insides began to tighten. Once the Edomites viewed Jews as not human, feudal rules wouldn't apply, and they would lose their protected status. Maybe that's why the baron had tried to cheat Papa last winter.

"This suspicion and loathing works the other way too," Eliezer continued. "Whenever I met a German burgher, I couldn't help but wonder if he helped open the gates for Emicho's men. Or if he would do so, should a future opportunity present itself."

"This is terrible. Everyone's fear and suspicion will feed on itself," Rachel said.

"None of this occurs in Sepharad," Eliezer said. "Jews, Moors, and Spaniards of Toledo are on excellent terms with one another. Few have even heard of the great bloodshed."

Rachel took a deep breath to calm herself. "Notzrim and Jews are on excellent terms in Troyes, even if grain prices are high. I see no reason why this should change just because Jerusalem has substituted one foreign ruler for another." Eliezer had to be wrong about hatred for Jews in Troyes. Without the Jewish community there would be no fairs, and without the fairs, no prosperity.

"Rachel, I see another problem. Right now Jews have a monopoly on trade between Edom and the Levant." Eliezer spoke quietly, as if imparting a great secret. "Our livelihood depends on buying cheap produce from the Notzrim and selling it for a profit to the Saracens, then turning around to buy cheap goods from the Saracens that we mark up for sale to the Notzrim."

"Don't lecture me. I've been a merchant longer than you."

"I just wanted to make sure you understood."

"I do. So what's your point?"

"Right now we charge prices as high as we like because nobody knows our costs. But assuming the Edomites aren't ousted from the Eretz Israel immediately, they will soon discover what Jews pay for the silk and spices we sell so dear." Eliezer paused for Rachel to digest his words. "And when the Venetians or Lombards realize our profit margin, how long do you think it will take before their ships start transporting merchandise as well as pilgrims?"

"But the Notzrim can't even communicate with each other," she protested. "How will they possibly negotiate with Saracens?" All Jews knew Hebrew, an enormous advantage in facilitating Jewish trade.

"If the profit is sufficient, they'll manage." Before she could find a new objection, he added another argument. "And if the Notzrim have a choice between buying from us or from other Notzrim, whom do you think they will favor?"

Rachel's heart sank as she considered her children's future. "Edomites won't become merchants overnight; maybe the Saracens will unite and expel them first."

From what Eliezer had seen of the Moors, this was unlikely. "It will be too late. Once enough Franks know the low cost of our goods, they will resent paying so much for them."

"Even if you're right, and I'm not saying you are, why should the children and I go with you now?" She knew he wouldn't have a good answer this time. "Why not wait a few years until Rivka is married and Shemiah has finished his studies?" *And Papa is in Gan Eden.*

"How I love to argue with you." He leaned over and began kissing her neck. "You should come with me this year because I can't live without you," he whispered as he reached out to caress her breasts.

Her breath quickening, Rachel gave herself over to the pleasure his hands and lips were generating. She couldn't refute his final reason—not that her *yetzer hara* wanted to.

A storm blew in the next day, causing Rachel to insist that it was too cold for Salomon to go out, and that she and Rivka would pray with him at home. While waiting for the men to return, Rachel helped Rivka with her spinning and told her about their plans. "You can't imagine all the wonderful things you'll see on the trip, Rivka." She gave the girl a hug.

"But Alvina and I have just started to study Mishnah." Rivka protested.

"I'll teach you Mishnah." Now Rachel would have someone to study with while Eliezer was out. She turned to Salomon. "You mustn't overexert yourself while we're gone, Papa."

"Don't worry, *ma fille*." Salomon stretched out his good hand to pat hers. "With Shmuel's help, I can revise my *kuntres* and resume my duties as rosh yeshiva. The only thing you need to fret over is what we're going to feed everyone during Hanukkah."

"Promise you won't spend too much time in the vineyard, especially in bad weather." Her voice rose with alarm. The demon had attacked him last year just after the Cold Fair.

"I won't. I'll let Baruch, Pesach, and Samuel do most of the pruning."

She sighed and turned her attention to Rivka's spindle, praising the quality of her daughter's wool thread. There was no way to keep Papa out of the yeshiva or the vineyard.

"I will miss you," he continued. "But a woman's place is with her husband. You've been a tremendous help by showing me which psalms need my attention; now you can relax with Eliezer in Toledo while I revise them."

"I won't be relaxing in Toledo, Papa. Rivka and I will be studying together, and I'll be writing more commentary on Nedarim." While Eliezer spends all night at the observatory and half the day sleeping, she said to herself, having second thoughts about leaving. Did she want their children to see him devoting his time to secular studies instead of Torah?

Before she could decide whether to share her misgivings with her father, the door swung open, silhouetting Miriam and Joheved against the swirling snow. They had their arms around each other as if neither could stand without support. Tears streamed down Joheved's cheeks and Miriam's pinched face was white as the snowflakes on her veil.

Rachel hurried to close the door behind them. "*Mon Dieu!* What's the matter?"

Miriam held out a letter as if it were a dead rat. "From Yom Tov."

His hand shaking, Salomon scanned the parchment. Then he passed it to Rachel and opened his arms to comfort his distraught older daughters.

Rivka ran to her side, and with great trepidation, Rachel began to read. Yom Tov assured his mother that he was well before offering regrets for bearing such evil news, but he knew she would want to be warned.

Winter storms had brought the pox to Paris.

With all the travel to and from Troyes during the Cold Fair, it would only be a matter of days, weeks at the most, before the pox struck here as well. Observing her sisters' terror, Rachel began to tremble. Shemiah and his older cousins had barely survived the previous outbreak, but children born since then would be vulnerable: Joheved's Shlomo and Jacob Tam, Miriam's Alvina and . . .

Rachel hugged Rivka tightly as potential tragedy loomed before her. *And my daughter.*

twenty-six

As one child in Troyes after another was stricken, Rachel spent an anxious January watching her daughter for any sign of poor health. Once they'd learned of the pox in Paris, there was no further talk of Rachel going to Toledo. Rivka would have the best chance of surviving if she became ill at home, and of course her mother must be there to care for her. Only pruning the vineyard with Papa and Shmuel, where they discussed how to revise Papa's commentary on Genesis, succeeded in diverting Rachel's mind from the approaching plague.

Papa was adamant that his very first question would address the heretics. "Shmuel tells me that several of their scholars ask why scripture begins with an account of Creation, and indeed our own sage Rabbi Isaac says the Torah should have begun with the first commandment given to Israel."

She smoothly cut off a shoot that grew toward the center of the plant. "How will you answer them?"

"Should the nations say to Israel, 'You are robbers who took the land of Canaan by force,' Israel may reply to them, 'All the earth belongs to the Holy One, Who created it and gave it to whom He pleased.'"

"But won't the *minim* say that He has now given it to them?"

Salomon dropped another trimmed branch on the pile behind him. "Just as when He willed, He gave the land to Canaan, so when He willed He took it from them and gave it to us."

"But the plain sense of the text is not to show the order of Creation, that the Holy One created heaven and earth first," Shmuel said. "It shows that at the beginning of Creation, the earth was without form and there was darkness."

"All forces of nature were created on the first day and activated later at their destined time." Salomon slid his palms across each other, as if washing his hands of the matter. "Those who wish to explore this further may refer to *Sefer Yetzira*."

Rachel addressed both her father and nephew. "How else will you refute the *minim*?"

Shmuel answered her. "The second verse states:

> The *ruach* of Elohim was hovering over the waters . . .

Since *ruach* means 'wind' or 'spirit,' they say this demonstrates the Holy Spirit, part of their false Trinity. But *ruach* obviously refers to the wind, which gathered the water into two areas above and below, just as the Holy One caused a *ruach* to split the Red Sea so the Israelites could walk through on dry land."

Salomon nodded. "Unfortunately, the *minim* also see reference to their Trinity when it is written:

> The Eternal said, 'We will make man in our image.' "

"What can you say to them?" Rachel asked. "The text is clearly in the plural."

"This demonstrates the Holy One's humility. He consulted with the heavenly council before creating other beings in His likeness," Salomon explained. "Though they did not assist Him in forming man, and though this use of the plural gives the heretics an opening to rebel, yet the verse does not refrain from teaching proper conduct—that the greater should take council from the lesser in issues that affect them."

"As a refutation to the heretics," Shmuel continued, "it is written immediately after this verse:

> The Eternal created man in His own image . . . male and female He created them.

'He,' not *they*." Shmuel smugly crossed his arms over his chest.

Rachel clapped her hands in approval. "What about the heavenly host, the angels?"

"Why is it written 'day one' [cardinal number], when all the other days are 'a second, a third, a fourth day' [ordinal numbers]?" Salomon asked. "Because on that day the Creator was the One, Sole Being in His world. The angels were not created until the second day."

"But the sixth day isn't called 'a sixth day,' like the others," she pointed out. "It's written 'the sixth day.' "

Salomon smiled at her. "This teaches that all of Creation stood in waiting until Shavuot, the sixth day of Sivan, when Israel was to receive the Torah."

Shmuel couldn't resist adding, "In fact this entire section, concerning the six days of Creation, was written to anticipate the commandment:

> Remember the Sabbath and keep it holy . . . for in six days the Eternal made heaven and earth."

"Speaking of the sixth day." Rachel's voice grew serious. "How will you counter the heresy of original sin?"

Salomon winced. "Shmuel, how do the heretics explain what happened to Adam and Eve?"

"In Paris they teach that Adam gave names to the beasts three hours after his creation, that the woman ate the forbidden fruit and offered it to him in the fifth hour, and that they were expelled from Gan Eden by the end of the eighth hour," he replied. "Since the verse following their expulsion states that Adam knew Eve and she became pregnant, the *minim* consider their children, and all children born since, to be stained with original sin."

Salomon turned to Rachel. "Tell us what Rabbi Yohanan bar Chanina teaches about that day in Tractate Sanhedrin."

"You mean from the end of the fourth chapter?" When Salomon nodded, she stopped pruning to recall the text.

> "The day has twelve hours. The first hour Adam's dust was collected; the second it became a shapeless lump; his limbs reached out in the third hour; in the fourth his soul entered him; he stood up during the fifth, and named the animals in the sixth. Eve became his mate in the seventh hour; during the eighth the two went up on the bed and four came down."

Rachel paused and then explained, "This means that the two, Adam and Eve, used the bed, after which she bore two children, Cain and his twin sister, making four altogether."

"Correct." Salomon removed a few small, weak branches from his vine. "Please continue."

> "In the ninth hour he was commanded not to eat from the tree [of knowledge], yet he sinned and ate in the tenth; he was judged in the eleventh and expelled in the twelfth."

Rachel fell silent for a moment and then her face lit with understanding. "Adam and Eve had children before they sinned."

"Exactly," Salomon said. "My rebuttal will point out that in Genesis, 'the man knew' is written in the pluperfect, emphasizing that Adam had known Eve before the previous events; before they ate the forbidden fruit and were driven from Gan Eden. So also the conception and birth of their children came before."

Shmuel slashed off a branch that had grown too tall. "This is a complete repudiation of the heretics. Adam's progeny, born before his sin, are not stained by his action and do not require any atonement."

Hoping the clean air in Ramerupt would help to stave off the pox's effects, Rachel sent Rivka to Joheved's at the end of January. This was followed by an apprehensive week when first Shlomo, then his little brother, started complaining that their heads and backs hurt.

Upon hearing that the boys had grown feverish, Rachel left the pruning unfinished and hurried to her sister's. A few mornings later, just as Joheved noticed small red spots on Shlomo's tongue, Rivka and Alvina announced that they were too tired to get out of bed and that their bellies hurt too much to eat breakfast. One look in her daughter's listless eyes was enough to freeze the blood in Rachel's veins, even as she falsely assured Rivka that she and her cousin would be feeling better soon.

Determined not to leave her daughter's side, Rachel took Rivka into her bed. But her hopeful lie turned out to be the truth: the girls' malaise disappeared the very day the telltale rash appeared in their mouths.

Although Alvina's fever rose alarmingly as the girls' spots spread to the rest to their skin, Rivka got only slightly warm, and to Rachel's surprised relief the girls felt so well that they spent the next two weeks giggling over which of the many sores on their body looked most like another belly button.

By then Shlomo's pustules were scabbing over, and his appetite returned as his fever dropped. Jacob Tam recovered sooner; his scabs gone before his brother's. Rivka's were the last to fall off, and while none of the children escaped without some pitted scars, Rachel thanked Heaven that her daughter's were predominantly out of sight on her feet and lower legs.

One month after Shlomo first became ill, parents in and around Troyes heaved a collective sigh of relief that the pox epidemic was clearly going to be a mild one. Every day when the Torah was read at services, more children, along with the parents of those too young to speak, stood and recited the *gomel*, the prayer of thanksgiving one says at the first synagogue visit after escaping from danger.

Finally it was Rivka's turn to recite the words that, may the Holy One protect her, she would not say again until she'd survived childbirth. "*Baruch ata Adonai* . . . Who bestows good things on the unworthy, and has bestowed on me every goodness."

Rachel joined the congregation in gladly responding, "Amen. He Who has bestowed on you every goodness, may He continue to bestow on you every goodness. Selah."

As the Torah reading continued with Miriam translating for the women, Rachel recalled the times she'd recited *gomel*: after each of her children were born, after she'd recovered from the stillbirth, and after that terrible storm at sea when their ship had nearly sunk. Thinking of how tightly she and Eliezer had held each other on that heaving deck, preparing to die in each other's arms, tears came to her eyes.

Was he well? What was he doing right now in Toledo? He must be worried about Rivka, with no knowledge yet of whether she was dead or alive. Somehow she must find a fuller, so he won't need to travel anymore. Everyone thought her goal of becoming a clothier was futile, that she should accept defeat and be content with the weavers. But that would mean accepting Eliezer's separation from her, which she could not do.

* * *

By early March, everyone was in the mood for celebrating, and the Jewish calendar provided the excuse they needed. Purim was less than a week away.

Isaac, as grateful a young father as any, discovered a way to celebrate Purim twice. He pointed out that, according to Jewish law, people who live in a walled city observe Purim on the fifteenth of Adar, while those living in a regular town celebrate on the fourteenth. Meir's students quickly grasped that they were entitled to two days of Purim revelry, the first in Ramerupt and the second in Troyes, and they lost no time in communicating this information to their older classmates.

Salomon arrived early, to avoid traveling on the Fast of Esther. Seeing his young grandchildren and great-grandchildren arrayed to greet him, all having survived the pox, his eyes filled with grateful tears. "Blessed is the Merciful One, King of the Universe, Who has given you to us and not given you to dust," he said as he hugged each one, reciting the Aramaic blessing made upon meeting someone who has recovered from a serious illness.

The next day the student bodies of both yeshivot descended on Ramerupt for the yearly recitation of the Book of Esther, to hear how the beautiful Persian queen dramatically revealed her Jewish identity to the king and saved her people from annihilation. After the reading concluded with the evil Haman hanging from the very scaffold he'd planned for the hero Mordecai, everyone settled in for hours of feasting, drinking, and carousing.

Isaac and Shmuel, each wearing a fur mantle inside out, spent the early evening on their hands and knees, either giving the younger children rides on their backs or chasing them around. Once the moon was high and the children in bed, several students pulled out dice in anticipation of a night of gambling. Daytime was for playing ball, tossing horseshoes, or running races in the manor's large courtyard, while music and dancing would be the entertainment the following night in Troyes.

Like Salomon, Meir drew the line at gambling with his students. "It will be awkward whether I lose to them or they lose to me."

"I think it should be fun to watch the gamblers," Rachel whispered to Joheved. "We're always too busy at Papa's."

In less than an hour, Rachel had learned several new dice games. She was about to warn Shemiah against an imprudent wager when Joheved grabbed her sleeve.

"Why should we watch when we can play?" A slightly tipsy Joheved pulled her into the warm kitchen, where Miriam was waiting with Zipporah, Judita, and Salomon's granddaughters.

To Rachel's surprise, Joheved placed six dice on the table. "You have no idea how many Milo confiscates from villagers fighting over bets." She grinned and added, "These are some of the few that aren't weighted."

"What game are you going to play?" Rivka asked, her voice at once timid and excited. For the first time she and Alvina were allowed to stay up past the usual children's bedtime.

"Let's start with Marlota," Rachel replied. "That's a simple one."

Joheved nudged Judita. "I told you she'd know."

Rachel handed three dice to Judita and the other three to Zipporah. "You alternate rolling your dice until each of you gets a total between seven and fourteen. That becomes your mark." When they both nodded, she said, "Then you continue rolling until one of you rolls her own mark, and wins, or rolls the other's mark and loses. The rest of us place bets on which of you we think will win."

They took turns playing until Miriam turned to Hannah and complained, "This game takes forever before everyone gets a turn. Let's play chess and leave dice to the others."

"Please, Mama." Leah jumped up and held out her hand. "Can I get Grandmamma Marona's chess set?"

Joheved removed a key from the bunch pinned to her *bliaut*. "Be sure to lock the pantry when you're done."

Leah returned with a large inlaid box, and dice were temporarily abandoned as she arranged the silver and ivory pieces on the gilt chessboard. When Joheved nodded permission, Alvina and Rivka examined the minutely detailed king with his drawn sword and the knights astride their horses. But the girls' favorites were the tiny elephants, and they eagerly awaited their capture, so they could play with them until the next game started.

Dice were again thrown with enthusiasm, with the non-players placing bets on both Marlota and the nearby chess match.

Miriam and Hannah were reduced to only a few pieces when Meir stuck his head in the door.

"We should be getting to bed." He couldn't restrain a yawn. "It's past midnight."

The women reluctantly agreed to continue their chess game the next day. After all, they would have to get up early for the morning Megillah reading and the banquet that followed if they expected to get back to Troyes in time do the whole thing again the following night.

The month between Purim and Passover passed slowly. Miriam and Rachel made occasional trips from Ramerupt to Troyes, Miriam to attend a few early births and Rachel to deal with the tardy wine buyers who always showed up just before Passover. Despite Miriam's concern that their daughters might experience a relapse, it was impossible to keep Rivka and Alvina indoors. Especially not on sunny spring days when the meadows were overrun with frisky newborn lambs.

As guilty as Rachel felt for neglecting Nedarim, she couldn't resist the pleasure of watching her daughter play with the lambs. Rivka was almost ten and would soon be too old for children's games. So Rachel decided to accompany Milo as he checked the quality of the new lambs' wool.

"Our experiment has worked well," he said, running his hand over one lamb after another. "Every year the new lambs' wool is finer."

When Rachel received his pronouncement with a less than enthusiastic *oui*, his expression became puzzled.

"But this was for your benefit. Aren't you pleased?"

She saw no reason to keep the truth from him. "I hired, and later dismissed, two men I hoped would be competent fullers. Yet my chain from shepherd to dyer cannot be complete without one."

"Surely that one missing piece cannot be critical to your success," he said.

"The fullers' guild in Troyes seems determined to thwart my goal. They keep the best woolens under their control, and if Eliezer weren't a dye importer, it would be impossible to find a dyer to work with me once the fullers threaten to boycott him."

His next question shocked Rachel into silence.

"Do you think that's because you're a woman or because you're a Jew?"

She gulped and replied, "I assume it's because I'm a woman. After all, there are many Jews in the textile business. Why do you ask?"

Milo frowned. "When I first came to Ramerupt, I never heard any disparagement about Lord Meir studying strange books and not attending church. If anything the other lords might have complained that he treated his villeins too kindly."

"But lately things are different?" Rachel tried to keep her tone neutral; yet she couldn't forget Eliezer's concerns.

"I think so. Sometimes I hear things in the marketplace: how the monks were shrewd when they charged higher prices for grain after last year's bad harvest, yet a Jewish merchant is taking advantage." He shrugged. "Other criticisms too."

"And what do you say to them?"

"Nothing." He eyed her with reproach. "I still keep the oath I took for Lady Joheved."

How convenient, Rachel thought. But she said instead, "Do you fear for her safety?" Wasn't that why Milo hadn't gone on pilgrimage?

"I did when so many armed and angry pilgrims were here with Peter the Hermit," he admitted. "But now I merely feel uneasy. As though I used to hear noise in the night and assume it was harmless animals in the fields, but now I don't know what's out there and if it's dangerous or not."

"My husband worries too," she confided. "He wants us to move to Toledo."

"Perhaps you should," Milo said with a seriousness that chilled her despite the sunny day.

But Rachel refused to accept Milo's recommendation. The danger from armed pilgrims was on the road, not in Troyes. Once Eliezer stayed home, he'd be safe.

Rachel's letter was waiting for Eliezer at synagogue. He read it once, then twice more, before closing his eyes and reciting the blessing for receiving good news, "*Baruch ata Adonai* . . . Who is good and does good." He also thanked Heaven that Salomon had avoided another demon attack. Next year perhaps Rachel could finally stop fretting about her father's health, so she and the children could spend Passover with him in Toledo.

When he returned to his rooms, Gazelle informed him that Abraham bar Hiyya was waiting. When her undulating form reached the end of the hall, Abraham sighed and muttered, "Greater is he who has succeeded in training himself to abandon thoughts of worldly passion and longs only for the service and adoration of the Most High than he who has still to wrestle with the appetites of the flesh, though he overcomes them in the end."

Eliezer accepted his friend's implied criticism. "When my wife comes to live with me, I won't need a concubine." Gazelle satisfied his physical needs and never complained about his absence, but she wasn't Rachel.

"I meant no offense," Abraham replied. "I was speaking only of myself. Have you heard from your wife yet?"

"I received her letter just this morning." Eliezer reached over to hug Abraham. "Apparently our daughter and the other children in my wife's family have survived the pox—may the Holy One continue to protect them."

"I have news as well," Abraham announced.

Eliezer knew his friend was waiting to be questioned, but he couldn't resist joking first. "After hearing how I taught about the calendar's secrets in Troyes, you've decided to write your next book about intercalation?" Abraham was always in the middle of writing some treatise or another.

"An excellent idea," Abraham replied. "I'll start on it as soon as I finish 'Form of the Earth.' Now let's go to the observatory. I want you to meet someone."

Eliezer wasn't sure if Abraham was teasing him, but clearly his friend was in a fine mood. They raced through Toledo's twisting streets, walking too fast for conversation, until they reached their destination.

Abraham knocked three times on a closed door, which opened slowly to admit them. A small dark man hovered protectively over a table covered with pages of calculations; otherwise the room was empty. Abraham looked up and down the hall, which was completely unnecessary since every civilized person in Toledo was at home sitting down to his midday meal, and then, apparently satisfied, closed the door behind them.

"May I introduce Ibn Bajjah," Abraham indicated the Moor, who bowed in Eliezer's direction. "He has returned from several years of study in Baghdad and is most interested in your recent observations."

Ibn Bajjah scuttled around the table and pointed to one of the manuscripts. "There can be no doubt that Ptolemy's planetary model is incorrect. As I have demonstrated here, it is mechanically impossible for a physical sphere to move at uniform speed around an axis that does not pass through its center."

Abraham nodded approvingly, and Ibn Bajjah moved to another page. "This treatise discusses the precession of the equinoxes, and in it I propose a model of trepidation, rather than Ptolemy's simple uniform precession."

Eliezer leaned over for a closer look, but before he could finish the first sentence, Abraham pulled on his sleeve. "Look at this." A new page was shoved in front of Eliezer.

"These appear to be my results." Eliezer squinted at the small characters, which were not in his handwriting. "But this diagram of circles is not mine."

"I have added your observations to my own," Ibn Bajjah said. "And calculated an improved model for lunar motion."

Until that moment, Eliezer's preeminent concern had been how soon the three men would leave to continue their discussion over *disner*. But as he gazed back and forth between Ibn Bajjah's calculations and diagrams, trying to discern how each formula corresponded with a particular lunar motion, thoughts of food receded in importance.

"This is amazing," he finally said, slowly shaking his head. "Do you mind if I study these more carefully?"

"Study them all you like and check diligently for flaws." Abraham laid his hand on the manuscripts. "But do not remove them from this room, and lock the door after you leave."

The following week Eliezer hurried to finish all his business so he could devote himself to Ibn Bajjah's astronomical data. He began copying the Moor's calculations, verifying their accuracy as he wrote, and pointed out some minor errors. Whenever they were together, he plied Ibn Bajjah and Abraham with questions about the new model, to ensure that he understood it thoroughly.

All too soon it was June, time for Eliezer to return to Troyes. Abraham and Ibn Bajjah were hoping to apply their lunar model to the inner planets.

"Our progress will be slower without you," Ibn Bajjah complained. "Can't you return sooner, after your New Year's holidays?"

"Let your junior partner attend the winter fair," Abraham urged. "Then he can meet you here to collect the dyestuffs."

Eliezer shook his head in frustration. It wasn't a matter of Pesach's competence. "I would miss my family too much."

"So bring them here." Abraham held up his hand to keep Eliezer from interrupting. "I know. Your son must continue his Talmud studies. But surely your wife and daughter can join you."

"I've tried to bring Rachel to Toledo, but her father is not well." He sighed with resignation. "The last time she came with me, her mother died while she was away."

"A wife's place is with her husband, not her father." Ibn Bajjah's tone registered his disapproval.

Abraham was equally doubtful. "You know that a married woman is only commanded to revere her parents, not honor them. Besides which, you told me that your wife has two sisters to care for your father-in-law, both of whom live near him."

"And you know that I cannot force my wife to change her residence," Eliezer shot back. "It's written in her *ketubah*."

Ibn Bajjah rolled his eyes at this. "If you cannot make her move to Toledo, then leave her in France and take another wife."

Eliezer scowled. That was easy for Ibn Bajjah to say; he had wives in Baghdad and Toledo. "I have a concubine here, but it's not the same."

"What good is a wife if she won't live where you do?" Abraham bar Hiyya asked. "But surely you can find a way to convince her to move here without forcing her."

"Why be so attached to this wife?" Ibn Bajjah muttered to himself. "One woman is as good as another."

Before Eliezer could respond, Abraham's face brightened. "You don't need to force your wife to move. Announce that you can only stay in Troyes for the summer, making it clear that you want her to join you here. Then let her decide what to do."

Two months later, as Eliezer traveled over the Pyrenees, through Provence, and north to Champagne, each night he noted the movement of the moon and inner planets. At the same time, he seethed with frustration at thoughts of Abraham and Ibn Bajjah experimenting with new models and improving their calculations without him.

Who knows how far they would have advanced by the time he returned? And how long it would take him to catch up with them?

The days grew longer and his resolve strengthened. He would stay in Troyes only through the Days of Awe. Rachel could accompany him back to Toledo—or not. The decision would be hers.

twenty-seven

"Joheved, could you tell me what you think of the commentary I've written?" Rachel put down her spindle to pat the bench beside her. "I tried to remember everything we discussed when we studied this section before I got married."

Usually Rachel worked on Nedarim with Miriam. But Miriam was away with a woman in labor, while Joheved had come into Troyes for Shavuot and decided to remain in town through the Sabbath. Joheved, who'd been hoping for such an invitation, took her spinning paraphernalia from her belt and headed in her sister's direction.

First Rachel read the Talmud text:

> "They asked Ima Shalom why her children were exceptionally beautiful. She said to them: He [her husband] converses with me, not at the beginning of the night or at the end of the night, but at midnight. And when he converses, he reveals a *tefach* and hides a *tefach*; and it seems as if he were forced by a demon. When I asked him why, he replied, 'So that I do not set my eyes on another woman.'"

"I remember that passage," Joheved said. "It's from the second chapter."

"*Oui*. Here's how I explain it. 'Conversing' refers to marital relations, and a *tefach*, as we learn in Tractate Berachot, is the amount of skin a man may expose to urinate."

Joheved nodded. "I think you should clarify that it is a *tefach* of Ima Shalom's clothes that her husband is revealing and hiding, until finally they are naked. Otherwise a student might think a man should perform the holy deed clothed, only exposing the smallest portion of skin necessary."

"Good idea." Rachel pulled a handful of wool from her distaff, tucked them into the top of her spindle, then lifted it up and let it drop. She waited until the spindle had completely descended, twisting and stretching the fiber as it fell, before winding the yarn onto her spindle.

"I like what you wrote about him seeming to be forced by a demon: that he moves with *koach*, 'great power.' "

"Miriam thought it might mean that he performs the act under the blanket, so a demon can't see them," Rachel said.

Joheved scowled slightly as Rachel took an even larger amount of wool and spun it into a heavy length of yarn. But all she said was, "It won't hurt to put in both reasons."

"This next passage definitely requires some explanation:

> Those who rebel and those who transgress—these are the children of fear, children of a forced woman, children of hatred, . . . children of an exchanged woman, children of anger, children of drunkenness, children of a woman whose husband intends to divorce her.

But maybe I wrote too much."

"I agree that it is important to explain the difference between fear, when the woman is intimidated into allowing an act she doesn't want, and when she is physically forced or raped," Joheved said.

"And if a husband hates his wife, he doesn't care about her feelings, which makes it like harlotry," Rachel explained. She turned to Joheved. "Do you think I need to say that the husband of an exchanged woman has two wives, and that he went to one thinking he was going to the other?"

"*Oui*. And also that anger doesn't mean that the couple hates each other, only that they had a fight first."

Rachel's cheeks flushed. "I'm not sure about that. Some couples may enjoy relations more after they've been arguing."

"I wonder if drunkenness refers to the husband or the wife," Joheved said. "We'll have to ask Papa."

"Papa says another fault that can create bad children is when one of them is asleep."

Joheved burst out laughing. "One of them is asleep? Surely this can only be the wife."

Rachel couldn't help but giggle. "Actually Papa meant that a man shouldn't attempt relations when he is too exhausted to fully desire his wife; otherwise he will come to resent her."

When Rachel stood up to let her spindle drop, twisting her wool into yarn as thick as a fuzzy caterpillar, Joheved couldn't restrain herself. "Why are you spinning such fat yarn? You'll use up all the wool and have only half the length I've spun."

Instead of bristling at being caught misbehaving, Rachel replied calmly. "Most spinsters believe as you do, that the longer the yarn the better. But thin yarn is too weak for warp threads and can only be used for the weft." She shook her head. "If the weavers' family and mine didn't spin it, we'd never have enough warp yarn for our looms."

Joheved was immediately intrigued. "Tell me more."

"The warp threads, which run the complete length of the broadcloth, must be strong enough to withstand being pulled taught on the loom."

"Of course." Joheved nodded slowly. "And to support the entire material."

"Sometimes, when we don't have enough thick yarn spun, we have to wind several thin threads together."

"But that must be inefficient."

"*Oui*," Rachel replied. "Not only do those who spin the thin threads waste their time, but also the one who winds them."

Joheved took some wool and awkwardly tried to spin a thicker yarn. "Oh dear. If I have to think about what I'm doing, I won't be able to study Talmud and spin at the same time."

Their conversation was interrupted as the gate opened and Zipporah stumbled in. "It took almost an entire day and night, but Menachem's youngest child is safely born," she announced, followed by a large yawn. "Get ready for a brit next week."

Joheved jumped up to assist her exhausted daughter-in-law, leaving Rachel to bask in the knowledge that, for the first time, she and Joheved had studied Talmud together without Miriam. And Joheved had treated her as an equal.

* * *

A week before the Hot Fair opened, Rachel received a message from Guy that a group of pilgrims had arrived from Spain. Those desirous of making a pilgrimage had to obtain permission from their bishop, which meant that Guy was well informed on their comings and goings.

She hurried to the local hospice, where a burly priest eyed her lewdly before handing her several letters bearing a Hebrew recipient's name. One of them was in her husband's hand, addressed to Shemiah, as was the custom in Sepharad, where women's names were never mentioned in correspondence.

Rachel quickly scanned the short missive, which said he might be delayed, but gave no reason. "Do you know if the man who wrote this was ill?" she asked.

"I didn't see him myself, but when his wife gave me the letter, she assured me he was well," the priest replied. "In case any of his relations should ask."

"His wife?" Rachel managed to choke out. Surely the pilgrim was mistaken. "But he already has a wife in Troyes."

"*Non*. I'm sure the woman said she was his wife. I've heard it's quite common for the Moors and Jews there to take more than one." His tone sounded more envious than critical.

Stunned, the only thing Rachel could think of to ask was what Eliezer's "wife" looked like.

"She was an unusual creature, taller than most men, with skin as black as soot. That's why I remember her so clearly." He closed his eyes and nodded appreciatively. "Yet not at all unattractive—quite the opposite in fact."

Rachel walked home in a daze, her fury rising as she suspected what really lay behind Eliezer's sudden interest in new positions for using the bed. By the time night fell, she was determined to divorce the lying, traitorous dog as soon as he stepped foot in Troyes. But in the morning, she had calmed sufficiently to realize that she needed more evidence than the word of a lecherous priest.

So she attended services at the New Synagogue, near the fairgrounds, where she was more likely to find a merchant from Toledo. There she enlisted Simon and Nissim's aid, telling them only that Eliezer was delayed and she wanted to make sure he was well. After a short consultation, they pointed out two swarthy men, one with a bushy beard and the other wearing red hose.

Her stomach tight with anxiety, Rachel approached the bearded one, asking what color fabric he thought would best suit Eliezer's new wife. The fellow scratched his head and admitted that he had never seen Eliezer's concubine and that she should ask Yusef. He indicated his compatriot with red hose.

Part of her wanted to go home, lock herself in her room, and cry her eyes out. But another part pushed her to question Yusef, to find out the truth, no matter how damning. So she took a deep breath and, putting on her most innocent expression, asked, "I'd like to get some nice woolens for Eliezer's new concubine." This was easier to say than wife. "What color would you recommend?"

"Let me think." Yusef looked at her as if it were the most natural thing in the world for one wife to buy clothes for the second. But then where he came from, no man took another wife or concubine without the first wife's permission.

"Red would suit Gazelle admirably, but it wouldn't do for a concubine to wear kermes scarlet." He shook his head. "Far too luxurious. But you can undoubtedly find some excellent cloth dyed with madder. Remember that with her height, you'll probably need a third more fabric than is usual for a woman."

"*Merci*. You have told me all I need to know." Rachel hurried off in the opposite direction. She didn't care if she appeared rude. She had to end this conversation and get away from this man who had put a name to her worst fears.

"Glad to be of help," Yusef called out after her.

Desperate to avoid anyone she knew, Rachel headed to the nearby Paris Gate and left the city. As she strode past the lush wheat fields, conflicting voices warred within her mind.

My husband, who says he loves me, has taken another wife. How could he betray me like that? But she's not a wife, only a concubine, a maidservant. *Her status doesn't matter; she lives with him and shares his bed.* He's a man, with a man's normal urges—would I prefer that he visits harlots? *How dare he do this to me? I'll divorce him.* Non! Make him divorce her. *Nobody needs to divorce anyone. Once I've hired a fuller Eliezer won't need to go to Toledo anymore.*

Slowly her rage cooled. Instead of confronting him as soon as he arrived, she'd wait and see what he said. And she'd redouble her efforts to find a competent fuller.

Rachel had her first opportunity when Simon came looking for Eliezer the following week.

"I hope he'll be here soon." The dyer shifted his weight from one foot to the other then back again. "I'm completely out of indigo and have almost no alum either."

"I'm sure he'll arrive any day now," Rachel said with more assurance than she felt.

But Simon made no effort to leave. He continued to pace the courtyard, leaving Rachel wondering how to get rid of the man without insulting him. For lack of a better subject she asked, "I don't suppose you've heard of any fuller who's looking for employment."

Simon stopped in his tracks. "Now that you mention it, I heard a rumor about Othon; that he's treated an apprentice so badly that the fellow may leave."

"I'm not interested in another apprentice, not even Othon's." Yet the man was one of the best fullers in Troyes.

"Don't be hasty. From what I've heard, this apprentice knows everything his master does, perhaps more."

Rachel approached Simon, getting a bit closer than she usually stood to a man. "Find out more about this apprentice, and you can be sure I'll send for you immediately when Eliezer arrives."

As soon as she saw Simon turn the corner, she grabbed her veil and headed for Albert and Alette's house. Their salon was a whirlwind of activity; Alette and her daughters busily spinning while Albert and Jehan sent the shuttles between the warp so quickly that their hands were almost a blur.

Alette's face lit with pleasure. "You've saved me a trip," she addressed Rachel. "We'll be out of wool next week."

"We should have some from the new shearing at Ramerupt by then, and you'll find the quality even better than last year's."

"Is that what brings you to visit, Mistress?" Jehan was always polite, but his fingers no longer slowed when he spoke.

"I need some information about Othon the Fuller," Rachel said. "Actually, I want to know about his apprentice."

"Othon will never allow one of his apprentices work for a competitor," Albert replied.

"I heard that one of them is unhappy," Rachel countered.

"Perhaps," Alette said. "Othon's a hard man to deal with and has only gotten worse as he's aged."

Rachel laid a handful of coins on the table. "Find the weavers who supply Othon's cloth and the women who spin for them. Buy them some ale at the fair and see what you can learn."

When Rachel delivered the new wool to the weavers the following week, Jehan told her that one of Othon's apprentices was so proficient that he practically ran the place for his master, whose gout was forcing him to spend more and more time in bed. But there were no signs of the apprentice's unhappiness, Albert warned her. In fact everyone expected him to marry Othon's daughter and carry on the business. But they assured Rachel that they would continue to ask about him.

Eliezer arrived a few days later, catching Rachel without a fully formed plan for how to confront him. Upon discovering that she'd immersed in the Seine only the day before, he showered her with affection, and Rachel found it easier to enjoy his attention and say nothing about Gazelle. She convinced herself that fighting with Eliezer would solve nothing and only distract her from searching out the elusive fuller's apprentice.

Thus she found time to stop in at the dyer's while Eliezer napped. "My husband has returned with an excellent supply of dyestuffs," she told Simon. "But I suggest you wait until tomorrow to come by, after he's had time to rest."

He flashed her a salacious grin. "I'll give him two days."

She forced herself to smile back. "Have you learned any more about Othon's apprentice?"

"Now that Eliezer's home, I'll have an excuse to talk to the other dyers." Simon chuckled. "Once they know I have access to his best merchandise, I'm sure I can loosen their lips."

The next two weeks passed with no word from Simon, and Rachel was thankful that she'd been too upset about Gazelle to tell Eliezer about the fuller's apprentice. Not that they had time to talk about her textile business or his concubine. Eliezer was adamant both that Shemiah begin learning about the dyestuffs and fur trade, and that the boy's betrothal be finalized that summer. Their son was in his sixteenth year and needed to have his future settled.

Rachel, still surprised to see Shemiah towering over her instead of looking up, was forced to agree. Soon she was too busy negotiating his engagement contract, as well as working in the summer vineyard and lending women money, to think about anything else. As Papa had done when she'd become engaged to Eliezer, Moses refused to allow Glorietta's betrothal upon learning that Shemiah would be traveling on business. In addition, Moses demanded a heavy financial penalty should Eliezer breach the engagement contract.

Eliezer took this setback with more grace than previously. "Let us have *erusin* and *nisuin* together at the wedding. I'm not worried that Moses will find a better match than our Shemiah for Glorietta," he confided to Rachel in bed one evening. "She's not nearly as attractive as you were . . . or as you are now."

That was the end of talking and the beginning of conversing.

As if Rachel weren't occupied enough, summer always brought more correspondence for her father than Simcha could handle. One evening, as the others were reviewing the day's Talmud lesson before returning to synagogue, Papa handed her some letters.

"I'd like you to respond to these queries." He pulled out the bench next to him for her to sit. "More questions about apostates and *anusim*. Almost four years since the great bloodshed; when will they end?"

She scanned the first one, relieved to find it rather straightforward. A man and woman, both *anusim*, performed *erusin* during the time they'd been compelled to forsake the Law of Moses. The witnesses had similarly been forced to apostatize. The couple had since left that locale and wished to repent. Was their marriage legally binding?

"Of course their marriage is valid." Rachel looked to her father, who nodded vigorously. "Although the couple committed a serious sin, they are still considered Israel. Their hearts remained faithful to Heaven, and they escaped as soon as they could—their *erusin* is most certainly binding."

Salomon shook his head sadly. "So many of our people wish to punish the *anusim*; yet who knows how they would act with the sword at their throats?"

Rachel read the next letter, a short one, and scratched her head in confusion. "A young man, whose only brother has apostatized, cannot find a woman who will marry him."

"A difficult problem." Salomon stroked his beard quite a while before continuing, "I'm not sure I have a solution."

"I don't understand."

"If our questioner should marry and then die before having children . . ." he left the sentence for Rachel to finish.

"Of course." Her face lit with understanding. "His wife would be left an *agunah*, chained to his apostate brother, who can neither marry her nor free her through *chalitzah*."

"There may be some hope for the poor fellow."

"What hope? No woman would want to assume that risk, not when there are unfettered men available."

"He could possibly find a convert to accept him." Salomon didn't sound confident of his answer.

"Or if he were of less-saintly character, he could get a maidservant with child first," Rachel said.

Salomon shook his head. "Most fathers wouldn't want their daughters marrying into a family tainted by apostasy, and even less so if the prospective groom is lacking in morals."

By the end of the summer, Rachel and Moses had almost completed their children's engagement contract. It was an amicable process, a relief from Moses's demanding patients and Rachel's desperate debtors, one that each had secretly prolonged as a pleasant contrast to the rest of their business dealings. Eliezer, recognizing that he couldn't return to Toledo without signing the document, fumed with frustration at their lack of progress. When they agreed to suspend negotiations until after Sukkot, Eliezer could barely hide his exasperation.

Rachel had no sympathy for his bad moods; she was exulting over the information she'd received from Alette and Simon. First came a visit from the weaver.

"We have almost finished two more bolts of broadcloth." Alette put her hand on Rachel's when the latter reached for her purse. "No need to pay until the fair's over, but I couldn't wait to tell you what I heard about Othon's apprentice."

Rachel poured her a cup of wine. "What have you learned?"

Alette's eyes twinkled with excitement. "You know how some tavern wenches take advantage of the fair season to earn extra coins from the merchants."

"*Oui.*" Proper women didn't like this by-product of Troyes' fairs, but the fact remained that there weren't enough harlots to service all the visitors. Prices naturally increased, drawing local amateurs to supplement their incomes in this fashion.

"Sybille's younger daughter works in a tavern near the Vienne Creek, so she knows all the dyers and fullers," Alette said. "One night Othon's apprentice comes in, and he's picking quarrels with the other patrons, which is quite unlike him, says Sybille's girl. So the tavern keeper tells her to quiet his bad temper or get him to leave before a fight starts, and since the fellow is good-looking, she tries to cheer him up."

"I understand what happened," Rachel cut her off. "What did she learn from him?"

"To make a long story short," Alette's tone revealed her annoyance at being interrupted, "the fellow worked years for Othon under the impression that he would be rewarded with the hand of Othon's daughter and a partnership in the business."

Like Jacob had worked for Laban, Rachel thought. And this man was about to be similarly cheated.

"Except that Othon decided to marry his daughter off to another master fuller, one at least twice her age," Alette announced. "Sybille's girl said the apprentice had some choice curses for Othon."

"Perhaps he would be willing to sell his skills elsewhere. By the way, what's his name?"

"*Mon Dieu*, I don't know." Alette looked at Rachel hopefully. "But surely you can find out."

Rachel lost no time in dispatching a message to Simon, but it was several days before the dyer sent word to meet at his shop. She arrived to find him stirring a vat of boiling blue liquid. Between indigo's normal stink and the addition of horse urine as binder, the stench was horrific.

"I apologize for making you come to me," Simon said as he wiped his hands. "But I need to get these finished if I'm going to sell them before the fair closes."

"And I apologize for interrupting your work," Rachel said, trying not to gag from the fumes. "But the rumor about Othon's apprentice appears to be true."

"I've made some discreet inquiries, and I believe that with the proper inducements Othon's apprentice can be persuaded to ply his considerable skills elsewhere."

"We keep calling him Othon's apprentice. Doesn't the man have a name?"

Simon avoided her gaze. "His name is Dovid."

"Oh my." Rachel slowly let out her breath. "I wonder if that improves or decreases my chances of hiring him."

"Dovid may have been born a Jew, but he's not one now," Simon said. "Not that he's big on worshipping the Hanged One; he only attends Mass on their major feast days."

"Maybe Dovid's not a Jew. Maybe his father fancied the name."

"He's a Jew all right. He's circumcised."

"That hardly sounds like a discreet inquiry." Rachel smiled and added, "*Merci beaucoup*."

On her way home, Rachel pondered this surprising turn of events. Had Dovid been converted as a child or more recently? And if the latter, was he one of the *anusim*? She needed to speak with Dovid, but, assuming she could locate the man, how should she approach him and when? One thing was certain. If he were that angry with his employer, she might not have much time.

When Sukkot arrived and it became evident that Moses and Rachel would not reach an agreement for several weeks, Eliezer swallowed his resentment and decided to use the time to make a fur-buying trip and for Shemiah and Pesach to accompany him. Part of his anger was with himself, knowing that he'd been too cowardly to confront Rachel about leaving early. And each time they used the bed, he felt less inclined to bring up the subject.

Finally he decided to wait until the Cold Fair closed to leave for Toledo—like usual. In the meantime, he could ask Salomon to intervene on his behalf. Relieved at his reprieve, Eliezer was determined to appreciate his son's company and the scenery as the threesome traveled to Kiev. He would probably never see those lands again.

Rachel's eyes filled with tears as her husband and son turned the corner and disappeared from sight. Seeing them on horseback together was a shocking reminder of how Shemiah had grown, for the two silhouettes were nearly identical. When they returned, Shemiah would be affianced to Glorietta. Rachel wiped away the wetness on her cheeks and sighed.

She had been craven not to challenge Eliezer about Gazelle, but their summer together had been more pleasant because of it. And was the fact that her husband had a concubine in a foreign land truly so terrible? Gazelle was merely one of Eliezer's servants; why was this so different than if she'd been his cook? Rachel didn't quite convince herself; yet she sensed that the wound, while not healed, would eventually only be painful if prodded.

Perhaps the best thing to do would be to give up her clothier ambitions and travel with Eliezer. Dovid had left Othon's employment less than a week after the Hot Fair closed, and all her efforts to find him had failed. He was probably halfway to Flanders by now.

Rachel was too consumed by nostalgia and regret to notice the man who'd stopped at her side. A soft cough above made her aware of his presence, and she quickly backed away. But he closed the distance between them.

"Mistress Rachel?" he asked.

Dumbfounded, she nodded and looked up at a dark-haired stranger. His wide-brimmed hat was pulled down low over his forehead, shading his face—the most handsome face she'd seen in some time.

"My name is Dovid. You've been looking for me?"

twenty-eight

he door banged open just as Salomon was rubbing his eyes and collecting the manuscript pages scattered across the table. After he'd put them away, a habit he maintained despite the many cats that now kept the yeshiva free from mice, he'd hoped to take a nap before services.

"Papa, Papa." Rachel raced into the salon and gave him a hug. "I have marvelous news."

Salomon smiled and resumed his seat. He hadn't seen Rachel this happy in . . . well, in a long time. "You and Moses have completed Shemiah's engagement contract."

"We have, but that's not what I wanted to tell you."

"So tell me."

"I've finally found the fuller I've been looking for." Rachel saw her father's doubtful expression, so she hurried on. "Dovid's not like the other apprentices. He's been fulling for fifteen years, since he was a child. He knows more than most masters, and he's going to work for me."

Salomon raised an eyebrow. "Dovid? Where's he from?"

"He's from Rouen." Grimness replaced Rachel's enthusiasm. "When he was a boy, marauders attacked the Jewish Quarter and massacred its inhabitants, including his parents. The surviving children were raised as *minim*, with Dovid taken in by a monastery. That's where he learned to full cloth."

"And where he learned to worship the Hanged One," Salomon said. "You're sure he doesn't mind working for you?"

"Quite sure. You see, he wasn't happy with the monks—that's why he left them and came to Troyes—and these days he doesn't go to church much anymore." Her eyes shone with excitement. "Papa, maybe I can bring him back to Judaism."

"Does Dovid have a shop already?" Salomon suspected not, but he asked to see if Rachel's focus was in the clouds or on earth.

"*Non*, but that's a good thing." Rachel was ready for her father's skepticism. "We're going to build a fulling mill in Ramerupt, like at the monastery. Dovid already found the perfect site—a narrow stream, just before it widens out into one of Joheved's creeks."

Salomon looked at Rachel with respect. "And before then?"

"Until the mill is ready, Dovid and his apprentices will walk the cloth in troughs. I'm sure Eliezer can get us all the fuller's earth we need."

"Speaking of Eliezer, we have another matter to discuss."

"*Oui*, Papa." Rachel sat down beside him.

"Some women, perhaps most women, don't mind being separated while their husbands travel for business. But I perceive that you are not one of them."

She nodded.

"You should return to Sepharad with Eliezer," he admonished her. "A wife's place is with her husband, not her father."

A giant knot twisted Rachel's stomach. "Papa, Mama asked me to take care of you, and I won't leave until you're healthy again. Besides, Eliezer doesn't need me in Toledo. He has work there that doesn't include me."

Papa would never understand how she abhorred the separate spheres that men and women occupied in Sepharad—men studying, praying, and doing business while women remained at home, ignorant. She would never subject herself, or her daughter, to that life. Papa was scowling at her, so she decided to give him a reason he would understand.

"I will not share Eliezer with another woman, and I know he has another wife there."

"He told you this?" Eliezer had certainly not told Salomon.

"*Non*." She paused, her chin quivering, to control her emotions. "I questioned some merchants from Toledo this summer."

"Are you going to tell him that you know?" Salomon was filled with an aching sadness. In her determination to ferret out her husband's perfidy, his daughter had not considered the pain that such knowledge would cause her. Salomon held out his arms to comfort her, miserable that he, who had always tried to make her happy, was helpless to do so now.

"I'm not sure. I haven't told anyone except you."

"You realize that because your husband has taken another wife, you can demand a divorce without forfeiting your *ketubah*."

Rachel nodded. Until Rabbenu Gershom, Light of the Exile, issued his decree a hundred years ago, a Jewish man might take more than one wife, as the patriarchs Abraham and Jacob did.

"But, Papa, I can't go before the *beit din* and tell them, 'I find this man repulsive; I can no longer live with him.' It's not true." She found Eliezer as attractive as always, curse him.

"You don't need to. Once Eliezer admits to another wife, the *beit din* will insist that he divorce one or the other."

"I don't want a divorce," she wailed. "I want my husband to live in Troyes with me year-round. That's why I've worked so hard on our woolens business."

Salomon sighed heavily. Rachel usually got what she wanted, especially from men, but he didn't see that happening in this case. Eliezer had asked him to talk to Rachel, to convince her to travel to Toledo, but that wasn't going to happen either. *Such willful children, my daughter and son-in-law, each one the spoiled youngest child of their family.*

Yet though he suffered for his daughter's plight, he had to be honest and acknowledge his relief that she would be staying with him in Troyes again this year.

Rachel took a deep breath as she realized that, for the first time in her marriage, she was going to deliberately lie to her husband. *But hasn't he been lying to me all year, deceiving me about Gazelle?* Her guilt hardened into resentment. Who knows how long he'd been living with that woman, using the bed with her? *Mon Dieu, maybe she was carrying his child. Maybe they already had children.* A calculating smile played on her lips. Pesach was going to Toledo with Eliezer this year; there would be no more secrets when he returned.

So when the Cold Fair ended and Eliezer began laying out items to take to Toledo, she put on her most frustrated expression. "Curse these snowstorms." She slammed her fist against the wall. "The fulling mill should have been finished weeks ago, and now I find that they've only just begun building the waterwheel."

Eliezer didn't look up from his packing. "Don't worry. It will be done when you come back."

"You don't understand. I can't leave until it's built and I'm satisfied that it's functioning properly."

"What?" He stared at her in alarm. "I thought this mill was Joheved's responsibility."

"*Oui*, it's on her estate, but Joheved knows nothing about fulling cloth." Rachel tried to keep calm. She must appear disappointed and not lose her temper no matter how angry Eliezer gets. "It's not fair, but I have to be here to supervise the workers."

"Isn't that Dovid's job?" Eliezer said with sarcasm. With all Rachel's talk about the new fuller, Dovid this and Dovid that, you'd think he could at least run the mill by himself.

"Eliezer, please be reasonable. Dovid is just our employee." She carefully said "our" instead of *my*. "No matter how much I want to, I can't disappear and let him run the business, not until I'm convinced that he's reliable."

He nodded slowly. "And how long will that take?"

"If it stops snowing long enough for us to start producing decent woolens, material worth dying with indigo and kermes . . ." She paused for effect. "I might be able to leave with the pilgrims and get to Toledo by Passover."

When he said nothing, she came up behind him and put her arms around his chest. "Maybe sooner."

To her relief, he turned around and began kissing her. "I suppose it's wise not to jeopardize all the work you've done, not so close to reaching your goal."

"I'm going to miss you terribly," she whispered. Though she never intended to go to Toledo, that much was true.

Unfortunately Rachel's complaint about the weather was also true. Joheved pressed her villeins into service building the fulling mill, and whenever snow delayed its construction, Dovid taught them the fulling trade.

As soon as she'd hired Dovid, Rachel began stockpiling unfinished woven cloth. Now, bundled in furs, she watched as Dovid directed two men to unroll a bolt of broadcloth into a long rectangular trough filled with fuller's wash, a mixture of warm water, sheep fat, fuller's earth, and urine. When the material was completely submerged, Dovid directed the men to climb into the steaming vat and trample the cloth. Again Rachel thanked Heaven for giving her a noble sister; Joheved's villeins owed three days of work a week doing whatever she wanted, from building a mill to digging fuller's earth to collecting piss.

The mixture stank worse than Simon's dyes, but the men seemed content to stomp back and forth through the warm liquid on this freezing day. Soon another cloth was undergoing similar treading in a second trough. Dovid carefully observed the four walkers, occasionally directing them to turn the cloth over. At the end of the day, clean water was bucketed into the trough until the foul-smelling wash was rinsed away.

"That's why fullers' workshops are best located near a source of running water," Dovid explained to Rachel the next morning as fresh, warm wash refilled the troughs. "In cold weather like this, it will take five days of treading until the cloth is completely scoured and thickened. Even in summer, it takes three days."

"Why so long?" she asked, pretending ignorance of the fulling procedure.

Dovid was happy to educate her. "Fulling accomplishes three goals. First it cleanses the cloth of dirt and grease. Second, and most important, it felts the cloth by forcing the fine, curly wool fibers to interlace and mat together. This gives the cloth its necessary cohesion and strength."

"And third?"

"During fulling the cloth shrinks and compresses until it becomes impervious to weather and so durable that one mantle may last a man's lifetime." Dovid's face shone with pride.

"What happens next?" Rachel just wanted to hear him talk.

"Once it's fulled, we stretch the cloth out to dry on great wooden tentering frames, held tight by tenterhooks." Dovid smiled and said, "It takes a strong man to lift the wet cloth and stretch it so taut that all wrinkles are removed."

"I look forward to seeing it done."

"While the cloth is still wet, we repair minor holes, remove knots or burrs, and shear off loose ends."

Rachel blinked as snow blew into her eyes. "How can you do this in bad weather? Won't the cloth take forever to dry?"

"Most fullers erect a tent over the frames, but your sister's steward says we can use the barns."

Tentering in the barns became the norm as one snowstorm after another descended on Ramerupt. The year before last had also been stormy, resulting in severe crop failures, and with only the previous year's surplus grain stored, Joheved's estate began to anxiously anticipate more poor harvests. But Rachel was too occupied with fulling, and the fuller, to notice.

Once the tentered cloth was dry, the next steps, teaseling and shearing, required more skill than strength and stamina. Dovid was thrilled to discover that Joheved's shepherds needed merely a little extra training.

He gathered them around the stretched cloths and held up a small wooden frame packed with prickly teasel plants. As he gently pushed the device across the cloth, he explained, "Our goal is to raise the nap of the cloth, to lift up all the straggly loose ends of the wool fibers so they can be shorn."

Dovid then took up a pair of shears and demonstrated how to cut off the raised nap. As the others watched closely, he repeated the process of teaseling and cropping until he was satisfied. Then he took Rachel's hand and placed it on the finished textile.

She gasped with delight and bent down to scrutinize the material. Dovid's efforts had totally obliterated any sign of the weave, producing a texture nearly as fine as silk. No wonder he was a master fuller; look at the dexterity it took to crop the cloth so evenly without damaging it.

The sheep shearers crowded around to examine Dovid's shears and study the results he'd produced. This was clearly a skill worth learning, one a man could ply in Troyes whenever he needed extra income. Several women nodded at each other. Strength was unnecessary for this part of fulling, and a gentle hand might be an advantage.

In mid-February the weather cleared for the entire week before Purim, and finally the fulling mill could be finished. Miriam was already in

Ramerupt for the lambing, but Shemiah, Rivka, and even Salomon rode out to see the new contrivance in operation.

At first view the fulling mill was a disappointment, for it looked exactly like a common grain mill, waterwheel and all. But inside, instead of a grindstone, the waterwheel powered great wooden hammers. Below the hammers sat tubs to hold the cloth and wash liquid, their edges somewhat rounded on the side away from the hammer, so that the cloth was gradually repositioned, ensuring that it was milled evenly.

"You see, Papa," Rachel waxed enthusiastic. "The fulling mill increases our efficiency at least threefold, and this is in addition to the improvement we've achieved with the horizontal loom."

"It is a great success." He nodded in appreciation. "Soon you will be a very rich woman."

Rachel looked across the room, where Joheved, Meir, and Isaac were talking. "My sister and I now control the entire cloth-making process, raw wool to dyed cloth. As our enterprise grows, our children's and grandchildren's futures will be assured."

Salomon suddenly realized what else Rachel had achieved. "Between producing wine and woolens, none of the family will need to leave Troyes to earn a livelihood. They can all become Torah scholars."

Shemiah joined their conversation. "But Papa wants me to come to Sepharad and import dyestuffs with him."

Rachel couldn't bring herself to ask her son to choose between her and Eliezer, but Salomon saw only one choice—Torah. "And what do you want?" he asked.

"I want to stay here and study Talmud with you, Grandpapa," Shemiah promptly replied.

Rachel proudly watched her son and father embrace. It wasn't only her sisters' sons who'd become scholars; Shemiah would be a *talmid chacham* too. And he wouldn't have to be separated from his new wife either.

Rachel and her children returned to Troyes for Purim, where another storm kept her at home for a week. One afternoon they dined with Moses haCohen's family, forcing her to miss Guy de Dampierre's visit.

At home Salomon pulled out a chair for the canon, but Guy excused himself. "I'm afraid I can't stay. Tomorrow is the feast of St. Matthias the Apostle, so I must fast today."

"What can we do for you then? Does the bishop need more wine?" Salomon asked. "Or do you bring some news?"

"I do have some news, but I was looking for your daughter Rachel." Guy gazed around the room, clearly disappointed at her absence. "The last of the pilgrims are leaving for Compostela, and usually she sends a letter with them for her husband."

"I'll give her your message." Salomon tried to hide his surprise. Surely Rachel hadn't forgotten to write to Eliezer.

"Perhaps she sent word with an earlier group." Guy turned to leave.

"You said you have news," Salomon reminded him.

"Of course." Guy took a seat. "Now that most knights have returned from Jerusalem, reinforcements are urgently needed. Pope Paschal has called for a new pilgrimage, particularly exhorting those who previously took the pilgrim's vow but never fulfilled it."

"That applies to Count Étienne of Blois," Salomon said. "Or has our Count Hugues decided to go?"

Guy leaned closer to his audience. "If it were up to their wives, both noble brothers would be gone already. However, it seems that only the elder is undertaking the journey. I've heard that Countess Adèle is so ashamed that she will not permit Étienne to remain at home. He left for the Holy Land with Hugh de Vermandois, Duke Odo of Burgundy, and others who returned early."

"So despite the French princess's urging, Count Hugues remains at home?" Salomon asked.

"For the time being," Guy replied, reaching for his ermine-lined cloak.

"Just a moment, Guy," Shmuel called out, halting the cleric at the door. "Do you have any news for me?"

"I'm afraid I do. While I agree that the Vulgate translation is imprecise compared to *Hebraica veritas*, there's nothing I can do to change it."

"At least you tried," Shmuel said as they walked to the gate.

Salomon, concerned about Rachel's behavior, said little during *disner*, leaving Shmuel to deal with the yeshiva students' questions. When she arrived home, he immediately gave her Guy's message and waited for her response.

"There's no need to waste precious parchment on a letter to Eliezer," she replied. "You and the children are well, may the Holy One protect them, and the fulling mill is working. He knows I only write if something's wrong."

Salomon raised his eyebrow skeptically. If Rachel were deliberately leaving Eliezer uniformed, then she must want him to worry. "You might make him more anxious if you wrote a letter full of praise for your new fuller," he said.

To her father's disappointment, Rachel blushed. "This way Eliezer will agonize over all the possible reasons I haven't written." *As well as why I haven't come to Toledo.*

Shmuel interrupted their tête-à-tête. "Grandpapa bet that Guy couldn't get the *minim*'s translation of the sixth commandment changed, and he was right."

"What are you talking about?" Rachel asked.

"They translate 'You shall not murder,' as *Non occides,*" Shmuel replied. "I pointed out that Latin verb *occidere* refers to killing in general, while the Hebrew *tirtza* always means 'murder,' an unjustified killing. For if the Holy One had merely wanted to say 'kill,' He would have used the Hebrew *hereg*, or if He meant 'put to death,' He'd have said *mot yumat.*

"Guy admits the translation is careless?" Rachel's eyebrows arched in surprise. Maybe she should have asked him to teach her Latin too?

"As do many of the Notzrim scholars I studied with in Paris," Shmuel replied. "But they say it doesn't hurt for men to believe that killing each other is forbidden."

"Not that it stops them from killing or murdering anyone," Salomon added bitterly.

At the first sign of decent weather, Rachel hurried back to Ramerupt, where Dovid proudly presented her with rolls of finished cloth, ready to be dyed.

Abandoning her usual caution around strange men, Rachel was so happy that she danced a little jig. "This is wonderful. I can't wait to hear how much they're worth."

"It will be a goodly amount, I'm sure." He rubbed his hands gleefully. "I can't wait for Othon to see me now, a successful clothier."

She smiled back. "I can't wait to see his face when he realizes what a tremendous mistake he made."

Dovid's expression hardened. "And to see his daughter's face when she realizes what she lost."

"Unless she's an idiot, she realizes it already. After all, where is she going to find another man as handsome, intelligent, and industrious as you?" Rachel declared vehemently.

Dovid fell silent and Rachel suddenly wondered if she'd said too much. "Did you love her?" she asked softly.

"Love her? Don't be absurd." He scowled. "She was attractive enough to wed, but it was her father's shop I loved."

"I don't understand. You're such a skilled fuller, one of the best in Troyes. Why wouldn't Othon want you as a son-in-law?"

"Don't you know my impediment?" he stared at her intently. "You of all people should know, since it's marked in my flesh."

Her mirth dissipated. "Because you were born a Jew."

"I don't know who I curse more—the parents who saddled me with this defect or the men who murdered them."

Horrified, Rachel raised her voice. "Being Jewish is not a defect. We are the Holy One's Chosen People." She strode to his side. "Look at me. Am I defective? Is my family defective? Compared to the *minim* we are better off in every way."

He was looking at her face, but his eyes didn't see her. "*Minim*—I remember that word. It means 'heretic.'"

"Of course they're heretics. They took our Torah, given to us at Mount Sinai, and misinterpreted it to support their lies that the Holy One is not One but three; that He has abandoned us and chosen them in our place; and that the Hanged One, whom they worship as the Messiah, is the son of God, born of a human woman, and, even more absurd, that she was a virgin."

She stamped her foot so hard that snow fell from the mill's eaves. "Then if we don't accept these lies, they murder us and steal our children."

Dovid stared wide-eyed as Rachel continued to vent her spleen. She finally slowed and fell silent. "I apologize," he said gently. "I didn't mean to upset you."

"I owe you an apology," she replied, appalled at having revealed her true opinion of the Notzrim to one of them, especially to an apostate. Her stomach knotted in fear. *What if he no longer wants to work for me?* "Please forgive me."

Each one was waiting for the other to speak when Joheved peeked in the door. A relieved expression appeared on her face when she saw her sister. "There you are, Rachel."

As Joheved closed the distance between them, Dovid walked to the fulling tubs, leaving the sisters to speak privately.

"I am so glad you got our estate involved in the fulling business," Joheved said, not that Rachel thought she looked particularly happy. "All this foul weather has ruined the winter wheat, and if it continues, the spring sowing will either rot or not geminate at all."

Observing Rachel's dismayed expression, she continued, "Don't worry. We'll have sufficient grain to eat; Milo saved some from last year. But we won't have much, except lambs, to sell this summer."

Rachel nodded. "Then it's a good thing you'll have both raw wool and woolens instead."

"Plus fulling keeps my villeins occupied and out of trouble when they can't work the land."

"When I saw Simon in Troyes, he suggested that you grow woad or madder," Rachel said. "Then we can dye the raw wool."

Joheved paused to think. "We could grow woad on a fallow field. It doesn't need a fixative and it matures in one season."

"What about madder? It would make a good base for scarlet."

"Marona told me that they used to grow madder, but it takes years before the roots are big enough to harvest their dye." Joheved chuckled. "She thought the sheep might eat the leaves and have pink wool, but they ended up giving pink milk instead."

"I guess we should just plant woad then."

Joheved hesitated and glanced toward the fulling tubs. "I was thinking about asking Dovid to celebrate Passover with us."

Rachel almost choked. "Here? With our family?"

"Why not?" Joheved replied. "He's living in Ramerupt now."

"Because he's not Jewish, that's why not." As soon as Rachel spoke, she knew it wasn't true. Papa always said that although a Jew might sin, he remained a Jew.

"But you told me he was—"

"All right, he is a Jew," Rachel conceded. "But he's an apostate now."

"How better to bring him back to the Law of Moses?" Joheved asked. "If Dovid has any happy childhood memories of his parents, they would likely include Passover."

"But our seder is on their Good Friday. He'd have to choose one or the other."

"I hadn't thought of that." Joheved paused, her hand on her chin. "I have an idea: why don't you drop some hints and see how he responds? Then if he seems interested, you can invite him."

"I'll try to do that," Rachel replied, knowing she wouldn't try very hard. Dovid was provoking too many strong feelings in her, feelings she hadn't sorted out yet, and she wasn't going to take any chance of displaying them in front of her family.

Eliezer stared in awe at all the well-dressed folks who'd come to his wedding. Before he could ask what they were all doing there, the music started and he was pulled into the dance. Two small rings of people moved to the left in front of his circle, and three larger rings behind him, with Gazelle seated in the center. Watching all these dancers spinning around him, each at their own speed, made him dizzy, but he couldn't stop.

The musicians increased the pace, and suddenly Abraham bar Hiyya grabbed him by the arm, forcing the two of them to twirl around each other even as their circle, and the others, kept going. Eliezer felt like he was falling, but Abraham held him upright. His vertigo increased as the dancers spun even faster, until Eliezer realized that he could no longer identify individuals. Everything was a blur of swirling color.

Finally the music slowed, but when his vision cleared, the people dancing had disappeared. Each circle now contained only a shining sphere. Even Abraham and Gazelle had been thus transformed. The scene looked familiar somehow; yet Eliezer couldn't recall where or when he'd seen it before. But he knew it was something important.

"Eliezer." Abraham was calling him.

Eliezer shook his head and looked up at his friend, who was yawning and rubbing his eyes. "It's nearly dawn. You can sleep here if you want, but I'm going home to my bed. If Mercury and Venus do orbit the sun, they will continue to do so after I wake."

Suddenly wide-awake and furiously trying to interpret his dream's significance, Eliezer bid Abraham good night. "I'll stay a little longer." What if he'd been the earth, Abraham the moon, and Gazelle the sun? Then the five spheres circling her would be the planets. *All of them orbiting the sun. Including Earth! Was that possible?*

"Are you sure? You were snoring hard just a moment ago."

"I just thought of a different algorithm I want to try, and if I stop now I'll lose track of what I'm doing." He reached for a fresh piece of parchment.

"I'll see you later then." Abraham started for the door and then halted. "By the way, I assume you'd like to spend Passover week with me in Barcelona again."

"Passover already?" *How has the time passed so quickly?* "My wife said she'd be here for Passover."

"Have you heard from her?"

"No. But she would have written if she weren't coming." Eliezer tried to suppress his budding anxiety.

"They say winter was very hard in Ashkenaz. Perhaps bad weather prevented her from traveling and delayed her message."

Eliezer sighed. A bad winter would mean another year of poor harvests. He'd better procure some grain to bring back, even if the prices he'd charge to make a profit would have even more Edomites hating him.

"I doubt very much that your wife is coming," Abraham continued. "But you can tell your partner that you've gone to Barcelona and if she does arrive, she can join us there."

Abraham closed the door behind him, and Eliezer returned to his work. But it was no use. Between speculating over what could have happened to Rachel and how another famine might inflame anti-Jewish feelings in Ashkenaz, it was impossible to focus on astronomy. The calculations would have to wait, he thought, as he locked the manuscripts away and headed home.

The nearly full moon was a visible reminder that Passover was indeed approaching. If Rachel weren't here, he might as well celebrate Passover with Abraham. But if she weren't coming, and his gut told him this was the case, why hadn't she written to him? Could she have left Troyes and been forced back by bad weather? Had Salomon taken ill again? Or had one of their children? Perhaps she'd written and her letter had gone astray. Eliezer could think of numerous reasons why she hadn't arrived, both terrible and benign.

It did not occur to him that his wife never had any intention of going to Toledo.

twenty-nine

achel waited an entire month after the men returned for the Hot Fair before questioning Pesach about Eliezer's second wife. Still she approached the subject gingerly as they walked together, first discussing the kinds of merchandise available in Toledo, what they cost, and the young man's impression of economic conditions in Sepharad.

"Eliezer has no trouble finding buyers for his furs and woolens; they were just waiting for him to arrive," Pesach said proudly. "And his agent in Maghreb brings the finest dyestuffs via the winter caravan. Honestly, I don't see why he needs me."

"Since he completes his business so quickly, I wonder what my husband does all day in Toledo." She spoke lightly, as though the idea amused her.

"As far as I can tell, he sleeps."

"Of course. He stays up all night studying the stars."

"I don't understand why he finds them so interesting." Pesach shrugged. "I mean, what difference does it make if the planets go around the earth or they go around the sun?"

"It makes a big difference to him," Rachel said. Eliezer had always been desperate to know more than other men: about Talmud, once, and now astronomy.

Pesach lowered his voice. "They say his friend Abraham knows when the Messiah is coming."

"Nonsense. Nobody can know that."

"Eliezer says Abraham may be right."

Rachel hesitated before springing her trap. "So how is Eliezer's second wife?"

As she expected, Pesach cringed at her question. "Please, Mistress Rachel, don't ask me about that."

"I know," she said gently. "My husband told you not to say anything about her. But you needn't say a word. I'll ask you a few questions; then you nod or shake your head in reply."

Pesach's eyes were wide with fear, but he nodded.

"Does he have any children with her?" She held her breath, waiting for the answer she dreaded.

Pesach shook his head and Rachel sighed with relief. If Eliezer hadn't gotten this woman pregnant after three years, then perhaps he was the barren one.

"One more thing. Was she with child when you left?"

He shrugged, which was probably the best answer she could expect. "That wasn't so bad," she said. "Now if Eliezer asks, you can honestly tell him that you didn't say a single word to me about her."

Pesach remained silent until they arrived at Simon's. The dyer was working in his shop instead of a smelly vat.

Simon grinned upon seeing her. "Mistress Rachel, your latest woolens are even finer than earlier ones, and they were fine indeed. Let me show you."

"They should be," she replied, accompanying him and Pesach outside to where racks of brightly colored cloth were drying. "The wool is from this summer's shearing."

Simon displayed his work. "As you authorized, I chose the dyes personally, according to the fabric's quality. You will be pleased to hear that all were worthy of imported dyes. Dovid's work for you surpasses anything he did at Othon's."

"Excellent. I expected nothing less." Rachel restrained the joy she felt at hearing her fuller praised.

"Since this fellow brought back so much kermes scarlet," Simon inclined his head toward Pesach, "I utilized it wherever I could. For the slightly lower quality wool, indigo and saffron."

He pointed out the red, blue, and yellow woolens, whose colors were vivid despite the bright sunlight. Every cloth's shade was without variation.

"They're beautiful." Pesach couldn't hide his delight. "But why are some black?"

"The abbess at Notre-Dame-aux-Nonnains was inquiring after fabric, so I asked Simon to prepare some for her," Rachel explained. Nuns took a vow of poverty, but the local abbess came from a noble family and refused to wear anything but the highest quality fabrics.

Simon turned to Pesach. "True black is one of the most difficult shades to obtain. Each dyer has his secret formula; mine involves lamp soot." He motioned the pair back indoors, where he slowly unrolled a small bolt of brilliant purple.

Rachel gasped. "This is exquisite." She couldn't resist stroking the material. "I thought Eliezer couldn't find any Tyrian purple, or did you mix scarlet and indigo?"

Simon allowed Pesach to answer. "I found some, although Eliezer judged it too expensive. But the other dye merchants in Toledo said Tyrian purple was particularly scarce this year, so I gambled and bought some on credit."

"A successful gamble, I may add," Simon said. "Several merchants have expressed interest, each outbidding the last."

"You did well, Pesach," Rachel said as he beamed at their praise. *Better than Eliezer, who is apparently more interested in the heavens than in our business profits.*

For his part, Eliezer spent the summer simmering with concealed anger, biding his time until Sukkot was over and he could return to Toledo. While Rachel responded to his embraces as enthusiastically as ever, she was not interested in anything he had to say. When he tried to explain how important and revolutionary it would be to prove that the heavens did not all revolve around the earth, she practically yawned in his face. She dismissed his calculations with a wave of her hand, saying she would look at them later, yet never finding the time.

All her attention was focused on woolens. She disappeared to Ramerupt for hours at a time, even spending the night when she was *niddah*. Yet when he offered to accompany her to see the fulling mill, to finally meet the new fuller, she always found some excuse why he should wait. Fed up with her delays, and suspicious about what lay behind them, he decided to visit Ramerupt on his own, about an hour after she'd left.

The estate, which should have been awhirl with the taking in of the harvest, was moribund. Shepherds leisurely tended the sheep, but the sparse, spindly sheaves in the fields were a sad testament to the recent poor weather. This being the height of the Hot Fair, Joheved and Meir were in Troyes, but Milo and Isaac's very pregnant wife, Judita, came out to greet him.

Both seemed alarmed to see him.

"Would you like some refreshment while I send someone to the mill for your wife?" Judita asked, a little too eagerly.

"*Merci, non*. I'll go see her directly."

Milo and Judita exchanged glances, and Milo said, "The fulling mill is some distance away; I'll take you."

Eliezer thought that Milo could just as easily have given him directions. The fulling mill would have to be downstream from the manor, and Eliezer was perfectly capable of following the creek alone. But he said nothing and accompanied the steward.

He could hear the mill long before it came into view, its thumping hammers reverberating through the trees. He frowned slightly as Rachel came down the stairs, her hair hidden under her veil, waving to him. So much for catching her and Dovid unawares—assuming the fuller was still there.

He was, following Rachel at a respectful distance. A handsome young devil too. Eliezer observed Rachel closely as she approached him, a big smile on her face. But he knew his wife well enough to recognize the annoyance in her slightly squinting eyes and tightened lips.

"Eliezer, I thought you and Shemiah were studying with Papa today." Her unspoken reproach was clear; he was taking time away from Torah.

"I've heard him teach this *sugia* at least twice, and the weather is so fine that I thought I'd go riding." He turned to the fuller and held out his hand. "You must be Dovid, the finest fuller in Troyes, the man behind our successful woolen business." Two could play this dissembling game.

Dovid shook Eliezer's hand and clasped him around the shoulder. "Come see our new mill. The fullers in town must be mad as wet cats; we're finishing our woolens at least three times faster than they are." He eagerly led Eliezer up the stairs.

Eliezer detected no guile in Dovid's voice, so he responded, "Excellent."

Rachel at his side, Eliezer followed Dovid through the mill, past the incredibly vile smelling troughs, and then quickly, thank Heaven, out into the fresh air where a great many lengths of wool cloth were stretched out drying in the sun. It was an impressive sight.

"It's good to see where all the dyes I bring back will go." Eliezer turned to Rachel. "It's almost time for *disner*. Shall we ride back or dine here?"

Rachel hesitated only for a moment. "Let's go home."

They rode through the forest with minimal conversation, their few words short and curt. Tension built between them, both knowing a quarrel was imminent and neither wanting to instigate it.

In the end, their son precipitated the argument by refusing to leave for Toledo in the fall, which sent Eliezer charging home in the middle of an evening Talmud session. One look at his furious countenance and the servants scattered. But the object of Eliezer's fury was upstairs.

"How dare you contradict my wishes for Shemiah?" Eliezer slammed the door behind him.

Rachel carefully put down the folio of Nedarim she'd been reading and stood up to face him. "If our son wishes to study Talmud with his grandfather, I will commend him, not discourage him." She tried to appear calm, but her insides were quaking.

"It is the Talmud that says a father must teach his son a trade, which I intend to do in Toledo."

"He is perfectly capable of earning his livelihood as a clothier in Troyes." Her eyes narrowed. "As are you."

"What if I don't want to be a clothier in Troyes?" he challenged her. There—now it was out in the open.

"How can you say that?" Rachel's chin began to quiver. "After all I've done to build this woolens business for our family."

"I didn't ask you to do it. You never consulted me about whether I wanted it."

"But I did it so we could live together in Troyes." Tears streamed down her cheeks. "So we wouldn't be separated."

"I told you before that I have no intention of living in France. Jews will never be as safe here as in Sepharad," he retorted, unmoved by her sobs.

"You're not interested in us living together; otherwise you'd have come with me to Toledo."

Rachel blinked back her tears, anger overpowering her pain. "You expect me to live in Toledo, to share you with another wife? Never!" she hissed.

Eliezer was silent; his face flushed bright red.

"Don't blame Pesach. He never said a word to me," she jumped in before he could speak. "I've known about her for years. You're not the only merchant from Toledo who attends our fairs."

"I have every right to another wife in Sepharad if that is their custom," he finally replied. "Rabbi Gershom's edict doesn't apply there."

"If you're so proud of having two wives, why didn't you tell me about her? Did you honestly think I would accept a rival in my husband's bed?"

Of course Eliezer hadn't thought that, which is why he hadn't told her. "What if I divorced her? Would you move to Toledo then?"

Now it was Rachel's turn for silence. Slowly she shook her head. "I can't leave Papa, not at his age. I couldn't bear it if he died while I was away."

This was Eliezer's opportunity for rapprochement, for responding with his own vulnerability. But instead he snarled, "Are you sure it's not that new fuller you can't leave?"

Rachel sprang forward and slapped his face. "How dare you distrust me? You who've kept another wife in secret."

"A woman is supposed to leave her parents and cleave to her husband," Eliezer quoted Genesis, his voice heavy with sarcasm.

"Don't you quote Torah to me," she shot back. "You know very well that a man may not force his wife to move to another city against her will."

"And if his first wife refuses to live with him, he is permitted to take another."

"Not in France he's not."

"I won't be living in France."

"But I will be." She stared at him defiantly.

"Because you don't love me enough to move to Toledo."

"On the contrary. It's you who don't love me enough to remain in Troyes."

Eliezer returned her gaze, observing her flushed face and flashing eyes. Her pulse beat visibly on her neck, where a trickle of sweat slowly slid down her skin and disappeared into the cleft between her breasts. Lust merged with fury, and with a quick bound he closed the distance between them.

She recognized the look in his eyes and tried to step back, but the bed was behind her. His arms were around her before she could dart away, pulling her close. His lips fastened on hers, her body clasped firmly against his. Abruptly one of his hands began fondling her breast, searching for a nipple beneath her thin chemise.

When he found it, desire flooded her. Drowning in passion, she franticly pulled him down onto the bed. Yet at the same time that she was reveling at Eliezer's caresses, a voice in her head was screaming that she hated him, hated how he could always make her body respond, and hated needing him so much. But though her mind could fight him, her flesh could not—would not. All her traitorous body wanted was to feel him, hard and throbbing inside her, pounding his flesh against hers until finally, in a great explosion, all desire drained out of her.

Even so, she would never move to Sepharad.

Normally a time of celebration, the New Year's approach filled Rachel with melancholy. Once Sukkot was over, in less than a month, Eliezer would depart for Toledo, not returning until Shemiah's wedding next summer. There had been no more arguments between them after that terrible and exhilarating night, each one accepting the other's implacability.

The day before Yom Kippur, both sought and received the other's forgiveness. But despite the Holy One's commandment to celebrate Sukkot with gladness, the holiday was heavy with gloom. Eliezer had agreed to delay his departure until she became *niddah* again, causing Rachel to pray for a child with a fervor she'd never experienced before. But her flowers arrived on schedule at the end of September, and she could barely restrain her tears as Eliezer packed.

"You're sure you can't stay in Troyes and study astronomy here?" Rachel asked one last time. It was no use expecting him to give up his secular studies.

"I need the observatory in Toledo." Eliezer's voice was heavy with resignation. "And I need other astronomers and mathematicians to work with."

"Just as I need my father and sisters for Torah study," she replied. "I would never be able to study Talmud outside Troyes."

He gazed at her sadly. He understood the Talmud's powerful attraction; it used to be his passion too. But now he was hungry for new knowledge. "You might be able to teach Torah to some women in Toledo."

She shook her head. "Like you, I prefer learning to teaching others." *As long as Papa is still alive to teach me.* "Besides, women don't study Torah in Sepharad." *And I want both our children to be scholars.*

"Just as men don't study astronomy in Troyes."

"Pesach will leave for Toledo with furs and woolens when the Cold Fair closes," she assured him. "And Shemiah will come after Passover to meet your business associates and escort you both back for the wedding."

"If everything is arranged, I should get to sleep. I have a long ride ahead of me tomorrow."

They lay down together, each wrapped in their own linens, with what felt to Rachel like an enormous space between them. Restrained from touching him, she couldn't help but think of sayings from the first chapter of Tractate Sanhedrin.

> Rav Huna said: Discord is like a waterway formed by a flood. Once it begins to widen, it will continue to widen . . . When our love was strong, we could lie together on the edge of a sword; now that it has become weak, a bed of sixty cubits is not wide enough.

All that autumn Rachel tried to avoid thinking about Eliezer, but she couldn't help recalling how he'd taught about the calendar's calculation when she noticed that both Heshvan and Kislev were full that year. As Joheved predicted, the fall harvest was poor, forcing Count Hugues to release grain from the town stores. Papa's grape harvest was only mediocre, and nobody was surprised at Hanukkah when the new vintage proved mediocre as well. Meat at least was cheap, owing to the high cost of feeding animals over the upcoming winter.

There were also benefits for Rachel's business. Quite a few new clients needed to borrow money until the spring harvest, while Pesach brought back the plushest furs anyone had seen for some time. She also found that more people than usual were buying new woolen clothing, complaining that their old ones didn't keep them warm enough or no longer shed the rain. Her bolt of Tyrian purple sold for an excellent price, after bidding from several royal houses. Thus when the Cold Fair closed and Pesach left for Toledo, she was able to provide him with sufficient credit to repay his loan and purchase whatever dyestuffs he wanted.

She did not, however, send a letter to Eliezer. Everyone at home was in good health, which Pesach could report to her husband in person.

Rachel kept her body occupied by pruning the vineyard and her mind engaged by studying Tractate Nedarim with Miriam. They had arrived at the sixth chapter, where she was pleasantly surprised to find another telling of the story of Rabbi Akiva and his beloved wife, Rachel, this one longer and more detailed than what they'd studied in Tractate Ketubot.

"Did you know this was here?" she challenged Miriam. Both Rachel's sisters knew how much she enjoyed learning about her namesakes in the Bible and Talmud.

"*Non*, Papa has never taught this section."

"Then let's have him explain it to us," Rachel said, never doubting that her father would do so.

And thus Salomon put aside his *kuntres* for a while to teach his daughters about this obscure piece of Talmud.

The *sugia* began, as did Ketubot's, with Akiva, an uneducated shepherd, becoming betrothed to Rachel, daughter of his employer, wealthy Kalba Savua. Disinherited immediately, she sent Akiva away to study Torah despite their poverty. Twelve years later, he returned home a great scholar with thousands of disciples, only to hear one of her neighbors disparage him.

> Your father behaved correctly to you. First, your husband is not your equal. And in addition, he has left you in living widowhood for all these years.

Salomon closed the book. "Let me explain this before we continue. Kalba Savua loved his daughter and was pressing her to initiate a divorce so she could marry someone more worthy. After all, Akiva was much older, had a son from a previous marriage, and was so ignorant he didn't even know the alphabet."

Miriam and Rachel nodded. They too would have been horrified if their daughters had run off with such a man.

"Even worse," Salomon continued, "and this is what 'not your equal' means, Rabbi Akiva was a descendant of converts."

They read further:

> She [Rachel] replied, "If my husband listened to me, he would stay at the yeshiva another twelve years." [Hearing this] Rabbi Akiva declared, "Since she has permitted me, I will return." So he studied there another twelve years.

The text continued with Rabbi Akiva finally returning, this time with twenty-four thousand disciples. But when his wife went out to greet him in her tattered dress, his students pushed her away, thinking she was a beggar. Rabbi Akiva stopped them, telling them that everything he, and consequently they, had acquired was due to her.

The happy ending, which Rachel and Miriam knew, followed. Kalba Savua, upon hearing that a great scholar has arrived in town, begged for release from the vow he made to impoverish his daughter. Rabbi Akiva reveals his identity, after which the grateful Kalba Savua gave his daughter and son-in-law half his wealth.

The text in Ketubot concludes with Rabbi Akiva and Rachel's daughter marrying Ben Azzai and sending him away to study, but in Nedarim there is no further mention of Kalba Savua's daughter or granddaughter. Instead the Gemara cryptically lists six ways in which Rabbi Akiva became wealthy.

> Rabbi Akiva obtained his wealth from six sources: from Kalba Savua, from the figurehead on a ship, from a treasure chest, from a certain noblewoman, from the wife of Turnus Rufus, and from Ketia bar Shalum.

"I've never heard of these." And Rachel thought she knew all about Rabbi Akiva.

Salomon explained how Rabbi Akiva found gold coins in a ship's figurehead and a chestful of treasure that washed up on the seashore. In addition he profited from a noblewoman's loan and from a Roman convert, Ketia, who left Rabbi Akiva half his estate.

The tale of how he'd become wealthy through the wife of Turnus Rufus was more complicated, and for Rachel, problematic.

"Turnus Rufus was the Roman governor of Eretz Israel, and he would often challenge Rabbi Akiva to debate the meaning of Torah," Salomon began. "When Rabbi Akiva won, Rufus was embarrassed in front of his court."

Neither daughter had any questions so he continued: "One day when Rufus returned home in a particularly nasty mood, his wife asked why he was so upset. He complained about Rabbi Akiva, who taunted him, and his wife proposed a strategy to humiliate the scholar."

"What did she do?" Rachel asked.

"She told her husband, 'The God of the Jews hates lewdness. If you allow me, I will cause him to sin.' Now Rufus's wife was very beautiful, so she adorned herself and went to visit Rabbi Akiva. There she lifted her skirt to show her legs, in order to seduce him. But he recognized what she wanted and, in turn, spat, cried, and laughed."

"How strange," Miriam said. "What was he thinking?"

"That's exactly what Rufus's wife asked him," Salomon replied. "He said that he would explain the first two, but not the third."

Rachel and Miriam leaned forward to hear more.

"Rabbi Akiva spat with disgust because, despite her great beauty, she had come from a putrid drop of semen. He cried because her lovely body would one day lie rotting in the dirt." Salomon paused and smiled. "What he didn't tell her then was that he'd had a divine vision showing that she would eventually convert to Judaism and marry him."

"Marry him?" Rachel exclaimed in dismay. "What happened to his other wife, Kalba Savua's daughter?" Surely Rabbi Akiva would not take a second wife in addition to his adored Rachel?

"I don't know. The Talmud tells us nothing more about her. Rabbi Akiva lived for 120 years: 40 as a shepherd, 40 studying, and 40 as a leader. Perhaps Kalba Savua's daughter was already dead at this time."

"Is there any more to the story?" Miriam asked.

"Indeed. When Rufus's wife realized that her plan was obvious to Rabbi Akiva, she asked if she could repent. He assented, so she began to study for conversion. When Rufus died, Rabbi Akiva finally explained his laughter to her."

"So once she became a Jew, they wed." Rachel glumly finished the tale. "Which is how he became rich from the wife of Turnus Rufus."

She slept poorly that night, terribly disappointed at how Rabbi Akiva's romance with Kalba Savua's daughter Rachel had come to naught. How could the Sages retell the couple's tender story and then not explain what happened to her? Rabbi Akiva was the greatest scholar of his generation—his colleagues must have known her fate. Could Rabbi Akiva have divorced her? Had she come to a bad end, like Meir's wife Beruria, and thus they chose to ignore her demise? Rachel took comfort in the knowledge that Papa had never heard anything else about her, good or evil, although he had been taught about Beruria's suicide.

The next morning she decided to go to Ramerupt, where the sight of lambs frolicking in the new grass never failed to cheer her. She was not ready to admit that the sight of Dovid the Fuller also raised her spirits; yet she avoided stopping at the manor house and rode straight for the fulling mill instead.

She could hear the hammers thumping, but the place looked deserted. Fighting her disappointment, she rode around to the back, convinced that she'd find no one there as well. Her heart leapt to see Dovid, alone, teaseling a woolen.

As he helped her dismount, she asked, "Where is everyone?"

Dovid showed no sign of resentment. "Now that the ground has thawed, the villeins are busy plowing furrows and planting spring crops."

"Can't Joheved find you at least one helper?"

"Not today. It's the feast of the Annunciation."

Rachel rolled her eyes. The heretics had so many feast days it was impossible to keep track of them. "What is this one for? And why aren't you in church?"

"The feast of the Annunciation celebrates the revelation to the Virgin Mary that she would conceive a child without sin, who would be the Son of God. This Incarnation took place nine months before Jesus was born, and thus is observed on March 25." Dovid ignored her second question.

"How can you believe that a virgin, who had no relations with a man, conceived a child?" she demanded. The very idea of the Holy One impregnating a woman was repugnant.

"Because the prophet Isaiah clearly states, '*Ecce virgo concipiet, et pariet filium, et vocabitur nomen ejus Emmanuel.*'" He emphasized the word *virgo.*

"That can't be what Isaiah said," she retorted. "Isaiah spoke Hebrew, not Latin; and if he'd meant a virgin, he would have said *betula*, the Hebrew word that appears many times in the Torah and always indicates a virgin."

Surprisingly Dovid's response was curiosity, not anger. "What word did Isaiah use? How would you translate the verse?"

"Isaiah said *almah,* which means a young woman," she said. "So the true translation would be, 'Behold, a young woman has conceived and will bear a son. And she will name him Immanuel.'"

"A young woman . . ." Dovid stopped to think.

"Not merely a young woman, who might be a virgin or not." Rachel added her father's explanation. "But a young wife, a newly married woman, whom no one would expect to be a virgin."

"How do you know that?"

She paused to think of another time *almah* appeared in scripture. "In the Song of Salomon, the king speaks of the sixty queens, eighty concubines, and *alamot* without number in his harem. Surely these are not virgins but merely young women."

"Even if you're right, the Church would never admit it."

Rachel nodded. It would undercut their entire heresy that the Hanged One was conceived without a carnal father.

"Suppose I were to grant that Isaiah does mean a virgin," she continued. "Still the verse cannot refer to Mary, because the word *harah* is in the past tense. Thus the young woman meant here has already conceived the child in Isaiah's time. If Isaiah were speaking of the future, he would say *tahar,* 'she will conceive.'"

"I believe you," Dovid replied after some thought. "For even in the Latin, it is not *virgo* but *puella* and *virginem* that mean virgin. *Virgo* could mean just a young woman."

"How is it that you know Latin so well?" Rachel asked.

"I was brought up in a monastery, remember?"

"They taught you fulling and Latin, how very useful."

"Since the Bible was written in Hebrew, it would have been more useful to learn that language."

"I have it." Rachel clapped her hands in excitement. "I'll teach you Hebrew and you can teach me Latin."

Dovid's smile lit his entire face. "With pleasure."

thirty

s soon as her younger sister came through the gate, Miriam stopped weeding the herb garden and hurried to greet her. "It's good that you're home. Papa has been asking about you all afternoon."

"I was in Ramerupt," Rachel replied, as though that explained everything.

"I know where you were, and so does Papa. He wants to know what you're doing there all the time."

"Why?" Rachel made no attempted to hide her irritation. "Does he think I'm neglecting my duties here?"

"I haven't complained, if that's what you mean," Miriam said. "I just wanted to warn you."

Although Miriam had observed Rachel's frequent absences of late, she couldn't deny that her sister was performing an appropriate share of familial responsibilities. Certainly Rachel's woolens brought in far more of the family's income than Miriam's midwifery. But their father was not so tolerant.

Miriam gave a nod toward the front door, where Salomon stood waiting. "*Merci*," Rachel replied, taking her sister's hand. At least she wouldn't be facing Papa alone.

The kitchen was empty, so they sat down at the table. Miriam poured them each a cup of wine.

"You must try this cheese." Rachel unwrapped the parcel she'd been carrying. "It's fresh from Joheved's sheep."

"Is that what you've been doing in Ramerupt these days?" Salomon's tone was skeptical. "Making cheese?"

Rachel took a deep breath. She wasn't going to hide what she'd been doing; it was nothing to be ashamed of. "*Non*, Papa. I've been teaching Dovid Hebrew and he's teaching me Latin."

Salomon and Miriam were taken aback by her proud reply. "Teaching him Hebrew is much easier than with Guy and Étienne Harding," Rachel added.

"How so?" Miriam asked.

"True, Dovid had to learn the Hebrew alphabet, just as a small child does." Her face lit with enthusiasm as she continued, "But speaking Hebrew comes so easily for him that I'm convinced his family must have spoken it at home." She was in the same position learning Latin; the letters were unfamiliar, but the language resembled her own vernacular French.

So far Papa hadn't objected, so she turned to him and added, "Since we use scripture as our text, I also teach him your explanations."

"How does he respond?" Salomon asked, his curiosity stronger than his disapproval. "Does he argue with you like Guy and Étienne did with Shmuel?"

Rachel shook her head. "Dovid finds it interesting. He says your exegesis is very different from the monks'."

Salomon stroked his beard and squinted at Rachel, who felt as though he were trying to peer into her heart. "*Ma fille*, you are a married woman whose husband is far away. You must be vigilant against the *yetzer hara*."

Miriam patted his shoulder as if he were a child. "Rachel is an expert at thwarting a man's *yetzer hara*."

"Don't worry, Papa. We always study outdoors where people can see us," Rachel assured him. Although not where they could be overheard, thank Heaven.

He smiled wanly. "You can't expect a father to stop worrying about his daughter just because he's gotten old." It was Rachel's *yetzer hara* he was worried about. Still, he couldn't deny the fuller the opportunity to repent his apostasy, despite the risk to her reputation.

Rachel gave an inward sigh of relief. Papa might not be happy with her teaching Dovid, but he wasn't going to forbid it.

To avert their father from lecturing Rachel further, Miriam made an announcement that was sure to change the subject. "Speaking of getting old, Avram the Mohel has asked me to consider taking on a new apprentice. He's concerned that his fingers aren't as nimble as they used to be and that it will take years to train another mohel."

Rachel groaned. Finding the last apprentice mohel had been so difficult that Troyes had been forced to accept Miriam. The community had been torn apart and was only now recovering. "Can't we import one?"

Miriam shook her head sadly. "There are even fewer mohels now than when I began training."

Rachel blanched at her own stupidity. *Of course there are fewer mohels—the German ones are dead.*

But Salomon had a twinkle in his eye. "You've chosen an apprentice already, haven't you?"

"*Oui.* Now that our woolen business is established, there's no need for Elisha to leave Troyes other than an occasional visit to his brothers in Paris."

Rachel gasped with pleasure. "My future son-in-law is going to be our next mohel? What an honor for Rivka." Now neither of her children would be moving away.

"I assume my grandson has agreed," Salomon said.

"Elisha is eager to begin his circumcision training," Miriam replied. "Judah is so proud."

"That's a relief." Rachel said aloud what they were all thinking. "I may prefer a woman circumciser myself, but the Jews of Troyes don't need any more troubles than we have already."

Between the busy springtime vineyard, her studies with Dovid, and readying their woolens for the Hot Fair's cloth market, Rachel was busy from dawn to dark. Dovid had accepted Joheved's invitation to the family's Passover seder, where he sat in silence like the child too young to ask questions. He declined to attend Shavuot services in Troyes, but Rachel was still pleased with his progress.

She had a feeling that Eliezer, loath to leave his astronomical calculations, would be late again this summer. So she was astonished when Shemiah walked into afternoon services a full ten days before the opening of the Hot Fair. Thank Heaven they'd returned safely, but curse her bad luck: she'd just begun her flowers.

Rachel was leading services for the women that day, but she hoped that Eliezer would be at home unpacking for some time and not notice that she hadn't rushed home to greet him. Not that they could do much greeting with her being *niddah.* Shemiah was pacing back and forth at the bottom of the stairs to the women's gallery, and immediately, when his troubled gaze met hers, she knew something was wrong. As soon as services were over, instead of hurrying to embrace her, he led her into an alley near the synagogue.

"What's the matter?" Rachel's heart was pounding. "Why aren't we going home to Eliezer?"

Shemiah swallowed hard. "He's not at home, Mama. He didn't come back with me and Pesach."

Rachel's knees began to buckle, and she would have fallen if her son hadn't supported her. "Why not? What happened to him?"

"Nothing happened to him." Shemiah's voice was bitter. "Gazelle is due to give birth next month, and he didn't want to desert her at such a time. He said you'd understand."

Overcome with outrage and pain, Rachel stood speechless in her son's arms. How could Eliezer choose a concubine over her? Because she had never forgotten how he'd left her to suffer a stillbirth alone, did he imagine that she'd appreciate him not allowing his other wife the same fate?

"I understand that he's a selfish cur," she spat out the words. "Putting his own needs above those of his family, even missing his own son's wedding—"

"He'll be here for the wedding," Shemiah interrupted her tirade. "He'll leave Toledo as soon as the baby is safely born."

"And how long will he stay here if he won't arrive until August?" She burst into tears.

"Mama, please don't cry so loud. People are stopping to see what's wrong."

Part of her wanted to scream. *Let them watch me cry! Let them see what kind of fiend I married.* But she came to her senses. Eliezer coming late to their son's wedding would be cause enough for gossip; who knows what people would say if they learned he had another wife in Sepharad? Heaven forbid his despicable behavior make her an object of ridicule and pity.

Rachel choked back her sobs and blew her nose into the dirt. "We mustn't let anyone know that I was surprised by his late arrival." She paused to clear her mind. "Let them believe that some business opportunity delayed him."

"What about Grandpapa?"

"Unless he asks directly, we say nothing," she declared. Then she gave her son the hug he deserved and took his arm. "So how did you enjoy traveling? What did you think of Toledo? Tell me everything."

They walked aimlessly through the streets, sharing stories of Sepharad, until they arrived at the courtyard gate. Rachel hurried to the well and splashed her face with cold water. Somehow she would survive the next two months until Eliezer arrived. *And if he doesn't show up for the wedding?* Her blood froze at the thought. Then she might just take her conditional *get* to the *beit din* and make it a real divorce.

When the wedding week arrived with no sign of Eliezer, Rachel made Shemiah and Pesach agree to say as little as possible about his absence. Thankfully it was no falsehood to say that they'd expected him for the ceremony and were now concerned at what could have delayed him. But she needn't have worried. The population of Troyes, indeed of the entire province of Champagne, was more concerned with the politics of their feudal lord's succession.

After braving another trip to the Holy Land, Count Étienne had died there in May. This time he'd reached Jerusalem, so instead of the wife of a coward, Countess Adèle was now the proud widow of a knight who'd fallen defending the Holy City. She further cemented the family's position by sending their ten-year-old son, Thibault, to the Troyes court as presumptive heir of childless Hugues and Constance.

Rachel, however, was too occupied with wedding details to listen to gossip. Tradition called for the groom's family to provide meals and entertainment, and, hoping that Eliezer would handle such things, she'd neglected planning them. In a panic, Rachel consulted her sisters, who, thank Heaven, had the combined experience of marrying off four sons.

"I can provide all the lambs we need," Joheved declared as they walked home from synagogue. "Once we find sufficient hearths in which to roast them."

"There are at least five hundred Jews living in Troyes, none of whom will be leaving town until after the Days of Awe." Miriam began counting the potential guests. "In addition to the hundreds of merchants who will still be here when the fair closes."

Rachel stopped in the middle of the street. "*Mon Dieu*, do we have to feed a thousand people?"

"Not only that, but we need benches for them to sit on, tables for all the food, plus people to prepare and serve it," Joheved pointed out. Obviously the banquets must be held in the streets of the Jewish Quarter; not even the synagogue courtyard was large enough.

"Maybe we should postpone the wedding a month?" Rachel asked in desperation. "Then the merchants will be gone and my husband might have arrived."

Miriam shook her head. "We can't. It will be Rosh Hashanah. And if we wait two weeks, Glorietta might be *niddah*."

Joheved had the final word on the subject. "We can't delay even a week or we risk interrupting the grape harvest."

Rachel's shoulders slumped in defeat. "It's going to be so much work." *And my husband won't be there.*

"Shemiah's wedding shouldn't be any more difficult to arrange than Isaac's." Joheved's voice was confident. "Moses and Francesca are delightful to work with."

Miriam took Rachel's arm to get them moving again. "Don't worry. Everyone in the community will provide a dish, so you'll likely end up with more food than you need."

Rachel sighed with relief. At least she wouldn't have to buy new clothes or a house for the newlyweds. She had traded Giuseppe a bolt of scarlet wool in exchange for his finest Palermo silk, for the wedding outfits, and offered Shemiah and his bride her own chamber.

After all, she'd been sleeping in her old room at Papa's house most nights since the demon first attacked him. And if Eliezer weren't coming home, their four-poster marital bed would only be a painful reminder. But enough self-pity. She must hire musicians, caterers, and all the other professionals necessary. One thought cheered her: for his bridal gifts Shemiah would have his choice of the jewelry she and Miriam had taken in pawn.

Joheved coughed delicately, sending Rachel out of her reverie. "Since Eliezer isn't here to instruct Shemiah, shall I ask Meir to share a copy of

Tractate Kallah and answer his questions? Or would your son prefer to talk to Isaac?"

"Eliezer already gave Shemiah a copy," Rachel replied. At least her husband hadn't completely abandoned his paternal obligations. "But Isaac should probably talk to him anyway."

Tractate Kallah, the Jewish Sages' treatise on marital relations, contained everything a bridegroom needed to know in order to provide carnal pleasure to his new wife. This was a necessity because, not only was a Jewish man obligated to fulfill his wife's sexual needs, but to conceive a son she must emit her seed first. Meir's father had given him a copy of Tractate Kallah shortly before he married Joheved, and Meir had done the same for his sons and nephews.

"Shemiah should start sleeping with others in the room besides Elisha," Miriam said. "I'll ask Judah to send some of his most pious students down from the attic."

Rachel nodded. Normally two people together were sufficient protection against *mazikim*, but bridegrooms were particularly vulnerable as the wedding approached. Lillit considered them her special prey, attacking the young men at night and stealing their semen to spawn her demon offspring. Eliezer had admitted to visiting harlots before their wedding: a precaution against Lillit, he'd maintained.

A pox on Eliezer. How could she plan this *simcha* without him intruding on her thoughts? And how could she possibly get through the wedding without his absence draining all the pleasure from it?

As it turned out, Rachel was so busy during those two days that she barely had time to use the privy, which only reminded her to tell the servants to be sure to keep them restocked with fresh moss. The moment she heard the first rooster crow on Friday morning, long before the sky began to lighten, worries prevented her from going back to sleep.

Soon the *shamash* would be pounding on their courtyard gate to summon Shemiah and his attendants to synagogue. Who was responsible for providing the torches? Hopefully not her. What if the musicians she'd hired overslept? How would she find more at the last moment? Yesterday had been clear, but what if a sudden end-of-summer hailstorm arrived? Immediately she peered out the window, but it was still too dark to see any clouds.

The windows of both houses across the courtyard were lit, and she watched with relief as Anna exited below her and headed to the well. Alvina and Rivka, who had given up their beds to cousins from Paris, were still asleep, snuggled up like kittens in the bed she'd once shared with Joheved and Miriam. Rachel tiptoed into the hall, nearly bumping into Meir and Isaac, already in their wedding finery.

The comforting smell of stirabout wafted up from the kitchen, but Rachel's stomach was too tight to eat, so she headed to Joheved's room instead. Her sister was still in bed, and Judita was nursing the new baby, so Rachel quietly slipped out. She longed to cross the courtyard, to the room where Shemiah would be getting dressed, surrounded by his male relations, but it was no place for a woman. When it was time, they would bring him to her.

She slowly descended the stairs, mulling over the details of the next two days and contemplating all the myriad ways in which things could go wrong. She took a deep breath before entering the kitchen, dreading the moment at which she would be swept into the whirlwind of her son's wedding. But the room was empty except for Papa. The servants must be outside already, preparing for the first banquet.

He smiled and patted the seat near him. "Don't worry. Your sisters will make sure everything goes smoothly. This is your eldest child's wedding—you should enjoy yourself."

"I don't know if I can, Papa," she replied, surprised at her honesty. "I know I'll keep looking for Eliezer to walk in."

"Here, have some stirabout and fruit." He ladled some into a dish. "And some of your sister's excellent cheese."

He was trying to cheer her up, and to please him she took a spoonful of cereal. "I can't eat all this. I'm not hungry."

"You must keep up your strength," he insisted, pushing the bowl back toward her. "You won't have time to eat later."

"Papa is right. You probably won't get a chance to sit down again until bedtime, so take advantage of it now," Joheved said as she and Judita bustled into the kitchen. Alvina and Rivka, rubbing the sleep from their eyes, soon followed.

Rachel forced herself to swallow the food in front of her, but the pungent cheese and sweet preserves tasted as flavorless as matzah. Suddenly there was a commotion outside as a gaggle of men dressed, like peacocks, in every color of the rainbow poured into the courtyard and headed for the open kitchen door. In the center, she knew, was her son.

Salomon stood up to welcome them. Each grandson, son-in-law, and grandson-in-law got a hearty hug as he passed him. By the time Shemiah finally entered, every piece of cheese was gone, as was nearly all the fruit. Miriam was the last to come in, carrying her sewing basket.

The crowd divided so Shemiah could sit next to Rachel. One at a time, he held out his arms to her, so she could sew his chemise sleeves closed. He looked resplendent in his glowing yellow silk *bliaut*, which Giuseppe assured her had been dyed with pure saffron. His orange cotton chemise was beautifully decorated with autumn leaves whose outlines glittered with real gold thread. Rachel knew her mediocre embroidery skills could never do justice to such an expensive fiber, but Miriam had stitched the golden strands as fearlessly as if they were flax.

Not expecting Rachel to have a steady hand at such an emotional moment, Miriam threaded the needle for her. These stitches didn't need to be perfect; they would only last until sunset, after which Rachel would remove them so Shemiah could easily shed his clothes before bedding his bride.

Rachel choked up as she gazed at her son. What had happened to the little boy she used to sing lullabies to at night? How had he suddenly turned into this good-looking young man? And today he was getting married. She sighed at memories of her own wedding night, before Eliezer's absence stabbed at her once more.

Thankfully Rachel had little time to indulge her emotions, for the sounds of musicians and men's loud voices could be heard in the distance. She'd barely finished sewing when they were at the gate, and only had time for a quick buss to Shemiah's cheek before he, along with the men, were gone. She raced to the gate to wave good-bye, but all she could see was a crowd of people holding torches and moving swiftly toward the synagogue.

Now it was the women's turn to dress, providing Rachel with another reminder of her missing husband. As long as she had hope of his appearance, Rachel had anticipated wearing her emerald silk wedding outfit. Now she couldn't bear to look at it.

"Miriam, may I borrow your red silk *bliaut* today?" she asked, as if by a whim. "I'm tired of always wearing green."

Miriam hadn't worn her wedding clothes since Judah's mother died, and she doubted they would fit her buxom sister. "Why don't you wear that lovely *bliaut* Marona gave me, the one that used to belong to Meir's sister?"

"Its embroidery also resembles autumn leaves," Joheved said. "So you'll match the wedding party."

"Please wear it, Mama," Rivka begged as Rachel tried it on. "Then our family will all be dressed the same."

Rachel thought yellow made her complexion look sallow, but she gave in to her daughter's entreaties. Recalling how frustrated she'd felt at Miriam's wedding, confined to wool while everyone else wore silk, Rachel had bought Rivka an outfit to go with Shemiah's. Rivka was in her thirteenth year, so there was little risk of her outgrowing the expensive *bliaut*. Amazingly Alvina fit perfectly into the blue silk outfit that Joheved had become betrothed in.

Next came the task Rachel had always enjoyed before, choosing which jewelry to wear. A family wedding, especially one on the Sabbath, called for the finest in a woman's collection. Rivka and Alvina watched in awe as their elders unlocked the jewel case and sorted through its contents. Rachel rejected everything Eliezer had given her, and she couldn't work up much enthusiasm for the other sparkling baubles. To her sisters' surprise, she let them choose first, contenting herself with gold and pearls rather than gemstones. Both Joheved and Miriam were wise enough to avoid anything with emeralds.

The doctor's house was on the way to the synagogue, so the women waited there for the musicians and torchbearers to escort Glorietta to morning services. From that point on, the day passed in a blur. Rachel accompanied Francesca and the bride to the synagogue courtyard, after which, Papa placed ashes on Shemiah's forehead, where tefillin were worn, as a reminder of the destruction of Zion. Though she knew that Shemiah must have put the betrothal ring on Glorietta's finger, said the *erusin* blessing and drank the first cup of wine, all she remembered was the cup shattering when he threw it against the wall and a crowd of girls, including Rivka, rushing to grab pieces to ensure happiness in their future marriages.

That and the squawking chickens swinging over Shemiah and Glorietta's heads—how did anyone find more poultry? Surely she'd bought every chicken in Troyes. The rest of the day was a whirlwind of receiving congratulations and checking regularly that they weren't running out of food or wine.

Saturday, the Day of Rest, was even more hectic. Dancing wasn't supposed to resume until the Sabbath ended, but the Edomite musicians showed up after *disner* and people began dancing anyway. Finally it was time for Havdalah, the ceremony marking the official close of Shabbat, after which the witnesses signed the *ketubah* and Glorietta received it. Rachel frowned in confusion; where had she been when the *ketubah* was publicly read yesterday?

Soon came the moment she'd been dreading—a couples dance started by the bridal pair and followed by their parents. Rachel's impulse was to hide in the wine cellar, where she could claim to be verifying supplies, but when the music started it was too late. A wall of people surrounded the dancing area, and how would it look if she tried to force her way through them? Suddenly there was a hand on her elbow, leading her to the center, and she looked up into her father's loving face.

"Papa, I didn't know you could dance," was all she could say.

"You're welcome," he replied with a grin. "Don't you remember us dancing together at your wedding?"

"Of course I do. I didn't know you could still dance."

He paused and expertly spun her around, much to the crowd's delight. "Apparently I still can."

"I love you, Papa." She squeezed his hand as they rejoined the guests when the dance finished.

Immediately the empty area was filled with alternating circles, either male or female, dancing in opposite directions. Periodically the music would change and the circles would reverse direction, allowing a man to briefly bow to the woman in front of him, while she curtsied in response. If the couple happened to be related, they linked arms and twirled. Rachel, who hadn't eaten *souper*, was growing dizzy from all the circling when the old tune abruptly stopped and a new one began. She paused to see who her partner would be, her eyes opening wide in astonishment at the attractive young man standing before her.

Dovid the Fuller was dressed in a magnificent indigo wool *bliaut*, cut short enough to display an almost indecent length of leg encased in bright scarlet silk hose. He flashed her a wide grin, bowed deeply, and as the tempo increased he circled away from her into the shadows.

thirty-one

even months after Shemiah's wedding, the two things Rachel remembered most clearly were dancing with Papa and standing for some time in shocked silence after discovering Dovid among the guests. Later he'd admitted to attending both days of celebration, but not the ceremony itself.

Her family had barely recovered from the wedding when Count Hugues announced the grape harvest, sending them into a frenzy of wine-making to get the vintage finished before Rosh Hashanah. At first Dovid was eager to help out. But after Rachel explained the significance of this action—that because non-Jews were forbidden to handle kosher wine, his participation would affirm his Jewish status—Dovid withdrew his offer.

Rachel told herself that this was nothing to feel so unhappy about, and then, one after another, things got worse. Though she had no reason to expect him, Rachel was bitterly disappointed when Eliezer not only failed to show up for the Cold Fair but didn't even send a letter with the Spanish merchants. *How could he not at least write to Shemiah after missing the wedding?* So when Pesach left for Toledo with his usual load of furs and woolens, she made him promise to write immediately upon arrival.

During the following two weeks, Rachel woke up each morning to the sounds of Zipporah vomiting into the chamber pot in the next room. A whispered talk with Miriam confirmed that Shmuel's wife was pregnant again and, should the pregnancy continue, would give birth before Shavuot. To Rachel's knowledge, Zipporah had miscarried twice already, both males, and it looked as if she were as cursed as Brunetta. Too late to pray for a girl, there was nothing to do but wait apprehensively until the birth.

It was mid-January when Rachel heard the worst news. To encourage his vassals' loyalty after Adelaide's death, Hugues had embarked on a grand tour of Champagne, visiting every castle, abbey, and estate that owed him fealty. But what should have been an extravaganza turned into disaster instead.

Joheved's family was among the first to learn the details when Milo returned from visiting Emeline. Since Rachel was in Ramerupt at the time, she too became privy to his tale.

"You're back soon," Meir exclaimed when Milo entered the manor's great hall. "We thought you'd be gone at least a month."

Milo swallowed hard. "I did intend a longer visit, but circumstances prevented me."

"I hope you found Emeline well," Joheved said anxiously.

"My stepmother couldn't be happier," Milo replied in a voice that belied any happiness. "She's been eager to return to the convent for some time and is grateful that my father gave her permission to enter Avenay during his lifetime."

"So what's wrong, Milo?" Rachel couldn't stand waiting through all the pleasantries. "Obviously some problem forced you home early."

Milo blanched and Joheved quickly poured him a cup of wine. "While I was visiting at Avenay, they brought Count Hugues into the infirmary, gravely injured."

Milo's audience stood in shocked silence as he drained his cup and held it out for more. "One of his servants tried to slit his throat in the night." He shook his head in disbelief.

"*Mon Dieu.*" Joheved covered her mouth in shock.

"Lady Emeline, who tended his wounds, said the cuts were so deep it's a miracle he's still alive."

"Who could have done such a thing?" Rachel burst out.

"The count's entourage included Alexander, a young foreigner that Hugues had personally ransomed from captivity," Milo replied. "Hugues was quite fond of the fellow, who often ate and slept in the count's personal quarters. They were staying at Dontrien when guards heard this terrible cry from the count's room, and, finding Alexander attempting murder, they killed him."

"So no one was able to question Alexander about his motives," Meir said.

From the gossip Rachel heard from Ganymedes in Troyes, Hugues preferred men to women, which was probably why he'd remained childless. In Rachel's opinion, which she wisely kept to herself, the count's injuries were likely the result of a lover's quarrel. Joheved, however, saw a more sinister motive.

"Obviously the traitor was in the pay of the count's enemies," Joheved said. "With Adelaide and Étienne dead, all the lands once ruled by Count Thibault will be ripe for picking now that Hugues is gone—Blois, Chartres, Meaux, and Champagne."

"I'm afraid you're right, milady," Milo said soberly. "Any greedy nobleman could attack at will, for we would have no sovereign to protect us."

Rachel stared in horror as the enormity of the danger dawned on her. "The Champagne fairs make Troyes and Provins a fat prize," she whispered. "Every count and duke on our borders must covet them."

"King Philip will not let his vassals harass us," Meir said. "His daughter is our countess, so Champagne goes to the crown if Hugues dies."

"The king is too weak," Milo replied. "Until his excommunication is lifted, his vassals are not required to support him."

"And they won't," Joheved added. "Not if they think they can take Hugues' lands for themselves."

"But Count Thibault's widow is sister to the king of Angleterre," Meir said. "Anyone who attacked her family's lands would have King Henry at his throat."

Milo shook his head. "From what I hear, Henry is too busy fighting his brother, Robert, over Normandy to spare any men to protect us."

"Are we helpless then?" Rachel asked in despair.

None of her companions could disprove her, and the conversation concluded on this unhappy note.

That night Rachel slept restlessly, worrying when and from whom the first blow would fall—the count of Anjou, duke of Burgundy, count of Flanders, duke of Lorraine? Or would it be any of numerous lesser but frighteningly ambitious nobles? What if Count André supported one of the usurpers? Where would that leave Joheved and Meir?

Would her new clothier's business be destroyed almost immediately after she'd finally established it?

For three months, she joined other Jews of Troyes in praying for peace and their sovereign's recovery. Each night when Rachel went to bed, she gave thanks that no enemy had attacked Troyes that day and recited Psalm 88 to invoke its magical power to save a city. Zipporah's pregnancy was now obvious, and thoughts of Eliezer receded in importance as Rachel worried about more immediate concerns. Not that she could do anything about them other than hope, pray, and wait.

Studying Talmud with her sisters provided Rachel some respite from these troubles, but it was her discussions with Dovid that gave her pleasure. The continual thumping of the fulling mill's hammers prevented any discourse inside, and it was too cold outdoors, so they met in the cottage Joheved provided for him, leaving the door ajar to maintain propriety.

Their initial task of learning texts in Hebrew and Latin, along with Papa's interpretations, had given way to a larger agenda. Dovid began offering the Church's explanations, challenging her to repute them, while she in turn questioned him about the *minim*'s heresies.

"Why do the Notzrim refuse to observe the Sabbath?" She was careful not to include him with the heretics. "How can they ignore one of the Ten Commandments?"

Always a gracious host, Dovid handed her a bowl of soup. "That's an easy one. Because Jesus rose from the dead on Sunday they observe the Sabbath on that day."

Rachel was pleased that he avoided using the word *we* for those following the Church. "Even so, they still work on what should be a day of rest."

"But it says in Genesis, 'On the seventh day God finished the work,' which implies that He was still working on the Sabbath," Dovid explained.

"And the next line says, 'He rested on the seventh day . . . and made it holy,'" she said triumphantly. "In any case, we both know that the fourth commandment explicitly forbids working on the Sabbath, no matter which day it is celebrated."

Dovid appeared more amused than angered at her victory and quoted verses from Isaiah, in Hebrew, that the Church said referred to Jesus and how his suffering expiated the people's sins.

> "He was despised and rejected by men . . . Surely he has borne our grief and endured our sorrows . . . he was wounded for our sins, crushed for our iniquities; he bore the chastisement that made us whole, and with his bruises we are healed. We all went astray like sheep, each going his own way; and Adonai has laid on him the guilt of us all."

"My father says this text speaks of the people Israel, who sinned during Isaiah's time and are often mentioned as one man by the prophets," Rachel said. "Thus Israel was made to suffer exile for their sins."

Dovid nodded, clearly not very impressed, and took her soup bowl back to the hearth for more. Rachel surreptitiously observed him, admiring his handsome features and wondering how old he was. Certainly he was younger than her, but was he in his early or late twenties?

"Perhaps you'd prefer a more forceful response." She took a sip of soup and smiled at him over the brim. "If the Church says Isaiah means forgiveness of sins, then weren't sins forgiven before Jesus was born? What of the myriad places in the Bible where the Holy One is described as 'forgiving iniquity.' And what of all the sin offerings, if they did not bring expiation?"

"The Church would say that while their sins were forgiven, this did not save them from hell," Dovid replied. "Only Jesus's suffering could do that."

Rachel's smile disappeared. "If they say that his death expiates the sins of those who believe in him and redeems them from hell, his believers are free of all commandments and may steal, murder, commit adultery, or any other crime. How is this anything other than a curse to the world?"

Dovid could only shrug his shoulders.

"Furthermore, how can it enter anyone's mind that the Holy One, Whom all agree is merciful to His creatures, condemns to hell all souls born before the advent of Jesus?" Her voice rose with outrage. "Even small children and newborn babes, who are surely innocent of sin?" *Including my poor baby Asher.* Rachel's only comfort over his death was the certainty that her little son now reposed in Gan Eden.

"Enough," Dovid threw up his hands. "I stand humbled and defeated by your vigorous argument."

Rachel saw the twinkle in his eye and chuckled. "You must try harder if you intend to vanquish me."

"Far be it from me to vanquish such a *femme formidable*," he said softly.

Rachel knew she was blushing under his frank gaze, but the more she tried, and failed, to think of a suitable retort the more her face flamed. All she could come up with was, "I'm impressed that a man can make such tasty soup."

"Another useful thing I learned from the monks."

After this, they began exchanging views on personal as well as religious subjects. Rachel learned more than she could imagine about life in a monastery and, in return, shared her experience in the household of a Talmudic scholar without sons. Dovid's cozy hut, with something delicious always simmering over the fire, became her shelter from all the worries outside. Yet despite their budding intimacy, Dovid never talked about his family, and she mentioned Eliezer as little as possible.

Passover arrived with some relief for Rachel's anxieties. Dovid acquitted himself well at the family seder and Count Hugues was recovering. Realizing that his survival was due less to physicians than to the intercession of the abbey's saints, Hugues showed his gratitude by donating some land to the nuns at Avenay. Among the many witnesses to the transaction were the count's nephew Thibault, Count André of Ramerupt, the nun Emeline, and the cleric Guy. It was from the latter that Salomon's family received the news.

"I suspect Countess Adèle is to be thanked for our continuing peace," Guy told them when he stopped in at Ramerupt on his way home from the ceremony in Avenay.

"How so?" Salomon asked skeptically. Étienne's widow was in her thirties, too young to have such influence.

"She is the daughter of a king, and sister of another," Guy said, "as well as a great friend to several prominent bishops and archbishops, whose churches she generously endows."

Meir nodded. "Growing up in the English court, exposed to politics and intrigue since infancy, no wonder she plays her vassals and rivals against each other so expertly."

"Luckily her adversaries see only a young woman without a husband and thereby underestimate her," Guy said.

"Lucky for her and for us," Joheved spoke for them all.

"Is Troyes out of danger then?" Rachel asked.

"Perhaps not out of danger, but in less danger than before," was all Guy would say until he abruptly slapped his thigh. "Oh *non*." He turned to Rachel. "Pilgrims brought a letter for you a while back, but with all the excitement over Count Hugues, I forgot about it until just now, when I saw you."

Rachel's heart leapt to her throat. "Do you have it with you?"

"A thousand apologies, but I left it in Troyes."

Rachel, unable to leave Ramerupt until the festival was over, was ready to cry with frustration when Milo came to her rescue. "I would be pleased to ride to Troyes with you, Guy," he offered. "Then you can give me news of my Lady Emeline and I can return with the letter."

Rachel thanked Milo profusely and, having no desire to speak with anyone, retired to her room. But her mind was too flighty to read or study, and she didn't dare search out Dovid with all her family in residence. She was about to lie down when there was a knock on the door.

Shemiah poked his head in. "Would you like to go for a walk, Mama? I can't abide sitting here waiting."

She sat up immediately. Of course Shemiah would be anxious to hear from Eliezer; her son was due to leave for Toledo in a week. Together they trod the forest paths that bordered the road to Troyes, discussing the Talmud passages he'd been learning. But her concentration kept faltering as she listened for the clip-clop of horse's hooves.

The slightest forest creature's movement sent her racing back to the road, Shemiah right beside her. Finally there was no point in walking anywhere except down the road toward Troyes. Their conversation turned to Shemiah's marriage and how he was appreciating his new status. More than his words, her son's blushing smiles told Rachel that all was indeed well with the newlyweds, and she began to wonder how soon Shemiah would make her a grandmother. Joheved said it was far more enjoyable than motherhood.

The day wasn't warm, but Rachel was sweating profusely when they glimpsed movement in the distance. Now that someone was finally approaching, her legs turned to jelly, forcing her to reach out to Shemiah for support. Together they watched as the rider drew close enough to be identified as Milo.

He dismounted and handed her a stained and travel-worn letter, its seal barely holding it closed. The handwriting was not Eliezer's, so it had to be from Pesach. Rachel wished she could peruse its contents in private, but she couldn't wait a moment longer.

The message was short, and after reading it, she passed it to Shemiah. Following the usual salutations and hopes that everyone was in good health, Pesach had written, "Master Eliezer sends his love to his family and regrets that he was not able to attend his son's wedding. The birth was difficult, resulting in the child's death shortly thereafter and a lengthy recovery for the mother. I have every hope that he will return with me for the Hot Fair."

Pesach continued with assurances that he'd gotten a good price for Rachel's woolens and that he looked forward to seeing Shemiah the following month. He closed by sending his regards to his parents and to Dulcie and wishing them all a good Passover.

Rachel closed her eyes and exhaled. *Thank Heaven Eliezer is still alive.*

Shemiah put his arm around her. "That's welcome news . . . not about the baby, I mean." Although he did mean the baby.

Mother and son walked slowly back to the manor house. By the time they reached it, Rachel's grateful relief was giving way to resentment. Her husband was alive and well, though apparently not concerned enough about his family to have written himself. Or was he still holding a grudge over her not writing to him the previous year?

"I want to know why Papa hasn't sent us any letters." Shemiah kicked a rock in the dirt.

"I'm glad you'll be seeing him soon," she said. "I'm worried."

"I am too. It's bad enough that Papa didn't come to my wedding, but now he hasn't studied Talmud for almost two years."

"Surely he's reviewing his studies in Toledo."

"*Non.*" Shemiah's voice hardened. "He says that Talmud study is doomed, that with all the other yeshivot gone, Grandpapa's is too small to make a difference. The only thing left of Jewish Law will be codes, each stricter than the last."

Rachel's eyes blazed. "The Holy One won't let Talmud study cease. Papa's *kuntres* will save it. You'll see."

The Mai Faire de Provins was held without incident, but the inhabitants of Troyes continued to worry that their Hot Fair would be an opportune time for an attack on the city, exactly when the plunder would be greatest. Rachel grew increasingly irritated, as she both dreaded and anticipated seeing Eliezer again. She snapped at the servants and was cross with Rivka, who began spending days at a time at Miriam's.

Finally Salomon suggested that she help him in the vineyard, thinking that some work outdoors might calm her or at least tire her out. There, hidden from watchful eyes, Rachel vented her frustration at weeds growing among the vines, vigorously uprooting them with her hoe and hacking them into pieces.

The week after Shavuot, work in the vineyard was at a frantic pace. All were aware that the grape blossoms would soon be opening and thus all activity must cease to ensure complete pollination. Rachel was hurrying to finish her row before sunset, when she heard Miriam frantically calling for her.

Heart pounding, Rachel dropped the hoe and ran toward her sister. Had Shemiah and Eliezer returned already? Was an army advancing on Troyes?

Non. Zipporah was in labor.

"I need you to ride to Ramerupt for Joheved." Miriam urgently propelled Rachel toward the road home. "Zipporah's water has broken."

Rachel rushed off to the stables and, grateful for the fine mare she now owned, managed to return with her sister before it was completely dark. The men were praying psalms in Salomon's salon, and Shmuel jumped up to give Joheved a hug as she headed upstairs. Rachel hesitated at the doorway, praying that she wouldn't have to endure hours, perhaps days, of Zipporah's painful labor process.

But when she stepped into the lying-in chamber, she saw that her prayers had been answered. Zipporah was already on the birthing stool, sweat dripping down her face, grunting with exertion. Brunetta sat on one side and Joheved on the other, taking turns whispering protective Torah verses in her ears. Three sets of tefillin were tied to the bedposts, which

Rachel assumed must belong to Papa, Meir, and Shmuel. Or was one of them Joheved's?

Out of habit she inspected the circle chalked on the floor, but there were no breaks in the protective ring surrounding Zipporah. All four walls, plus the door, were clearly chalked against demons with the magical inscription "Sanvi, Sansanvi, and Semangelaf, Adam and Eve, barring Lillit." There was nothing else to do except pray Psalm 120, and, just in case, Rachel also whispered Psalm 126, for a woman whose children die.

Their ministrations were successful, for the church bells had not yet chimed Compline when Zipporah was delivered of a healthy baby girl.

"Mazel tov!" Rachel joined the women shouting congratulations.

Their happy voices carried to the men downstairs, who in normal circumstances might have thought the child was male to merit such joy. Brunetta broke down weeping, and tears filled Joheved's eyes as she made the blessing *Baruch ata Adonai . . . Hatov Vehametiv,* "Who is good and does good."

Joheved stared defiantly at Miriam and Rachel, as if daring them to correct her for saying the blessing a parent traditionally makes at the birth of a son. But if Zipporah's sons were under a curse, the Holy One was indeed doing a good thing in giving her a daughter.

Shmuel must have thought so too, because he and Meir hosted a banquet the day of the baby's naming as extravagant as any given after a brit milah, an especially generous gesture since the Hot Fair opened the following week and Troyes was full of merchants. So little Marona, named for her Meir's mother, was joyously welcomed into the world.

All agreed that her future was assured. Born on a Friday, she would grow to be pious; under the dominion of Venus she was destined to enjoy wealth and physical pleasures. Not that one needed any knowledge of astrology to predict that the daughter of Shmuel and Zipporah would be pious and wealthy.

Rachel, however, was not destined to enjoy Marona's naming feast. Midway through morning services, Rivka tugged on her sleeve and pointed to Shemiah pacing the synagogue entry hall below. Rachel tried to leave unobtrusively but tripped over a bench in her hurry, so that when she reached the bottom of the stairs, her foot was throbbing, adding physical pain to her considerable emotional turmoil.

Shemiah had returned without Eliezer—again.

"I brought a letter for you from Papa," Eliezer said. "I left it on your bed so you could read it in private."

Rachel leaned on her son's arm as they headed home, Rivka holding her other hand. "Have you read the letter, Shemiah?"

"*Non*, I haven't. But Papa discussed it with me."

She could have asked him how business went in Toledo or told him about Zipporah's baby girl, but her tongue seemed frozen to the roof of her mouth. Rivka and Shemiah were silent as well, until they reached her bedroom door.

"I'll wait downstairs," Shemiah said, his somber tone fueling her trepidation.

"So will I," Rivka added. "I want to know what Papa wrote too."

Rachel kissed each of them, thankful for their support, then limped inside and closed the door. The folded piece of parchment lay on top of the covers, pale in stark contrast to the dark blanket. She hesitated to touch it, as if it were poisoned, but eventually put her fear aside and picked it up. With nary a word, Eliezer hadn't come home in almost two years; what could he say now to hurt her more?

Abruptly she unfolded the missive and held it up. "Dearest Rachel," it began. "There is not a day when I don't long to see you. I have learned of Troyes' precarious position as your sovereign recovers from his wounds and believe more strongly than ever that there is no future for our people in Ashkenaz. So I urge you one more time to join me in Toledo, for I have no intention of returning to France."

Rachel wiped away the tears brimming in her eyes. "You still have the conditional *get* I wrote you years ago. If you cannot bring yourself to live with me here, you should take it to court, obtain a divorce, and be free of me. Between the house and jewelry in Troyes, there are ample funds to pay your *ketubah*. I myself am content to remain married to you, since a wife in France makes no difference to my life in Sepharad. But you are too young to be left in living widowhood."

Here the letter closed abruptly, with no wishes for her good health or any other casual chitchat. Rachel dropped the letter on the bed, then lay down next to it and wept.

Divorce! It has finally come to this—Eliezer isn't coming home again, ever.

She never wanted to leave this room. How could she endure the shame of being abandoned by her husband? How could she endure the pain of this rejection?

Sometime later there was a soft knocking on the door, followed by Shemiah's pleading voice. "Please, Mama, let us in."

Wordlessly she handed Eliezer's letter to her son, who scanned it and passed it to Rivka. Neither child shed any tears.

"Are you moving to Toledo?" Rivka's voice was trembling with fear. "I don't want you to go."

Rachel pulled her daughter close, not sure who was comforting whom. "I'm not moving anywhere."

"I don't care if Papa never comes back," Rivka said. "Uncle Judah's been nicer to me than Papa ever was, and I'm glad he's going to be my father-in-law."

Rachel sighed at Rivka's misguided effort to be supportive. There was nothing Rachel wanted more than for Eliezer to return to her, but she would not display her weakness to her children.

"Are you going to get divorced?" Shemiah sounded more angry than frightened at the prospect.

"I don't know; I just don't know. I need to think about it."

thirty-two

or six months Rachel told no one about Eliezer's letter. She tried to learn more from Shemiah and Pesach, but, surprisingly, neither had spent much time with her husband. Both reported that Eliezer was like a man possessed, spending nearly every waking hour at the observatory.

"Even his own son could not drag him away from his calculations for a decent conversation," Shemiah complained. "All Papa wanted to talk about was how he was going to prove that the planets moved around the sun."

"How did he look?" Rachel asked. "Was he well?"

Shemiah shook his head. "He's lost weight, and he's as pale as you'd expect for someone who never goes out in the daytime."

"What do you think I should do?"

"Divorce him." Shemiah was adamant. "He's taken another wife and made it clear that he's never coming back to Troyes. And considering how much time he spends looking at the stars, you'd never see him even if you did move to Toledo."

Rachel was certain that Joheved would agree with Shemiah, especially once her sister knew about Eliezer's second wife. But maybe Miriam could help her decide what to do; after all, Miriam had rejected a divorce from Judah despite his refusal to use the bed with her. But finding private time to consult her sister was not easy. Rachel was forced to wait until they were collecting the vine props on a windy autumn afternoon.

"Miriam, I need to talk to you about something important." Rachel looked around to be sure no one was within hearing distance. "Just the two of us."

Miriam raised an eyebrow and moved to the row behind Rachel.

Rachel didn't waste time. "Why did you refuse Judah a divorce when he wanted one?"

"That was over ten years ago. Why do you want to know now?"

"Just answer me, please."

"I don't regret my decision." Miriam pulled her mantle closed as the wind blew a swirl of grape leaves around them. "I would have lost my children to Judah, and if he'd moved away, I might never have seen them again."

"That's the only reason?" Rachel asked in surprise.

"In nearly every way, Judah was, and is, an exemplary husband. Living with him was not so repulsive that I would have preferred to live alone." Miriam waited for Rachel's response, but when none was forthcoming, she continued, "You didn't answer my question. Why do you want to know?"

Rachel took a deep breath. "Eliezer has offered me a divorce, and I need your advice." When Miriam gasped, she added, "He wants to live in Toledo and I want to live in Troyes." She wanted her sister's reply without mentioning his second wife.

Miriam hesitated, her expression reminding Rachel of their father stroking his beard. "Since you and Eliezer are already living apart, I can think of only one advantage for you to divorce him. And that is if you intend to marry again."

"Marry again?" Rachel pulled up a vine prop so vigorously that she nearly fell over. "What do you mean?"

"Your children are grown, so he can't take them away, and you don't need his income to live comfortably," Miriam said. "So there is no disadvantage to your getting divorced."

"Other than the shame and gossip," Rachel interrupted.

"Since when have you cared about shame and gossip?" Miriam pointed out. "Frankly, the only legal difference between being married to Eliezer and not is the freedom to marry someone else."

"So you think I should accept his conditional *get*?"

Miriam's voice softened. "It depends on how you feel. Do you want to be married to him, even if you will never live with him again?"

"I want to be married to him and live with him, but I want to live here." As soon as she spoke, Rachel knew Miriam would hear a spoiled little girl, pouting because she couldn't have what she wanted.

Miriam said gently, "But Rachel, that doesn't seem to be what Eliezer wants."

Rachel sighed. "Do you think Papa would be disappointed if I got divorced? Nobody else in our family has."

"He might be, but I'm sure his main concern would be your happiness."

"So as long as I don't intend to remarry, there's no reason for me to divorce?" Rachel asked. *Except that Eliezer has another wife, and he's only allowed one.*

Miriam nodded and Rachel made her decision. "Then I may as well stay married for the time being."

Rachel spent much of the winter in Ramerupt, continuing her studies with Dovid. They had completed the Bible twice, and both felt confident in their ability to understand the other's language. Rachel was hoping to concentrate on Salomon's commentary during the upcoming cycle, but Dovid surprised her.

"I've been to two of your family's Passover feasts," he said. "And while I have vague memories from my childhood, much of the ritual was a mystery to me. According to my understanding of the Torah, Jews were supposed to bring their Passover offering to the Temple in Jerusalem and sacrifice it there. There's no mention of a home ceremony."

"That's correct," Rachel said slowly. Did she dare explain how the seder is described in the Mishnah?

Papa had strongly cautioned her and Shmuel to never mention Talmud to the *minim*. As long as the Notzrim believed that they and the Jews shared the same holy text, they viewed the Jews benignly, rather like an ignorant younger brother who would eventually become educated. They would be shocked to discover that Jews had postbiblical works that solidified Jewish beliefs and traditions, compiled after the Hanged One's death and therefore heretical.

"But it's clear that all Jews celebrate Passover the same way, even with the same words," Dovid continued. "And from your family's discussions at the feast, I can tell there's another book this comes from."

Rachel merely nodded, unprepared to confirm his conclusion.

"I want to study that book in Hebrew," Dovid declared.

"Why?"

"So I can be prepared for Passover this year and not sit there like an ignoramus."

Impressed with Dovid's reasoning, Rachel began to consider his request in spite of her father's warnings. Dovid was a Jew, after all, and the Talmud was his patrimony. Besides, with so many recent forced converts, some of whom had not returned to Judaism, the Talmud wouldn't remain a secret. But it was Dovid's stated desire to study in Hebrew that gave her an escape. She could teach him Mishnah from the last chapter of Tractate Pesachim, the one that describes the seder. He wouldn't have to know how much more there was in the Talmud.

"There is another book where the ritual is presented," she admitted. "It's written in Hebrew, and not very long, so I could probably teach it to you before Passover."

Dovid grinned triumphantly. "I was right; I knew it."

"We'll start with you writing down the words I dictate," she said. "Then you can study them and prepare questions." She would teach him Mishnah the same way she'd learned it.

> "On the eve of Passover, from the afternoon offering time, one may not eat until nightfall. Even the poorest in Israel must not eat unless he reclines, and they should give him not less than four cups of wine, even if they come from charity."

"What and when is the afternoon offering time?" Dovid asked exactly the question Rachel expected.

"It is the ninth hour after sunrise, at which time the priests in the Holy Temple sacrificed their animals," she replied. "If we eat nothing in the afternoon, when it comes time for the Passover meal that evening we'll be hungry and eat the matzah with a good appetite."

"I remember your father explaining why the poor recline," Dovid said proudly. "Reclining at the table is the mark of a free man and Passover celebrates our freedom."

"Papa teaches that there are two ways of interpreting the part about wine," Rachel said. "It could mean that those distributing wine to the poor should not give them less than four cups of wine. Others say that it applies to all Israel, that none should drink fewer than four cups of wine during the seder, even if they have to accept charity for the expense."

"Surely no Jew in Champagne is that poor."

"Maybe not today. But Joheved told me that when Papa was away studying in Mayence they could only afford enough wine at Passover because their family were vintners."

"According to three of the four gospels, Jesus's last *souper* was on the eve of Passover," Dovid said. "There Jesus explains that the wine represents his blood, and the matzah his body."

Rachel shuddered at the idea, and Dovid quickly added, "I'm only telling you what the monks taught me."

After they'd been studying a few weeks, Joheved caught up with Rachel on her way to the fulling mill. "You didn't tell me you were teaching Dovid Mishnah." Joheved's voice wasn't condemning, more as though Rachel had kept good news a secret.

"He wanted to learn more Hebrew, so I thought he could try the last chapter of Tractate Pesachim." Rachel tried not to look like a guilty child. "How did you know?"

"Dovid asked me a question about the seder." Joheved's eyes gleamed with excitement. "But never mind that. Since you're teaching him Pesachim, would you mind if Jacob Tam joined you? He's been out of sorts since Shlomo started studying with Meir at the yeshiva."

At that moment Rachel realized that she would mind a great deal, but she couldn't refuse her sister's request. "Not at all. It will give Dovid someone to review his lessons with." If Joheved thought she and Dovid required a chaperone, they could do worse than young Jacob.

Rachel and her two students slowly worked their way through the Mishnah, sometimes in Dovid's cottage and, as the weather warmed, more often at a table outside. To her relief, Dovid didn't mind appearing more ignorant than an eight-year-old boy, particularly when the boy was a prodigy like her nephew.

> They bring him matzah, lettuce, and *haroset*, and two cooked dishes, though the *haroset* is not mandatory. Rabbi Elazar son of Rabbi Za-

> dok says it is mandatory. In the Temple, they bring him the Pesach offering.

"After the appetizers, the servants bring in the special festival foods," Rachel said. "Matzah, of course, is explicitly commanded in the Torah. The lettuce is the *maror*, the bitter herb also mandated by Torah."

"But *haroset* isn't in the Torah," Jacob pointed out. "Where does it come from?"

Rachel hesitated. If Jacob had been her only student, she would have given him the Talmud's answer. But she was reluctant to do so in front of Dovid. "There's more written about Passover than what I gave you, but it's not in Hebrew." She turned to Jacob. "It asks the same question you do.

> Why is *haroset* mandatory? Rabbi Levi says it is a symbol of the apple tree, but Rabbi Yohanan says it is a symbol of the mortar."

"I assume Rabbi Yohanan means the mortar the Hebrew slaves used to make bricks for Pharaoh," Dovid said. "But I don't recall anything about apple trees in the seder."

"Apple trees aren't mentioned in the seder, but that's where the Hebrew women gave birth without pain in Egypt, away from Pharaoh's men who wanted to kill the baby boys," Rachel explained. "As it says in Song of Songs:

> Under the apple tree I roused you; there your mother conceived you; there she who bore you conceived you."

Dovid stared at her in bewilderment, but before Rachel could respond, Jacob asked, "Is that why *haroset* is made with apples, to remind us of the brave Hebrew women who defied Pharaoh and kept having children despite the danger?"

Rachel nodded. Her gaze lingered on the curve of Dovid's lips until she abruptly realized that Jacob might notice her lapse. "In addition *haroset* contains spices such as cinnamon and ginger because its sticks resemble the straw used for bricks."

Her other concern, Dovid discovering Talmud, was realized when Jacob asked, "Is your answer from the Gemara on this Mishnah?"

"What is the Gemara?" Dovid asked, now more confused.

Jacob Tam looked at Dovid as if he had asked what bread is. "The Gemara and Mishnah together make up the Talmud, the Oral Law, which was given to Moses on Mount Sinai along with the written Torah."

Rachel had no choice but to interrupt. "Jews only discuss Talmud with other Jews, Dovid. Then Notzrim can't criticize us by accusing the Talmud of distorting our Torah, preventing us from realizing the truth about—" She caught herself just before saying "the Hanged One" and said, "Jesus."

"Grandpapa says that Dovid is Jewish." Jacob turned to the fuller. "But if you're Jewish, why aren't you married? Only Notzrim don't marry."

Rachel thought she'd die of embarrassment, but to her surprise Dovid smiled and tousled the boy's hair. "Your grandfather isn't married."

"But Grandpapa is old," Jacob replied. "And besides, he was married for a long time."

"So who would you have me marry?" Dovid asked. "Jews consider me Jewish, and the Church considers me a Christian."

Jacob squinted at Dovid. "What do you consider yourself?"

Rachel thought to chastise Jacob for such a personal question, but she was curious about Dovid's answer.

"I don't know, I haven't decided." He was silent a while before adding, "I suppose that's why I'm not married."

"Let's get back to our studies," Rachel broke in. Then she said to Dovid, "The Talmud is a fence around the Torah. Since all the commandments are spread throughout the twenty-four books of the Bible, a little here and a little there, one who learns a particular law may forget it before he reaches the next. Thus our Sages established tractates and arranged all the laws of Passover together in Tractate Pesachim, just as all the laws of Sabbath are explained in Tractate Shabbat."

"The Mishnah contains the laws," Jacob added. "And the Gemara answers the questions the Sages asked about the Mishnah."

"To answer your question, Jacob Tam," Rachel said sternly. "What I explained about the apple tree and spices did come from the Gemara on our Mishnah."

* * *

Studying Mishnah with Dovid and little Jacob was both pleasant and frustrating. On one hand, Dovid and Jacob asked the most intriguing questions. But on the other hand, Rachel longed for the idyllic hours she and Dovid used to spend studying alone in his cottage, where there were no witnesses if she covertly admired his countenance while he spoke. In the weeks following Passover, her feelings grew more conflicted. Shemiah left for Sepharad, and she anxiously awaited the report he would bring.

The Jewish Festival of Freedom served to drive home the message that neither she nor Dovid were free to marry. He would not find a bride until he settled in one religion or the other; she was tied to Eliezer until she accepted his *get*. As the weather warmed, she was increasingly presented with the enticing sight of Dovid's muscular body, clearly outlined beneath his wet chemise in the fulling tank. At night, when she grew restless and her hand slipped between her thighs to give her relief, it was often Dovid she imagined in bed with her, not her husband.

Yet when she thought of accepting Eliezer's divorce, she couldn't see how she could break the news to Papa until he'd regained his health. For no sooner had he returned home from Passover at Ramerupt than he was attacked by the fever demon Kadachas. Moses haCohen recommended a diet rich in wine and red meat to strengthen his blood, but Papa insisted on following the regimen found in the Talmud at the end of Tractate Shabbat's sixth chapter, a cure based on reciting verses from Exodus that describe Moses's encounter with the burning bush.

> Rabbi Yohanan said: For an inflammatory fever let him take a knife made of iron, go to a thornbush, and tie a strand of his hair on it. Then he must notch the bush and recite the verses, *The angel of the Eternal appeared to him . . . and Moses said, "I must turn aside to see."* On the second day he cuts another notch and recites the next verse, *And when the Eternal saw that he had turned aside to look . . .* The third day he cuts another notch and concludes with the verse that follows, *And He said, "Do not come closer."*

Salomon's students scoured the neighborhood for the nearest rose bush, which was farther away than Rachel thought he should walk in his feeble condition. But he managed the effort each day, leaning heavily on her arm, and was twice able to invoke the miracle of the burning bush not consumed by fire. The third day was difficult, but Salomon was eventually able to recite the final verse that warned the fever demon to approach no closer.

Then, sweating profusely, he chopped down the bush and said the Talmud's incantation, "Even as the fire in the furnace for Hananiah, Mishael, and Azariah fled before them, so too shall the fire afflicting Salomon ben Leah flee from him."

At first this magic remedy appeared successful, but the fever returned a few weeks later. Now the doctor recommended herbal infusions and more frequent bloodletting, but nothing could vanquish Kadachas, and each new attack only weakened Salomon further.

For the first time in Rachel's memory, her father did not visit the vineyard even once during the six weeks between Passover and Shavuot. He no longer woke at dawn but rose two hours later; plus he went to bed immediately after *souper* and took naps on weekdays in addition to Shabbat. Despite many prayers for his recovery, his health continued to deteriorate. Some of the scholars arriving for the Hot Fair recommended treatments detailed in the seventh chapter of Tractate Gittin, but others decried these as dangerous because nobody knew exactly how to prepare them anymore.

"What Papa needs is a continuous treatment," Rachel complained as she and Miriam walked home from synagogue. "Not something that wears off gradually."

Miriam shook her head. "But he can't eat or drink a medicine continuously, and all prayers and incantations have a beginning and an end."

"I wish there was an amulet against fever." Rachel paused to think. "Wait. Doesn't a topaz protect against fever?"

"You're right." Miriam increased her pace, Rachel right behind her. "How did we forget that?"

At home, Rachel and Miriam sorted through their jewels, eventually settling on a large topaz brooch to be reset as a ring. And thank Heaven, after Salomon began wearing it, his condition stabilized.

Still, Rachel approached Miriam and Judah about Rivka and Elisha marrying after the Cold Fair. "I think it would give Papa pleasure to see his two grandchildren wed." She couldn't bring herself to say that Papa might not live long enough to enjoy the wedding if they waited longer.

"I agree that we can't wait for Eliezer to decide to come home," Judah said. "Elisha will be eighteen soon."

"Rivka has already told me she doesn't care if her father attends the wedding." Rachel made no effort to keep the bitterness from her voice.

With Salomon out of danger, Rachel wanted to speak with him about Eliezer, but whenever she tried, he was either resting or deep in conversation with Shmuel or Judah. In her frustration, she would ride to Ramerupt instead.

Meir's nieces had written that Meshullam would no longer be traveling as far as Ramerupt since plenty of excellent wool was available in Flanders. "Are you sure you can take all our wool this year, now that my brother-in-law has no need for it?" Joheved asked.

"Dovid says that if I can procure enough spinsters and weavers, he'll provide the fullers," Rachel replied, as much to allay her own anxiety as her sister's. "Spinsters are plentiful, and we should be able to attract sufficient weavers if we supply them with horizontal looms."

Jehan had married Alette's daughter and established his own weaving shop. Both he and Albert had apprentices, with Albert boasting that he could train others if he had additional looms.

"It will need a large investment," Joheved warned her.

"One that should reap a large reward." Rachel tried to exude confidence. "Don't worry."

"How can I not worry when Papa has asked Shmuel to lead the yeshiva this summer?" Joheved said. "He's barely twenty-four."

Salomon, while confined to bed, had consulted with Meir and Judah as to his successor. Both asked to retain their current responsibilities, Meir teaching the younger students and Judah editing his *kuntres*.

That left Shmuel.

"If the foreign merchants object to your son's youth, Papa said to remind them that when he founded the yeshiva he was only a year older than Shmuel is now. And that Shmuel knows just as much Talmud as he did at that age."

Joheved smiled. "I'm not sure that's true, but it's a nice thing for Papa to say."

This would have been a good time to ask Joheved's opinion on divorce, but Rachel couldn't bring herself to broach the subject with her judgmental older sister. Instead she went to visit Dovid, telling herself that she'd make her decision after Shemiah and Pesach came home.

But the news her son brought the following week left no hope for her marriage. Eliezer's concubine was pregnant once again.

Still Rachel waited until the Hot Fair closed, until the vintage was fermenting in the cellar, until the week before Rosh Hashanah, to take Eliezer's conditional *get* to the *beit din* and officially accept it in front of witnesses. She would start the New Year a free woman.

Her fears of shame and gossip turned out to be greatly exaggerated, mainly because everyone had more scandalous topics to discuss. In nearby Tours, Archbishop Ralph had prevailed upon King Philip to name as bishop of Orléans a young man named John. Normally such a mundane matter would be of no interest in Troyes, except that Ivo de Chartres had taken it upon himself to complain to both the papal legate and the pope that John was currently the archbishop's lover, as well as a former bedmate of the French king.

Worse, John was only twenty-two years old and therefore far more likely to act the part of Ralph's puppet than that of an independent bishop. However much the new pope, Paschal, may have agreed with Ivo, he declined to challenge the king's choice, seeing as Philip had finally returned to the Church's good graces by putting Bertrade aside.

Closer to home, Count Hugues' wife, Constance, had left him and demanded a divorce, an annulment actually, based on consanguinity. Rumors abounded that she was smitten by Bohemond, Prince of Antioch, who had returned to France for reinforcements, enthralling audiences with tales of heroism and gifts of relics from the Holy Land.

Some said that Constance wanted a manlier husband, that Hugues had failed to both give her a child and prove his courage by fighting the infidels. Others said that her father, King Philip, hoped to use her new availability to recruit more powerful allies than Champagne.

Guy, who visited Salomon regularly now that the scholar was disabled, had his own opinion. "Count Hugues' natural inclination is toward the ascetic. Unfortunately it is only now that we see that he should have been chosen for the Church."

"Who could know that Eudes would die so early in his sovereignty?" Salomon mused. "Otherwise Hugues might have become a bishop."

Rachel quailed at the thought of what else might have happened had someone not killed Hugues' older brother.

"Do you think Hugues will marry again?" Miriam asked.

"I don't know," Guy replied. "Adèle of Blois must hope that he doesn't, so her son Thibault will remain Hugues' heir."

"Have you any news of Robert?" Salomon asked. "Is he content back at Molesme or does he intend to defy the pope and return to Cîteaux?"

"Apparently Robert's monks have accepted his discipline this time," Guy said.

Salomon sighed. "I hope that Robert finally finds the peace he seeks in Molesme."

"Robert thanks you for helping Étienne Harding establish the *Hebraica veritas*," Guy said. "Étienne is confident that he will be able to produce an accurate Latin translation of the Bible."

"So I understand from my grandson and daughters," Salomon said, followed by a yawn.

"I have tired you." Guy stood and bowed. "I will say adieu and visit another day."

Rachel accompanied Guy to the gate, where he had an odd question for her. "Does your husband by any chance know Latin?"

"I don't think so. Why do you ask?"

"I've heard that the king of Toledo is looking for scholars who know Latin, Hebrew, and Arabic," he replied. "He wants to translate the ancient Greek texts in his library from Arabic into Latin so the Church can study them."

"Eliezer knows Arabic," Rachel said. "And he's studied many of the Greek masters' works in that language, so I suppose he could translate them into Hebrew for another Jew to translate into Latin."

"That's the king's intent." Guy sighed. "Ah, what I wouldn't give for a Latin version of Aristotle's *Metaphysics* or *Ethics*." His voice was full of longing. "Or even better, *De Anima*, his great treatise on the soul."

* * *

Dovid considered Hugues and Constance's divorce the height of hypocrisy. "At least the Jews who divorce are honest about it," he muttered as they studied the Mishnah from Tractate Sukkah in advance of that festival. "While our so-called Christian nobility change spouses whenever they please, in spite of the Church's avowed prohibition of divorce."

"You disapprove of divorce then?" Rachel asked cautiously. She had told only her children and sisters that she'd accepted Eliezer's *get*. If her neighbors knew, they hadn't learned of it from her family.

"The monks taught that marriage is a sacrament; that a husband and a wife must cleave to one another only, until one of them dies."

Rachel blanched at his harsh reply. "But what if a husband abandons his wife or treats her cruelly? Jewish Law says no one should be forced to share a basket with a snake."

"I don't know. I'm not a scholar." He looked at her pleadingly. "Can't we discuss a more pleasant subject, such as our previous passage from Tractate Sukkah?"

"You are a scholar, or at least you're becoming one." She smiled. "And I too would rather discuss sukkah building than divorce."

Listening as he ardently explained the difference between a valid sukkah and an invalid one, a daring idea came to her. She would encourage Dovid to study, just as the Talmudic Rachel had encouraged Rabbi Akiva. And then, when Dovid became a *talmid chacham*, she would marry him. Even better—unlike Rabbi Akiva, Dovid wouldn't have to leave home for his education. And unlike Rabbi Akiva's wife, Rachel, she wouldn't be living in poverty.

thirty-three

Troyes, France
29 Tammuz 4865 (July 13, 1105)

achel stared out her window at the dark, moonless sky. Downstairs the last of the yeshiva students were climbing up to the attic. She had gone to bed early, soon after sunset, but again sleep eluded her. She ventured onto the landing, hoping that Papa was awake as well.

To think that only a few months ago, at Rivka and Elisha's wedding, she'd been so happy. Now her world was in ashes.

Her relationship with Dovid had developed nicely as they continued to study together, with and without Jacob Tam, and she thought he acquitted himself well at the family seder. Two weeks later, she rode out to Ramerupt one Sunday morning, anticipating that Dovid would be alone at the fulling mill while the villeins attended church.

When she arrived he was outside, inspecting a still-dripping cloth that had recently been tentered. He stopped to greet her, and they had closed perhaps half the distance between them when she heard a low rumbling noise. Rachel slowed to listen when she felt the first trembling beneath her feet. She told herself that it was just an earthquake, most likely a small one that would be over in an instant, but her mind screamed panic. Then the ground jerked abruptly and she stumbled forward—into Dovid's arms.

The shaking stopped a few moments later, but they continued to stand together like statues, Rachel's heart pounding and Dovid's eyes wide with terror, until the unearthly silence was broken by birdsong. They simultaneously let out their breaths, Rachel acutely aware that she hadn't felt a man's strong arms around her in far too long.

Dovid immediately released her, apologizing, "I shouldn't have taken hold of you like that. You're a married woman."

Some demon must have possessed her, Rachel thought later, because instead of adjusting her veil, which had come loose in the quake, she removed it and replied, "I'm not a married woman. I accepted Eliezer's divorce last summer."

Dovid stared at her flowing curls with undisguised appreciation, and Rachel felt her cheeks grow warm. She would never appear on the street bareheaded, but exposing her hair outside of home was part of acknowledging her new unmarried status.

After that she began to tell Dovid about Eliezer, their courtship and early years together. He was fascinated by their travels and plied her with questions about the foreign lands she'd seen. Rachel increasingly found her thoughts returning to Dovid's earthquake embrace, and it seemed that an affection was growing between them. She began to eagerly anticipate the future.

Until that unhappy day, just before Shavuot, when everything changed.

As often happened, their scholarly discussion had veered into personal subjects.

"I know my sisters envy that I'm Papa's favorite," she said. "But it's not my fault that he was away studying when they were small and home while I was growing up."

Dovid's eyes clouded as he recalled his parents. "As the youngest, I was my mother's favorite. But my father preferred my oldest brother."

It took a moment for Rachel to realize the significance of what he'd said. "How many brothers did you have?"

"Two brothers and one sister," he replied, clearly unaware that anything was wrong.

"What happened to them?" She tried to keep her voice from shaking. Why had she assumed he was an only child?

His expression hardened. "The same as to me, I expect. After our parents were killed, we were separated."

"I meant did you ever see them again or do you know where they went?" Rachel held her breath waiting for his reply. *Please let his brothers be dead.*

"*Non*. Our captors saw to that." Dovid sighed. "My sister could be married already or she could be locked away in a convent. I suppose I'll never know."

Or she could be in a brothel, Rachel thought. But it was Dovid's brothers she cared about. "Do you think your brothers went to monasteries too?"

"Perhaps. Though my eldest brother was big enough to make a useful worker, so some tradesman may have apprenticed him."

Rachel's blood froze in her veins. Dovid had two brothers, in unknown locations, both raised as heretics. If she married him and he died without issue, she would become an *agunah*, never able to remarry. First it would be nearly impossible to locate the brothers to perform *chalitzah*, and, second, even if one were found, an apostate couldn't perform the ritual. Eliezer had gotten his second wife pregnant twice, so Rachel had to be the barren one.

Her stomach felt filled with rocks. Did she want to marry Dovid so badly that she would risk being chained to his corpse? She told herself that there was no hurry to decide; she could keep studying with him and see how she felt later. But deep inside she knew the answer, terrible as it was to contemplate.

Better stop things immediately, because the longer they continued the more painful it would be at the end. And it was painful enough already that she cried herself to sleep for a week.

As the Hot Fair drew closer, Rachel reluctantly left Dovid and Jacob Tam to study without her. When she did see the fuller, she kept their conversations focused on business, whose great success now gave her little pleasure. Dovid never questioned her increasing absence, and if he were disappointed, he hid it well.

She was desperate to see Shemiah again, to assure herself that nothing had happened to him and to hear news of her now former husband. So another blow struck when Pesach returned from Sepharad alone. The moment Rachel saw him washing up in the courtyard she ran to question him.

"Your son is well," Pesach replied. "But Eliezer is ill, so ill that Shemiah felt he shouldn't be left alone in such a perilous state."

"Alone?" Rachel asked. "What happened to Gazelle?"

"She died in childbirth some months back." Pesach dried his hands on a towel hanging at the well. "And the child with her."

Rachel sank down on a nearby bench. She wasn't sure she wanted to know the answer, but she had to ask, "How serious is this sickness?" *Is Shemiah planning to stay until Eliezer recovers, or until he dies?*

Pesach had been warned not to worry Rachel. "Your son thought Eliezer's recovery would happen sooner if he were there to direct the physicians."

"How long will that take?"

"Shemiah assured me he would be home for the New Year." When he saw Rachel's face crumble, he added, "But he hoped that it would be much sooner."

The Hot Fair had been open a month with no sign of her son, and, worrying over him and Eliezer, each night Rachel got less sleep. Strangely enough, Papa was also staying awake longer. He too would go to bed after *souper*, but he'd get up when the students came home so he could question Shmuel about that day's studies. Then, completely awake, he and Judah would work on his *kuntres*.

Rachel discovered this activity late one night when she went downstairs for a cup of wine to help her sleep and saw the light in Papa's room. He'd welcomed her company and she in turn had found a few hours of solace in the night, listening drowsily as Papa explained a complicated section of Gemara from the third chapter of Tractate Makkot.

Tonight the Sages were discussing the punishment, *makkot* being the Hebrew word for "lashes," for eating tithed or sacrificial foods outside Jerusalem. Those who ate certain tithes while *tamei*, or "ritually impure," were also to be punished.

Rachel sat down as Papa repeated what he'd been explaining to Judah. "When the Torah commands a farmer to declare that he has not eaten tithed food in *tumah*, 'impurity,' it means two things: that he has neither eaten any while he was *tamei* and it was *tahor*, 'pure,' nor while it was *tamei* and he was *tahor*."

Then Papa was silent. At first Rachel thought he was waiting for Judah to finish writing. But Papa's jaw had dropped open and his eyes were unfocused. Something didn't seem right, and she stood up to get a better look. But her father made no effort to follow her movement, and when Rachel came closer, she could see saliva trickling from his mouth.

"Papa," she said nervously, and when there was no response she asked, "Papa. Are you all right?"

Judah put down his quill and parchment, an expression of alarm on his face. "Papa," he said loudly.

Salomon remained silent, not looking at either of them. Judah waved his hand in front of Salomon's face, and when this drew no reaction, he bent his head down on Salomon's chest.

Only then did Rachel begin to suspect what was happening. Fear propelling her, she dashed to the kitchen and returned with a shiny steel knife, holding it under her father's nose while Judah brought the lamp near. They waited in vain for the blade to cloud over from Salomon's breath, until Rachel finally dropped the knife, let out a shriek, and burst into tears.

Judah frantically tried to find a pulse, first in Salomon's wrist and then in his neck, but both efforts were futile. Tears streaming down his face, he closed Salomon's eyes and mouth. "*Baruch Dayan Emet*," he whispered: Blessed be the True Judge. Then he turned to Rachel. "Wait here while I wake the household."

Her voice trembling, Rachel choked out the same blessing, one Jews make when first learning of a death. Yet her mind was protesting that Papa couldn't possibly be dead; surely he was just sleeping and would wake like usual in the morning.

Judah opened the door to find Shmuel standing in front of him. "I heard a cry. Is anything the matter?" Shmuel peered into the dimly lit room.

Rachel's weeping and Salomon's closed eyes were all the answer he needed, and the next moment Shmuel was crying as well. They were soon joined by Joheved and Miriam, who encouraged her to recite psalms with them as they guarded their father's body. But Rachel could only get out a few words at a time before grief stopped her speech.

It was also difficult to concentrate on her prayers with people stomping up and down the stairs, doors opening and slamming, and a continual hubbub outside in the salon. Anxious voices kept asking if all the water in the house had been poured out, while others inquired if Salomon had died smiling, looking up, or facing people, all of which were good omens for his ease in the World to Come.

At dawn the sisters' prayers would cease and Papa's male relatives would begin *tahara*, preparing his body for burial. Students would dismantle Papa's study table for wood to construct his coffin, while others procured reed mats on which the mourners would sit for the next seven days. There were no tasks awaiting Salomon's daughters, as it was the community's responsibility to care for mourners. So the three went upstairs to rest before the funeral.

Rachel somehow dozed off, waking with surprise to Rivka's announcement that it was almost time to leave. She dressed in a daze and headed for the courtyard, carefully stepping over the muddy puddle at the doorstep, where water had been dumped to prevent reentry of Papa's ghost or any *ruchot* drawn to his corpse. Simcha, Samuel, and a large group of Papa's students bravely joined Meir and Judah at the head of the coterie, their presence to protect Rachel and her sisters from demon attack as they accompanied the coffin. There were plenty of pallbearers, the six being assembled from the oldest of Salomon's grandsons and grandsons-in-law. Rachel sighed with regret that neither Shemiah nor Eliezer were there to represent her family.

Outside in the street, an enormous crowd waited. Rachel blinked several times in the bright sunshine, but she could not see to the end of the long line of people. It seemed forever before the unwieldy mass reached the cemetery, and then there was confusion over who should be chosen as the seven pious men to recite Psalm 91 while Papa's body was lowered into the grave. Clearly all of Salomon's relatives qualified, so rather than offend anyone, seven foreign merchants who studied with him every year, each representing a different country, were honored.

In this nightmare that was Papa's funeral, returning home from the burial took longer than getting there, for it was customary for the procession to pause seven times along the way. There the congregation prayed the anti-demonic Ninety-first Psalm through verse eleven, which consists of seven words. They added one word of that verse at each stop to ward off *ruchot* following from the cemetery, until, at the final stop, they concluded with the complete seven words of the eleventh verse:

> *His angels guard you wherever you go.*

Someone must have realized that all these guests would never fit in Salomon's house and courtyard, for tables and benches were also set up on several adjacent blockaded streets. Rachel had no idea how many she greeted—hundreds wanted to pay their respects to her father. She sat alone and miserable on the floor, bereft of solace save an occasional hug by her daughter. Her isolation grew, threatening to choke her, as she watched Miriam consoled by Judah plus their sons' families, all of whom summered in Troyes, and saw Joheved surrounded by Meir and their dozen-plus children and grandchildren.

The day after the funeral was Friday, the first of Av, and Rachel woke to a few precious moments before she realized that yesterday had not been some terrible dream. Papa was dead. She spent the day miserably sitting on the floor next to her sisters, in their hot, stuffy home, while the parade of pitying strangers and acquaintances offered condolences that served only to remind her how alone she was. Dreading four more days of the same, she gratefully attended Shabbat services.

Despite the Sabbath, the atmosphere at synagogue was subdued. Besides mourning the loss of their rosh yeshiva, the community was observing the final week of semi-mourning that preceded Tishah b'Av. No Jew in Troyes would be bathing, cutting their hair, drinking wine, or eating meat that week, not just Salomon's family. Rachel found no solace in this, resenting that her special role in mourning her father should be so diluted.

As was customary for mourners, Rachel, Joheved, and Miriam could not walk to synagogue unaccompanied, and once inside, they took different seats than usual. Below, in the men's section, Salomon's mourners also made a point of not sitting in their regular places. None of them would return to their old seats until *sheloshim*, the first thirty days of mourning, was over.

During the rest of the shiva week, Rachel felt as though each day would never end; yet when Shabbat came again, it was too soon. Since the Ninth of Av fell on a Saturday, the fast day would be observed on Sunday, making for another joyless Shabbat experience. But when she arrived at services, the congregation was buzzing.

Salomon's ghost had been seen at synagogue during the previous night.

Spirits of the recent dead took a while to leave their bodies behind, and the pious among them gathered in synagogue late Friday night for their own ghostly worship. That was why additions were made to the Friday evening liturgy, to ensure that no one remained in the synagogue alone to finish his obligatory prayers. That was why Shabbat hospitality was compulsory on the community. On other nights travelers might lodge in the synagogue, but not Friday. Heaven forbid that a man be alone in synagogue if the ghost congregation needed one more for a minyan.

Despite the danger, two yeshiva students—nobody said which ones—decided that both of them together might, in such a large city, visit the synagogue that night in relative safety. For further protection, they waited until the moon was high to sneak into the courtyard, and only viewed the spirit worshipers through the windows.

The rumor continued that the students had witnessed flickering lights and shadowy forms within, two of whom they recognized. One was a Flemish cloth merchant who had taken ill and died shortly after arriving at the fair, and the other was Rabbenu Salomon. Joheved rejected the account immediately, but Rachel wasn't so dismissive. It lessened her despair to imagine Papa's spirit nearby, watching over her.

When she got home, she entered Papa's room for the first time since his death, hoping to sense his presence. His clothes were gone, for it was bad luck for anyone in his family to wear the dead man's clothes. But Judah's notes lay on the chest, and, curious, she picked them up. There, under Papa's explanation of why the tithed foods must be eaten in purity, was written:

> Rabbenu's body was pure and here his soul departed in purity. He did not explain further; the language from here is from his *talmid*, Rabbi Judah ben Natan.

Rachel began to look forward to the next day, Tishah b'Av proper, when she could spend a peaceful afternoon at Papa's grave. But everyone else in Troyes had the same idea, and his burial site was a mob of people, jostling each other and clamoring to be closest to his tomb. She refused to yield until sunset, her disgust and sadness mounting with each passing hour.

All these strangers cared about was losing their teacher; yet they would have new teachers tomorrow. She had lost her father, and nobody would ever love her as much as he had.

The next morning, too despondent to get out of bed, she instructed the servants that no one should disturb her. So when she heard the knock at her door after the bells chimed at midday, she called out irritably, "Go away. I don't want any *disner*."

But the door opened anyway, and in a moment she was sobbing wildly in Shemiah's arms. She'd missed him and worried so much, but now her son was finally home.

"I'm so sorry I missed Grandpapa's funeral." Shemiah wiped his tears away as they walked to the cemetery.

"There's no way you could have known to return earlier," Rachel said, her grief more easily borne in his presence. "Your father needed you, and you did the right thing in staying until he recovered."

"He is still very ill."

Rachel halted and turned to face him. "What? You left Eliezer to die alone?"

"Never. I came back to send you to him."

Rachel stared at her son in shock. "But he's not my husband anymore. You know that."

"Have you married anyone else?"

She thought of Dovid and sighed. "*Non*."

Shemiah's voice grew urgent. "You could resume relations with him and be married again."

"How could we resume relations if he's on his deathbed?"

"His sickness is a result of all the heartache he's suffered. I'm sure he'd recover if you were there."

"If Eliezer is so anguished over his concubine's death, I don't see how I can cure him." *Or why I would want to.*

They arrived at the cemetery and Shemiah opened the gate. "Forgive me, Mama. I'm explaining this badly."

She resolved to listen patiently. "Please start again."

"Of course Papa was unhappy about Gazelle and the babies' deaths. But he didn't get sick until the other astronomers rejected his work."

Rachel found Salomon's grave and sat down on the grass. "How could they do that? Eliezer is a brilliant scholar."

"I admit I don't understand most of what Papa says when he talks about calculating how the stars and planets move in the heavens," Shemiah said sadly. "But I always believed that he knew what he was talking about."

Rachel sighed. "And the others didn't believe him?"

Shemiah nodded. "At first he was so excited and proud of his discovery. He showed me pages and pages of calculations: proof, he said, that not only do the inner planets orbit the sun, but the outer ones as well."

"His friend Abraham bar Hiyya believed that too; it was Abraham's idea."

"Abraham gave up that theory to prove that the Messiah is coming in 250 years."

Rachel's jaw dropped. "He's calculated the exact date?"

"Abraham says the Messiah will arrive in the year 5118. But never mind that. Papa's troubles began when he declared that the earth and the planets circle the sun."

Rachel was stunned into silence. *Impossible—everyone knows the earth is the center of the universe, and that the sun and stars go around her.*

"Every single one of his colleagues insisted that he was wrong, including Abraham. Nobody even wanted to see his proofs," Shemiah said. "The harder Papa tried to interest the other astronomers in his work, the more they rejected him. Some called him a heretic."

"Poor Eliezer. He must have been crushed."

"But the final blow came when I arrived and told him that you'd accepted his *get*, and that you were going to marry the fuller."

"What? I have no intention of marrying Dovid, or anyone else for that matter." Rachel glared at him. "How could you say such a thing?"

"From what I saw at Passover, I assumed your marriage was imminent." Shemiah's tone softened to mollify her. "So I was wrong about Dovid. But I know Papa still loves you, and I thought if I told him about a rival it might spur him to come home."

"Eliezer told you that he loves me?" *Could that be true?*

Shemiah hesitated before replying, "Not in so many words. But he always asks about you when I arrive—are you well, what are you doing, do you have any plans to visit him—questions like that."

"Perhaps he's being polite," she said skeptically.

"It's not mere politeness," he insisted. "I can tell by the way Papa talks about you, the expression on his face and his tone of voice, that he harbors a great affection for you. Please go to him, Mama. He'll die without you."

"I don't know, Shemiah. I'm still in *sheloshim* for my father." Surely her son was exaggerating Eliezer's illness, in addition to Eliezer's fondness for her.

"The root of Papa's problems is that he has abandoned Torah for astronomy and all those other secular subjects so popular in Sepharad. As Rabbi Yohanan taught in Tractate Berachot:

> On one who has the means to study Torah but does not, the Holy One brings afflictions that will pain him to his very depths."

Shemiah locked eyes with her. "You must bring Papa back to Troyes so he can study Torah again. Only that can save him."

Rachel shook her head. "I tried that a few years ago, but it didn't work."

"Because Papa hadn't suffered enough yet."

"I need to think about it." Had Eliezer finally lost the protection of Torah study? For also in Berachot,

> Reish Lakish said: He who studies Torah, painful sufferings are kept away from him.

"Please don't think about it for too long," he pleaded. "I considered Papa's condition so perilous that I rode on Shabbat to get here faster."

For two weeks Shemiah said nothing about Eliezer, but his reproachful looks were like arrows in Rachel's breast. She knew her son believed what he'd told her; otherwise he'd never have traveled on the Sabbath. But was Eliezer really that sick or had he manipulated Shemiah to force her to come to Toledo against her will? Could she possibly convince him to return to Troyes and study Talmud again?

Yet she knew the only question that mattered was if Eliezer truly loved her, and only by seeing him would she know if the answer was yes. But how could she decide without her father's advice? And she needed to make up her mind soon, for no decision would be a decision. The end of *sheloshim* would coincide with the close of the Hot Fair, when she could travel safely with the many merchants returning to their native lands.

The thirtieth day after Papa's death was a Friday, and Rachel solemnly accompanied her sisters to the bathhouse to acknowledge the end of this period of bereavement. Now they could return to normal life for the most part, with only the few strictures imposed on those mourning their parents. As Rachel gratefully washed a month's worth of dirt from her hair, she wished something would happen to push her one way or the other.

The Hot Fair would be over in five days.

She considered going to the synagogue that night, to consult with Papa's ghost, but she didn't dare. Every day at the cemetery she'd begged his spirit, who must know her future, to give her a sign, but she neither saw nor heard anything unusual. So while her sisters were celebrating Shabbat with their husbands, Rachel went to bed alone with a heavy heart.

The next thing she knew, it was daytime and she was outside watching Miriam weed the herb garden. But wait, it was Mama, not Miriam—Mama as she looked when she was young. Mama turned around at Rachel's approach and opened her arms to embrace her.

"You were a dutiful daughter to take such excellent care of your father." Mama was beaming. "He is very pleased with you."

Unable to speak, Rachel waited while her mother continued, "He told me to release you from my deathbed request so you can tend to your husband. It is your obligation to care for Eliezer, to see that his needs are met so he can study Torah without worrying about worldly concerns."

Rachel wanted to say that Eliezer wasn't her husband any longer, but her mother waved her hand in dismissal. "A mother knows her daughter's heart, and there he is still your husband. Just as in Eliezer's heart you are still his wife."

"He is alive then?" she was able to ask.

Mama nodded. "Your father says Eliezer is not so ill that you should violate the Sabbath for him."

"Let me see Papa. Let me talk to him," Rachel cried out.

"He's at Shabbat services now: I can't disturb him."

"But I never got to say good-bye," she pleaded.

It was too late. Mama and the herb garden were disappearing in a fog. "He says to pray Psalms 138 and 140 on your trip," were Mama's fading words.

When Rachel woke up, she remembered that these were the psalms invoked to reawaken love between a man and a woman.

* * *

Saturday night, the first of Elul, Rachel was about to blow out her bedroom lamp when Miriam called through the door, "Rachel, I hope you're not asleep yet."

Rachel quickly let her sister in. "*Non*—I was just about to get in bed though."

"Elizabeth needs help with some twins she's delivering, so I wanted to say adieu to you tonight, as I doubt I'll be home in the morning."

"I'm glad you've come." Rachel gave Miriam a warm hug.

"Shemiah says you refused to let him go with you," Miriam said with a frown.

Before Rachel could reply, Joheved peeked through the slightly open doorway. "I thought I heard voices." She tiptoed in and closed the door behind her. "I don't think you should travel alone either."

"Don't worry. I'll be safe with all the merchants." Rachel's voice conveyed her determination. "My son has already spent too much time away from his wife, and I want him to be here with her, especially if I'm delayed for several months until Eliezer is well enough to ride."

Joheved's eyes opened wide in surprise. "You mean . . . ?"

Rachel smiled and nodded. "Rivka told me that Glorietta hasn't immersed in the pond with her all summer."

"I'm glad you're bringing Eliezer back." Miriam's expression clouded. "Papa's death hit Judah very hard, and I don't know if he can finish Papa's *kuntres* without Eliezer's help."

"I'm not sure Eliezer and I will stay in Troyes all the year." When Rachel saw her sisters' disappointment, she quickly added, "Of course we'll be here most of the time, making sure the yeshiva thrives and visiting our grandchildren. But I'd like to travel in between fairs, for there are so many places we haven't seen together."

"What if Eliezer still insists on living in Toledo?" Miriam asked.

Rachel had prepared herself for that possibility. "We could spend part of the year there, with Eliezer opening a small yeshiva."

They might even work on the king's translations together. After all, why should all that Latin she'd learned go to waste? For if she, a woman, could study Talmud, why couldn't she study Ptolemy or Aristotle?

"That's a good idea," Joheved said. "Meir and I are concerned that the only yeshivot left are in France." She hesitated and lowered her voice. "If things go badly for the Franks in Jerusalem, I'm afraid they may take vengeance on the Jews here."

Rachel sighed. So Eliezer wasn't the only one afraid of what those who worshipped the Hanged One might do in the future.

"We must have faith in the Holy One, Who will never forsake us as long as we keep learning Torah."

"You're right," Joheved replied, as Miriam nodded in agreement. "And we must work to send Papa's commentaries to all the foreign communities, so his words won't be lost no matter what happens."

Miriam stepped forward and embraced Rachel for a long time. "I mustn't keep Elizabeth waiting. Please be careful, and write us as soon as you arrive."

"And my little sister needs a good night's sleep before her long journey," Joheved added before following Miriam out the door and closing it silently behind them.

The next morning Rachel rose to the sounds of one shofar after another blowing throughout the Jewish Quarter, their raucous calls intermingled with the peals of Troyes' many church bells. Her necessities for the long journey were packed, but Rachel realized there was something she'd forgotten. She unlocked the chest at her bedside and took out her *get* from Eliezer. She noticed her hands were shaking and took a deep breath to calm herself. When she saw Eliezer again, she would return the divorce decree to him so he could destroy it.

Don't worry, she told herself, as she rode through the narrow streets leading to the fairgrounds, where the merchants from Sepharad were assembling. Wherever there were Jews in the world, there would be Torah study. And no matter what happened with Eliezer, no matter where she ended up living, Papa's spirit would watch over her.

And so may the spirit of Rabbenu Salomon ben Isaac continue to watch over all the daughters of Israel who study Talmud.

epilogue

SALOMON BEN ISAAC'S LEGACY CONTINUED through his eleven grandchildren and numerous great-grandchildren. By the time Joheved died in 1135, outliving her sisters and brothers-in-law, her son Jacob, now called Rabbenu Tam, was recognized as the undisputed head of Ashkenaz Jewry. Interestingly it was Hannah's son who became the outstanding scholar and leader of the next generation, not one of Salomon's grandsons' sons, as his family's greatness continued through the female line.

Sadly the erudition, creativity, and tolerance of the Twelfth-Century Renaissance were to be short-lived. As Rachel and Eliezer feared, the Crusades opened the Levant to Christian merchants, and by the thirteenth century, the great Italian city-states had supplanted Jews as long-distance traders.

In early 1171, the first accusation of ritual murder in France was leveled against the Jews of Blois, resulting in thirty-one Jews being burned at the stake—including Count Thibault's Jewish mistress, who refused to forsake her people. In that final year of his life, Rabbenu Tam unleashed his formidable influence to provoke such widespread condemnation of the events in Blois that even King Louis publicly proclaimed his refusal to believe such scandalous charges against the Jews.

But in 1187, when Saladin united Egyptian and Turkish armies to recapture Jerusalem, nobody could save the Jews after that.

The failed Third Crusade demoralized France, and after the disastrous Fourth Crusade, which ended with the sack of Constantinople, Christian fighting Christian, the Church turned its eyes toward Europe.

The Fourth Lateran Council of 1215 decreed that Jews must wear special badges to distinguish them from the rest of the population, an edict enforced in England and royal France, but ignored in Provence, Spain, and Champagne. The thirteenth century saw a growing concern with heresy, leading to the Talmud being burned in Paris in 1242.

Worse was yet to come. In 1267 the Inquisition was established to punish Christian heretics, as well as Jews who "induced" Christians to convert. Champagne was no longer a haven. In 1268 the count confiscated all Jewish goods and loans to finance a crusade that ended dismally with the death of King Louis in Tunis. Ritual murder accusations came to Troyes in 1288, where thirteen Jews were turned over to the Inquisition, found guilty, and burned alive.

The final blow came when the entire Jewish population of France was expelled in 1306, forcing more than twenty thousand Jews to leave Champagne. Thus, just two hundred years after his death, Salomon ben Isaac's many descendants abandoned their homes and fled to every corner of Europe: Germany, Bohemia, Hungary, Provence, Italy, and Spain. More expulsions followed, scattering his seed further. A statistician at Stanford has calculated that someone with European Jewish ancestry today is almost certainly descended from Rashi.

As his descendants spread throughout Europe and the Levant, they brought with them his Torah and Talmud commentaries. Eliezer may have been correct in his predictions of the Crusades' devastating effect on Ashkenaz, but he was wrong in saying that Salomon's words would die with him.

Today more Jews study Rashi every day than all other Jewish scholars together—in synagogues, yeshivot, and Jewish homes throughout the world. Some say that without Rashi's *kuntres*, Talmud would be lost to Judaism and the Jewish religion would be very different, if indeed it existed at all.

And just as Talmud study has continued to thrive in our generation, as women find the subject no longer closed to them, so there is a new future for the Jews of Troyes. Empty of Jews for five hundred years, the city has been repopulated by a community of Sephardim expelled from Muslim Algeria when the State of Israel was established in 1948. Across the street from their synagogue sits the Rashi Institute, founded in 1989 to study the history of French Jewry.

Indeed some of my own research was done within its walls.

afterword

ONE QUESTION MORE THAN ANY OTHER INTRIGUES my readers: what is fact in *Rashi's Daughters* and what is fiction?

Salomon ben Isaac was a real man, whose commentaries and responsa contain thousands of words about his life, his community, and his opinions. Regarding him, I have made every attempt to be as historically accurate as possible, and when forced to be creative, I have used the wealth of information contained in his writings to stay true to his character as I know it.

His daughters, sons-in-law, and grandchildren are also historical figures, as are the various clerics and feudal lords who appear in this book, and I used their real names whenever they were known. I did have to invent a name for Rashi's wife, and for some of his granddaughters as well, because the names of most Jewish women in history have been lost to us. I also fabricated a few grandchildren who would die young, ensuring that my tale reflected this sad historical reality that was the eleventh century.

In my first book, I built upon two popular legends about Rashi's daughters—that they studied Talmud and prayed with tefillin. But there is a less-well-known legend that says they wrote the commentary on Tractate Nedarim that has come down to us as Rashi's, which is clearly not in his usual terse and pithy style. To this day, the author of this text remains unidentified, but my careful study suggests a feminine point of view.

Not everything written about Rashi's daughters is legend. Much is recorded about Joheved and Meir, including when they died and what Meir said at her funeral. Less is known of Miriam and Judah. We know the names of their children and that their eldest son, Yom Tov, served as rosh yeshiva in Paris. And in Rashi's commentary on Tractate Makkot 19a, we find the words Judah wrote upon his father-in-law's death.

But so little data exists concerning Rachel and Eliezer that some scholars doubt Rashi had more than two daughters. The main evidence comes from a letter Rabbenu Tam wrote to his cousin Yom Tov that mentions the divorce of their aunt Rachel from Eliezer, plus the existence of a grandson of Rashi's named Shemiah, who is neither Joheved's son nor Miriam's.

Not much from which to write a historical novel.

My first challenge was to create a plot involving Rachel and Eliezer's divorce; yet I knew I had to take care in making them both sympathetic and heroic figures. There could be no villains in Rashi's immediate family. Aware that some of the eighteenth century's finest yeshiva students abandoned their Talmud studies when the Enlightenment opened the great European universities to them, I decided to make Eliezer similarly tempted by the ancient Greek knowledge being rediscovered in Spain during his lifetime. To my surprise, I learned that Arab astronomers had postulated a heliocentric planetary system hundreds of years before Copernicus.

With Eliezer committed to his secular studies, Rachel would be forced to choose between the two men she loved most—her father and her husband. She would face the choice of leaving her family and moving with Eliezer to Spain, where women were hidden away at home and certainly didn't study Talmud, or staying to care for an increasingly enfeebled Rashi in Troyes, where the massacres of the First Crusade threatened the Jews' very existence.

Ah yes—the First Crusade. Since I planned that my trilogy would end with Rashi's death in 1105, there was no avoiding the First Crusade and its disastrous consequences for Rhineland Jewry. So I carefully salted the first two volumes with imaginary characters who'd be living in different Rhineland cities in the third—Catharina and Samson, Aunt Sarah's son Elazar, Judah's early study partners Daniel and Elisha. Then I took Jewish historical descriptions of the horrific events and had my characters experience them, using the original wording as much as possible. I apologize for the graphic violence, but I wanted to stay true to the eyewitness reports. It was a truly terrible time.

How the martyrs of Mayence, Worms, and Cologne died is factual, as is the fate of Emicho's men and the pilgrims who followed Peter the Hermit. However, the legend of a dying Rabbi Amnon writing Unetanah Tokef, one of the most powerful prayers of the Days of Awe, is completely unfounded. In fact, the prayer seems to have been composed, not in eleventh-century Mayence, but in Eretz Israel hundreds of years earlier. But the legend is so pervasive and compelling that I reworked it into a version that might have happened, or at least cannot so easily be disproved.

My portrayals of life in Tunisia and Sepharad are taken from documents in the Cairo Geniza, but there is no evidence that either Eliezer or Rachel ever stepped foot out of Troyes. All of their travels are the product of my imagination, as are their occupations. Yet we know that in addition to being vintners, some of Rashi's family earned a living from wool. Research showed that Rashi's description of the horizontal loom in his *kuntres* is the earliest mention of such a device and that the first fulling mill appeared in northern France during his lifetime.

Also during the twelfth century, wealthy clothing entrepreneurs emerged who employed all the laborers involved in the production of these expensive fabrics, eventually eliminating the previous system in which workers bought their own raw materials and equipment and then sold their product to the next craftsman in the chain. Amazingly, 80 percent of international trade in the Middle Ages consisted of luxury woolens and silk.

For other events in Rachel and Eliezer's life, I borrowed liberally from the medieval responsa literature. The incident where Joheved put the milk spoon in the meat pot is from Rashi's own responsa, although he doesn't state which daughter was responsible. Rashi also answered many questions about forced converts after the First Crusade, and I used the responsa from the man with an apostate brother to complicate Rachel's life. Eliezer's capture and self-ransom in the forest actually happened to another merchant, but it was too good a tale to ignore. Jewish women had little difficulty obtaining a divorce from their husbands at this time—unlike today—so I had Brunetta demonstrate the procedure.

I tried to incorporate many of the local political events. Young Count Eudes died mysteriously on New Year's in 1093, his successor Hugues barely survived an assassination attempt by his favored servant, and Érard of Brienne launched his attack soon after. The scandal of King Philip leaving his queen for the beautiful Bertrade is well known, as is the influence of Countess Adèle in Champagne's affairs.

In Spain, where Jews thrived despite (or because of) the constant battles between Spaniards and Moors, I placed Eliezer in the thick of the cultural and historical milieu. King Alfonso's conquest of Toledo was a turning point in the Reconquista, and I couldn't resist including El Cid as well as the poet Moses ibn Ezra, astronomer and philosopher Abraham bar Hiyya, and Arab mathematician Ibn Bajjah (the concentration of intellectual giants in Sepharad at the dawn of the twelfth century was extraordinary). It was quite an effort for me to assimilate the ideas of Ptolemy, Aristotle, and Philo well enough that I could then convey their essence to my readers.

As in the first two volumes, the magical and medical remedies, as well as the astrology and demonology, came from the Talmud itself or other medieval sources. I could never have invented such bizarre stuff.

Speaking of the Talmud, the passages quoted are: Berachot 10a and Shabbat 23b and 34a (chapter 2); Kiddushin 29b, Rosh Hashanah 33a, and Niddah 31b (chapter 4); Berachot 55b (chapter 6); Eruvin 100b and Shabbat 73a (chapter 7); Ketubot 51b (chapter 8); Shabbat 21 (chapter 9); Berachot 55a (chapter 10); Avodah Zarah 18a (chapter 14); Shabbat 66b and Kiddushin 33 (chapter 15); Shabbat 75a (chapter 16); Avodah Zarah 18a and Moed Katan 20b and 22b (chapter 17); Berachot 55a and Sukkah 29a (chapter 18); Taanit 30b (chapter 20); Rosh Hashanah 20–21 (chapter 24); more Rosh Hashanah 21 (chapter 25); Sanhedrin 38b (chapter 26); Nedarim 20b (chapter 27); Nedarim 50a and Sanhedrin 7a (chapter 29); Shabbat 67a (chapter 32); and Makkot 19a and Berachot 5a (chapter 33). All translations are my own.

For those readers interested in my many sources, a bibliography is located on my Web site, www.rashisdaughters.com, under "historical info."

I thank you for sharing this journey with me. My hope is that, just as I enjoyed and learned a great deal from writing Joheved, Miriam, and Rachel's stories, so you did as well while reading them.

glossary

Adar Final month of the Jewish year: Purim falls on the Fifteenth of Adar. An extra month, Adar II, is added in leap years.

Allemagne Germany

Angleterre England

Baraita A source cited in the Talmud that is not found in the Mishnah.

Bavel Babylonia

Beit din Jewish court

Bima Pulpit. The raised platform in synagogue where Torah is read.

Bliaut Tunic. The outer garment worn over a chemise by both men and women.

Brit milah Ritual circumcision, performed when the baby boy is eight days old.

Chacham Jewish scholar

Chalitzah Jewish ritual that frees a childless widow from levirate marriage.

Compline Last of the eight canonical hours, approximately 3:00 a.m.

Dinar Gold coin. A unit of money equal to 240 deniers, silver pennies.

Disner The midday meal in medieval France, usually the largest meal of the day.

Distaff The stick that holds the raw wool or flax to be spun into thread.

Edomite European non-Jew (Talmudic term for Roman)

Elul Sixth month of the Jewish calendar, the month prior to Days of Awe.

Erusin Formal betrothal that cannot be annulled without a divorce but does not allow the couple to live together.

Flowers Medieval French term for menses, used both as noun and verb.

Ganymede Mythic prince of Troy seduced by Zeus, and a medieval word for male homosexual.

Gemara Questions and discussion about the Mishnah, later part of Talmud compiled between 200–500 CE.

Get Jewish bill of divorce

Halachah Jewish Law

Havdalah Saturday evening ceremony that marks the end of the Sabbath.

Heddle Any of the vertical cords in the frame of a loom used to guide the warp threads.

Herem Excommunication

Heshvan Eighth month in Jewish calendar, the month after Days of Awe.

Kavanah Serious intention before praying or performing a mitzvah.

Ketubah Jewish marriage contract given by the groom to the bride, specifying his obligations during the marriage and in the event of divorce or his death.

Kislev Ninth month of the Jewish calendar; the month in winter when Hanukkah occurs.

Kriah Tearing one's clothes as a symbol of mourning.

Kuntres Notes and commentary explaining the Talmudic text.

Lillit Demon responsible for killing newborn babies and women in childbirth; Adam's first wife.

Matins The first canonical hour: midnight.

Matzah Unleavened bread eaten during Passover.

Mazikim Demons or evil spirits.

Midrash Genre of rabbinic commentary that expands and explains the biblical text, generally used to refer to nonlegal material.

Mikvah Ritual bath used for purification, particularly by women when no longer *niddah*.

Minim Heretics, derisive Jewish word for Christians.

Mishnah Second-century collection of Jewish Laws, arranged by topic; earliest part of Talmud.

Mitzvah (plural: mitzvot) Divine commandment

Mohel (feminine: *mohelet*) One who performs a ritual circumcision.

Niddah A menstruating woman.

Nissan First month of the Jewish calendar; Passover starts on the Fifteenth of Nissan.

Nisuin Ceremony that completes the marriage, followed by cohabitation.

None Sixth of the eight canonical hours, approximately 3:00 p.m.

Notzrim Polite Jewish word for Christians; literally those who worship the one from Nazareth.

Pâques Easter, also the French word for Passover.

Parnas Leader, or mayor, of Jewish community.

Prime Dawn, third of the eight canonical hours, approximately 6 a.m.

Responsa Questions sent to a rabbi asking for a legal decision and his reply.

Rosh yeshiva Headmaster of a Talmud academy.

Ruchot (singular: *ruach*) Ghosts, spirits of recent dead.

Seder Ceremony observed in a Jewish home on the first two nights of Passover.

Selichot Prayers for forgiveness, also the special religious service that takes place at midnight on the Saturday night preceding Rosh Hashanah.

Sepharad Spain

Sheloshim First thirty days of mourning following the death of a relative.

Shema Central creed of Judaism, verses from Deuteronomy said twice a day and ideally upon one's death: "Hear O Israel, Adonai is our God, Adonai is One."

Shiva First seven days of mourning following the death of a relative.

Shuttle Bobbin of thread that goes back and forth through the loom's warp, weaving in the weft.

Souper Supper, evening meal.

Sukkah Booth in which Jews dwell during the harvest festival of Sukkot.

Tahara Preparation of a corpse for burial.

Talmid chacham Great Jewish scholar

Tefillin Phylacteries, small leather cases containing passages from scripture worn by Jewish men while reciting morning prayers.

Tekufah Solstice or equinox, one of the sun's four turning points in the Jewish year.

Tierce Fourth of the eight canonical hours, 9:00 a.m.

Villein French serf, a slave belonging to whoever owned the land he lived on.

Warp Threads running lengthwise in a fabric, crossed by the weft.

Weft Threads running from side to side in a fabric, crossed by the warp.

Yeshiva (plural: yeshivot) Talmud academy

Yetzer hara Evil inclination, usually refers to the sexual urge.

Experience the lives and loves of the three daughters of the great Talmud scholar...

978-0-452-28862-1

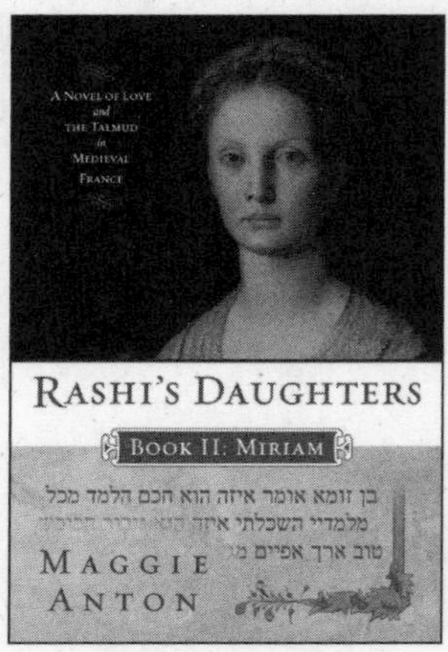

978-0-452-28863-8

978-0-452-29568-1

www.rashisdaughters.com

Available wherever books are sold.

Plume
A member of Penguin Group (USA) Inc.
www.penguin.com